PRAISE FOR
If I Fall

APR 2 7 2013

"Thoroughly winning." —*All About Romance*

"A unique tale . . . *If I Fall* is one to read."
—*The Season for Romance* (Top Pick)

"Noble mixes humor, poignancy, murder, and mayhem in a quick-paced charmer . . . There's plenty of action to keep pages turning." —*RT Book Reviews*

Follow My Lead

"If Austen were alive and writing novels today, the result might be something exactly like *Follow My Lead*, a wickedly witty and superbly satisfying romance." —*Chicago Tribune*

"Believable and captivating . . . An outstanding and memorable tale." —*Publishers Weekly* (starred review)

The Summer of You

"How many romances really, and I mean *really*, stir the heart? This one did." —*All About Romance*

"Vivid and touching . . . Something new, something real, something genuine, something special and alive. It is worth savoring and appreciating." —*Smart Bitches, Trashy Books*

"Will touch your heart and wring your emotions until you find yourself laughing and weeping simultaneously."
—*TwoLips Reviews*

continued . . .

Revealed

"[A] terrific tale of 'love and war' that contrasts . . . Regency high society with the dangerous world of espionage."
—*Midwest Book Review*

Compromised

"Noble's clever and graceful debut Regency romance is simply sublime."
—*Booklist*

"A delectable and delightful debut! Every word sparkles like a diamond of the first water. I can't wait for Kate Noble's next treasure of a book!"
—Teresa Medeiros, *New York Times* bestselling author

"Kate Noble's writing is smart and sparkling . . . Wonderfully entertaining, delightfully effervescent romance."
—Amanda Quick, *New York Times* bestselling author

"An amusing historical romance . . . A lighthearted late-Regency romp."
—*Midwest Book Review*

"Ms. Noble is a talent to watch. I look forward to her next book."
—*Romance Reviews Today*

Berkley Sensation titles by Kate Noble

COMPROMISED
REVEALED
THE SUMMER OF YOU
FOLLOW MY LEAD
IF I FALL
LET IT BE ME

Specials

THE DRESS OF THE SEASON

Let It Be Me

KATE NOBLE

B
BERKLEY SENSATION, NEW YORK

THE BERKLEY PUBLISHING GROUP
Published by the Penguin Group
Penguin Group (USA) Inc.
375 Hudson Street, New York, New York 10014, USA

USA / Canada / UK / Ireland / Australia / New Zealand / India / South Africa / China

Penguin Books Ltd., Registered Offices: 80 Strand, London WC2R 0RL, England
For more information about the Penguin Group, visit penguin.com.

LET IT BE ME

A Berkley Sensation Book / published by arrangement with the author

Berkley Sensation Books are published by The Berkley Publishing Group.
BERKLEY SENSATION® is a registered trademark of Penguin Group (USA) Inc.
The "B" design is a trademark of Penguin Group (USA) Inc.

For information, address: The Berkley Publishing Group,
a division of Penguin Group (USA) Inc.,
375 Hudson Street, New York, New York 10014.

ISBN: 978-0-425-25120-1

PUBLISHING HISTORY
Berkley Sensation mass-market paperback edition / April 2013

PRINTED IN THE UNITED STATES OF AMERICA

10 9 8 7 6 5 4 3 2 1

Cover art by Judy York.
Cover design by George Long.
Interior text design by Kristin del Rosario.

ALWAYS LEARNING   **PEARSON**

*For those who believe that
just because something is difficult,
doesn't mean it's impossible.*

Prologue

BEFORE there were ever words, there was music. A language in and of itself, music is the background to life, where emotion dwells. Through time, words evolved, and music—while ingrained in the flesh of every living thing—became a language only for those inclined to study it. To mold it into new formations, push the limits of what was known and what evoked feeling—but ultimately, anything created, no matter how technically perfect, has to be imbued with life. And that life, its presence, could be ascertained by the king most high or the peasant most common—because music, no matter the words put upon it, belongs to everyone.

Bridget Forrester believed that. She discovered it as a child, when the staccato rhythms of horseshoes on cobblestones set the beat to which she skipped. She practiced it over and over, the pianoforte her companion as she grew and became the woman she was meant to be. And during a lifetime of study, of listening and learning and feeling, no piece of music brought more life to the world than the four movements of Beethoven's Ninth Symphony.

Long after her voyage to Italy was complete, music and love both made and stolen, yet returned in full, Bridget Forrester would look back on her life and realize that for a brief magical moment, she had owned the qualities of each of the movements of the Ninth Symphony, when she had needed them most: The first, *allegro*: quick and intense. *Scherzo*, second: rigid structure, but able to vary. Third, *adagio*: stately, but hopeful . . . and the fourth movement, the culmination of all that came before.

Over the course of her life, Bridget would hear Beethoven's Ninth played dozens of times—on every occasion that it was being performed within fifty miles of London, her husband would arrange for them to attend. They heard it at least once a year. It was their piece. It was the sound to which they fell in love.

It was the culmination of all that came before.

In 1895, at age ninety, Bridget was nearly blind, confined to a wheeled chair, and missing her darling husband every day of the six years he had been gone. But she still had her ears. She could still hear when the door to her music room creaked open. She heard as her children's children's children would practice their scales on her beautiful pianoforte—careful to be delicate with it, as its keys were nearly a century old. Her own hands had long since failed her—their bones freezing in pain from playing the complicated rhythms that had once flowed from her fingertips. But her memory held. And, as she was too frail to attend concerts, it was her memory that sustained her—until the day of her ninety-first birthday.

Bridget's youngest granddaughter, who was in her first Season and very keen on what was new and the latest, woke Bridget up from her afternoon nap by having burly men haul a massive contraption into her suite of rooms.

"It's a phonograph!" her granddaughter cried, obviously very pleased with herself. "The latest invention from America!"

Bridget had heard of such things, of course—sounds recorded, as a photographic camera would take a person's likeness. But surely it could not compare. Daguerreotypes always looked still, frozen and cold. Not like real people, or places in time. A phonograph was certain to be as disappointing.

But her granddaughter was very enthusiastic. And in the anxieties and trials of a first Season, it was all too rare to see the girl enthusiastic.

Thus, she squinted, watching her granddaughter as she put a waxed cylinder on a horizontal spindle, and set the needle.

The sound was tinny, a single violin, like an echo of music being played from another room. But Bridget—her mind still sharp, her ears still perfect—slipped into memory, fell back in time, and heard the music of a full orchestra.

She heard Beethoven's Ninth.

One

London, England
January 1824

IF Bridget Forrester had one wish in life, it would be one day, when introduced to someone new, *not* to hear that person cry in surprise and delight, "Oh, you must be Sarah's sister!"

It was not a grand wish. She had no desire to be the most admired girl in the room, be festooned with diamonds and silks, or have sonnets written to the color of her eyes. But she did like to think that she was enough of her own person to be recognized as such, instead of an extension of her elder sister.

The problem was, of course, that her sister Sarah *had* been the most admired person in the room, festooned with diamonds and silks, with sonnets written to the color of her eyes—which technically, was also the color of Bridget's eyes, but no one thought for a moment that those lines were composed to her.

And as she stood in the ballroom of the Newbury town house off Berkley Square, Bridget had to admit to herself that her one wish was not likely to be granted. Even when her sister was absent.

"Oh, so you are Miss Sarah's younger sister!" Lady Newbury cried, taking in Bridget's brown, curly hair with a skeptical eye. It was the opposite of her sister's fair, straight locks. Nor did she have the long, easy grace that Sarah did. But she did have her mother at her elbow, and she at least would attest to having birthed both of them, strange as it might seem.

"Yes, my lady," Bridget replied, the only betrayal of her true feelings being a double blink at Lady Newbury's exclamation.

"We should say Mrs. Fletcher now," Bridget's mother, Lady Forrester, corrected. Now it was Lady Newbury's turn to double-blink.

"Yes, of course," she replied smoothly. "And how is Mrs. Fletcher—Sarah—settling in to married life?"

As her mother launched into polite small talk about the town house Sarah and her new husband had purchased, and how it was a mother's duty to help with the decoration, Lady Newbury kept her smile pinned neatly on her face, but Bridget knew she was thinking about how such a bright star as Miss Sarah Forrester could possibly have chosen a naval lieutenant over any number of wealthier, more aristocratic gentlemen that vied for her hand. (Even though Jack was a family friend and proved an excellent match for Sarah, and with his new position at the War Department was well able to keep Sarah in comfort, none of those things mattered to the likes of Lady Newbury.) Bridget simply wanted to shake her head. It was that curious quality that Sarah possessed and Bridget did not—even after all the dramatics were said and done, people still wondered about Sarah, her name on the tips of their tongues.

"I do hope you enjoy yourself, Miss Forrester," Lady Newbury said, and Bridget realized she was addressing her. "A girl's first Season is always a wondrous occasion."

"Yes," Bridget replied, her eyebrow going up, "it certainly was."

But her use of the past tense went unnoticed by Lady Newbury, who tittered on. "And I'm certain you will make a splash just like your sister. Why, I remember her sitting in my ballroom, just last summer, surrounded by men, and choosing of all of them her lieutenant to dance with." She sighed. "So romantic."

"It wasn't romantic," Bridget replied, bluntly. "He left her in the middle of the dance floor, causing a stir."

"He did?" Lady Newbury's brows came down. "I'm certain you heard it wrong."

"Possibly, but I *saw* it correctly." Bridget would have defiantly crossed her arms over her chest if her mother hadn't been squeezing her elbow quite so tight. "I was there, after all."

"Lady Newbury, thank you for inviting us. I'm certain we shall see you later in the evening," Lady Forrester interrupted, before their hostess's face could change from confusion to embarrassment at her faux pas. But even though she couldn't help setting Lady Newbury back on her heels a bit since she had overlooked the fact that Bridget was not in her first Season and had in fact attended functions of Lady Newbury's in the past year . . . Bridget was somewhat thankful that she had been overlooked. Perhaps it meant that everyone would think that she was new to the social scene.

Maybe, Bridget thought hopefully, she was about to be awarded a clean slate.

Sadly, it took only an hour to dispel that notion.

For girls who were completely unknown would at least get asked to dance at least once or twice.

But not Bridget.

The closest Bridget got to the dance floor was when being introduced to one Mr. Hartley, the son of a Baronet in Yorkshire whose pleasant appearance was marred by a lack of chin, which he tried to make up for with an incredibly complicated cravat. But he was nice and spoke passionately (about his sheep farm, but passionately, still) and seemed very eager to talk to Bridget. In fact, Bridget had thought he might ask her for a dance. That perhaps it was even on the tip of his tongue.

"Miss Forrester, might I ask . . ." Mr. Hartley was saying, when a firm hand clapped him on the shoulder.

"Hartley, where did you get off to?" came the friendly voice of Mr. Coombe—a young man not too long down from Cambridge, who Bridget remembered dancing attendance upon Sarah last Season. At least he wasn't one of the cadres of men that had stood outside their doors at all hours, hoping for a glimpse of her sister, the Golden Lady, but instead confined his fawning attentions to various ballrooms.

"I was just having a pleasant conversation with Miss Forrester here," Mr. Hartley said, and Bridget offered a smile and curtsy to Mr. Coombe, as he gave a short bow over her hand.

"Miss Forrester, happy to see you again." Mr. Coombe said quickly before turning to Hartley. "Where have you been, old man? My aunt has been waiting a quarter hour for you to come partner her at whist, as you promised."

"I did?" Mr. Hartley replied, before hastily amending, "Er, so I did! Miss Forrester, if you will excuse me?"

And with that Mr. Hartley, and the possibility of dancing, left Bridget.

It wasn't long before she knew why. Without a dance partner, Bridget had no reason to remain in the ballroom, despite her mother's insistence that she stay there "just in case." She successfully pleaded thirst and excused herself to find the refreshments. After all, no one would be fetching anything for her, so she would simply have to do it herself.

At the refreshment table, Bridget procured herself a glass of lemonade and a small respite behind a potted palm tree, into which she and her green dress blended quite nicely.

One should beware of potted palm trees. They yield only unwanted information.

"I say, why did you pull me away from Miss Forrester?" she heard Mr. Hartley's voice as he took a gulp of his own freshly procured lemonade. He was decidedly *not* playing cards with Coombe's aunt.

"Don't worry, I promised I'd introduce you to many eligible young ladies, and I shall," Mr. Coombe replied. The thud she heard was likely him slapping Mr. Hartley on the back again. Coombe seemed inclined to back slapping.

"But you're the one who told me that Miss Forrester was the catch of the decade! In fact, I was remarkably surprised to find her unattended."

"That's her sister, you fool! And that was *last* Season. Miss Forrester—the one worth talking to, at any rate—married herself off to a navy lieutenant last year." Mr. Coombe then lowered his voice to a grumble. "The Golden Lady, married to a man with no prospects . . ."

Bridget could not contain an eye roll. Coombe was unaware of just how illustrious Jackson Fletcher's prospects had become with his new, pivotal role within the War Department, but it wouldn't matter to him if he did. He was still stuck on the idea of the Golden Lady going to someone else, like a prize won at cards, instead of it being *her* decision. But the eye roll was stopped short when she heard the next exchange.

"Then what do you know of Miss Bridget Forrester? I have to say she seemed pleasant enough to me. Pretty, too, in a freckled sort of way," Mr. Hartley offered, and Bridget silently thanked him (freckles aside) for his kindness. Because she knew—knew to her toes—what Coombe's answer would be.

"Yes, well, don't let that fool you. She is an absolute shrew. Last Season, whenever anyone approached her, she said either something snide or nothing at all. Shocking that she's related to the Golden Lady."

"Oh," was Hartley's only reply. And with that single word, Bridget knew that any chance of dancing with Hartley—of dancing with anyone this Season—was next to nothing.

"Don't worry, chap," Coombe replied, their voices getting fainter as they moved away from the refreshment table, "this town is full of lovely young ladies for you to converse with. I'll steer you around the unpleasant ones. Perhaps we'll even find one who likes sheep as much as you do."

Bridget stood quietly behind the fronds of the palm. She did not sink back against the wall. She had too much pride for that. Her eyes remained quite dry—indeed, to cry over the opinion of someone as low in her estimation as Coombe was a waste of perfectly good salt water. Instead, she let a wave of resignation move over her, straightening her spine, setting her jaw defiantly.

No, she would get no second chances. No blank slate. Instead her character was fixed as "unpleasant." And there seemed little she could do but endure it.

It was going to be a long Season.

Two

Two things came in quick succession that would change Bridget Forrester's fortunes and alter the course of her second Season.

The first was a letter.

The second was a tree.

Bridget was where she always was when the first of these life-altering objects made their arrival: the music room. And it was hand-delivered by her little sister.

"I knew I'd find you here!" Mandy—Amanda, as she preferred to be called now, Bridget quickly admonished herself—exclaimed as she raced into the room, her face flushed, eyes sparkling.

Bridget did not pause in the minuet she was practicing. "And what new bit of gossip have you heard?"

Amanda pulled off her bonnet, her bright, shiny curls bouncing as she did so.

"Why would you think I have gossip?" Amanda frowned.

"Because you rushed in here from shopping with Mother, and you didn't even pause to take off your cloak and bonnet," Bridget replied, unable to hide a smirk.

"Well, if you don't want my gossip, I shan't give it to you." Amanda said in a huff. At sixteen, Amanda had reached her full height—at least everyone hoped she had, since she had outstripped their father and most men of their acquaintance. But her features still maintained the roundness of girlhood, and her hair still bounced around her shoulders. Mother never let any of them put their hair up before seventeen, no matter how much they had all whined and begged.

"Fine," Bridget said, smiling to herself, wondering how long Amanda could hold out before the dam burst.

Amanda came to sit next to her on the bench. Idly, she tapped her finger against the wood, then leaned her elbow against the pianoforte's frame, her head against her hand. Staring her sister down.

"That's a pretty piece. What is it?"

"It's a Bach minuet," Bridget answered, her fingers hopping over the keys in their happy rhythm. She'd always found the piece rather wistful, even though it employed staccato.

"Really?" Amanda asked, her brow coming down. "It sounds different."

"Well, I'm fiddling about with a variation," Bridget admitted. Indeed, the Minuet in G Major was a clean but somewhat simplistic piece. Its bass clef was little more than long-held chords. Today, Bridget wanted a challenge.

Bridget had always found that the easiest way to put away her social failures was to lose herself in a challenging bit of music. To let her fingers flow over the keys, moving and mutating the sounds she knew, took all of her will, so that she had none left over to reflect on how Mr. Coombe had denigrated her to Mr. Hartley the night before, and how Mr. Hartley had believed him so faithfully. How she had not received one single request to dance. How she had kept a smile pasted on her face until it became strained, painful, and still it was for nothing.

It was all her sister's fault.

Not Amanda's of course—as she was not yet out, she could not really have any effect on Bridget's social successes or failures—but Sarah's. If Sarah had not spent all of last Season—Bridget's first—being so popular . . . If Sarah had not seemed to shun Bridget when she proved less popular than she . . . If Sarah had not had so many suitors they left none for poor Bridget, and she was sought out only by those wishing to charm inside information about her sister out of her . . .

But really, it was difficult to blame Sarah when she was

now married and living in her own town house a few streets away, and not at all involved in the Little Season's social whirl.

Luckily, as she played the Minuet in G Major, and her variations on it, Bridget did not have to think about such trying things.

Until, of course, she ran out of music. Which she did far too quickly.

"Are you finished?" Amanda asked excitedly.

"Apparently," Bridget replied, lifting her fingers off the keys.

"Good, so now I can tell you my news!"

"You made it thirty-two measures, I'm impressed."

Amanda shot Bridget a look of sisterly exasperation.

"Fine," Bridget said, holding up her hands. "What did you learn today on Bond Street?"

Bridget braced herself for being told of some wonderful salon to which she would not be invited, or the announcement of some young lady's engagement, a girl who had come out at the same time as Bridget. But instead, Amanda launched into a breathless narrative that, surprisingly, turned out to be all about Bridget.

"We didn't learn anything on Bond Street; in fact, we only made it to one shop before it began to snow so heavily that Mother insisted we come back before the roads became impassable, although I did get a new bonnet ribbon, which will hopefully last me through St. Valentine's Day because one simply cannot wear bright spring colors in winter, it just seems lazy. But anyway," Amanda plowed on, taking a deep breath, "when we got home the post had been delivered, and since Mother was occupied telling the butler to make sure the front steps were swept of the snow in a timely fashion, I looked through it myself, and there was a letter that was addressed to the Forrester Family *from Venice* of all places, and since I'm a Forrester I decided I should be allowed to open it and so I did."

And with that, Amanda took the letter out of her pocket and held it out to Bridget.

"Mother will be absolutely livid that you took a letter without her permission!" Bridget admonished.

"Bridget, just read it!" Amanda bounced in her seat. "Hurry!"

Bridget took it with some caution. "But we don't know any-one in Venice."

"That's what I thought, too! But apparently, you do."

"Me?" Bridget replied, perplexed.

She unfolded the letter. And as she read the words, each more fantastical than the last, a buzz of anticipation and excitement spread through her core.

Dear Lord and Lady Forrester—

I am writing this note on behalf of my good friend Signor Vincenzo Carpenini, the musician and composer, who, I am told, is well-known to you. His written English is unfortunately unequal to the task. Signor Carpenini and I are currently planning a tour of his latest compositions in northern Europe and England. He has mentioned several times that your daughter, Miss Brittany, has great raw skill at the pianoforte, and perhaps—should she be of a mind to further improvement—you would be amenable to having her become a pupil of his. Be aware, the Signore rarely takes on students but felt her natural talent worthy of his instruction. If it is agreeable to you, the Signore will call at your household upon his arrival in London.

Yours, etc.—
Oliver Merrick, Esq.
Rio di San Salvador, Venice

Bridget stared for some minutes at the letter, letting its words flow over her, some fragments of sentences making sense, and then others not.

"You remember Signor Carpenini, don't you, Bridge?" Amanda said, gleefully.

Of course Bridget remembered Signor Carpenini. It had been one of the pinnacles of her short life, meeting the Signore.

It was five summers ago. A few years before Sarah's first season. They were at their home near Portsmouth, which, as a major shipping city, always had people passing through. And their father, Lord Forrester, had a propensity to take in strays. Thus, people of the thinnest connection to the Forresters were always invited to stay at their beloved Primrose Manor while they waited for passage on a ship that had been delayed, or for friends who were at sea two days—or sometimes two weeks— longer than expected.

Lord Forrester at least had discretion enough that these people were, in general, incredibly interesting. There was the time a young painter, Mr. Turner, came for lunch while he waited for a colleague to come in on the ship from Spain. Mr. Turner became quite taken with the rolling hills of Primrose and the violence of the sea at their far edge. There was another time that Bridget's mother's second cousin's four nephews came in from the wilds of America and stayed the night, before beginning the long trip up to Scotland, where their mother's second cousin lived, as they were sent to help him build a manufactory. Bridget, Sarah, and Amanda beat those four strapping young boys soundly at bowls. (Sarah was, Bridget had to admit, a rather fierce bowl-player.) And Sarah's own husband, Jack, had once been such a stray, as a midshipman at the nearby Royal Naval Academy. But having a house opened to unexpected visitors her whole life in no way prepared Bridget for the arrival of Signor Carpenini.

She had been in the music room—which was not uncommon at any point in her life, but especially at the age of fourteen. She preferred to hide there. From her governess, who would no doubt try to make her learn more Latin. Really, she should be learning Italian, given the amount of musical terminology written in that language—but no, Miss Pritchett insisted that Latin was the root of all romantic languages, and therefore it was better to learn that stuff and nonsense. She hid as well from her mother, who would undoubtedly try to tie another bow in her hair, no matter how much she had exclaimed that her unruly, curly dark hair was statement enough and did not require any frills or furbelows. And from her sisters, who would try to rope her into widening pursuits—be it a walk to town, or shopping, or playing a game. Right at that moment, at fourteen, she just felt like playing music.

Of course, the fact that she was hiding didn't mean that she hadn't been found.

Sarah had entered abruptly, interrupting what Bridget had been playing—an étude, if she recalled correctly—and wheedled, whined, and cajoled Bridget into accompanying her while she practiced singing a new tune.

Bridget grumbled but complied. After all, Bridget didn't sing. Sarah did not sing much better, but she insisted on trying.

"*For tho' his body is under hatches, his soul is gone aloft . . .*" Sarah sang in her soft, thin voice, finishing out the strains to the not particularly feminine tune "Tom Bowling." Bridget let her chords resolve . . . then, struck by a moment of impishness, played a few runs and triads—a flourish to finish off the piece. Though it was completely incongruous to the theme of the song, after playing accompaniment for the past half hour, it felt good to let her fingers run free.

"Why must you always do that?" Sarah had asked, her brow coming down. "It's a sad song!"

"Would it be better if I did this?" Bridget asked, playing a range of minor chords in a progression that could only spell out doom for the poor sailor, Tom Bowling.

"*Si*, that is better," came a thickly accented voice at the door. Both Bridget and Sarah turned and saw in the doorway a dark-haired, dark-eyed stranger. Behind him an equally dark-haired but hazel-eyed man hovered, anxiousness apparent in his tall frame.

"Vincenzo, Lady Forrester has had luncheon laid for us. If you will excuse us, ladies," the lighter-eyed, anxious one spoke, his voice the epitome of aristocratic English.

"No, *uno momento*, Oliver," the first man said, as he angled his way into the music room and came to stand over Bridget. She craned her neck to see up into his face.

"Play it again," he intoned, his hand behind his back. "But this time, *calando, ritardando*."

If Bridget was slightly confused why this man would be dictating how she played, she was also too curious about his critique to voice objection. She put her fingers to the keys and played the same minor chord progression that he had deemed better than before. But as per his request, she gradually lessened the pressure, the intensity, the music becoming slower and softer, as if drifting away to sea. When she lifted her fingers from the pianoforte, the note faded away, and all that was left was . . .

"Melancholy," came the British voice of the light-eyed man—Oliver, he had been called—by the door. "Beautiful."

Bridget noticed that all the tension had left his shoulders for those few moments, and his line of sight went straight through the window to somewhere far, far away. The continental man who hovered over her, however, wore a smirk on his face.

"*Si*, Oliver! Exact!" he cried triumphantly. "You do well! I will hear more later!" And with that, he slapped Bridget on the back—a shocking gesture, not only for its impact but its intimacy—and made for the door.

"*Ciao, signorinas*," he said, with a flourishing bow, and made his way past his friend, then disappeared down the hall, following where his stomach took him.

"*Ciao*, Signor Carpenini, Mr. Merrick," Sarah replied, giving a small wave. The man who remained in the doorway— the light-eyed English one—snapped out of his reverie, tension returning to his shoulders as he gave a stiff bow, and made to follow his friend. But Bridget could only pay cursory attention to him. Because, if she was not mistaken, Sarah had called the Italian man . . .

"Did you say Signor Carpenini?" she asked, breathless.

"Yes, I did."

"Vincenzo Carpenini? The *composer*?"

Sarah nodded. "He and his friend Mr. Merrick are on their way to Italy, but their ship was delayed until tomorrow. Why do you think I wanted to practice this song? Mother intends to have us play after supper."

"Oh my goodness." Bridget's voice came out a squeak. "Oh my goodness."

"Bridge—are you all right?" Sarah asked, looking queerly into her face. "You haven't blinked in the last two minutes."

"What? No! I mean, yes, I'm all right!" Bridget said finally. "But what are you doing just standing there? We must practice!"

And they had, Bridget working her fingers over the keys long after Sarah had felt she had practiced her fill and abandoned Bridget to the pianoforte. Bridget, of course, did not limit herself to playing droning chords for Sarah while she sang "Tom Bowling," but instead, once dinner was over, she rushed to the piano and was ready to play the entirety of a Haydn concerto. When she was finished, and after Sarah had dutifully sung "Tom Bowling," both guests had clapped enthusiastically, and then . . .

Bridget would never forget it.

Signor Carpenini made his way over to the pianoforte, kissed her hand, and declared to the room, "Marvelous! Send her to me, and I will make a virtuoso of her!"

Of course, she was not to be sent to Signor Carpenini. She knew this immediately. He was going to Italy the next day, after all, and Bridget was but fourteen. And no girl, especially not one of aristocratic birth, would be allowed to travel to Italy alone to study music.

But she had been so *proud* when he had said it. Practically glowing with it, her mother commented to her later. So full of . . . confidence.

It had been a long time since Bridget had felt such confidence. To know that *she* was the one, for that briefest moment in time, standing at the center of the universe and succeeding at the task in front of her.

But again, that was more than five years ago.

"Of course I remember the Signore," Bridget answered her sister. "But he apparently doesn't remember me. My name is not Brittany," she murmured, on a frown.

Amanda rolled her eyes. "He certainly remembers your playing! Who else could he mean, silly?" She snatched the letter back, before Bridget could stop her. "You're the only one of us he heard play—and besides, you're the only one who could have 'great raw skill' . . . Sarah and I are abysmal."

"He thinks my skill raw," Bridget said dully. Then a terrible thought wretched through her. "Oh Lord—does that mean he thinks I play *poorly*? As if I am too unformed a player to have any true talent?"

Amanda blinked at her twice before shaking her head. "How is it possible that you heard only that one word? Instead of *great* and *skill*?"

Instead of answering, Bridget snatched the letter back. "Hold on. I have to read it again. I have to make certain—"

"Make certain of what? Yes, you play excellent pianoforte. Yes, he wants to tutor you. Yes, yes, yes!" Amanda cried, grabbing Bridget by the shoulders and giving her a small shake. "And most importantly, yes, you have to tell Mother that you rifled the mail without her knowledge."

"Oh, hang that!" Bridget said, her heartbeat finally catching up with her shock as excitement coursed through her body.

"You tell her *you* rifled the mail, and then I'll tell her I am about to become a student of the great composer Signor Carpenini!"

ॐ

Lady Forrester was duly annoyed at her youngest daughter and duly enthusiastic for her middle child upon hearing about the letter.

"Of course we will receive him when he comes, darling!" Lady Forrester cried. "He doesn't list a date of arrival, does he? Hmm . . . well, for now I suppose there is little to be done but wait."

And so they waited. Bridget practiced and practiced while she waited. She went to boring teas and dances where she was rarely asked to partner anyone. But now, it was actually tolerable. Because she had this shining, glowing ball of light inside her. A secret, better than anything anyone had ever had happen to them.

Well, it was inevitable, wasn't it, that such a shining glowing secret could not stay secret for long.

It happened casually. Some first-Season debutante, her mother hovering gently in the background with Lady Forrester, asking Bridget in the awkward silence of polite small talk if she played music.

"Oh, yes," Bridget replied smartly. "I've played forever."

"Oh, as have I," the debutante—a Miss Parrish, who had in a few short weeks in the Little Season gained a reputation as a silly girl with as voracious an appetite for gossip as her mother had for food—said on a very dramatic sigh. "I absolutely loathed it as a girl. All those lessons, and music masters forcing me to spend hours on a hard bench, bored to tears— why, it was only when I pointed out to my mother how ugly and curled my hands were becoming that I was permitted to stop!" She finished on a laugh and glanced pointedly at Bridget's hands.

Bridget stretched out her gloved fingers. They were long and elegant, nothing cramped or ugly about them. Granted, they were a little smaller than ideal—she could barely span an octave, no matter how much she stretched her hands—and the constant practice kept her nails blunt, but out of everything that could possibly be wrong with Bridget, her hands were certainly not one of them.

"Actually, I've found that constant practice keeps my fingers dexterous and nimble. Perhaps your music master had you positioning yours incorrectly," Bridget replied, unable to keep a hint of archness out of her voice. Then she let her gaze slide to Miss Parrish's hands, which were so plump, they looked like sausages in her gloves.

"Oh, so you still take lessons?" Miss Parrish continued, seemingly ignorant of any askance looks on Bridget's part. "One would think that such instruction would have ended with the schoolroom. But if you require extra lessons . . ."

"Oh I wouldn't call them a requirement," Bridget responded, her reaction to the smugness in Miss Parrish's voice strong and swift. Her own voice rose in volume, ever so slightly. "But when Signor Carpenini asks to take one on as a student, the extra instruction seems worthwhile."

"Signor Carpenini?" Miss Parrish repeated, blinking in surprise. Mrs. Parrish, who had suspended her conversation with Bridget's mother and taken a half step closer to them, blinked, too.

"Yes," Lady Forrester said, jumping into the fray. "When the man returns to London, Bridget is to be one of his pupils."

"You must be incredibly accomplished, Miss Forrester," Mrs. Parrish replied.

"Er, yes," Miss Parrish added, after a pointed look from her mother. "Perhaps you should put on a musicale, Miss Forrester. Show everyone your talent."

"Perhaps we shall," Lady Forrester replied. "But most likely in the regular Season. Bridget darling, I see your father calling us."

And with that curtsies were made, and Lady Forrester excused them from the Parrishes.

"Mrs. Parrish grew her daughter's penchant for gossip," Lady Forrester muttered, taking Bridget's arm while pulling her silk shawl tighter about herself. It was remarkably cold for a ballroom full of people, but the winter so far had no intentions of being mild. "It will be all over before tomorrow. I told you, we should keep this to ourselves for now."

Bridget grimaced as her mother's fingers unwittingly bit

deeper into her arm. "I know, Mother, I'm sorry. I couldn't stop myself." Then she looked up, as if raising her eyes to the heavens. "Surely it isn't a terrible thing to have known. After all, he *is* coming back, and I *will* be his pupil."

"I know, my dear, I know." Lady Forrester squeezed her hand as they threaded through the crowd. "But it invites trouble to brag about future accomplishments. I simply do not wish to put the cart before the horse. Do you take my meaning?"

Bridget grasped her mother's meaning—but she did not understand the full measure of her social mistake until a week or so later. Yes, indeed, Miss Parrish and her mother had managed to work Bridget's stunning news into every conversation they had. For a few days, it actually had a positive effect on Bridget's popularity. She was asked to dance once at a public ball, and twice at small soirees. Granted, both times there was a scarcity of other partners to be had, but Bridget was strictly admonished to "not look a gift horse in the mouth." (Her mother's recent overuse of horses in metaphors merited some attention, however.)

But the most unfortunate surprise was when Lady Worth, a leading society matron and a dear friend of her sister Sarah— and a lady whose very voice set Bridget's teeth on edge— asked Bridget to play the pianoforte.

"My dear, you simply must!" Phillippa, Lady Worth, said, as they milled around her alarmingly pink drawing room, waiting for dinner to be rung. Lady Worth's dinner parties, as with all of Lady Worth's activities, were the height of fashion. Therefore one could expect to be served fashionably late. "After we dine, I should love to hear what you've been working on!" Then she turned to Lady Chatsworth, a woman of Mrs. Parrish's social circle who seemed appropriately cowed to have been invited to a party by Phillippa Worth. "Of course, I've heard Miss Forrester play many times when I have visited her home, and she is so talented. But she so rarely accepts invitations to play publicly!"

A trickle of fear ran down Bridget's spine. Yes, since coming out, she rarely accepted invitations to play in public, with good reason.

"I find it so odd that you would not wish to play in public, Miss Forrester," Lady Chatsworth was saying, a glint of suspicion in her eye. "Especially considering the status of tutor your playing apparently attracts."

Bridget blinked twice, hesitating. Luckily Lady Worth was there to fill the void.

"Precisely why she does not! Indeed, I think we should be thanking her," Phillippa smiled easily. "Think of how all the other young ladies, like your own Henrietta, who practice their scales and trills and whatnot, would have felt having to play after someone of such refined skill?"

"Yes . . . well . . ." Lady Chatsworth said, her cheeks becoming florid. "Henrietta's playing was proficient enough to win her a fine fiancé. Without the help of fancy Italian tutors."

"I would never say otherwise!" Phillippa cried. "Indeed, I am all astonishment that you would think so! I should never say something so rude about one of my guests. As I know, neither would you." Steel had laced her sweet words, and Lady Chatsworth was smart enough to concede to the more socially influential lady in the room.

Perhaps Lady Worth's voice was not so grating after all, Bridget had to admit to herself.

"You simply have to play for us after supper," Lady Worth said graciously, turning back to Bridget. But her smile was firm and insistent.

Dread. Cold, pure dread started in the base of her stomach. But no, she would turn it away. Force it into submission. It was ridiculous, and more to the point, utterly vain to be nervous about playing. Thus she forced a smile that matched Lady Worth's, and replied, "With pleasure, ma'am."

As the eavesdropping vultures moved off from their little circle, Lady Worth turned her full attention to Bridget. "You are suddenly quite alarming pale, Miss Forrester," she assessed, keeping her smile for appearances' sake. "Dare I assume you suffer from a touch of nerves?"

Heat flushed across Bridget's face. She *hated* being so transparent. Especially to someone like Lady Worth, whose manipulations were partially to blame for Sarah's success the previous Season. Bridget had resented the highly polished woman for her interference, no matter that Sarah had flourished under it. And Lady Worth had tended to regard her—at least in Bridget's estimation—as little more than a bother-some fly.

Although why she would concern herself with how Bridget felt now, she had no idea.

"I do not think my playing is a good idea, Lady Worth. I have nothing prepared . . ." Bridget began to demur, but Lady Worth cut her off with a wave of her hand.

"Don't be ridiculous. You sister tells me you have hundreds of pieces memorized. And your mother tells me you play hours every day, so one must assume you have something in your repertoire."

Bridget's mind looped back over the course of the past week. The occasional dances, the gushing from one lady who said she was *sooo* lucky to have such a tutor, the pointed glances, and then her mother insisting on fitting this dinner party into their incredibly empty schedule. Bridget sought the eyes of her mother across the room and found her suspicions confirmed in Lady Forrester's guilty look.

"You mean . . . did you throw this dinner party so I would have a stage upon which to exhibit?" Bridget asked, her entire body freezing in fear.

"Of course not," Phillippa replied. "Although it is the only reason I would invite Lady Chatsworth. She is the most musically inclined of her little group. And it is why I invited Lord Merrick, of course."

"Lord Merrick?" Bridget asked. The name was incredibly familiar.

"Yes—the father of Mr. Oliver Merrick, Signor Carpenini's friend. The one who wrote you. Heavens, child, you mean you have not been introduced? That will be remedied shortly. You are seated next to him at dinner. To my knowledge, he is not particularly musical, but his late wife was," Lady Worth continued. "So you should be able to impress him with your knowledge."

Bridget was going to demur further, try to talk her way out of this situation that had put a hole in her stomach, but Lady Worth took her by the elbow and steered her to a more private corner of the room, where her smile instantly dropped.

"My dear Miss Bridget, if you are to convince the populace that you have what it takes to be a student of Signor Carpenini, you *must* play. There is simply no other way around it. Now, if you are as good as I assume you to be, then you have nothing to worry about."

Spoken like someone who had never worried about anything, Bridget thought, her mind a huff. Never worried about how she was being perceived, about how people were *judging*, looking, peering closely to see if the cracks lined up as they should.

Bridget was a marvelous player. She never had loved anything like she loved music, and never would. But at some point, early in her first Season . . . music had failed her.

She had stood up to play at her first party—certain that this would be the thing to make her shine, the thing to make her stand out from a crowded field of young debutantes of refinement. She had smiled as she sat at the beautiful, expensive showpiece of a pianoforte, and . . .

And her eyes had caught on her sister Sarah across the room. Flirting with some man, some group of men, who all only had eyes for her. And for the first time in her life, Bridget had felt fear upon placing her fingers on the keys.

It wasn't bad at first. She had played the opening stanza beautifully. But then she flubbed an arpeggio, and her fingers stumbled a bit on a key change. One thing building on another, like a snowball rolling downhill, becoming a boulder, and suddenly, Bridget was glancing wildly about her and finding herself . . . lost. By the end, the polite applause Bridget received was just that . . . polite. Not the triumph she had expected, that she needed.

The weight of judgment had fallen, and Bridget had been crushed beneath it.

She tried again, of course, but the second time was almost worse than the first, as she had that pit of dread in her stomach from the beginning. It was utterly bewildering, as Bridget had played in front of people loads of times! When people visited Primrose, they begged for a performance! Signor Carpenini, for heaven's sake!

It was only at that time, in her first Season, when she was being judged on *everything*, that her playing was affected.

She was tempted to give up—but how could she give up the one thing that acted as solace? So she played at home, practiced, intent on rediscovering perfection. And with only her family to overhear, the family who had listened patiently through her first scales a decade and a half ago, she was completely fine. Better than fine, actually. She was . . .

"I am that good, Lady Worth," Bridget replied fiercely.

"Are you certain?" Lady Worth replied, her eyebrow going up.

"Yes. I am brilliant," Bridget stated. Her words might be full of bravado, but there was conviction behind them. At least enough to fool Lady Worth, who leaned in close, and whispered:

"Then play like it."

❧

She would. She would play like there was no tomorrow. The pit in her stomach, that cool dread making camp there, dissipated and howled against the fire now in her belly.

I can do this. I can do this.

All through dinner, Bridget repeated this mantra to herself, willing away that nervousness. She would play the Bach minuet she had been practicing the other day—perhaps she would even be so bold as to play the variation she had been fiddling with. No—that would be a mistake. Instead, let them see how perfectly she could play the original. Every note, every run, would fall perfectly in time. She could do that, she told herself.

Bridget held fast to the mental fever, to the focus that she needed to get through the meal—both interminable and too short!—and play. She was good enough. For heaven's sake, she was going to be a student of Carpenini, wasn't she?

"What did you say, my child?" Lord Merrick—an older, gruff man seated at the table next to her—asked in between bites of mutton. "Something about Carpenini?"

Oh dear Lord, had she been muttering her mantra aloud? Bridget blushed, mortified, hoping that no one would be paying their section of the table any attention. But Bridget's luck had never been that good, and at the word *Carpenini*, several people in their immediate vicinity grew silent. The gentleman with little pieces of mutton stuck in his long sideburns did not seem to notice, however. Instead, he nudged his elbow into Bridget's arm, attempting to prompt her to speak.

"Cat got your tongue, child?"

"More likely she was simply talking to herself, Lord Merrick," came the voice of Henrietta Chatsworth—Lady Chatsworth's eldest, snobbiest daughter—from the man's other side. Bridget feared for the girl's fiancé; her hearing was too sharp and her nose too pointed to make for a pleasant life. "After all, whom else would she talk to?"

Bridget's eyes narrowed at the taunt. But as much as she wished to stare daggers at Henrietta, she knew it would only cause her reputation to further deteriorate, and therefore, she would have to try to be—*ugh*—sweet.

"We cannot all be as talkative as you, Henrietta," Bridget replied, her tones so saccharine they would have turned lemons into lemonade. "I'm sorry, er, Lord Merrick," she continued, turning her attention to the gentleman between them. "Miss Chatsworth is correct that I was talking to myself."

"About Carpenini?" Lord Merrick replied, surprised. "Whatever for?"

"Well," Bridget began. "I am a great admirer of his music . . ."

Merrick harrumphed at that.

"As I would assume your son is?" Bridget's brow came down in confusion. "After all, he must be great friends with the composer, if he is bringing him with him to England . . ."

"No, he is not!" Lord Merrick exclaimed. "Fortunately or unfortunately, take your pick."

His words came out with a measure of hurt behind them. But Bridget was far more concerned with the content of his speech than the emotions behind it.

"He's . . . not?" she stuttered, dread driving her heartbeat faster.

"He's not?" Henrietta injected herself into the conversation. "But how can that be?" Her voice dripped with the same acidic sweetness that had colored Bridget's earlier tones. "When Miss Forrester here has been telling everyone that Carpenini asked if she would be his student?"

Bridget turned her mortified gaze to Lord Merrick. "I . . . that is, we . . . had a letter. Written by your son on behalf of Signor Carpenini, saying that they were coming to London."

"And when did you receive this letter, Miss Forrester?" Lord Merrick regarded her with a gleam of interest in his eye.

"A few weeks ago, sir," Bridget replied, only to watch Lord Merrick's face fall abruptly, then reconstitute itself into resignation.

"I thought so. Your letter predates mine." Lord Merrick shook his head and heaved a great sigh. "I'm sorry, my girl; I had a letter from my son not two days ago. It was brief, but in it he expressly said since he is not needed at home, he is extending his stay in Venice—and Signor Carpenini with him."

"But . . . but . . ." Bridget couldn't tear her eyes from Lord Merrick's face. If she did, she knew she would see Henrietta Chatsworth positively crowing with delight.

Lord Merrick gave her a pitying pat on the shoulder. "Neither my son nor Carpenini is coming to England anytime soon."

I can do this. I can do this.

She still had to play. If fact, as Henrietta whispered her delicious piece of gossip to the person on her other side, and it spread in a loop around the table, it became even more imperative that she show them all that she was imbued with real talent and skill. Or at least that was what Lady Worth whispered in her ear before she could slink away into the background.

"Let them know who you are, Bridget," Lady Worth had said. "Make them eat their words."

And so Bridget, her back straight and proud, still holding on for dear life to the focus she needed to play, walked through the crowd to the far side of Lady Worth's pink sitting room and seated herself at the gleaming cherrywood pianoforte that had been placed there for her benefit.

The room grew quiet, stilling itself as the audience arranged themselves in their seats. Bridget felt a nervous giggle bubbling up and stifled it. After all, when was the last time any of the ton was so attentive to a debutante's musical efforts? They were all so serious, so terribly curious!

But instead of giving in to a small hysteria, Bridget lifted the smooth hinged lid, revealing the ivory keys.

She took a deep breath and let her fingers rest lightly on the cool ivory, finding her first position for the Bach minuet as easily, as instinctually as breathing.

She let her muscles flex—not moving the fingers, mind, not yet ready to play. But just enough that she could map out where she wanted her force and power to go. She let the piece play in her head, let it wash over her, so much that everyone else in the room faded away.

I can do this.

Bridget played. She let the melody flow from her fingertips. And for once, it felt as if she might have it. As though the people who were staring at her were not there to judge her, and she were allowed to simply play the way she liked. To lose herself in the music.

But then . . .

A giggle intruded on her thoughts. But Bridget could not afford to let it distract her. So she played on, wiping it from her mind.

It was probably Henrietta Chatsworth who giggled.

It probably was, and she was probably giggling with Lord Merrick, who had been so sad himself and yet had regarded Bridget with pity.

Bridget suddenly realized her pace was too fast. Oh dear, this minuet would be over before too long, and Lady Worth would make her play something else, something longer. Better to slow down.

She changed her pace for the next stanza. But this just made her feel off. The G-major minuet was lively, spritely. But then again, its tempo was *moderato*; perhaps she should aim for somewhere in between?

A cough from somewhere in the back of the room jolted Bridget's fingers, and she missed the F-sharp at the bottom of a long string of eighth notes, turning the entire run sour.

No, this mustn't happen. I can do this.

. . . Can't I?

At the refrain, she felt like it was a new start. But so much had come before it, it was impossible to undo all the damage. It was like a snowball rolling downhill—only getting larger and larger in her mind, a number of little mistakes adding up. Henrietta's giggle, Bridget messing up the tempo, Lord Merrick telling her that Carpenini wasn't coming . . .

Carpenini wasn't coming.

Another note missed, another half rest not held right. Basic music, things taught to children in the nursery, was abandoning Bridget. Until finally, she could not take it anymore.

The piece still had sixteen measures left to it. But they didn't matter.

She lifted her fingers from the keys as if they burned.

"I'm sorry," she croaked out, with tears in her eyes.

And then, before she could see her mother's dismay, Lady Worth's disappointment, Henrietta Chatsworth's glee, or Lord Merrick's pity, Bridget ran from the room.

That night, as Bridget lay awake in bed, her wretchedness acute, Mother Nature decided she agreed wholeheartedly with the ton, and that it was futile for Bridget to continue the farce of being a London debutante, and delivered that second thing that would in quick succession forever alter Bridget's life.

She dropped a tree on their house.

Three

"WELL, this cannot possibly get any worse!" Lady Forrester cried as they surveyed the damage the next morning.

The tree in question—usually standing strong and elegant on the edge of the square, just across the thin street from the Forresters' front door—thanks to the thick ice weighing down its branches and a suspiciously strong breeze that had exploited a weakness within the tree's trunk, now resided in the drawing room of the Forrester house.

"I tell you, my dear, I have absolutely had it!" Lady Forrester continued huffing to her husband. Lord Forrester stood in the doorway to the drawing room next to his daughters, staring into the wreckage while stroking his mustache in a nervous habit. Lady Forrester was working herself up into a good lather. The crash that had come in the wee hours of the morning had awoken the entire household, but only now, after the sun was well up, were they able to properly assess the damage.

The two large framed windows facing the street in the drawing room were completely smashed in, broken glass mixing with melting ice and shards of wood from the window frames. Additionally, the masonry work of the Forrester town house must have been atrociously shoddy, since parts of the stone facade and bits of wall littered the now utterly ruined carpet, too.

"How could we have possibly been living in a house as badly constructed as this one?" Bridget's mother cried, as she paced. "We should take the builders to court!"

"Considering the house was built sometime before George the Third's ascension, I doubt the builders are still alive, my dear," Lord Forrester replied, but a swift kick from his youngest daughter, Amanda, stilled him from making further comment. A look passed between them told Bridget it was best to not poke the grumpy bear.

The grumpy bear in question shot her husband a dangerous look as she continued gesticulating from the doorway. None of the family had been allowed in the drawing room until all of the broken glass could be cleaned up, and thus they were relegated to the hall outside.

"Look at the mess! It looks like a cannon fired through the house!"

"That's only because you refuse to wear your spectacles," Lord Forrester muttered, and received swift kicks from both his daughters. "Er, I mean, my love, it's not that bad. Just a few broken windows. We will simply close this room off until repairs can be made . . ."

"Close the room off? We cannot very well close it off from the street, can we? What will people say about us living in such conditions? Why will young men want to call when they have to weather that eyesore to do so?"

Bridget's heart sank at her mother's words. She was too tired, too sad to contradict her by saying that no young men were going to come calling—at least not until Amanda made her debut in two years' time.

The situation was disheartening all around.

"All right, all right," Lord Forrester was saying, holding up his hands. "We can remove from the house, then. I'm certain we can find a suitable one to rent, or perhaps Sarah's new home can sustain us until the repairs are done . . ."

But a furious look lit his wife's eyes. "I am not about to impose on my newly married daughter with our entire family! I doubt Jackson would much appreciate the intrusion, either. As for letting a house—nothing would be available on short notice. Oh! Why don't you understand? I've absolutely had it with winter altogether!"

The sisters, meanwhile, watched their parents' heated conversation in a mild state of shock.

"Bridget," Amanda whispered, taking a small step back and pulling her sister with her, "have you ever seen them argue like this?"

"No," Bridget whispered back. "Not in front of us, at least." Indeed, their parents were usually very good about presenting a united front to their children, keeping any heated discussions behind closed doors. But now, with the pressures of a failing Little Season; a daughter who was not only "not taking," but seemed to prove repellent; and a tree through the house, cracks were beginning to show in their mother's usual practicality.

And Bridget knew it was her fault.

Not the tree, of course, but the other failures and catastrophes rested on her shoulders. After all, she had been the one who couldn't help telling the Parrishes that she would have Carpenini for a teacher, and she was the one who let her doubts overcome her on the stage when she had learned of the Signore's changed travel schedule.

When they came home after last night's musical debacle, her mother had said nothing. No recriminations, no lectures. And Bridget felt worse for it. It was as if through silence, her mother had said she finally realized that Bridget was beyond saving.

Yes, Bridget was tired of the winter, too.

"Well, then," their father was saying, stepping bravely back into the fray and trying to fix things, "perhaps you ladies should return to Primrose! I have to stay in London on Historical Society business, I'm afraid, but it must be much more cozy to the south."

Their mother snorted. "Primrose Manor is practically on the sea! The winds alone are freezing, and they've likely knocked another dozen trees into our home!"

"My dear, short of hibernating or removing winter altogether, I can see no way around the season but to wait it out!" their father harrumphed. Apparently the cracks were beginning to show for him, too.

"Remove winter altogether?" Amanda asked quietly, in their own corner of the hall. "What a strange notion."

"Indeed, how might one remove winter, do you imagine?"

Bridget replied as brightly as she could manage. "Setting large fires at appropriate intervals?"

"Building a large ship that takes you away from it?" Amanda tried, wrinkling her nose.

"Far more practical than my suggestion, but I fear that would be removing *from* winter, not—"

Bridget's voice caught in her throat. Could it be that simple? Was it possible there was a solution to all their woes, right in front of them?

For after all, it *was* possible to remove from winter—one simply had to go to a place where these early months were relatively mild. And what such land was renowned for its mild climate?

"*Italy*," she breathed, earning a quizzical stare from her sister.

"Bridget, what on earth . . . ?" Amanda began, but was cut off by Bridget's hand squeezing her arm.

"Mandy, do you want to spend the next few months with Miss Pritchett in the schoolroom at Primrose?" she whispered hurriedly.

"I doubt I'll have much choice in the matter . . ." Amanda replied, her brow coming down in confusion.

"I know I wouldn't. In fact, I would rather spend them learning from the world than reading about it. Wouldn't you?"

"Er, I suppose so . . ."

"Then agree with everything I say for the next five minutes." Bridget went on tiptoe to peck her sister on the cheek, then turned to her parents, who were still grumbling and staring daggers at each other.

"Father, what a marvelous solution you have struck upon. Mother, isn't it simply wonderful?" she cried, crossing the hallway to them, Amanda in tow.

"What?" her father replied. "What solution, child?"

"Why for the removal of winter! Or rather, for the removal *from* winter."

And with a tremulous smile, the largest of which had been seen on Bridget Forrester's face in nigh on a year, a plan was laid out that suddenly made a tree through a drawing room look like a stroke of good fortune, instead of the worst of luck.

"Husband," Lady Forrester cried when Bridget was done, "forgive me, but I must see to our trunks. We are off to Italy!"

Four

February 1824

A T *last*, Bridget thought, her body vibrating with excitement, *Italy*.

But not just Italy, no. *Venice*.

Although, she thought, wrinkling her nose in the salt air as they were transitioning from the large passenger ship that had borne them from Rome to a smaller skiff that would take them to the mass of islands that made up this miraculous city, Venice was not necessarily Italian at all.

While on board the *Tromba*, the Italian-owned merchant vessel that Bridget, her mother, and her younger sister had boarded in Portsmouth nearly a month ago, Bridget had been without what usually took up most of her time—a piano on board an oceangoing vessel was pure folly, after all.

Thus, she and Amanda had taken to wandering around the ship, pestering the captain of the *Tromba* (which meant "trumpet" in Italian, which Bridget took as a good sign). Well, Amanda was pestering. Bridget could not pester, as she couldn't get a word in edgewise, with Amanda peppering the captain with her questions about what was Italian, and what was not.

"But it says in my guidebook"—when they had decided on this trip, Amanda had immediately devoured every travelogue of Italy she could find in their family library, not to mention in London's bookshops—"that Venice is not *really* Italian!"

Captain Pirelli, a kind man, scoffed at the notion. "Venice, not Italian! That is like saying Rome is not Catholic!" And thus he humored their lack of knowledge about the world stage and took out his maps.

It seemed the wars at the beginning of the century had turned what had been a conglomeration of kingdoms that most Englishmen thought of as Italy into a bit of a redistricted mess, and Venice, at the very northern edge of the Adriatic sea, was no longer Italian at all, but part of the kingdom of Lombardy-Venetia.

"And since Lombardy-Venetia is ruled by Emperor Francis of Austria," Amanda concluded, "one could argue that Venice is . . . Austrian!"

"But do not worry," Captain Pirelli had said, his eyes crinkling to the superior Amanda and the blinking Bridget from behind his bushy beard. He must have been smiling in there, somewhere. "The city of Venice has survived the assaults of Turks and pirates and raiders for a thousand years. One little Austrian government is a minor thing in its history."

"But, Captain," Bridget had replied. "Who owns Venice?"

"The Venetians, my little *uccello canoro*." He tweaked her nose then, a gesture that in England would have earned him a strong reproof, not to mention the possibility of a duel for disgracing her so, but on board an Italian ship, the rules of Italy seemed to apply. And Italians *touched*. Even sheltered English ladies, who had their mother, three maids, and three footmen traveling with them for protection. (Lord Forrester, who could not accompany them on the trip because of "Historical Society business"—although Bridget suspected that her father's dislike of traveling farther than his library weighed more than business in his decision—refused to allow his ladies to travel with anything less.)

Italians also apparently called people by pet names. It took an Italian-to-English translation book and Captain Pirelli's own indulgence for her to figure out that *uccello canoro* translated to "warbler" or "songbird." Apparently, Bridget, without a pianoforte on board, had taken to getting the melodies that took up space in her mind out of her body by humming them under her breath—as her singing voice left much to be desired. According to Amanda she did this all the time, and as they shared a stateroom she had to beg her to stop humming as she fell asleep.

The pet names Bridget could get used to. The constant touches were a bit more disconcerting.

Really, between the little tweaks to the nose and the *uccello canoro*, Bridget would have half believed that Captain Pirelli was in love with her. If he weren't old enough to be her grandfather and didn't show off the miniature of his wife of thirty years to anyone who showed the slightest interest, that is.

She was sorry to say good-bye to Captain Pirelli when they docked in Rome. Indeed she was sad to say good-bye to the entire crew. (Their mother was less sorrowful, as she spent the first week of the journey "getting her sea legs" and never fully adjusted, practically kissing the ground as they disembarked.) But she was far too excited for what was to come to mourn for long.

It was as if, with each passing league away from London, she felt herself shedding the old Bridget as a bird molted feathers for the summer. The closer she got to the warmth of the Mediterranean, the farther she was from the wretched, scowling thing she had become over the course of the past year, watching her sister Sarah's success at the expense of having any herself. The Bridget whose fingers failed her when anyone other than her family watched her play.

It was her second chance. Her blank slate. She could be new again.

And, she had thought determinedly, with the help of Signor Carpenini, she would become the musician she was meant to be.

They had stayed in Rome for two days. Not long enough for their mother, who, after weeks at sea, was loath to board a ship again, and not nearly long enough for Amanda.

"But the Pantheon!" Amanda had cried, flipping to the appropriate page in her guidebook. "The Colosseum!"

"We will get to them." Bridget had tried to placate her sister. "After Venice."

As they had planned their trip in those frantic days in

London, Bridget had done her best to steer her family into the opinion that it was best to go to Venice first. "It will be much easier to start at the top and work our way down. That way, we will have less to travel on the return trip," she had said, as nonchalantly as she could manage.

This logic looked sound on paper, and therefore it was agreed on at the time. But now, having already docked in Rome, less than two days' travel by sea around the island of Sicily and up the Adriatic to her intended destination, Bridget could not let something as little as her mother's weariness and her sister's sightseeing enthusiasm stop them.

"But Venice will be crowded," Amanda warned. "It says right here in my guidebook—" But Bridget cut her off with a wave of her hand.

"Yes, yes, the carnival. I don't know why that worries you so; I think a carnival will be fun," Bridget said smoothly. "And of course it will be crowded; Venice is supposed to be the most beautiful city there is, and the most pleasant in temperature."

Amanda frowned a little and flipped pages, looking for any information that might relate to Venice's weather.

"Well, hopefully it will be warmer than Rome," Lady Forrester replied. "Their winters may be milder than England, but one could hardly call this gray atmosphere balmy or exotic."

Bridget nodded, and hoped that neither her sister nor her mother would realize that, being to the north, Venice's weather was likely similar to if not slightly cooler than Rome's. And since the English winter had been the excuse given for their escape, Bridget's fragile fiction could fall apart at the seams.

"Besides, we have already arranged for rooms in Venice, haven't we, Mother?" Bridget said finally.

Thankfully, this last little bit of persuasion did the trick, as Lady Forrester sighed and rang for the footmen to come and make sure their trunks were ready to be loaded onto the smaller ship that would take them to Venice in the morning.

Because it was in Venice that Signor Vincenzo Carpenini, master musician and composer, currently resided. And thus it was to Venice that Bridget would go.

"I told you we should have stayed in Rome."

Amanda puffed out the words on a sigh, low enough so

their mother wouldn't hear her frustration. Although their mother was already frustrated enough.

"What do you mean you have no rooms for us? We sent a messenger ahead to arrange for them!"

"Si, Signora, you did," Signor Zinni, the proprietor of the Hotel Cortile, located right off the winding Grand Canal, stammered, wringing his hands. His English was very good (and not surprisingly, so was his German), which was likely why the establishment was recommended to them as being very friendly to travelers of the Forresters' station and nationality. "But you arrived too quickly to receive our reply. The hotel is booked months in advance for Carnival!"

Carnival—not "a carnival," as Bridget had been quick to dismiss it—was the festival of indulgence that preceded Lent. And it was something for which Venice, according to Amanda's guidebook, was well-known.

For the months of January and February, before Ash Wednesday descended and ushered in forty days of penance, Venetians took it upon themselves to make certain they had something to repent. Well, at least they *had*, before Napoleon and Austria took the stuffing out of the city. Now, the custom was limited only to those who had the funds and the time to do so—that is, the wealthy and the tourists. Which seemed to make up the entirety of the Hotel Cortile's clientele.

White masks, faces blank and frozen, made to hide the sinners from the consequences of their sins, had stared back at them from other gondolas—some made out of plaster, some heavy ceramic. Yet all were strangely beautiful and grotesque. People danced in the streets and on the footbridges that arched over the narrower canals. And the music! There was music pouring out of every window, on every corner. No matter their exhaustion at travel, it made Bridget's senses awake with wonder, made her body vibrate with melody.

"Just wait until my husband's friends at the Society of Historical Art and Architecture of the Known World in London hear about this," Lady Forrester was saying in grand, tragic tones. It had taken two ships and a gondola to get them to this hotel, and Bridget knew her mother was not about to set foot on another waterborne vessel without putting up a fight. "They are the ones who recommended your establishment, Mr. Zinni. And they travel. Quite often."

Zinni blanched, as was appropriate. "Signora, the Carnival will be over after this Tuesday," he replied, thinking quickly. "Indeed, in four days time, you can have an entire floor of the hotel to yourselves." Lady Forrester squinted, then raised one imperious eyebrow at the little man. "At no additional cost, of course," he murmured.

Their mother, who relished negotiating more than was seemly for a lady of quality, preened a bit at winning that battle. But then she steadied herself and raised her eyebrow again at the hotelier. "That is all well and good, but what do I and my poor daughters do in the meantime?"

"I . . . I know not, Signora." Zinni shrugged. "Perhaps some of our gentlemen customers can be persuaded to share a space for a time? But it would take some lire . . ."

While their mother metaphorically rolled up her sleeves and set about haggling for a room like the very best fishwife, Bridget turned to Amanda, who was waiting by their luggage, trying to stay out of the way of the numerous people passing through the hotel's main entrance.

"Is Mother still negotiating with that poor man?" Amanda asked, her eyes never leaving the guidebook except to occasionally peek out the window, as if confirming something she had read.

"Intimidating him is more like it." Bridget threw her eyes over to her sister. "What are you reading about now?"

"Where we are," Amanda said. "Did you know that there are no carriages in Venice? No buggies? The narrowness of the streets and all the steps on the bridges don't allow for it. If you rode in a carriage, you'd never get anywhere." She nodded to the window, which opened up onto a smaller canal. "Everything has to be transported via those little flat boats. That or walking."

"Mother will be so pleased," Bridget said under her breath. "To have the choice between boats or walking." Amanda giggled. "Why do you have your nose in that thing constantly?" Bridget asked, suddenly struck by how often she had seen her sister buried in that book of late.

But Amanda just shrugged. "I like to know things. You and Mother and Sarah never tell me anything, so I have to figure it out on my own."

Bridget blinked in surprise. Although she supposed it was true. Last Season, Amanda was shielded from most of the dramatics, which drove the girl crazy with curiosity. And when she had decided to persuade her mother to take them to Italy, Bridget had simply told her sister to follow her lead, not giving her any more information than that. Surely she deserved a little more consideration.

"So," Bridget exhaled, seating herself next to Amanda. Amanda looked up, slightly surprised at this newfound attention. "Where are we? Precisely."

Amanda flipped the pages in the guidebook and found one with a detailed map of the streets and canals of the main island of Venice. The Grand Canal bisected the picture, and Amanda pointed to a small canal just to the east of it. "Here. Rio di San Marina."

Bridget dutifully looked to where Amanda's finger pointed, but her eyes found themselves falling on another *rio*, just a few canals away.

Rio di San Salvador.

Her breath caught as little pinpricks of awareness spread across her scalp. In the letter they had received from Carpenini's friend Mr. Merrick, regarding taking lessons with the Signore, he had given his address as the Rio di San Salvador.

And Mr. Merrick would know where she could find Carpenini.

Bridget peered closer at the map, her nose coming close enough to touch the pages.

"Good heavens, Bridge, do you need to borrow Mother's spectacles?" Amanda said, startling Bridget out of her reverie.

"What?" Bridget asked, her focus blurry as her head came up from the page. "Oh, no—ah, may I borrow this for a moment?"

Without waiting for an answer, Bridget grabbed the guidebook from Amanda's hands and quickly crossed the room to their haggling mother.

"Mother!" Bridget said breathlessly. "Look, we are on the Rio di San Marina."

"Yes, my dear, that's lovely. But I am trying to deal with our arrangements, as you see . . ."

"But, look how close we are to the Rio di San Salvador!"

Bridget could not keep the excitement out of her voice. "We could go there this very afternoon and ask Mr. Merrick to help us find Carpenini . . ."

"Bridget," her mother said on a sigh. "We just arrived. Surely it can wait."

"But we could walk there easily—"

"I don't think so, my dear. Now, Signor Zinni, surely such a sum would be by week, not by night . . ."

"But Mother!"

"Bridget, I said no!" Her mother ordered, turning her attention fully to her daughter. Her gaze was straight and focused— albeit slightly squinted, without her spectacles. "It would be utterly unseemly for us to impose upon the man, without any notice." Then, with a little more kindness, "I know you are excitable, but do keep in mind this holiday is not solely for the purpose of your musical instruction. We are in Italy to . . . take a respite. And I personally think you would do better to show more of an interest in our surroundings than in the prospect of being taught by Carpenini."

The words stung. "You . . . you don't wish me to study with him?"

"I did not say that, my dear." Her mother laid a hand on her daughter's shoulder. "Once we are settled in, we shall send a note to Mr. Merrick. I promise. You've waited this long. What's another day or two?"

A day or two. Her mother wanted to wait a day or two, when Mr. Merrick, who knew where to find Signor Carpenini, was a mere two canals away? Bridget clamped down on an automatic, panicked reply, instead taking a deep breath and settling on what she needed to do.

She had waited this long, as her mother had said. But that was precisely why she could not wait another minute longer.

"I'm sorry, Mother. You are right," Bridget said meekly, once she found her voice. "I think the madness of travel and this busy room has unsettled me."

Her mother smiled at her daughter but then turned sharply to Zinni. "You see that? Your Carnival madness has unsettled my daughter."

"Signorina, you can rest in the dining room; surely it will be less crowded . . ."

"No, thank you. Mother, if it is all right with you, I think I shall stand outside the front door. Take in some fresh air."

Her mother looked worried for a second. But since all of her attention was on Zinni, it was possible her focus was on her next counteroffer. "Do not leave sight of the door. And keep Molly with you," her mother said finally. Bridget slid her glance to where Molly, the girls' lady's maid, was chatting with one of the footmen and gesturing toward the trunks, likely trying to ascertain which one should go where. "And," her mother continued, "do not let your reticule off your wrist. Tie it twice if you must. Now, Signor Zinni, about that dining room—is it private?

"Oh, and wear your bonnet!" her mother called back, as Bridget headed for the Hotel Cortile's entrance, grabbing Molly on her way. "If you get any more freckles you will be one big spot!"

"All right, miss, it's that one," Molly said, pointing to a crumbling redbrick structure as she rejoined Bridget on the path that ran alongside the buildings on the north side of the Rio di San Salvador. They could not walk on the *rio* itself, as the buildings abutted right up against the water, but there were footpaths and alleyways on the back side of the houses.

"Are you certain, Molly?" Bridget asked nervously. The house looked very plain from this side. Very nondescript.

"Well, frankly, no, miss, I'm not. But I went over to that chap and said, 'Signor Merrick?' and he said a string of Italian I didn't understand and then he pointed to this house. And then he tried to pinch my bum," Molly finished darkly. "I still canna believe your mother let you to go off on your own like this and find the letter-writing gent."

"She was busy with the hotel proprietor and said I should take a walk," Bridget lied smoothly.

It had not taken long to get here. With the help of Amanda's guidebook, she and Molly had made their way from the hotel to the Rio di San Salvador. They could have taken a gondola, but neither Bridget nor Molly had much money, and none of the local currency at any rate. So they walked. Molly had expected to get lost, but Bridget had always been able to read a map. Music, maths, and maps were all things at which she excelled, and all were connected in her mind somehow. After all, finding where you were going in music was akin to finding where you were going on the streets, wasn't it?

However, one minor flaw in the plan was that she hadn't known which particular house was Mr. Merrick's, and thus they had spent a considerable length of time walking the footpaths on the other side of the canal, crossing back and forth when there was a bridge, asking people in the crudest of Italian if they spoke English and consequently if they knew which home was Signor Merrick's, and getting Molly's bum pinched.

But, Bridget thought, she was finally here. A thrill of anticipation went through her. It was better that she came here herself, not sending a note and waiting days to hear a reply. And it was better that she came alone. Her mother, Amanda, they did not understand. None of her family really understood how she felt about music.

She *must* play again—because without the music, what was she? The melodies in her head would dry up and the silence would be intolerable.

And she must play better, too—because she knew she could. Knew it in her bones that she had it in her.

And Carpenini had seen it. Five years ago, before her nerves overcame her, before the tortures of the London Season, he had heard her play one song and seen that she had it in her.

And with that surety giving her strength, she squared her shoulders and went to knock on the little door on the side of the brick house.

"Frederico, get the door, would you?"

Oliver Merrick stamped down the stairs of his house, his eyes on the papers in his hand. Bills, bills, a letter from his father, more bills. Damn it all, but none of this was ever going to be under control, was it?

Oliver reached the landing just as another tentative knock came from the door to the street.

"Frederico?" he called again for his erstwhile valet/butler/footman/occasional cook. But Frederico did not respond, lazy bastard. Indeed, the only sound Oliver heard was the same phrase of music, repeated over and over again, coming from the main sitting room. It would stop between playings, a scratching of a pencil could be heard, and then it would start again.

Oliver knew this was a bad sign. If his friend was on a good streak, the music would never stop.

"I'll just get the door myself, shall I?" he grumbled under his breath in his fluent Italian. Even if his mother hadn't been the classic dark-haired, olive-skinned (both of which he'd inherited), passionate firebrand that typified the race, he'd spent enough of the past decade in Venice to speak like a native.

Strange, he thought as he crossed to the door, it couldn't be a caller. His friends from the theatre and any prospective commissions for Vincenzo would come by gondola via the canal. The latter of which were very few and far between.

The only people who ever came by the street door were the grocer and . . .

Oh no. Not again.

He knew what he would find. "Goddammit, Vincenzo," he breathed, as he threw open the doors. "You are out to drive me insane with your whores, aren't you?"

But his self-ramblings were cut short when he found himself staring down into the greenest eyes he had ever seen.

Like the lagoon when it caught the sun just so, making the water turn jewel toned and alive, those eyes stared up at him, wide and trembling with nervous resolve. Freckles danced over her nose and cheeks like someone had reached down from above and sprinkled them there. Freckles that he found oddly familiar but could not place. Dark curls were tucked up in her bonnet, but a tendril behind her ear had escaped, trailing down her neck. She had a kind of delicate prettiness rarely seen in the streets of Venice, where bright colors and extravagant beauty seemed the fashion.

Oliver was halfway to enchanted in the space of a breath. But then he remembered he was supposed to be annoyed.

"Sorry, ladies," he said in Italian, his face as stern as he could make it, "he's not taking visitors today, nor is there coin to pay for your services." When those green eyes just blinked, then looked nervously back at the older, more practical-looking woman behind her, he let out a breath.

"Look, Carpenini might have sent for you, but I'm sending

you away. I'm sorry, but the best I can do is pay for a gondola to take you back where you came from."

"Carpenini!" the green-eyed enchantress finally said, her language and accent decidedly English. That was shocking enough. What was more shocking was what she said next. "That is exactly why I am here!"

English. She was English. He blinked twice. And by her cultured tones, she was a lady. One who, considering what he had assumed her to be, he fervently hoped did not know the Venetian dialect.

"Er . . . can I help you, miss?" His English, so rarely used here, felt thick and awkward on his tongue. He suddenly became very aware of the fact that he hadn't put shoes on yet that day.

"Yes," the girl replied, unable to keep the excitement out of her voice. "I should like to see Mr. Merrick, please."

"You are seeing him," Oliver replied, in shock enough to only wonder where this conversation would lead.

"I thought you looked familiar," she said, and smiled.

And she had one hell of a smile. Seemed a bit rough, though, somehow. As if the muscles in her face had briefly forgotten how to arrange themselves. But smile she did, and Oliver again found he was losing himself in her impish countenance.

"Might we come in, sir?" the practical, stiffer one said from behind the green-eyed one. "My lady has been traveling for weeks, after all."

Oliver shook himself out of his reverie and stepped back to admit them to his foyer. He felt immediately awkward about the surroundings. The rugs were threadbare and the plaster was crumbling in a way he found charming, but he supposed young ladies of good family might not.

"You seem familiar, too," he finally blurted. "Er, your freckles."

A delightful blush spread across her cheeks and Oliver found himself wishing it would happen again. And again, and again.

"We have met before, briefly, Mr. Merrick," she said, her eyes meeting his. "I am Miss Forrester, and you wrote me a letter."

As she worked at the fierce knot of a reticule and then

began to rummage in it, a sense of the familiar began to mingle with a sense of dread. "Miss . . . Brittany Forrester?"

A small frown flashed across her face. "Bridget," she replied tersely, and then handed him a piece of paper from her reticule. A letter written in his own hand.

Oh, hell.

"You wrote me on behalf of your friend Signor Carpenini, who heard me play some years ago, and wondered if I would be amenable to taking instruction from him when he—you—came back to England. Unfortunately I learned that you would not be coming to England after all, so . . ."

"Miss Forrester," he interrupted her. "Please do not tell me that you came all the way to Venice because of this letter?"

"No." The word came out weakly, and Oliver knew it was a lie. "My family is taking a holiday . . . and since we were in Venice and you were here, we thought . . . I thought, that maybe . . ."

Oliver wanted to let his head come down into his hands. Oh, hell. Oh damn, and blast. He cursed profusely under his breath in Italian, which was a language much better equipped for the current predicament.

"Miss Forrester, I am afraid there has been a terrible misunderstanding. You see, I did write this letter, yes, but Vincenzo—Signor Carpenini, that is—is in the middle of a composition. And when he's composing, he does not take on stude—"

But Miss Forrester was not listening to him. Instead her face had taken on a dreamy faraway look, and her fingers began to twitch in time to the music, as if playing imaginary keys.

The music.

"Is that," she finally asked, "the Signore? Is Carpenini here?"

Her face lit up with the possibility, and she took a few unconscious steps toward the door to the drawing room.

"Miss Forrester, please do not disturb him," Oliver cried, then reached out and grabbed her arm just as she reached the closed door.

"I won't," she replied, stilling beneath his touch. "I just wanted to hear better. Is that an A-minor key?"

"I don't know," he began to say, and drew her back a little. But, unfortunately, the damage had already been done.

It could have been the sound of voices in the hallway, especially female ones, that drew his attention. It could have been Oliver's doing, speaking too loudly or too near the door. It could have been the gentle touch of Miss Forrester's hand on the drawing room door latch. But in any case, the music abruptly stopped, footsteps sounded as they crossed the room, and the drawing door was flung open from the inside.

"What the hell is going on out here? Don't you realize I'm composing?" the short-tempered man who emerged from the drawing room said in grunting Italian.

"Signor Carpenini," Miss Forrester breathed.

Oliver straightened and kept his hand on Miss Forrester's arm. Then, his mind remembering better manners than he'd known he had, he turned to the girl at his side. "Miss Forrester, this is Signor Vincenzo Carpenini. Vincenzo, this is Miss Forrester."

Miss Forrester—and the woman with her, whom Oliver decided was her maid—dropped to a curtsy. He still kept his hand on her arm—for some unknown reason, he knew that touch was the only thing keeping her from flying away—and he could feel her shaking.

"Signore, this is a great honor," she began, but was cut off by Carpenini as he crossed the room and grabbed her under the chin.

"Vincenzo!" Oliver cried, pulling Miss Forrester back.

"English, eh?" his friend said, his dark eyes going cold. And then, in his own English, he turned to Oliver. "If you are to bring a whore for me, Oliver, at least be sure she is beautiful. This one is too small to be of any use."

And with that, the great composer stepped back into the drawing room and slammed the door, rattling the dusty chandelier in the foyer.

"I am so sorry; he's a bit—" But as Oliver looked down into Miss Forrester's face, he knew his apologies would be for naught. She was utterly and completely shattered.

"Molly." Her voice shook. "We should go."

The maid—Molly—nodded, and before he knew it, she had whisked Miss Forrester out the door to the street.

"Miss Forrester, wait!" he cried, jolting out of his shock.

He ran after them, into the street, heedless of his lack of shoes. "At least let me see you home—this is no city for a lady alone!"

But it was too late. Miss Forrester and Molly moved quickly from the alley into the main street, disappearing into the crowds of pedestrians going about their day.

"Damn it all," Oliver breathed, as he walked back to his house. *No*, he thought, his vision going red. *Not damn it all. Damn Vincenzo Carpenini.*

He walked straight into the drawing room, any tentativeness about disturbing his friend gone.

"Vincenzo, you bastard!" he growled, and his friend looked up from the score on the pianoforte. "Do you have any idea who that was?"

"No." The composer blinked at him. "Should I care?"

Five

"THAT," Oliver seethed, "was your last best chance of making any money this month."

"Making money?" Vincenzo replied, as if he had never heard of the concept. "Was that child going to pay me for a composition? A tune to commemorate her first communion, perhaps?"

"No, she was a prospective student," Oliver sighed, collapsing onto the red velvet chaise that occupied the corner of the drawing room. Well, really the music room, ever since Carpenini had come to stay with him. "A determined one, at that."

"A student?" Vincenzo recoiled from the keys. "I'm not going to take a student I've never heard play. Besides, once I complete this opera, money will not be a consideration anymore."

"Yes, if you would please hurry up and finish the opera, I would be most grateful," he sighed. "But by the by, you *have* heard her play. That was Miss Forrester. When you came to get me in England? Five years ago?" At Vincenzo's blank look, Oliver rolled his eyes. "We stayed with her father, Lord Forrester, for a day while awaiting our ship in Portsmouth. She played while her elder sister sang 'Tom Bowling.'"

A light of recognition filled Vincenzo's eyes. "But what on earth is she doing in Venice?"

"That . . . is my doing, I'm afraid."

Vincenzo's dark eyebrow went up. "Indeed? You called a little lamb to me from the coast of England?"

"Not exactly." Oliver's face went hard. He refused to turn red. This would all have been easier a year ago, when Vincenzo was the toast of Venice—not now, when he was practically barred from every patron and musical venue in the city. Every venue except Oliver's. "Do you recall, a few months ago, my father sent for me, calling me home?"

Vincenzo's eyes returned to the keys in front of him, and he began softly playing the same tune that had been haunting him all morning. As if he could escape the conversation by slipping into music.

"And when I told you of it," Oliver continued, heedless of his friend's inattention, "you said you would love to see England again—and I said I could likely manage your passage, but you would need some kind of income once there."

If Vincenzo was listening, he did not acknowledge it. But he did continue his playing, as if giving Oliver permission to continue speaking.

"And you said—and I quote: 'I'll find a few students, stage a few concerts, and sell a few operas. It will be a triumph!'"

Vincenzo's hands came off the keys. "I do remember something about you trying to force me to leave Venice," he replied, shrugging. "But then you changed your mind."

"It was not I whose mind was changed," Oliver replied darkly. Oliver had been packed; he had broken off ties with his work at the Teatro la Fenice, the premier theatre in Venice, and was ready to return to London when he received another letter from his father, stating that Oliver was not needed at home after all.

Not needed. Stay away.

Oliver had admitted to himself a certain disappointment. Not for his sake, he told himself, but for his friend. Vincenzo could have had a fresh start in England. Overseas he was still regarded as a master. Miss Bridget Forrester's appearance here today made that clear.

But Vincenzo was nothing if not stubborn.

Suddenly the music stopped with a slam on the keys. Vincenzo stood and began pacing. "I could not leave Venice, my tail between my legs, surely you see that!" He rubbed the growth of beard that had taken over his features since his fall from grace. "If I cannot compose in the city of my birth, then I can compose nowhere! I will not be in disgrace forever—and this"—he threw his hand out to the half-written pages on the pianoforte—"will be what saves me from it. This symphony will be my triumph!"

"Oh, it's a symphony now? A moment ago it was an opera."

Vincenzo shot Oliver such a look of loathing that Oliver felt momentarily compelled to be contrite. Or he would have, had he not remembered that Carpenini was living in Oliver's house, on Oliver's income, as the only person in Venice who would accept him.

And that was the quandary in which Oliver had found himself stuck. Carpenini had promised him a new composition to stage. But a year after Carpenini's fall from grace, he was still living on Oliver's goodwill and depleting what funds Oliver had to possibly stage said opera.

Unfortunately, Oliver owed him too much to do otherwise.

"The Marchese prefers symphonies to operatic histrionics," Vincenzo replied. "And you will benefit as much as I from the Marchese putting me back in favor."

It was true. However, until then, Oliver was stuck.

Oliver was resigned to putting up with supporting his friend (financially as well as emotionally) until he wrote a piece that would impress all of Venice into loving him again. But it was not just the city that Carpenini had to impress. It was his former patron—the Marchese di Garibaldi.

"But if you wish to travel to England," Vincenzo continued blithely, "go. Do not worry about that warehouse you purchased . . ."

"It's a theatre—the Teatro Michelina," Oliver answered automatically.

"Right now it is a warehouse," Vincenzo answered back. "At any rate, you can tell your father you have invested your allowance in real estate. I am sure he will be pleased. But I release you from any obligation. I will be fine here by myself."

Oliver rolled his eyes. If he could only believe that Vincenzo would be fine without him! The difficulty was he had no notion as to the man's ability to take care of himself. There were too many days he did not eat, and absolutely no money coming in to pay someone to remind him to do so or to pay the rent on this house. His artistic fever would overtake him, and he would compose, compose, compose. Or his artistic fever would leave him, and he would wander aimlessly into trouble with women, women, women.

Just watching it, Oliver—who himself enjoyed such troubles, in moderation—was exhausted.

"You know I'm not going anywhere." He gave in to the impulse to pinch the bridge of his nose. When he had first come to Venice, the excuse he had given his father was that he wanted to know the land of his mother's birth. He had not intended to stay this long. But now it had become his home—if only because his father did not welcome him back in England. And it was here that he had determined to have a future. It was here that he had learned the business of the theatre from every angle—even appearing on stage. It was where, discovering his position at La Fenice had been filled after his aborted trip to England, Oliver decided to attempt a long-held ambition, sinking most of his savings into his own warehouse . . . er, theatre. It was where he would someday stage works of his own choosing, starting with Vincenzo's newest. Whenever he happened to finish the damn thing. "Can we move forward, please?"

"But you still have not explained the girl," Vincenzo broached, his fingers returning to the keys.

"Ah—well, she seemed a good prospective student. You even offered to teach her when you originally met. So, when I thought we were going to England, I wrote a letter on your behalf, exploring whether her family would allow her to be taught by you."

Vincenzo looked up at him in horror. "So you're my procurer now?"

"I was attempting to be practical." Oliver's brow thundered down. "I apologize, it won't happen again."

"How many letters did you write? Are there going to be a dozen English schoolgirls showing up while I am trying to write my masterpiece?"

"I only wrote the one, because that was the only English girl I ever heard you offer to teach." Granted, they had not been in England together for very long five years ago. But after spending the last five years in Vincenzo's company, he hadn't often heard the man offer to teach anyone. He'd had students, of course—back before his fall from grace. But those had been children of the highest nobles in Venice, people who did not wait to be asked. For Carpenini to *want* to teach someone, they had to display something special.

"Was she that good, then? This Miss Forrester?"

As Vincenzo kept playing variations of his tune, Oliver took himself back in time to that afternoon they had spent at the home of the Forresters, Primrose Manor, waiting for their ship to be ready to sail with the tide.

His father was going to try to stop him. He had been sure of it, and it made him one raw nerve during the long carriage ride from London to Portsmouth, where they would catch their ship. But while he had been taking furtive glances out the window and constantly rearranging his long legs, trying to get comfortable, easy, he had also been sitting across from the great composer Vincenzo Carpenini, who—after a concert at which the man had received three ovations—upon learning who Oliver's mother was, and Oliver's desire to see Italy, offered to take him back with him.

Lord Merrick had been furious. He saw it as a personal betrayal, a rejection of everything English that Oliver had been raised to be. His older brother had just blinked in confusion—how could Oliver want to go to *Italy*, of all places? Wasn't it horribly hot and dirty? But his brother Francis, both of his parents having been English, never knew what it was like to feel like you had one foot in one world and one foot somewhere else. Oliver was the second son, from the second wife. England was where he was raised, but perhaps, he'd thought, perhaps he belonged elsewhere. Why else did he reject the notion of a career in any of the three places—the law, the military, or the church—where a gentleman's second son can thrive? Why would he be so unnatural, as his father had said more than once, to take a liking to music, to the stage?

So there he was, on a mad adventure away from the only place he knew, with a man he knew of but did not know. One who kept smiling at him and trying to converse about the bright and beautiful city of Venice in broken English, and Oliver kept trying to answer in barely remembered Italian from his mother.

They had come to Portsmouth a day earlier than the ship departed, and Oliver was numb with fright that his father might come and try to stop him. Worse yet, Oliver was afraid that he himself would have time to rethink his flight. Italy? Had he gone mad? He had no funds and didn't know a soul there!

He was doing this kind of second-guessing when he and Carpenini had run into Lord Forrester's personal brand of kindness in Portsmouth. And Lord Forrester, delighting in finding an Italian composer of renown wandering around looking for a decent spot of lunch, invited both of them back to Primrose to wait for the dawn and their departure.

Oliver had walked into Primrose Manor still unsettled, but realizing he had to play the gentleman for the next several hours, he kept it under wraps. And he found that—much as it did on the stage—playing the role helped ease his nerves. Not entirely, however. Primrose was a big, happy place, made more so by the hospitality that Lord Forrester and his family provided. It reminded him of his own home, the one he was leaving.

The second-guessing began again, and as he and Carpenini wandered the halls, he almost voiced his change of heart.

Almost.

Because at that moment, they passed the music room, and Oliver's ears were filled with . . . Tom Bowling?

Carpenini, like a bloodhound with a scent, turned on his heel and followed the music. And in the music room they had found two of the Forrester girls, one singing, one playing. It was a solemn tune, but the girl had been playing it in a joking fashion, as if she made fun of its overwrought lyrics by matching it with even more overwrought dramatics. Carpenini began correcting her immediately, of course.

"Play it again," Carpenini had said to the girl. "But this time, *calando, ritardando.*"

Oliver hadn't expected what came next. But there was something about the way the girl at the keys played, bringing the truth out of the music. Something about how she infused the music with some spark of life—even if she was just playing a phrase twice over, as she was doing now for Carpenini. Fine-tuning her playing, elevating the mood, the emotion behind her technique. But none of that mattered nearly as much as the feeling of being caught up. The way she was. In music. In a story.

That is why you are going to Italy. To be caught up in something.

"Melancholy." his voice came from somewhere outside himself. "Beautiful."

Later that evening, the Misses Forrester had played for them again, although the obvious talent had been the one on the pianoforte. Oliver knew enough about music to appreciate its being played well. There was no mistaking her playing in the music room as simply a passing moment. She was very, very good.

Yes, Miss Forrester had shown them something special.

Although now, Vincenzo seemed hard-pressed to remember it.

"She was very good." Oliver said, as if lost in a dream. Then, at Vincenzo's arched eyebrow, he cleared his throat. "She stood out in my memory for five years, and she was just a child then," Oliver tried again, venturing into the void of silence that had fallen. "Think of how much better she could have become in that time."

"Or so desperate for instruction that she crosses a continent to obtain a teacher." Carpenini shrugged. "But it does not matter. I will not have need of a student before long. It has been a year, and the Marchese has not given his patronage to a new musician. He has not found someone to match me. He is simply waiting for me to compose something that will justify my return. Thus, I will finish this sonata—"

"I thought it was a symphony."

"—and I will dedicate it to the Marchese, and he will have to forgive me. And then you will stage it to great acclaim!"

Once again, it was up to Oliver to pour ice water onto his fantasy. "Men forgive their mistresses being seduced, Vincenzo, not their daughters."

Vincenzo's expression darkened. "The Signora Galetti is a married woman; she should be her husband's concern, not her father's. But she feels badly enough about my circumstances that she has agreed to help me."

"*Now* she feels badly?" Oliver asked in disbelief. "A year after her seduction and betrayal caused you to lose your place?"

"It was not the seduction and betrayal—it was her telling of it."

Oliver refrained from allowing his judgment to show on his face. Again, when the muse left Vincenzo . . . women, women, women. The more troublesome, the better. And the beautiful, vain, and spoiled Signora Galetti had certainly proved troublesome. What did Vincenzo think would happen when he started up with her? And then started up with her maid?

"But she is making up for it now," Vincenzo continued. "With this!"

He stood up with his characteristic energy, his mood swinging into elation as easily as it could in high dudgeon. He rummaged through a pile of letters and scratched-out sheets of music that littered the top of the pianoforte, beneath it all finding two pieces of card and, with a triumphant flourish, handing them to Oliver.

They were heavy stock, ornately gilded around the edges. He turned them over in his hand. But it was what was written on them that was most interesting.

"This is an invitation . . . to the Marchese's ball."

"It is." Vincenzo smiled mischievously at him.

"I'm assuming that the Marchese does not know that you have this. Because if he did, either his guards would be here to take it back or all would be forgiven and his servants would be moving you back into the palazzo."

"True, he does not know. But I ran into the Signora Galetti the other day at the Piazza San Marco—"

"Because you just run into aristocratic ladies walking around the city all the time, do you?" Oliver interjected sardonically.

Vincenzo ignored him. "Her husband is at the villa near Padua for the winter. Antonia—the Signora—has been so saddened by his departure, she has taken to walking through the piazza. So I paid a call or two on her recently, to keep her company. She feels very badly for what happened between us, and said I should attend her father's ball."

"But if the Marchese doesn't know you are coming, he'll throw you out on sight."

"No, he won't."

"You have a greater faith in your ability to beg than I do, then."

"No, he won't," Vincenzo continued patiently, "because it is a *Carnival* ball. Everyone will be wearing carnival masks."

Oliver ruminated and had to admit there was some intelligence to that argument. Carnival masks, faces blank and frozen, were used for hundreds of years to hide the identity of anyone—thus, one could be dancing with a Duchess as easily as with a milkmaid. Some had been made of plaster, some heavy ceramic, some embellished with paints and gold, some austere and staring. Yet all were strangely beautiful and grotesque.

While they had been banned during Napoleon's reign, the tradition had begun to filter its way back in during the height of the Carnival season. And for someone of the Marchese's consequence, no Austrian Emperor was going to kick up any fuss.

The mask could make Vincenzo as anonymous as the next guest. And chances were the ball would be so crowded, one more person would not be remarked upon.

"So . . ." Oliver said slowly, putting together the pieces of Vincenzo's jumbled plan in his head. "You sneak into this party, find an opportunity to play your new piece. You tell the Marchese it is dedicated to him and only him. And once he sees that you and Antonia have mended fences, all will be forgiven?"

Vincenzo blinked at the mention of Antonia, as if he had not considered her as more than a stepping-stone on his path to the Marchese. But he then nodded fervently, latching on to the idea.

"*Si, si*, I will make it known the lady loves me once again. And when the Marchese hears this music, he will fall to pieces weeping, and I will once again live in the light of Venice!"

Vincenzo finished his speech with a flourish, his future triumph vibrating through his wiry frame. Oliver was always struck that such a lean, sinewy individual could have so much energy. Oliver himself was much more solidly built and seemed, therefore, much more grounded. Then again, Oliver had spent his formative years in boxing lessons, and Vincenzo had spent his at a pianoforte. And while Oliver could not help but envy Vincenzo's talent, there was one thing that went along with his grounding that Vincenzo never seemed to grasp. Practicality.

"Well, I had better get started, then," Oliver said on a sigh. "It's rather late for us to get proper costumes. There isn't a chance that any tailor could make something up in two days . . . our only hope of finding any masks is likely at La Fenice. I'll ask my friends there, although I have a feeling every opera singer in Venice is invited, and therefore their stores are likely well picked over."

"Us?" Vincenzo looked up at him, happy surprise in his voice. "You mean you will come as my guest, help me with the Marchese?"

Oliver sighed again. "Of course I'll help you. If you go by yourself I will likely end up paying for your release from prison. I figure the expense of a second costume is much cheaper."

Oliver was being glib, he knew, but deep inside, a spark of hope came to life. This could be the solution to their difficulties. If Vincenzo found himself back in the Marchese's good graces, Oliver could start putting his meager funds into his warehouse-theatre. It was far-fetched, but if Vincenzo could do it . . .

"Marvelous!" Vincenzo cried, clapping his hands like a pleased child, for all that he was in his thirties. "I will come with you to pick out costumes. The costumer at La Fenice adores me; they will have something for us."

"No. That is my part. You have your own work to do."

"Nothing that can't wait until the afternoon," Vincenzo replied with a wave.

But Oliver pushed him back firmly to his seat at the pianoforte.

"I will arrange the costumes. You have a masterpiece to finish." Oliver checked his pocket watch. "And seventy-eight hours in which to do it."

Six

THE Marchese di Garibaldi was not a man who did things by halves. It was an instinct bred by the generations of wealth and power that preceded him, the family name having been in the Golden Book for centuries before that document of Venice was forsaken. The Palazzo Garibaldi was evidence of that commitment to luxury. Built in the seventeenth century, designed by that god of Baroque architecture, Baldassarre Longhena, its three stories of white marble facade faced the Grand Canal. Lined with double colonnades, scrollwork, and flourishes, it spoke of greater wealth than anyone from the ancient lineage of the Merricks of East Sussex could dream of.

And that was just the outside.

The Marchese di Garibaldi was also one to hold to traditions. And as a product of the previous century, his version of Carnival was an echo of the old spectacle—bullfights in the streets, acrobats crowding the Piazza San Marco, and lavish, lavish parties that lasted from noon until dawn.

Even though the Austrians now controlled the city and so many of the old names had faded away, the Marchese liked to do what he could to keep the past alive.

"This is madness," Oliver breathed, making the close air under his mask hot and humid. The Palazzo Garibaldi was lit by a thousand torches, making it as bright as day, a beacon calling to all the boats on the Grand Canal. Long lines of gondolas stretched all the way back to the Rialto Bridge.

"This is Venice, my friend." Vincenzo clapped him on the shoulder, as they disembarked at the front steps of the palazzo. Oliver had to hold up his trouser legs up to keep them from dropping onto the wet stones.

They were each dressed in the only costumes the Teatro la Fenice had available, taken from her dusty attics. They were clowns, in the traditional commedia dell'arte style. Vincenzo had grudgingly taken the bright, diamond-patterned Harlequin with his cloak, cane, and nimble antics, while Oliver wore the loose white costume of the Pedrolino, with stiff ruffled collar and cone-shaped hat. However, they forwent the painted faces, instead wearing *bautas*, the traditional male Venetian Carnival mask.

With the dust and moths pounded out of the clown costumes and the *bautas* firmly in place, they looked as mysterious and anonymous as the next guest. But still—regarding the hulking guards at the door who silently took their invitation, a degree of caution was pragmatic.

Once they crossed the threshold, Oliver let out a small sigh of relief but refused to let his guard down for long.

The inside of the palazzo was no less opulent than the outside and would have been even without the festooned draperies and the trapeze artists hanging from the ceiling. Tintorettos lined the entryway; marble coated every surface. Unlike many of the palazzos that lined the Grand Canal, which had seen better days before the fall of the Republic, the Palazzo Garibaldi was still proud, still in its full flush of beauty.

And currently filled to the brim with a complete crush of men and women in seventeenth- and eighteenth-century costumes, drinking and dancing the last night of amusement away before they became penitent in the morning.

"Do you see the Marchese?" Oliver asked in Italian, scanning the room from behind his mask. "Or his daughter?"

"Hmm?" Vincenzo replied, distracted. "Oh, he will be found eventually. I would not worry so."

"The whole point of this endeavor is for you to play your new piece for him, and to show him you and Antonia have mended fences."

"Yes, yes." Vincenzo waved his hand in the air. "But we should not attack the man the minute we are through the door. He will be much more relaxed later on into the evening."

That made complete sense, of course, and Oliver nodded in agreement. But there was something about the way Vincenzo dismissed the notion with a wave and the barest quaver in his voice. It set alarms off in Oliver's head.

"How is it, by the by?" he asked, as nonchalantly as possible.

"How is what?"

"The piece. The symphony, the sonata, or whatever it turned out to be. I've been out of the house, trying to give you space to work, so I haven't heard you play it yet."

"Oh. The piece. It is marvelous, a triumph. Do not worry, all will be well."

Beneath the mask, Vincenzo was beginning to sweat. Oliver knew it like he knew the back of his hand.

"Damn and blast," he swore, and pulled Vincenzo to a stop. "You haven't written anything, have you?"

"Of course I've written . . ." Vincenzo blustered.

"Hum it."

"Hum it?"

"Hum the tune. What have you come up with?"

After a moment, Vincenzo began to hum, so softly that with the crowds and the mask, he was almost inaudible.

Well, at least one of those circumstances could be remedied.

Quicker than Carpenini could blink, Oliver reached out and ruthlessly pulled off his mask. Black eyes blinked back at him.

"Hum the tune, Vincenzo."

Instead of pretending, Vincenzo threw up his hands. "Fine! I have nothing. Are you happy now that I have confessed it? I have slit my wrists and bled onto the keys and yet the muse gives me nothing. I cannot find the theme for the piece; I know I could grow it into something beautiful if I had a theme, but I will not play something for the Marchese that is less than perfection."

Oliver shook his head. "You have nothing? Then what, pray tell, have you been doing for the last two days, locked in my house with your piano?"

"Vincenzo! Darling!" came a melodic voice, trilling high

above the raucousness of the crowd. "You naughty boy—masks are not meant to come off until morning."

Both Vincenzo and Oliver turned and caught sight of Antonia di Garibaldi—now Antonia Galetti—floating toward them. There was no doubt it was her. Only the spoiled daughter of the Marchese would be able to get away with such a costume. A wig in the style of the previous century, so tall that Oliver wondered how she kept her balance, was pinned through with stuffed birds, which had unceremoniously had their eyes replaced with fine jewels. Her dress was equally bejeweled—except, that is, for her bosom, which was unadorned and pushed up alluringly, catching the eyes of every guest, male and female alike, who marveled at her bodice for the cantilevered feat of engineering it was.

"But then how would you have been able to find me, my sweet?" Vincenzo replied in equally enthusiastic tones.

Antonia was wearing only a half mask, and thus she was not burdened at all when she leaned forward and gave Vincenzo a lingering kiss on the mouth. Then she pulled his mask back into place.

"Now, keep this on, at least until midnight. Oliver was out for days trying to get you this costume; the least you could do is wear it longer than ten minutes."

"Well, then he should have done better than a clown suit," Vincenzo grumbled, with a dark look at Oliver.

But Antonia saved him from any rebuttal by saying, "I quite like it, actually."

"You do?" Vincenzo asked, a smile playing on his lips.

"Yes, usually you are so overpowering, so forceful. It makes me quite nervous. But no one can be nervous in a circus, with a clown."

Whatever Vincenzo thought about being emasculated by a clown suit he kept to himself, while Oliver had to choke back his laughter. But as Antonia flashed a naughty smile at him and held out her hand to be kissed (although with the masks, it was more of a bend over than a kiss), Oliver suddenly knew what Vincenzo had been doing in the drawing room for the past two afternoons—and it had nothing to do with composition.

When the muse left him, Carpenini found trouble.

And Antonia Galetti had been trouble for him before.

Antonia was one of Venice's finest creations—a dark-eyed

beauty who was married at the age of twenty to a man four decades her senior. It was inevitable that she would take a lover; in fact, Oliver wouldn't have been surprised if that expectation had been written into the marriage contract. The only difficulty was, should that lover ever break with the girl, they had to face the wrath of not only Antonia but also her indomitable father.

"Antonia, my dear, introduce me to your friends."

Who, as it turned out, was right behind them.

"Father, I do not believe any introduction is needed," Antonia tittered, as she placed a far more chaste peck on her father's cheek.

The Marchese di Garibaldi had no need of a costume. He would have owned the attention of everyone in the room even in full masquerade, so why bother with fancy dress? Instead, he watched over the festivities like some sort of demigod, unafraid to show his face to the anonymous masses. Indeed, his lack of a costume only made it easier for everyone in attendance to bow and scrape before him.

A man about the age of his daughter's husband, the Marchese wore his age well. His frame was tall and strong, without an ounce of the weight that normally comes with a lifetime of excess. His face, tanned from living on the Adriatic, contrasted sharply with his silver hair. All in all his physical appearance was as imposing as his reputation, as one of the last standing members of the old guard of Venetian aristocracy.

Of course, the Marchese di Garibaldi's shrewdness with money and a well-timed third marriage to a German countess contributed to his survival. But not nearly as much as his reputation for supporting and fostering all the musical talent to be had in Venice.

"Marchese," Vincenzo said, as he bowed low. "It is wonderful to see you again. Thank you for inviting us back into your home."

The Marchese leveled his gaze at Vincenzo, then Oliver. "Mr. Merrick," he finally said, his face splitting into a calculated smile. "I enjoyed that little comedy you had a hand in at La Fenice last season. You, are of course, welcome here." Then he turned to the still somewhat bowed Vincenzo. "Signor Carpenini. The *Great Master.*" His words dripped with sarcasm, as if they could turn their recipient into the lowest form of vermin simply by hearing them. "My daughter told me she was inviting you. And I admit to discouraging it—if only to spare her another heartbreak."

"I assure you, Marchese, I have no intention of causing your daughter any more pain. Indeed, I found my heart hurting far more than I realized without her gracious presence in my life."

"See, Father, I told you." Antonia hung on her father's arm. "Now, can't you say something pleasant to him?"

"It has been less lively of late, I grant you. I even had to go to Vienna over the New Year to alleviate my boredom," the older gentleman admitted grudgingly.

"I am only too happy to do what I can to enliven things for you, Marchese. And for your beautiful daughter."

The Marchese gave a small smile, while his daughter giggled on his arm. Then, while the father and daughter turned away briefly to greet another newly arrived guest, Oliver leaned into Vincenzo's ear.

"Doing it a bit thick, aren't you?" he muttered.

"Shh! If this plays out as I hope, I won't need to have a new piece for the Marchese. Showering his daughter with the love she deserves will be enough to earn back my place," Vincenzo whispered. "Hell, he practically admitted to missing me!"

"'The love she deserves?' A consideration she should have had before she found you in bed with her maid."

But Vincenzo waved that away. "Just you watch. I will be at his daughter's side all night. And then I will engage him in conversation, which will naturally turn to music, and I'll have my place back before the night is over."

"What will happen before the night is over?" Antonia asked, her attention returned to her lover.

"Ah—wouldn't you like to know, my little pet," Vincenzo replied. Antonia giggled. Oliver rolled his eyes beneath the mask.

"Oh, Vincenzo," the Marchese said, breaking the focused concentration of the overly happy couple, "have you heard of a composer named Gustav Klein?"

Vincenzo perked up, obviously pleased to have conversation brought around to something musical. Perhaps his plan would take less time than imagined. "Indeed I have, Marchese—he composed variations on one of my concertos. He is young, but well regarded in Vienna, I believe."

"He's not in Vienna anymore." The Marchese smiled like a serpent and gestured to the newly arrived member of their circle, a blond masked man with a short, terse bow. "Gustav, this is Carpenini. Carpenini, this is Gustav Klein—my new protégé. Come listen to him play later; I would enjoy learning your opinion of him."

❧

Vincenzo Carpenini was a self-made man. His mother gone before he reached the tender age of four, raised by a kind but absentminded grandmother, Vincenzo learned early on that if you wanted something, you could not wait for it to be given to you. You couldn't hope it would land in your lap after you had been very, very good and worked very, very hard. You had to *take* it. By any means necessary.

Once he had achieved a certain level of fame, he had hoped to be able to enjoy that status. And for a time, he did. His music was his life, his soul, and sacrificing a part of his attention to scrambling for recognition made him weary. Even when he had toured the Continent and England, being feted as a master everywhere he went (his last opera, *The Virgin and the Chrysanthemum*, had been particularly artful, he knew without conceit), that feeling of always having to scrounge, always being chased by someone younger, smarter, better, would not leave him be.

Accepting the Marchese's patronage five years ago had freed him of the scrambling that came when you knew your work was brilliant but no one else did. With the Marchese beside him, *everyone* knew. His works were given a stage and performed for the world to see. He was the composer who defined Italian music of the age.

For almost three years, he had sat down and composed. It allowed him to be generous—Oliver had been a recipient of that generosity, ending up on the stage of La Fenice, of all things. But more than anything, it had allowed Vincenzo to enjoy the life he had earned.

And enjoy he did. He enjoyed the fine wines and dances. He enjoyed the women who admired him, the salons and the people who had no greater task than to think all day about abstract things like beauty, art, and the truth about love. People who had never had to trick the butcher into giving a growing boy an extra cut of meat, people who took for granted that life had always been this way and always would.

And then . . . he began to take it for granted, too.

His compositions, while still strong, began to drop off in frequency. Music was no longer what drove him; it was no longer his savior. It was his occupation.

When the Marchese noted at one of his infamous musical gatherings that Carpenini should sit out performing, as it was likely he did not have anything new from the past few months, it was taken by all assembled as a rebuke. As he was about to slink away, acid churning in his stomach, a reprieve came. The Marchese's newly married (and unhappy) daughter, Antonia, with her sparkling brown eyes, had taken up his cause, saying that anyone who had written such a masterpiece as *The Virgin and the Chrysanthemum* could not be rushed in composing his next.

And she had looked at him with such sweet intention, how could he help but fall into bed with the girl?

But unfortunately, his instincts for self-preservation abandoned him when he overindulged on wine, especially around Antonia's luscious little maid.

That was why, tonight, at the Marchese's Carnival ball, with Antonia back on his arm, her dark eyes twinkling at him from beneath her mask, he was not even risking a sip of wine. No, he needed to be sober; he needed his wits. The wits on which he had survived in his youth would now earn him back his place by the Marchese's side.

But damned if he knew how.

"I heard that your last opera was enjoyed, Gustav," Carpenini said drolly, by way of conversation. "Where was it performed again? Linz?"

The party had waged on. He danced endlessly with Antonia, greeting people gaily, all while he gritted his teeth beneath the mask. Now, in the early hours of the morning, he steered Antonia into the music room, where those who mattered gravitated.

Gioachino Rossini, visiting from Paris, was at the far side of the room, waxing rhapsodic about some new opera. He wasn't much of a composer, Carpenini scoffed, but he tried.

Caroline Unger, the young contralto, was down from Vienna and had her wig off, and was laughing with a masked man on a settee. Oliver leaned against the wall, listening to a hired harpist pluck away at her strings, giving the room a practiced air of lightness and formality, when it was anything but. At this point in the evening the masks were left off for the hot pretenses that they were, so Vincenzo felt justified in discarding his.

And in the center, holding court, was the Marchese. With young, pale-faced Gustav Klein at his side.

In that moment, Carpenini knew what he had to do. He had to, God help him, play nice.

Separating the Marchese from his new protégé was simple. Antonia simply flitted to her father's side and naturally drew his adoring attention. Leaving Klein to Carpenini.

"Not Linz. Vienna." Klein answered, his Italian clipped by his Austrian accent. He frowned in the direction of the Marchese's daughter, his scowl disapproving. "In the Theater an dur Wien—and yes, it was well received. In fact, the manager at the opera house told me he had not heard such applause since your *Virgin and the Chrysanthemum*."

"Yes, those were a marvelous four weeks that *The Virgin* played there."

"Only four? Mine played for six."

If Klein had said that with any trace of a smile, Carpenini would have been able to respect him, as it would be acknowledging another player in the same game. But the man was so terse, so humorless, that it was as if he did not even see Carpenini standing there. As if he were nothing.

Suddenly, he wanted nothing more than to crush this interloper—this child, this copyist, who had first gained attention by writing variations on *his* work!—like the bug he was.

"Well, the Vienna opera house has nothing on the acoustics of La Fenice. The sound floats to the ceiling and permeates the air."

"I look forward to finding out how my work sounds there. The Marchese is sponsoring a performance there next month."

His eyes shot to Oliver across the room. Had Oliver mentioned that La Fenice was preparing a new opera? If he had, surely he would have mentioned that it was one sponsored by the Marchese, and by this upstart Klein.

The Marchese had brought Klein all the way from Vienna. And now he was staging his latest opera. The situation was becoming more dire by the minute.

"Well, I confess I look forward to hearing it. In fact, I have no idea what this opera is about. What style is it in?"

Klein lifted a brow, then shrugged with decided Germanic stiffness. "It is an old tale. *The Odyssey*. Greek heroes long at war, one a secret king, lost at sea," he began, but Vincenzo waved him silent.

"No, no, what would be better than to *hear* it. I'm sure we would all love to hear what brought the house down in Vienna!" He declared this last sentence so loudly, the entire room could not help but turn and listen to him. Even the unnecessary harpist stopped plucking.

"Come, come, Gustav. You can play the ballet at least? The theme?" he smiled, challenging. "A stanza?"

Gustav's eyes flitted to where the Marchese stood with Antonia. The room had gone still, waiting. Then the Marchese gave a slight nod and held out his hand toward the pianoforte, inviting Klein to play.

As Klein stepped to the beautiful golden pianoforte that dominated a stage on the far side of the room, all eyes turned to him. And Vincenzo made his way to stand beside the Marchese.

"Dare I ask if you will be gracing us with a new work tonight?" the Marchese asked in a low voice as Klein put his fingers to the keys, the first graceful bars floating over the guests, perking them up and out of their dissipation.

"No?" the Marchese continued, when Vincenzo did not answer directly. "I did not think so. Vincenzo, I am happy to let my daughter be foolish with you, if you can afford her, but that doesn't mean I have to be. I would have kept you on if you had written anything worth performing while under my roof. But alas, you proved less than worthy."

Vincenzo could feel the blood rushing to his face, a fury of hate and self-loathing covering his skin like tar. But he could not let this man see. Thus, he schooled his features into passivity and pretended to listen to Klein play.

"Perhaps I did," he admitted, pressing a hand to his breast. "Although I am currently working on a piece that might prove more so. Tell me, what do you think this Klein will prove?"

And with that enigmatic statement, he bowed and left the Marchese to listen to the music.

Taking two steps back, he found himself against the wall, next to Oliver, who listened intently to the music.

"He's very good." Oliver whispered to him after a time.

"Hmph," was all that Vincenzo could reply. But secretly, that pit of worry that had settled into his stomach upon meeting Klein had begun to grow and churn since he put his fingers to the keys. Klein was good. Very, very good. His fingering was graceful, impeccable. He pulled down on the keys instead of striking them, making the sound less jarring and more of an element of the space they occupied.

The section of his composition that he had chosen to play was powerful, angry. Vincenzo could imagine the wind beating against the Greek sails as rain poured down violently on stage in a depiction of those tragic Greek sailors lost at sea. And then, suddenly, the mood of the music changed—calming, like the storm passing. Klein told a story with his music . . . and he held the attention of every person in the room.

It was a complete disaster.

Damn it all—if only he had known about Klein before!

"Oliver." Vincenzo turned to his friend, accusation unhidden in his voice. "Why did you not tell me about Klein's opera being staged at La Fenice? And that the Marchese is financing it?"

"Because I didn't know. I resigned from the theatre months ago. Remember?"

Oh yes. Oliver's thwarted departure. Those few weeks Oliver had thought he was headed home had a lasting impact. He had never understood the hold Oliver's family had on him. Perhaps it was one of the effects of having been raised by one. To his mind, Oliver and his father did not even get along—if they had, why would he have run to Venice at the first opportunity? So why Oliver should jump up to come home when called was beyond him. Family had its uses, Vincenzo supposed—gave one something to lean on when times were tough. But guilt and sacrifice were its pitfalls, and they just got in the way.

"But you still talk to some of the girls, the director," Vincenzo replied.

"Yes, well, perhaps the director refrained from mentioning the Marchese since he knows the topic is delicate for you. And the girls . . ." Oliver shrugged. "When they talk to me about the opera, it is only to gripe about the lack of female roles."

Vincenzo looked up, confused. "But doesn't *The Odyssey* have a wife, and a daughter? There are a number of women in the story."

"Yes, but Klein cut them all out of the libretto. Penelope, the wife, is mentioned but never seen. Even the role of Calypso is minor. Our friend Veronica barely has three stanzas to sing. The entire story is all about Odysseus and his men, longing to come home."

Just then, something began to ferment in Vincenzo's mind. It was barely more than an inkling, but he had been observing Klein as much as possible that evening, and there was more to his general rigidity than simply being Austrian. There was something almost puritan about his attitude. He regarded the partygoers—especially the ladies, with their soft forms and high-pitched laughter—with disdain.

And now, he writes an opera with almost no parts for women?

"Oh hell, what is it?" Oliver asked, peering at him closely. "I know that look. You are planning something, aren't you?"

"Not planning, no. I am very much making this up as I go along." Vincenzo replied, his face breaking into a smile. His first honest smile all evening.

"Vincenzo, I'm warning you. Don't do anything rash. If the Marchese expels you from his home again, there is no possibility you'll ever—"

"Stop acting like a grandmother," Vincenzo whispered vehemently. "Do not worry. I am simply going to test a theory."

Luckily, Klein finished playing then, lifting his fingers off the keys, allowing the notes to float over the room. Vincenzo made certain his applause was the first, and the loudest.

In his Harlequin costume, he was well positioned to put on a show.

"Bravo! Bravo!" he cried, as he moved through the crowd efficiently, coming to stand next to Klein at the pianoforte. "That was marvelous, Gustav, simply marvelous. I cannot wait to see the production at La Fenice. What an excellent selection you chose to play for us. Showcasing the two sides of nature."

"Thank you, Signor Carpenini." Klein gave another one of his short bows. "I am gratified by your compliments."

"Indeed, the beginning so forceful and powerful, and the calming of the storm so delicate, and . . . *feminine*."

The word struck home. Vincenzo could barely hold back his triumph as pure malice flashed over Klein's face.

"Feminine? Perhaps I did not understand you correctly. My Italian . . ." Klein said by way of excuse, stiff politeness in his voice.

"Feminine? Of the female nature? Although I suppose the angry crashing of the beginning could be described as feminine as well. We've all known a woman who is a force of nature." He found Antonia in the audience and winked at her. She blushed as the crowd tittered, knowingly.

"My work is not feminine," Klein ground out, his entire being shifting uncomfortably, trying to decide between deferment and engagement.

"What is wrong with feminine?" Vincenzo asked innocently. "Here in Venice, we have the tradition of the Ospedale della Pietà—female foundlings trained in music and regarded as angels. Feminine music is not an insult. Women are the more expressive sex—indeed, some might say it lends them to music and art far more than men."

Gustav Klein threw back his head and laughed at that. "Women are useful, I'll grant you. They can reach the higher notes, they can inspire men's work—but no woman has the education, the deep understanding of music that men have."

Vincenzo glanced at the Marchese. He had hoped that Klein's sentiments might earn him a blacker outlook, but the Marchese did not look angry. The man did not express more than mild interest in this sparring for his favor.

Clearly, Vincenzo needed to guide this confrontation through one more turn.

"I am sorry, Gustav, but that is simply not the case. I have female students who far outstrip my male ones."

"*Your* male students perhaps, Vincenzo. Not mine."

And there it was. The way to what he wanted. And Vincenzo would seize it like a man aflame.

"I accept your challenge." He smiled at Klein graciously.

"What challenge?"

"The challenge you just laid out, my dear fellow. One of my female students against a male one of yours." Vincenzo knew that every eye in the room was on him as he chanced a glance at the Marchese. The corner of the man's mouth had lifted ever so slightly. A thrill of triumph went through him.

"I made no such—" Klein began, but then he, too, chanced a look at the Marchese. He saw the same thing Vincenzo had. Quickly, he changed tactic.

"I had heard that you did not have any students—male or female," Klein stated blandly.

Vincenzo had to hand it to him; the man was smarter than he looked. But instead of letting his ire show, he simply smiled.

"If that's the case, then you will win the challenge quite easily." He laughed, and the crowd laughed with him. Including the Marchese, he noted victoriously.

"But how will one student be judged against the other?" Klein said. "Music is a subjective art. One person's perfection is another banality."

Vincenzo knew in that moment that he had him in the trap. Now, to get him to agree to the terms.

"Excellent question. I would submit that there be one judge. And there is only one person in all of Venice qualified to do so. Marchese?"

The Marchese gave a serene smile as all eyes in the room turned to him.

"An interesting challenge. Can a woman play with the same intensity, the emotional depth of feeling, as a man? It would be my pleasure to serve as judge."

Applause lit the room. Vincenzo's face broke into a wide grin.

"But"—the Marchese raised his hands to quiet the room—"what are the terms, gentlemen?"

"The terms . . ." Vincenzo thought a moment. "Each student plays his or her best piece."

"No," Klein spoke up. "They must play the same piece. If his student plays 'Twinkle Twinkle Little Star,' and mine plays the Waldstein, one can assume one will play better than the other. Then again, perhaps not."

A titter went up from the crowd again. Vincenzo felt his

smile cool. "I am perfectly fine with playing the same piece. As long as it is the Marchese who chooses it."

Klein seemed to think this over. "I agree to those terms."

"When shall the competition be?"

Everyone looked around the room, speculating a good date. Vincenzo heard "One week?" from someone murmuring in the crowd, and felt himself pale. It was a very tricky moment—he had to make certain that he got his way on this point.

"Marchese, tomorrow marks the beginning of Lent—and it would not do to have a fete in a time of penance." Vincenzo then looked to Klein, who seemed to be chewing on this information. "Also, in deference to you, Gustav, I would not want you to be distracted by this while you are trying to put on an opera. Thus, shall we say, mid-May? Just before you retire to the country for the summer, if I recall correctly, Marchese."

Everyone held their breath as the Marchese took this information in and, after a heart-stopping breath of time, nodded firmly.

The room went up in a cheer. People began speculating what the festivities would hold, which students would be performing, what musical piece would be selected. Vincenzo even saw one masked attendant running gleefully from the room, likely to tell everyone else at the ball what had just transpired in the music room.

As a finale to the show they had just performed, Vincenzo gave Klein a deep bow. And Klein was forced to return it.

"I don't know what you expect to come of this, Vincenzo," Klein said through gritted teeth.

"I expect to send you back to Vienna, Gustav," he replied, his smile going cold.

He left Klein's side and was immediately enveloped by the crowd. The crowd that loved him and his theatrics. He would rule them again; he would be hoisted on their loving shoulders some day soon. Shaking hands, accepting flirtatious touches from women, he cut his way to where the Marchese stood next to Antonia.

"Oh, Vincenzo, what fun!" Antonia cried, latching herself onto his arm and planting a hearty kiss on his cheek. "It's like a musical duel! And I'm so happy that you have a female student you feel worthy of this challenge."

"Yes," the Marchese drawled. "But the challenge is not solely about male versus female, my dear. It is about who is the better teacher. And, consequently, the better musician. Am I not correct, Vincenzo?"

Vincenzo simply shrugged one shoulder. "If the better student brings light upon the better teacher, certainly facility with music must have something to do with that."

The Marchese's small smile remained frozen on his features, as inscrutable as the masks they all had been wearing not hours before. "But the unasked and unanswered question is what shall the winner have as prize."

"Prize?" Vincenzo blinked innocently. "I thought only to entertain and inform, Marchese. After all, you did say that it has been too dull around here of late."

"Quite true." The Marchese raised an eyebrow. "Your costume may be that of a fool—let us hope your actions do not prove you to be one."

And with that, the Marchese smirked at him and took his daughter off Vincenzo's arm as they moved away from him. Antonia blew a kiss back at him as she and her father went to stand beside . . .

Klein.

Vincenzo watched as the Marchese stood next to Klein, on the stage in front of the whole crowd, and bowed to Klein, much to the delight of the crowd. As they feted and cheered the Marchese's newest protégé, Vincenzo felt his smile slip from his face.

The Marchese was publicly backing the horse he had already chosen. And as much as the crowd enjoyed Vincenzo's antics, they worshipped at the feet of the Marchese.

Just as Vincenzo felt all the blood in his body draining to the floor, a hand clapped him hard on the shoulder, holding him there. He turned and looked into the unsmiling countenance of Oliver Merrick.

"What the hell have you gotten us into now?"

Seven

"THIS is a mistake."

Oliver paced the length of the entryway of the Hotel Cortile, grinding his heels into the carpet on the turns. It had taken less time than he had hoped for Vincenzo to locate where Miss Bridget Forrester was staying. After all, there were only a certain number of places in the city where a young British lady of good family and comfortable means would feel at home. The Hotel Cortile was one of the many buildings that were near the Grand Canal that had, once upon a time, been the home of a great Venetian family. But like so much of Venice, the fall of the Republic had forced change upon it, and now its beautifully appointed rooms were used to board a full house of mostly British and Austrian visitors.

At least the proprietor, a Signor Zinni, told them that it *had* been full, up until the end of Carnival, two days ago. Now their only remaining guests were a family of ladies, the Forresters, who had somehow managed to requisition the entire second floor.

"I doubt they will stay much longer, however," Zinni had said with visible relief. "They have all of Italy still to see."

Then, at the faint sound of a bell, the little man had run up the stairs to the second floor with such speed that it left Oliver and Vincenzo blinking, wondering at Zinni's obvious fear of the Forresters.

Well, Vincenzo probably wondered. Oliver was too busy running over in his mind just what they were doing there in the first place.

"You know I have no other options," Vincenzo replied in his smooth Italian. He leaned lazily back in his chair in the empty foyer of the hotel. "The Marchese and Klein have let it be known to all of the lovely young female musicians in the city that I am in need of a student—none of them would even let me leave a card."

Oliver grunted. "I would place faith in your reasoning—if only I hadn't the suspicion that appealing to Miss Forrester had been your plan all along." He shot the only other occupant of the room a reproachful look. Vincenzo simply leaned back even farther, tilting the chair back on its rear legs. As the back of the chair bumped against the wall, Vincenzo gave a loud, long yawn.

A yawn. He *yawned*. Oliver stopped pacing. Perhaps Vincenzo was not overly concerned with why Zinni was so fearfully attentive to the Forresters. Perhaps he was not concerned about any bloody thing.

"How can you be so easy with the mess you've created?" Oliver rounded on him. "You remain undisturbed by the gauntlet you threw down to Klein; you have no fear about what will happen if you lose. You don't even seem to care about using Miss Forrester to your aim—that is, if you can persuade her to do so, given that you called her a little prostitute less than a week ago."

"I did not think she was a little prostitute. I assumed she was a whole prostitute, with no equivocation." Vincenzo chuckled at his own joke. "Who else would come to the street door?" But seeing that Oliver was not smiling, he sobered, letting his chair drop to all four legs with a thud that echoed across the empty foyer.

"I am not concerned about persuading the girl to become my student because she traveled across the Continent with that intention. I'm sure an apology will erase the previous misunderstanding." Vincenzo began studying his fingers, the picture

of a collected individual. "Besides, if she is still unhappy with
me, I'm certain I can find a way to . . . change her mind. A
young, impressionable thing like her."

Oliver felt all the blood in his body rage through his veins.
He knew what that meant. Vincenzo thought to persuade Miss
Forrester the same way he had *persuaded* Antonia Galetti to
forgive him. Suddenly, green eyes flashed through his mind.
As green as the lagoon at dawn. Wide, nervous.

Adoring.

A knife twisted in his gut.

"Miss Forrester is a young English lady," he warned, his
voice coming out cold as ice. "She is not like these Venetian
girls, who know the rules to those games."

"Then she will be all the easier to win over." Vincenzo
waved his hand dismissively. "Come, come, this is all a debate
about the thinnest of possibilities. Of course she will want to
be taught by me; I have no worries about the girl."

"No worries whatsoever?" Oliver's eyebrow rose skeptically. "What if she can't play?"

Vincenzo met his eye, deadly calm.

"You are the one who told me she could."

Oliver could not debate that point.

"Oliver!" Vincenzo called, breaking the silence that had
fallen. "You said the girl could play."

"Yes, I did, but—"

"And we both know I have no other options."

"For students, but—"

"Then that is all there is to it," Vincenzo stated with finality.

Oliver was on the cusp of vehemently disagreeing, as there
was very much more to the matter, but before he could, the
sound of a throat clearing brought their attention to the staircase, where Zinni stood, his back straight with propriety.

"Signora Forrester will see you now."

What were they doing here?

Bridget stood frozen at the door of their sitting room in the
Hotel Cortile, her eye glued to the keyhole. Normally, she did
not spy. She was far more likely to burst into a room and con-
front than stay behind curtains and listen.

Amanda, however, was far more accustomed to pressing her ear to walls.

"See!" her sister whispered excitedly. "I told you! Now aren't you glad you came out of your room?"

In the week since they arrived in Venice, Bridget had kept to her room as much as possible. Her brief and disappointing interview with Carpenini had crushed her spirits so thoroughly, Lady Forrester had wondered if she had caught some sort of wasting disease from the travel. Luckily, Molly the maid had managed to keep their excursion to themselves, and Bridget had not been missed in the half hour they had been gone, so when she had said she was simply overwhelmed by the crowds of Carnival, it was taken at face value.

But when Carnival ended and the Forrester ladies had an entire floor to themselves (which somehow, Lady Forrester had managed to overtake *before* all the other guests had vacated, persuading the gentlemen to give over and bunk two to a room to accommodate them), Bridget was still uninspired to go out, which made Lady Forrester call the doctor.

But when the doctor pronounced Bridget healthy, it made her throw up her hands.

"We rush here to Venice, and now you don't want to see it?" Lady Forrester twitched about the room in frustration. "You don't even want to send your note to Mr. Merrick? Bridget, you always were a fickle child, but I do not know what has come over you of late!"

Didn't they realize she was in the deepest mourning? For the hope that she had for greatness? For her lost illusions? Venice, the most beautiful city in Europe, had no color for her now! Its canals held no charm, merely inconvenience. Its buildings were no longer masterful works of architecture, they were instead overdecorated boxes falling to ruins. Food had lost its flavor. Music, its melody.

Carpenini had taken one look at her and dismissed her. Like everyone else did.

Well, no, not like everyone else did. He was far more base.

When she confided this in Molly, the only one who knew the true depths of her sadness, she was rewarded with a roll of the eyes and a request that she vacate the room for at least a half hour, so Molly could change the sheets.

But now Signor Carpenini, the master himself, was taking tea and biscuits in their hotel. With her mother!

"What is he saying?" Bridget whispered to Amanda. "I can't hear anything."

"Try this," Amanda replied, handing her a drinking glass. Bridget turned it over in her hand, unsure of what to do, until Amanda rolled her eyes and took it back, and showed her how to place it between the door and her ear.

". . . studies . . . pianoforte . . . biscuit? . . ." Words came through muffled, and out of place.

"I still can't understand." Bridget handed the glass back to Amanda.

Amanda sighed. "Well, there is only one thing more to do."

"What?"

And with the meanest possible little-sister smile, Amanda reached past her, opened the sitting room door, and let Bridget tumble through.

All eyes fell on Bridget. Her mother's. Mr. Merrick's. And . . .

There he was, smiling at her. Vincenzo Carpenini. His face lighting up for her, and only her.

She felt for certain that she had stopped breathing.

"Ah, there you are Bridget," her mother said blithely, as both men rose to their feet to make their bows. "I have some interesting news. Signor Carpenini has offered to become your teacher."

Oliver watched as the wide green eyes of the girl in front of them came to land on Carpenini and stay there. Her face paled, making the freckles that covered her skin stand out in stark contrast. There was little doubt that the young lady was surprised to see them—but what worried him more was the awestruck quality that had taken Miss Forrester over.

"I am sure you must be very surprised to see Signor Carpenini, and Mr. Merrick," Lady Forrester continued, squinting at her daughter slightly. "Especially considering that we had not yet gotten around to leaving a card with either of them."

Miss Forrester—Bridget—seated herself tentatively next to her mother on the settee, her gaze suddenly shifting from Carpenini's face to Oliver's.

"I . . . I am sorry, Mother," Bridget began, stumbling over the words in a soft voice. And suddenly, Oliver knew that his suspicion was right: Miss Forrester's visit to them had been clandestine. And he felt the overwhelming need to protect her from her mother's scrutiny.

"Miss Forrester did write a note," he blurted out, surprising everyone in the room, including himself. "Just a note. It was very proper, I assure you. She . . . she said your family was in Venice and wondered if I might have Carpenini's address, to apply to him about his offered lessons." Oliver tamped down the flush that was threatening to rise to his face. This was not a lie, he told himself. It was simply . . . an improvisation of his lines. "I thought it might be a nice surprise to bring you Carpenini instead."

"Bridget, is this true?" her mother asked.

"Ah . . . it is as Mr. Merrick says," Bridget replied hesitantly. Then, latching on to the fiction they were spinning around themselves, "Of course, you are Mr. Merrick. I recognize you . . . from when you came to visit us in Portsmouth."

"And I you," Oliver smiled at her. A smile that he hoped conveyed what he meant to say. *Do not worry. It is safe. I will protect you.*

"And I recognize you as well," Carpenini interjected smoothly. "How could I not recognize the girl who played so beautifully all those years ago? Of course, you are no longer a young girl." At this last, his face broke into a beatific smile.

That delightful blush that had captivated Oliver when he'd last seen Miss Forrester again spread across her cheeks. Its effect this time was no less potent. But this blush's cause set Oliver a bit on edge.

He knew that most women's reactions to a man of Carpenini's fame and talent were admiring. And that admiration usually bought the man a certain amount of forgiveness. But a girl who would cross a continent on a single letter . . . she would be in far more danger.

"I was so pleased to discover you were in Venice, Miss Forrester," Carpenini was saying. "Indeed, I was just saying to Oliver that I wished for a student of true talent, and it was so unfortunate that my business keeps me here, when such a student is in England!"

"What luck," Lady Forrester replied, as she poured herself

another cup of tea. "I'm certain Bridget would very much enjoy—and benefit from—your instruction while we spend the next few weeks in the city. What do you think, Bridget?"

The younger lady opened her mouth to speak, but Carpenini interrupted.

"Signora, I am afraid that I would want to instruct the Signorina for more than a few weeks. Now that I have the opportunity . . ."

"But we are on a tour of the Italian peninsula," Lady Forrester replied smoothly. Almost as if she were negotiating. "Confining ourselves to Venice would be criminal."

Carpenini shot a helpless look to Oliver.

"In fact, as Venice has so far unimpressed my daughter, we were contemplating traveling at the end of this week."

Miss Forrester sent a look of complete shock to her mother. Obviously, the girl was not expecting to leave Venice so soon. Especially not now that Carpenini was sitting in front of them.

"But, er, Mother," the girl ventured, "I would think that now, considering the opportunity . . ."

"Yes, my dear," Lady Forrester replied sharply, staring daggers at her daughter. "But perhaps if we traveled south and found warmer climes, your disposition might improve."

Oliver had to suppress a grin as he watched Miss Forrester suppress a snort.

"Besides," Lady Forrester continued, "I hate to be so gauche in front of company, but we hardly planned to have the expense of unending lessons. Traveling is so much more costly than one expects, isn't it?"

The command in Lady Forrester's voice, the sly way she played her cards, the way she said no but then invited them to argue against her: Oliver suddenly realized what this game was all about. Lady Forrester *was* negotiating with them, and by the gleam in her eye, hidden beneath a studiously resigned expression, she enjoyed it considerably.

"Lady Forrester, on that score you should have no worry," Oliver replied smoothly. "For Signor Carpenini is offering to tutor Miss Forrester gratis. For free."

"He is?" both ladies asked at once.

"I am?" Vincenzo asked, alarmed. "Er, that is, of course I am." He smiled at Lady Forrester, then Miss Forrester. "It has been long that I was allowed to teach someone with talent. I

will enjoy the opportunity." Vincenzo's Italian accent flowed
charmingly over his not-quite-fluent English, making the ladies smile, and not just politely.

Then, under his breath in rapid Italian, he laid into Oliver.
"What the hell are you doing? I could have made a fortune!
You are the one always complaining of funds."

"True—but if you are going to use her to save your career,
I would not have her pay for the privilege," Oliver fired back,
in the same language.

"Gentlemen." Lady Forrester's English broke into their
conversation, although she did not look pleased. For one
breathless moment, Oliver was afraid that the woman understood what they had said, but then he realized she was merely
disappointed by the lack of a fight over price. "I think that
sounds lovely."

"So we are agreed?" Carpenini's face broke into a smile.

But Lady Forrester simply turned to Bridget, regarding
her. Oliver glanced down and saw that the girl had taken her
mother's hand and given it a short, sharp squeeze. A message.
Apparently he and Vincenzo were not the only ones able to
have private conversations in company. "That, I believe is up
to my daughter," Lady Forrester answered. Then she rose.
"Would you all excuse me a moment? I should speak with Signor Zinni about the possibility of extending our stay."

And, with the light of bargaining once again restored to
Lady Forrester's face, she left her daughter to entertain the
gentlemen callers. But not before issuing a curt nod to the
maid just inside the door (the same one who had accompanied
Bridget to Oliver's home a week ago), a silent directive to keep
an eye on the goings-on.

When the door clicked shut, silence fell down onto the
room. Miss Forrester, her wide green eyes never blinking as
she turned to look from Oliver to Vincenzo, back to Oliver
again, and then, finally to the abandoned teapot.

"M–More tea, Mr. Merrick?" she asked, scooting over on
the settee to take her mother's place by the tray.

"No, thank you, Miss Forrester." He saw the nervousness
in the smallest shake of her hands, the uncertainty in her very
skin. "Er, I know it must seem strange, given the circumstances of the last time we met—"

"Oliver, she does not wish to speak of that," Vincenzo

broke in. "She was foolish to interrupt, and I was foolish enough to have such an angry temperament. But I promise, my dear, it is only when I am composing."

He smiled at her again, obviously hoping to put off her unease. But, to her credit, Bridget Forrester proved less malleable than Vincenzo probably liked.

"No, I think it should definitely be remarked upon. Especially considering what you are asking of me."

Both Oliver and Vincenzo went very still. "What do we ask of you?"

"I don't know!" The girl practically exploded from her seat, sending cups scattering to the floor. The maid leaped from her position at the door to gather the broken pieces.

"Oh, Molly, I'm so sorry," Bridget said suddenly, on the verge of tears.

"It's no difficulty, miss," Molly demurred. And then with a sharp look to the two men, she muttered, "I understand why you are so upset."

"Yes!" Bridget cried. "I am upset. But I am also confused. A week ago, you had no idea who I was, Signore, even though Mr. Merrick wrote to me on your behalf. And now you seek me out, and you wish to become my musical instructor? For free? This smacks of something underhanded, and I do not know what it could be." Her voice began to tremble with vehemence. "Are you planning to make fun of me? Because I have had plenty of that in my life and I could easily do without it, thank you very much."

On this last, Bridget's voice broke completely, and the smallest sob escaped. But she stifled it. She beat it back with an unseen resolve. But even that resolve could not stop her frame from shaking with every breath.

"My dear Miss Forrester," Vincenzo began, "there is nothing, as you say, underhanded—"

"Tell her," Oliver said bluntly, before he could stop himself.

Vincenzo shot him a look that told him he would prefer Oliver to be on fire at that very moment. But he didn't give a damn.

"If Miss Forrester is going to put her hand in with us, she had better well know what it is all about. About the mess you've gotten yourself into." He turned to meet those unblinking green eyes. "Miss Forrester, you are feeling badly dealt with, and you should be. You are right that Signor Carpenini does not remember you. Because he didn't. I wrote you that letter, because I remembered that you played very well, and thought to drum up some business for him, but that is beside the point at the moment. What is important is that Signor Carpenini finds himself in reduced circumstances in this city. He has lost his patronage." Vincenzo's face went red with fury, but he said nothing. Indeed, it seemed at that point that anyone would be hard pressed to stop Oliver from continuing his narration.

"And now, he thinks to earn his patron's favor back again by challenging the Austrian composer, Herr Gustav Klein, to a musical competition. Klein produces his best male student, and Carpenini produces his best female student, and whoever plays better is pronounced the winner. It's as simple as that. Except that Signor Carpenini has no female students. No students at all, in fact."

Oliver finished his speech, letting silence come into the void. Even Molly, the maid, had stopped scraping up pieces of china in the wake of these revelations. Miss Forrester slowly lowered herself back onto the settee.

"So . . . you need me to perform? In a competition?" she asked slowly. "In public. Now?"

"No. In May," Oliver answered, when Vincenzo refused to open his mouth.

"All . . ." she began, and then collected herself. "All I had wanted was to learn . . . to learn everything I could." She took a few more moments, swallowing the information, her eyes on the floor but darting back and forth as if reading something written on the rug. As if searching to come to terms with what had been said.

"Is this true?" she finally said, looking directly into Vincenzo's gaze.

"Yes," he replied curtly, his accent thick but his words unobscured. "I do find myself in a trouble that only you can help me out of. I am—how do you say—alone in Venice and no musician—man or woman—wants to work with me. I live on Oliver's charity. I even find myself in a bitter black humor because I . . . because composing does not come as easy as it once did."

Oliver's eyes shot to Vincenzo's face, surprised at this last admission. It was a vulnerability that he had not expected to hear. Neither, apparently, had Miss Forrester. She gazed at him with sadness and sympathy.

He's reeling her in, Oliver realized.

"It is all true," Vincenzo continued, his voice becoming low, mellifluous. "Except for one point. I do remember you."

Oliver's head came up slightly, surprised.

"You played while your sister sang a sad tune. 'Tom Bowling,' was it?"

"Yes," Miss Forrester replied. "I was playing it too cheerfully, and you corrected me."

"Yes, I remember." He sighed, somewhat wistful. And Oliver felt his brow come down. What were the chances that Carpenini actually remembered Miss Forrester's playing, instead of simply using what Oliver had told him?

"You were very good. I remember at the time wondering why anyone would ruin such excellent playing by having an inferior singer. Most people would only see your sister—older, is she? Pretty."

At Miss Forrester's stilted nod, Oliver knew that Vincenzo had found a wound to needle. And now, he was going to exploit it. Just as he had with Gustav Klein.

"It's very hard to be overshadowed by a sibling, but you would be used to it. Your friends, society—even your parents—they favor the other. But that does not mean you have to like it," Vincenzo continued, drawing Miss Forrester to him, bringing her to the edge of her seat, as he sat on the edge of his.

"If you come train under me, I will make you the best piano musician in England. Ladies' parlors will be too small a venue for your talents. You will be sought after, admired. People will want you."

Vincenzo, at some point in the conversation, had taken Miss Forrester's hand, which had gone limp in her lap, all sense of nerves gone. He now raised it to his lips and held it there.

"It will not be easy. I will work you harder than you've ever worked in your life. But in the end you will win this competition, the respect of Venice, and I . . . I will be forever in your debt."

He held her eyes. Oliver held his breath, hoping for a different answer, for some defiance that would protect the girl. But he knew her words, even before she said them.

Her voice was small but sure. On her face rested a look of desire, ambition . . . and endless adoration. She was completely under Carpenini's spell.

"I'll do it."

Eight

THERE would be rules.

First of all, the lessons would be conducted at Mr. Merrick's home. This surprised Bridget, as instruction was usually given at the student's place of residence. But, as Signor Carpenini pointed out to Bridget's mother when she returned, the Hotel Cortile, while well appointed, had a rather inferior instrument, out of tune and from the last century. Mr. Merrick's piano was apparently of the latest style, with a proper seven-octave keyboard.

"But my daughter must be chaperoned," Lady Forrester replied, unwilling to budge on this point.

"She has a maid, does she not?" Carpenini's eyes flew to Molly, who had retaken her place at the door. Molly's gaze remained steady and just slightly contemptuous. After all, she had heard every word of the true reason Carpenini wanted to teach her. Bridget could only silently plead with her to not blurt it out to her mother then and there. Later, she would plead verbally.

"A maid is hardly acceptable chaperonage in a *bachelor's* home," Lady Forrester wisely countered. "It would seem that I would be the only appropriate chaperone available."

Her mother, chaperone? How was she supposed to learn

anything with her sitting in the room, watching like a hawk? She would be too nervous to do anything. And she was already nervous enough, to be in the presence of Signor Carpenini!

Bridget shot a look of alarm to Mr. Merrick. Why Mr. Merrick, she did not know—perhaps because he was the one who had first breached honesty with her. But somehow, she knew that he was the person best suited to solving this problem.

He blinked twice, and then, miraculously, solve the problem he did.

"Er, luckily, it is not a bachelor's home," he blurted, seeming to surprise even himself.

"Are you married, then, Mr. Merrick?" Lady Forrester replied, blinking. "Your father never mentioned such good fortune when we met with him."

"No! I am not married. But my, er, my aunt lives with me. On my mother's side. Great-aunt actually. She hails from Milan and is very much a stickler for propriety."

By the way Carpenini looked at his friend and then smoothly covered his reaction, Bridget knew this to be a lie. It was a small wonder that her mother did not catch it as well. She could only attribute it to the fact that once again, Lady Forrester had left off her spectacles.

"My aunt will provide ample chaperonage."

"Well," Lady Forrester said on a sigh. "I still will not feel comfortable until a proper call is paid upon your aunt. We will attend her at your first lesson, Bridget."

"Oh, Mother, I don't think—" Bridget was about to demur and try to gracefully back Mr. Merrick out of being caught in his lie, but the upturned corner of Mr. Merrick's mouth—the smallest show of mischief—told her to keep still. Maybe he did have an aunt hidden away in the city somewhere who could be installed at a moment's notice.

But the problem of the aunt was quickly put aside when Carpenini laid down the second rule.

"Your lessons will be daily, except for Sundays. They will begin at nine in the morning and not end until three."

"*Six hours?* Are you intending to break my daughter's fingers?" Lady Forrester said, aghast.

"It is how I teach, Signora," Carpenini said simply, brooking no opposition. And then he added a third rule. "But I will not take all of the Signorina's time. In fact"—he leaned forward, a conspiratorial glint in his eye—"forbid the young lady from practicing outside my presence."

As much as his confiding tone (and the thought of six hours of Carpenini's uninterrupted presence) set Bridget's heart to *prestissimo*, she had presence of mind enough to ask: "But . . . why?"

"Because your mother wishes you to enjoy the delights of the city, and I will not take that away from you." Carpenini gave a generous nod to Lady Forrester, and she preened with the attention and the deference. "Besides, I would not want you practicing bad habits," he admonished Bridget. "So I must be there to make sure you are practicing good ones."

"So we are agreed? We begin *lunedi*, Monday," Signor Carpenini said as he rose from his seat, bringing an end to that afternoon's interview. Bridget had a dozen or so questions (Did Mr. Merrick really have an aunt living with him? Why couldn't she practice at the hotel? What should she play for the Signore first?), not to mention another dozen questions that were related directly to the competition (What piece would they play? How many people would be there? How was she ever going to play in front of a room full of people without her nerves failing her?), but no such questions emerged from her mouth as she and her mother stood and gave curtsies to Mr. Merrick's and Signor Carpenini's farewell bows.

Which was how, Monday morning at nine o'clock, Bridget found herself taking her first lessons from Signor Carpenini.

"Don't be nervous," Mr. Merrick said in her ear as he took her hand to help her from the gondola at the door to his home. Approaching the rough brick structure from the water had been different than approaching by foot. As if she were being delivered to her fate, instead of rushing headlong toward it. She managed to smile and nod at him as he led them through the main entrance.

Although she had been here for only minutes previously, there was now a charged air about the place. A sense of expectation.

"Your home seems different," Bridget whispered to Mr. Merrick as she took his arm and he escorted her to the music room—which, it seemed, was also the drawing room, wherein a beautiful scrolled ebony pianoforte took up the center of the room. Indeed, it was a far superior instrument to what the Hotel Cortile had.

"Yes. It's amazing what two days' worth of scrubbing can do to a place," Mr. Merrick whispered back, his eyes smiling at her. "But no more mentions of your last visit. We wouldn't want your mother to become suspicious."

"Yes, of course," Bridget said nervously as she glanced over her shoulder, where her mother had seated herself on a low settee and was busy conversing with, surprisingly, Mr. Merrick's ancient great-aunt.

"*Che?*" the old, bent woman kept saying, pulling her thick shawl tight over bony shoulders. "Lessons, *si?*"

"*Si!*" Lady Forrester yelled, taking another sip of the tea laid out for them. "For my daughter!" She pointed to Bridget. "With Signor Carpenini!"

"I think yelling is unnecessary, Mother," Amanda said, from Lady Forrester's other side. "She can hear, but she does not understand the language." Amanda was exhibiting all the signs of the energetic younger child forced into this visit. Her feet tapped, and her hand went from her chin to the armrest to her chin again, an endless fidget. "Where is Signor Carpenini, anyway?" she pouted. Amanda had been horribly affronted to be left out of the meeting with the Signore.

Bridget had been wondering that, too.

In all the jumble of questions since the meeting, in Bridget's mind, the memory of the direct gaze, handsome features, and passionate voice of Signor Carpenini played directly into her subsequent fractiousness. The fact that she had not seen him yet that morning only heightened the anticipation, and her fears.

Calm yourself, Bridge, she told herself. *Think serenely. Like . . . Mr. Merrick. He is always calm, always affable. Emulate that.*

"I am here," Carpenini's voice came from the entryway, and Bridget found that any calm she'd hoped to cultivate fled completely. And her scattered nerves returned in full force.

The first time she'd met with Carpenini in Venice, he had been bearded, scraggly, and angry. Like a feral dog scrounging bones, who growled at anyone that crossed his path. Then,

when he had come to the Hotel Cortile, he had been clean
shaven, handsome, suave, enticing. Now he bounded, com-
manding the attention of the room. His wiry frame made him
seem like a coiled spring. His eyes were focused, pinning her
to her place.

Out of all the incarnations of Carpenini, this one set her
pulse fluttering fastest.

She glanced around the room, her eyes finally finding the
calming gaze of Mr. Merrick. There was some comfort in his
strong, solid form. Everyone else in the room looked at her
with some expectation—Carpenini most of all. Mr. Merrick
just smiled merrily and began to direct Lady Forrester and his
aunt into quieting down.

Curious, that.

But there was little time to contemplate, as Carpenini
quickly trotted across the room, took Bridget's hand in his,
and brought it to her lips.

There went her pulse again, like a hummingbird's wing.

"Signorina Forrester, I so look forward to being your
teacher."

Was she supposed to say something? It seemed like she
was expected to say something.

"And I your student." Her voice came out small, demure,
even. Bridget did not think she had ever sounded demure in
her entire life. "Er . . . shall we begin?"

"*Si.* I would like to learn of your skill," he said, then
frowned, as if searching for the right word. "The level? *Si.* The
level. It has been some time since I heard you play."

Already. She knew she was going to have to perform, but
she was still steeling her nerves to do it. She had spent hours
practicing different pieces, not knowing what would be required of her. She figured she had not yet become his pupil,
and thus Carpenini's strange rule about not practicing at home
was not yet enforced. *Please don't let my courage flee. Don't
let me fail this first test.*

"All . . . all right," she stuttered, as Carpenini helped her to
her seat at the pianoforte. He drew back the cover, revealing
the most perfect, beautifully straight keys. "I have been working on a Bach concerto, or I know Mozart . . ."

"No, we will start simply. I would like to hear your scales."

"Scales?" she asked, surprised.

She almost missed it, such was her astonishment. But she was sure she saw Carpenini give the quickest of glances to Mr. Merrick. And saw Mr. Merrick give the smallest of nods in return. "*Si*, scales. Start with a C-major scale, then go up the octave by half steps. Then return."

Carpenini seated himself in a nearby chair, so he could watch her hands while she played.

Then, with no other recourse, Bridget shrugged and let her fingers fly over the scales. As she did so, Carpenini wound the Maelzel's metronome that sat on a nearby mantel. Its steady click became her beat. Soon enough, she was playing scale after scale, almost in a trance.

Carpenini would occasionally make small comments, such as, "Hands must be arched," or, "Good, good," but the one that came with regularity, whenever she reached the bottom of the octave, was, "Again."

"Is this really how he teaches?" Lady Forrester said loudly to Mr. Merrick's aunt, squinting at Carpenini.

The aunt simply turned and said something in Italian to Mr. Merrick. He responded conversationally, likely explaining what Lady Forrester had asked of her. Then the aunt turned back to Lady Forrester and said simply, "*Si*."

The drills were easy, her dexterity unhindered by the lack of practice from a month spent aboard a ship. But by the time an hour had ticked by, Bridget's fingers were beginning to cramp, Amanda looked bored to tears, and Lady Forrester was visibly twitching whenever Bridget began a new octave of scales, having given up long ago on conversation with Mr. Merrick's aunt.

But both Carpenini and Mr. Merrick were calm, and watchful.

"*Si, si, bellissima!*" Carpenini finally cried, clapping his hands to end her playing. Everyone in the room visibly relaxed. Bridget lifted her hands from the keys and took the opportunity to rub her hands.

Carpenini tsked. "If your hands are sore already, we must build your enduring."

"It's not the playing," Bridget was quick to assure him. "It's the repetition."

But Carpenini just shrugged as he rubbed his chin. "You need to strengthen! Now, we work on chord progression."

"No!" Lady Forrester cried, standing up. Every eye in the room flew to her, causing her to blush and fumble. "Er, that is, Bridget, my dear," she said, taking a deep calming breath. "I am afraid your sister and I must leave you."

"You must?" Bridget asked.

"We must?" Amanda echoed, perking up considerably.

"Yes, we have an appointment. Somewhere. But I have satisfied myself that you are in good hands with Signor Carpenini, and Mr. Merrick's aunt will be the most gracious of hostesses." She nodded to that lady, who smiled daftly back at her, showing a yellowed, decaying set of teeth. "We shall come and collect you at three."

"I will be happy to escort Miss Forrester back to the hotel," Mr. Merrick said, giving a bow.

Her mother must have been flustered enough by her haste to flee the forthcoming hour of chord progressions, because she abandoned negotiations and flouted propriety in one simple nod of the head. Then she took Amanda by the hand and practically ran to the front door, where Mr. Merrick, following behind, hailed a gondola for them with an expert's speed.

Bridget remained seated at the pianoforte—oddly, holding her breath. She wasn't entirely certain what was happening, but by the way Carpenini remained frozen, listening to the muffled sounds of her mother and sister's departure, neither was she about to move.

"Er . . . should I begin chord progressions?" she asked, tentatively. But Carpenini just held up a finger, silencing her.

Suddenly, Mr. Merrick came back into the room. He gently closed the door behind him.

"They're gone."

It was as if the room exhaled. Carpenini crossed over to Mr. Merrick and clapped his friend on the back. "Well done!"

"I think it should be Miss Forrester who is congratulated," Mr. Merrick replied. "After all, she is the one who did the hard work."

"*Si*," came a lovely, airy accented voice from the settee. "I would go mad, singing scales."

Bridget turned, and saw Mr. Merrick's aunt . . . but suddenly, she didn't seem ancient or decrepit. She had stood and was stretching her body—one that was longer and fuller than her hunched frame implied. With one quick movement, she unpinned her hair, letting surprisingly thick curls fall down her back. Threading her hand through the masses, she shook out a quantity of powder, revealing darker, shinier tresses, instead of the dull gray they had all assumed.

"Miss Forrester, this is Veronica Franzetti," Mr. Merrick said by way of introduction. Veronica dipped to a curtsy and, stunned, Bridget did the same.

"We should be safe for the rest of today," he said, turning to Veronica. "Could you do us the greatest of favors and come back in costume for a few more days? I think after that we should be safe, but I could not imagine the difficulty if Lady Forrester decided to accompany her daughter again, and my aunt weren't here." When she looked confused, he repeated himself in Italian and was rewarded by a huge smile.

"*Per te*, Oliver? *Naturalmente*." She twinkled up at him and then went up on tiptoes to buss his cheek, like he was her favorite schoolboy. When she noticed that some of the deeply etched lines that had painted her face had come off on his cheek, she touched her skin, horrified. "Oh, I must remove the terrible stuff!" and she fled the room with a brief, "*Scusi*."

Bridget could only stare at Mr. Merrick. "She's not your aunt, I take it?"

"Not at all," Carpenini replied for him, his voice an insinuation.

"Is she . . . is she . . ." Bridget did not know if she could even say it aloud.

"Is she what?" Mr. Merrick asked, with a trace of a smile.

"A *courtesan*," Bridget finally whispered, mortified.

Mr. Merrick and Carpenini both laughed aloud at that.

"No, of course not!" Mr. Merrick replied. "She is an actress, singer. She is an accomplished diva at La Fenice."

"But . . . aren't actresses often courtesans?"

He cocked his head to the side, questioning. "Sometimes they take lovers, but 'often'? I doubt they would have the time, what with rehearsals and performance schedules and the like." His eyes lit with amusement as Bridget felt her face go red. "What is your fascination with courtesans?"

She met his eye in exasperation. "Well, Venice is rather known for them."

"In the sixteenth century, perhaps," he countered, enjoying the banter. Bridget found herself enjoying it, too, in spite of the uncouth topic. Or perhaps because of it.

It had been, all in all, a very strange morning.

"Now that we have established Veronica's morals," Carpenini drawled, interrupting the conversation, "should we get down to the business?"

Bridget's eyes flew to the master. "Should I start playing chord progressions?"

Carpenini gave a little chuckle. "That will be unnecessary."

"But you said . . ."

"Yes," Mr. Merrick interjected. "I'm afraid that was also part of the ruse. We decided, and I'm sure you will agree, that it would be better to have the freedom to learn without your mother's watchful presence. Thus, it was determined that the fastest way to drive her out was—"

"To *bore* her." Bridget finished for him, the truth dawning. "Oh, Signore, that is absolutely brilliant," she cried, turning to Carpenini. He took her smiles with a pleased bow, making that little thrill run down her spine again.

But what he said next was like cold water on her skin, sobering her . . . worse yet, freezing her.

"No more scales, no more exercises." He seated himself in his chair next to the pianoforte again, indicating she should take her place at the keys. "Play your best piece for me. I will hear what you can do."

Bridget felt the cold, all-too-familiar dread begin to snake over her body. *Please, do not let me bungle this. Please—just don't let me fail.*

"Now," he said, "we will begin in truth."

Nine

SOMETHING was wrong. Oliver knew it the instant Carpenini instructed her to play.

Since the interview at the Hotel Cortile, Oliver discovered he was of two minds about the entire enterprise. On the one hand, now that Miss Forrester had agreed to become Carpenini's student, now that everything was in place, it was futile to try to persuade her against it. They could only move forward and make the best of it. And Oliver could not deny that he had a stake in the scheme's success. He wanted it all—the lessons, the competition—to go as smoothly as possible.

On the other hand, he knew that Bridget Forrester was here by his doing—his fault. Therefore, he felt an overwhelming sense of responsibility for her welfare in these strange circumstances. He knew how Carpenini could be. The man never saw the looks of utter adoration in the faces of his admirers—thus he didn't have to set out to seduce someone for them to wind up in his power. And often, in his bed.

Thus, while he found it expedient to find a way to remove Lady Forrester and any other unwanted observers to their lessons, he would be damned if he was going to leave the girl alone with Carpenini for a single second.

But at that moment, it was not Bridget Forrester's physical

welfare that concerned him. It was the way the blood drained
from her face, the way her lips thinned, when faced with
Carpenini's instruction.

"Now we will begin in truth," he had said, as the girl seated
herself.

It was not as if she had lost her footing, or swooned, or
something equally dramatic. But as someone who had once
found the study of people beneficial to his profession, Oliver
knew that something was . . . off.

She had skill, he remembered that with certainty. Not to
mention, an hour's worth of scales had proven her fingers
adept and strong—a result of the hours and hours of daily
practice that, at their interview, they had been informed was
Bridget's routine. Therefore her talents should not have become rusty with disuse. Quite the contrary.

So why the tremor in her hands? Why the fear?

"This is . . . this is, a Bach minuet," she said, her voice
coming out a touch too sharp, as if she were forcing herself out
of meekness.

She began. And to be fair, she began quite well. It was
a simpler piece, but one that was meant to be played with
feeling—and it was often the feeling that set a good musician
apart from a great one. Oliver could tell immediately when her
shoulders began to relax, when she began to throw herself
more into the piece.

But then her fingers stumbled.

Just once, and she recovered from it. Oliver saw Carpenini's face register a small frown, although he said nothing. But
Miss Forrester caught it out of the corner of her eye.

Swallowing hard, she recommitted herself to the piece. But
then the same descending run occurred, and the same flub.
Then another.

By the time she reached the end of the second refrain, what
had begun beautifully had declined into unfortunate medioc-
rity. By the time the last note died in the air, Miss Forrester's
face looked so distraught, Oliver wondered how her eyes remained dry.

But if Miss Forrester's face was complete ruin, Carpenini's
face was pure thunder.

They all held their breaths. The metronome ticked, its constant rhythm the only sound in the fragile air. Finally, Carpenini broke the silence.

"Please, excuse me a moment," he said tersely. And then, with no further explanation, he left the room.

As the door clicked shut, Oliver felt something in his soul begin to wake up. Something indefinably from his English half. Something . . . protective.

"It wasn't as bad as all that," he began, trying to comfort.

"Yes it was," Miss Forrester replied, her voice heartbreakingly final.

"No, I promise you, it wasn't. The Signore is likely getting some sheet music . . . trying to discern how to approach your instruction. Now that he knows where we are to start, it will be—"

"Don't lie to me!" she cried vehemently, stilling the next platitude on his lips. "That was terrible. *I know it.* And he knows it. I ruined my one chance with my own wretchedness. I have disappointed Carpenini, and now he'll never teach me—he'll be better off finding some other girl off the street who's never seen a note of music. At least he can train someone like that to overcome her own fears," she sighed, a watery sniffle escaping as she did so. "I should go."

She stood, her decision made. But Oliver found himself so lost in what she was saying, he almost missed it when she made for the door.

At least he can train someone like that to overcome her own fears . . .

"Miss Forrester!" he cried, leaping from his chair, following after her. "Miss Forrester, wait!"

She was out the door that led to the street before he managed to catch up with her. "Miss Forrester, if you insist on going back to the hotel, at least allow me to escort you."

"There is no need," she said, not turning to face him, her hand wiping at her cheeks. "I know the way."

"Don't be ridiculous," he replied sternly. "I am not about to let you get lost in the alleyways of Venice by yourself."

"I don't get lost," she countered, matter-of-fact. "Not on streets, anyway."

"Well, I've lived here for nearly five years, and I still do. Perhaps it is I who require your escort."

Despite the roundabout logic, she made no further objection, so Oliver fell into step beside her. But her gaze remained straight ahead.

"When did it start?" he asked, after they had gone a few blocks.

"Last year," she answered, resigned. "During my debut season. There was so much weight placed on everything. How I spoke, how I danced. How I played." She paused, let her eyes flit over the water as they crossed one of Venice's many footbridges.

"I used to love playing for an audience." She sighed after a moment. "It made people happy, or bereft, or wistful, depending on the piece. It's such an amazing sensation, being able to make people *feel something*."

"But now, you think you've lost that."

"After a year?" She surprised him by looking up into his face. "Mr. Merrick, I know I have."

"I wonder, then, that you play at all anymore," he said mildly. "I know many performers on stage who have given up their careers when faced with a bad case of nerves."

"I play because when I play really, truly well . . ." She came to a stop and rubbed her knuckles into her chest, just outside her heart. "There is this strange hollow that has never been filled by gossip, or flirting, or books. But music . . . music fills it." She paused, sniffing away tears. "Besides, I can still do it when by myself, or just with my family." Her face became bleak again. "But when people I do not know are waiting to hear me play—all their expectations written plainly on their faces . . ."

"Miss Forrester, I did not mean to upset you," Oliver was quick to reply. "I meant my last statement as a compliment. It takes a great deal of fortitude to push through when you have little to no hope."

"Oh," she replied. They began walking again. "Thank you."

"And I do understand that hollow feeling you speak of." He let a small smile creep onto his face. "Although I might describe it a little less dramatically."

"That was particularly overwrought, wasn't it?" she replied sheepishly, with a small laugh.

It was good to see her smile, however small.

"Miss Forrester, you say you can play in front of people you know. Now that you know both myself and the Signore, surely you can see that there is nothing to fear from us."

She shook her head. "Don't you understand? Every time he sees me now, he will expect me to disappoint him. And I will live up to that expectation. I will not be able to stop it. And he's just so . . ." Oliver wondered which adoring adjective she would choose. *Wonderful? Brilliant? Talented?* "Carpenini," she finished quietly.

She came to a stop again, and Oliver was surprised to see that they were standing in front of the Hotel Cortile. Bridget's steps had been sure, and she'd led him quickly through the complicated maze of Venice's streets and bridges. Perhaps she really didn't get lost. At least, not on streets.

"Mr. Merrick, thank you for your escort. I . . . I suppose it is best if I explain the situation to my mother."

"What situation?" he blinked at her.

"Why the Signore will no longer be teaching me." She shrugged. "Perhaps she will be pleased. She had hoped this Italian holiday would prove more varied."

Her resignation was so terribly sad that the protectiveness that was born in him earlier that day came raging back, full force. He wanted to wrap her in his arms and murmur comforts—she would never have to play again if she did not wish it, there would be no competition, nothing to make her afraid of people's stares again.

But there was another part of him, perhaps an even greater kind of protectiveness, that saw the truth. She had crossed a continent for the chance to learn from Carpenini, to overcome her own fears. She had come this far. He could not let her give up now.

"Miss Forrester, I beg you, do not say anything to your mother yet," Oliver said, taking her hand in his, a strange shock of warmth running through him at the touch. "Just come back tomorrow."

One skeptical eyebrow went up. "The Signore will not want to teach me . . ."

"Let me worry about Carpenini. Just come back tomorrow. And if after tomorrow, you still feel the same, I will be sorry for it, but I will understand."

Stunned, Miss Forrester nodded slowly. Then, after a quick bow over her hand, he released her, watching as she tentatively walked away, disappearing back inside the hotel.

After a quick walk back to his home (during which he took a wrong turn only twice), Oliver entered the drawing-cum-music room, his mind still turning over ideas for tomorrow. There he was not surprised to find Carpenini, returned once more to his place at the pianoforte, looking dejected. His fingers did not play but instead traced the ghosts of patterns left by Miss Forrester's fumblings not a half hour ago.

"So," Oliver said, making himself known.

"So," Carpenini echoed back at him in Italian. Then after a moment, he turned his head and eyed Oliver from over his shoulder. "Stage fright?"

"Quite so," he replied, also in Italian. "A rather ingrained case of it. She says it's been plaguing her for about a year now."

"Ah." Carpenini put his fingers back to the keys and this time pressed down lightly, letting chords seep into the room like morning light. "She did not have to run off. We could have continued the lesson."

"Well, perhaps if you had been a little more discreet in hiding your disappointment, instead of rushing out of the room . . ."

"You'll have to excuse my shock, Oliver. I have a great deal riding on Miss Forrester, and I had been told by someone whose opinion I trust implicitly that the girl could play, and quite well, too."

"She *can* play," Oliver began, but Vincenzo cut him off with a stern look.

"Is that your memory or your infatuation talking?"

"My infatuation?"

"I've seen you watching her. The way your shoulders tense when I get within six inches of her."

"That's because I know *you*, Vincenzo." Oliver replied darkly. "And if I become anxious when you get near to her, how do you think the girl feels? Someone with as bad a case of nerves as I've ever seen . . ."

Vincenzo stood up from his bench, shock written on his frame. "As bad a case of nerves as you've ever seen? And this is who I'm supposed to teach?" He began to pace. "Perhaps it is not too late. Perhaps we can set off for England. You can see your home again, and I can set the British on their ears with my new compositions!"

"What new compositions?" Oliver replied flatly. "The ones you've been promising me for a year? Besides, it won't work now. Before the Carnival ball, yes, you could have toured abroad. But since you have made this wager—if you back out of it, that disgrace will follow you wherever you go." Oliver watched as Vincenzo stopped moving and took in his predicament. There was no slipping out of this one. He cleared his throat and brought them back to the topic at hand.

"Miss Forrester says her nerves do not plague her as long as she is alone or with close friends—people who do not make her uncomfortable."

"Unfortunately, we do not have the month or so it would take to devote to making her comfortable with me," Vincenzo argued, resuming his pacing.

"I know—we need to shock her into not being afraid of you." Oliver said, a slow smile spreading across his face.

"And just how do we do that?" Vincenzo harrumphed.

"What was it you said to me at the Carnival ball?" Oliver mused. "Oh yes: 'Do not worry. I am simply going to test a theory.'"

 ❧

"I'll be right honest, miss: I do not like this. Not one bit."

Molly crossed her arms with such force, it caused the gondola to rock slightly in the current. The gondolier—the young man with strong arms who propelled the gondola on its path—shot an unhappy glare at Molly. The ride from the Hotel Cortile to Mr. Merrick's home on the Rio di San Salvatore was short and, since they went via the Grand Canal, beautiful, but Molly was determined to make it as torturous for Bridget as she could.

As if Bridget weren't torturing herself enough already for agreeing to come back.

"I promise there is nothing amiss about it, Molly."

"Nothing amiss about a young lady paying calls on a gentleman alone? We may not be in England anymore, but we are not in the savage lands neither!"

When Bridget had come home the day before, her mother and sister had not yet returned. Perhaps they actually did have an appointment to keep somewhere in the city, or perhaps they had simply decided to sightsee, but in either case, it was Molly who greeted Bridget with surprise, and then, seeing the worry on her face, suspicion. And it was Molly who had dug out the truth of what had happened that morning from a reluctant Bridget.

And out of everything that had happened—out of Bridget's horrible case of nerves and the Signore walking out of the room and playing scales for hours—what was the one thing that Molly had to harp on? It was the fact that Mr. Merrick's aunt was very clearly not Mr. Merrick's aunt.

"I don't know what your mother was thinking, declining to accompany you today. I told her in the strictest terms she should."

Luckily, even when faced with Lady Forrester and Amanda's sternest objections to sitting and listening to scales, Molly had held her tongue on *why* she felt Bridget required a chaperone. She simply insisted on accompanying her herself.

Lady Forrester and Amanda had returned home at nearly four, famished and in great need of repast. While Lady Forrester regaled Bridget with tales of all the sights seen and unseen (their mother really should not be without her spectacles) and Amanda went on and on about what the guidebook had said about the Piazza San Marco and the Doge's Palace, Bridget smiled and nodded and waited for an inquisition that did not come.

It seemed that Lady Forrester was content with the lessons as long as Bridget was content with the lessons and would not lay question to it.

For that Bridget was grateful.

And strangely, she was grateful for Molly, too.

Molly did not make her nervous. Molly did not look at her with expectation. Instead, Molly simply protected.

It was comforting. Even if such protection came with a degree of disapproval.

"I will not be sitting down in the kitchens, miss, I tell you that much," Molly was going on, her tight movements of fractious energy swaying the gondola, earning glances from the gondolier, thus repeating the cycle. "And if that Signore walks out of your lessons again, we will go right out the door and back to the hotel to pack. You don't need no lessons from the likes of him."

"Just . . . if anything like that happens, just please do not tell my mother about it. I . . . I can't disappoint him again," Bridget whispered to herself.

"You can't disappoint him? That man should be worried about disappointing you!" Molly practically jumped from her seat, like the best of guard dogs, ready to defend her miss from any slight, real or imagined. Unfortunately, while most guard dogs have four legs and can keep their balance, Molly had only two, and the rocking of the gondola was so severe that the gondolier actually held them in place beneath a bridge, put one hand on Molly's shoulder, and, with a string of Italian neither of them understood, forced her into her seat.

"Well," Molly said touchily. "There's no need to be so forceful about it!"

They remained silent—and, thankfully, still—for the remainder of the short trip, and before Bridget had even begun to muse on what the next few hours would bring, they found themselves at the front door of Mr. Merrick's home. There, they were greeted not by Mr. Merrick, nor by the Signore, but by someone new.

"Signorina Forrester?" the man asked, his Venetian accent thick over the English. When she nodded, he bowed. "I am Frederico, Signor Merrick's valet. The gentlemen are setting up; allow me to help you." Luckily, Mr. Merrick would have a valet with decent English.

"See, Molly?" Bridget whispered, once they had been handed onto the landing. "There are servants. I would not be alone in the house with the gentlemen."

"Yes, well, what are they 'setting up' as this Mr. Freddy says? A dungeon? A torture chamber? A kidnapping?"

"Molly." Bridget shook her head. "Have you begun reading horrid novels?"

But even Molly's lurid imagination was not prepared for what greeted them when they walked into the music room.

Jugglers, tossing batons into the air.

Acrobats, hanging from the ceiling.

Girls in costume, dancing in lines.

It was a circus. An actual circus, wedging itself into the

small music room of Mr. Merrick's house. Laughter, noise, movement, color. And at the center were Mr. Merrick and Signor Carpenini, dressed as clowns—the former in the white baggy costume and painted face of a Pedrolino, the latter in the bright diamonds of a Harlequin. Both broke into huge smiles upon seeing Bridget.

"There you are, Miss Forrester!" Mr. Merrick said merrily, as he bowed.

"Mr. Merrick, Signore . . ." Bridget fumbled, as she stepped forward. "What on earth is going on?"

"This," Signor Carpenini said, with a dramatic flourish of his cane (part of the costume, it seemed) as he came forward to take her hand, "is your first lesson."

Bridget stood in shock, her eyes moving from one thing to the next, finally coming to rest on Molly's equally surprised gaze.

"If you think I ain't telling your mother about this, miss," the maid said, shaking her head, "you're stark raving mad."

Ten

As first lessons went, Miss Forrester's instruction by Signor Carpenini would certainly rank among the oddest.

Oliver had to hand it to Vincenzo—while he might have scoffed at the idea initially, once it was in place he embraced it with his usual vigor.

"It is like Signora Galetti said," he reminded Vincenzo as they were setting up. "One cannot be nervous in the middle of a circus. And it just so happens, we know a few performers."

Dressed in his Harlequin costume, Vincenzo nimbly conducted the room of performers with his cane, as he would an orchestra. He took Miss Forrester by the hand, led her to the pianoforte, and said very simply, "Today we are helping them," as he pointed to the jugglers.

Miss Forrester tentatively took her place, and at Vincenzo's command, she began to play. The same piece she played yesterday, the simple Bach minuet. But this time, Vincenzo did not peer over her shoulder as she played. Instead, he turned his attention to the jugglers. "Signores, begin!" he commanded. And the jugglers, as they had been commanded to do, began their routine. While the dancers practiced their own steps in the background, as well as the acrobats doing their back bends, Bridget played, giving pace and tone to the cacophony of their rehearsals.

She had not come with her mother today. Oliver wasn't exactly certain how he would have explained the circus performers in his drawing room if she had. (It was bad enough that Veronica, in full great-aunt makeup, was currently practicing a routine with the chorus girls.) Instead, Miss Forrester brought the same maid who had trailed after her that first day—Molly, he recalled. But by the way she looked to Molly for reassurance, Oliver felt certain the maid would be no obstacle.

The obstacle would be Bridget herself.

After a few minutes of playing, Vincenzo stopped the jugglers. Bridget's hands came off the keys at the same time.

"What did I do wrong?" she asked, the fear easily read in the quaver of her voice.

"Nothing, Signorina. Carlos"—he addressed one of the jugglers in Italian—"you are half a beat behind. If you do not catch up, you will end up hitting your partner. Again!"

With that, they began again. And it was notable—or, perhaps, it was highly unnoted—that Miss Forrester's performance was, for once, perfect.

"I can't believe it," Vincenzo whispered to him in Italian, when Bridget's focus was squarely on the juggling team. "Your plan is actually working."

Oliver couldn't believe it, either. Or that it was working so quickly.

Being amid all the noise and movement that was the circus, Miss Forrester did not have time to worry about her performance. She was too busy watching everyone else's. Therefore, as everyone was looking for fault in the jugglers, the acrobats, and the dancers, the idea of looking for mistakes in her own playing became almost preposterous. It was taken for granted that she would play perfectly, and thus she did.

She spent her first hour with the jugglers. By the end of their time together, the jugglers had broken a new routine to the minuet, and Bridget had taken to issuing commands—although since both Carlos and his brother spoke nothing but Italian (and the Venetian dialect at that), the communication was a little shoddy.

"Signor Carlos!" she said once, stopping midstanza. "You must *catch* on the downbeat. *Catch*."

Carlos shook his head and shrugged.

Miss Forrester, frustrated, got out from behind the piano-forte, took the small bean sack from Carlos, and marched back to her place at the keys. Tossing the ball up in the air with her left and playing with her right, she demonstrated the note she wanted him to catch on. "See? Catch!"

Oliver could not help smiling. It seemed that when irri-tated, Miss Forrester's overwrought nerves ran for cover.

The next hour was spent with the dancing girls. Vincenzo asked for a piece of music that was lively. "*Allegro*," he re-quested, and she began with a variation by Pleyel. There was not a note that fell out of place as Vincenzo concentrated his instruction on the dancers, as opposed to the music.

The hour after was spent with the acrobats. For them she played Haydn.

After each hour, Oliver was certain that Miss Forrester's playing was becoming stronger—she was becoming more and more comfortable with them. They took a short break for luncheon—bread and cheese and some cold fish. A necessary repast, as conducting a circus was an exhausting business. After the repast was served, they said good-bye to the jug-glers, the acrobats, and the dancing girls, with promises that they would come and see them at the theatre soon.

"Now," Vincenzo declared, clapping his hands together, "let us turn our attention to you, Signorina."

This would turn out to be a terrible mistake. Oliver could see all of the good the morning had done falling away from her, as a snake shed its skin. In its place was raw vulnerability and uncommon fear.

But she covered as well as she could, straightened her pos-ture, put her nose to the sky, and went to the pianoforte.

"I would like to go back to that *allegro* piece, the Pleyel?" Vincenzo said, and immediately began instructing her on a certain section. Leaning far over her shoulder. Playing fast and talking faster. And immediately, Oliver could sense Bridget shrinking back, almost afraid to have her fingers on the keys.

"No . . . it is triplets, here," Vincenzo was saying, his frus-tration mounting.

Oliver wanted to hang his head in his hands. What had begun so well was turning quickly into disaster. And there was nothing he could do about it.

"Mr. Merrick, sir," came a rushed whisper from behind him. It was Molly, who had sat watchfully in the corner during the entire morning "lesson." "Miss Bridget seems to be losing her nerve."

"Yes, Molly. I tried to make her more comfortable with us, but I don't think it took."

"Forgive me for saying so, sir," Molly sniffed, "but a man who dresses up in a clown's costume to put Miss Forrester at ease doesn't seem the type to give over so quickly."

Oliver looked down at himself. He was indeed, still in his Pedrolino suit—loose flowing shirt and pants, uncomfortable frilled collar, and short pointed hat. His false smile was still painted on his face in white.

And the thought struck him. Maybe there was something he could do, after all.

Moving as silently as he could, he trotted across the room and found a few bean sacks left behind by Carlos and his brother, underneath a chair. Historically, Pedrolino was not the happiest of clowns, but he would have to make do. Then, crouched behind the settee, he took two breaths. One to steady himself, and the second for what came next.

And then he began his performance.

It started with simply popping up and giving a large smile. A smile that said, *I am shocked and pleased to find you here!* Pointing at Miss Forrester at the piano, causing her to look up from her keys. Then a silent, belly-splitting chuckle.

Miss Forrester frowned and stopped playing. Vincenzo was about to say something cross to Oliver, but with a single silent look between them, he changed tack.

"Ignore him," he said to Miss Forrester. "He will act to what you play; just concentrate."

She tried to do as he said, but her eyes kept flitting up to meet Oliver's. Usually while he was failing dramatically at juggling.

It was harder to make people laugh than it was to cry. That was one axiom of the theatre Oliver had learned quickly. His pantomime had never been subtle. In fact, it relied very heavily on bumping into things and falling over and failing at jug-

gling. It had been quite a while since he last played this role
(let alone any role), and he had seen it performed much, much
better. But he was in a clown suit, and in Bridget Forrester, he
had a captive audience.

And her playing immediately improved.

It was difficult to say why. That morning, having the focus
off her and on the performers had provided her with the relief
of not being able to worry about how she played. But with just
him in the room, being completely silly, it was different . . .

If Oliver was to guess, it was because his silliness allowed
her to let go of seriousness, of the weight of expectations.

One could never be nervous in the middle of a circus. Or
perhaps, just with a clown.

And then, it happened.

Bridget stopped paying any attention to Oliver and his antics. The music had her attention instead. Not her playing, not
the order of her fingers on the keys, the *music*. Oliver stopped
his pantomime for the barest of seconds, testing her.

She did not notice. In fact, he would venture to guess she
noticed nothing else in the room.

Her playing had been technically correct over the course of
the morning, but she had not played like this. A vapor, a spirit,
possessing her and moving through them all. This was feeling translated into music and then back again. This was
getting lost. And she was set free by it.

This was how he remembered her having played before,
five years ago.

By the time the final chords drifted away and she lifted her
fingers from the keys, the music room had gone completely
still.

Miss Forrester came out of her daze slowly, blinking her
way back into the present. Oliver found himself almost mournful as the trance she'd laid was lifted and time came back to
them.

"I . . . I am sorry," she stuttered, seeming to realize what
had occurred. "Did you want me to start again?"

"No, Miss Forrester, that is enough." Vincenzo held up his
hand and came to sit beside her. "Well," he said, "you must
arch your hands higher. And you were *allegretto*, not *allegro*.
We must work on your pace."

Her face fell, her mouth set into a grim line at the critique.

But Vincenzo would not allow that. He leaned in and lifted her chin with a gentle touch. Made her meet his eyes. "But I am so pleased to have *at last* heard you play."

Carpenini's wide smile spread to her, and warmth filled the room. Oliver exhaled the breath he hadn't known he was holding. "Now," Vincenzo continued, rubbing his hands together, "now, we get to work, *si*?"

"What a day," Bridget sighed, as she rolled her sore shoulders. Let out into the light of the early afternoon, Bridget felt as exhausted as if she had been working for a full twenty-four hours. Her limbs were languid, her knees shaky. But her mind was remarkably calm. She had poured out everything she had onto the keys, and it left her nothing more than a floating, peaceful vessel.

It felt very, very good.

"I could sleep for a week," she said dreamily, letting the salty air fill her lungs as she took a deep breath.

"I would advise against it," Mr. Merrick replied, keeping pace beside her. "After all, you are due back for lessons again tomorrow."

She smiled up at him. When Bridget had rejected the idea of taking a gondola back to the hotel, instead wanting to walk, Mr. Merrick had changed out of his clown clothes and insisted again on seeing her home, even though she had Molly to escort her.

In truth, she was glad for his company. The afternoon had brought out the sun and warmth, and that brought out an alarming number of people. Given Bridget's previous observations on board the ship about how *tactile* Italian men could be, the presence of a solidly built English gentleman did much to soothe any fears—as Mr. Merrick tended to do in general.

If it had been Carpenini who attended her, she would have been far too aware of it. Mr. Merrick was much safer.

Yes, she was glad for his company—but found his directional prowess somewhat lacking.

"Have you been in Venice long, Mr. Merrick?" Bridget asked suddenly.

"I've been in Venice for nearly five years, Miss Forrester."

"Ah . . . I only ask, you see, because we have now gone a

footbridge too far in our path back to the hotel, and I don't think the alleyway that we just cut through—quaint though it was—has taken us anywhere nearer our goal."

Mr. Merrick threw back his head in a deep-throated laugh. "Well, I did warn you yesterday that I might get lost."

True, on their walk back to the Hotel Cortile the day before, he had mentioned something about getting lost. But since yesterday's walk was vastly different (not only in direction) from this one, Bridget could not be surprised that such a detail had slipped her mind.

"And here I was thinking you made up your lack of a sense of direction in order to make me feel better about your company," she replied impishly.

"I happen to have an excellent sense of direction, Miss Forrester." Mr. Merrick bristled in an overexaggerated manner that made her giggle. Even though he had changed out of his clown face and costume, he still had some of the mannerisms. "But Venice is the one place that I find myself constantly lost. There is something new and interesting around every turn. How can one not?"

"One can not, by knowing where one is going," Bridget heard Molly grumble from three steps behind them.

"Take the alleyway—quaint, I believe you called it?" Mr. Merrick continued, without regard for Molly, if he had even heard her. "What did you find quaint about it?"

"Well," Bridget turned to look behind her, trying to jog her memory of the alley they had just left. "The . . . the cobblestones, I suppose."

"What about them are so quaint?"

"They . . . they are wet. Either from the rain or from the seawater that seems to permeate everything. They shine in the afternoon light," she ventured. "And the windows are so high but tumbled, stacked one on top of the other. Waiting impatiently."

"Exactly!" he cried. "When else would you have seen such a sight, if not for taking the less direct route? When and where else would the light have been right for you to notice the beauty of wet cobblestones and stacked windows?" He sighed then, a sound of utter contentment. "There is always something I haven't seen before in this city, and I find myself lost at least once a day because of it."

"Even after you've been here nearly five years?" Bridget shook her head.

"Even then," he replied. Then, thought creasing his brow, "Although, the fault could lie in the fact that I *came* to Venice to get lost."

Bridget came to a standstill at the top of the little footbridge they happened to be crossing. A narrow canal ran underneath their feet, people propelling themselves forward. "I am afraid I don't understand. Are you not on an extended European tour?"

"What in the world gave you that idea?"

"Your father." Her simple reply was met with the most thunderous crashing of Mr. Merrick's brow that Bridget found herself stammering. "Er . . . that is . . . I met him at a dinner party before we left London. He said . . . or rather, I guess I assumed . . . that you are on your European tour."

Mr. Merrick took two deep breaths through his nose before he answered, and when he did so, it was with his normal calm, affable demeanor.

"Is that what my father is telling everyone?" He smiled at her, attempting to reassure, but it did not reach his eyes. "Miss Forrester, you are aware that most young gentlemen's European tours don't last five years."

"Most, but not all," she countered.

"And that those young gentlemen tend to travel to more than one city."

"It is rare, but not unheard of."

"*And* that rarer is the young English gentleman who studies pantomime on such a voyage."

"That . . . that did give me pause, I will admit." She shared in his smile then, and enjoyed the warmth that it lent her— almost like the warmth of the sun on the waters of the canal beneath them.

"So, you came to Venice to get lost . . . by becoming a clown?" she asked, taking a step forward, slowly propelling them on a more correct path.

"Not exactly. I came to Venice to meet my mother."

Bridget felt herself stopping in her tracks again, not three steps taken since her last astonished stalling. He turned to her when he realized she was no longer keeping pace beside him.

"Mr. Merrick, I apologize; I was under the impression that your mother—"

"My mother passed, ten years ago," he answered simply.

"I am sorry."

"Thank you." His hazel eyes seemed to grow misty for a moment, but with true English stoicism, he quelled any display of emotion. "While I was growing up, my mother was the buoyant, beautiful light—always singing, always dancing. She would tell me stories about when she was an opera singer in Venice, and how she met my father when he was visiting Europe, and they fell madly in love. Three weeks later they were married, and she was on a ship bound for England, never to return—much I think, to her regret."

They continued walking again, moving slower now—lest Bridget feel the need to pull to an abrupt stop again.

"So, when Signor Carpenini—Vincenzo—and I chanced to meet, I took the opportunity to come to Venice and find out about my mother's life here."

"That I can understand," Bridget replied. "However, I'm still a bit unclear on how it translates into clowning."

He smiled again, the residual grimness from their sad conversation leaving him. Bridget realized suddenly that Mr. Merrick was not a man who could be unhappy or dour for very long. In contrast to the Signore, whose mood seemed to swing violently with his passions and fracture her pulse with it, Mr. Merrick's pleasant steadiness was a decided comfort. And, curiously, infectious.

"Well, my mother *had* worked in the theatre," he replied, with an impish grin. "I thought, how better to learn about her life than to work there? Luckily, Vincenzo put in a good word for me at La Fenice, and I ended up in the third row of the men's chorus."

"So, you are an actor!" Bridget cried, delighted. "I would not have guessed."

"Because I'm an English gentleman?"

"No because you are so solidly built," she said, then immediately blushed. "Forgive me, but I always picture actors as rangy, mobile fellows. Not so . . . tall."

Bridget's eyes flitted to his wide shoulders, to his reserved English bearing—in spite of his Italian coloring and startling light eyes. Her cheeks raged red at the awkwardly personal comment. But he saved her with a laugh and an explanation.

"That is likely from a youth spent as an English gentleman, pursuing those things my father thought an English lad should. One of which was boxing. When I proved adept at it, he threw me into that wholeheartedly."

Her eyes again focused on the way his coat fit across his shoulders. Yes, he would have done quite well in an arena.

"But you loved the theatre," she guessed, and he nodded.

"I boxed to please my father, and sang with my mother to please me."

"Ah . . . so you must have a marvelous voice."

"One thing that working in the theatre has taught me, Miss Forrester, is that my voice is depressingly ordinary," he replied in good humor. "Which is one of the reasons I am no longer an actor on the stage."

"That seems a shame," Bridget replied sadly. "Your pantomime was quite amusing."

"Thank you." He blushed at the honest compliment. "But not only was my voice not strong enough, I also did not have the hunger for it."

"Hunger?"

"Yes. There is this strange stagestruck ambition, an overwhelming desperation to be loved, that one must have to be cutthroat enough to be an actor."

"That sounds rather . . . violent," Bridget replied quizzically.

"Only to one's psyche," he answered jovially.

"So what do you do now?" she inquired. "I cannot imagine that someone who came to Venice and fell in love with the theatre is content to simply take a box for the season."

Oliver's eyebrow arched in surprise. "You are far more astute than most people find comfortable, aren't you?" Then he began to explain that many would assume that a young foreign-born man of means, after a few years of folly upon the stage, would resume his place among his peers of wealthy expatriates who had their own society, and content himself with a box (and a mistress) at the opera. But Oliver could not. It had gotten into his blood, the theatre—or rather, because of his mother it had always been there, just awakened by his time in the men's chorus. So he did something few men of his station rarely had done.

He had taken a job.

"At first," he said, "I took whatever job Bruno—the stage manager at La Fenice—decided to torture me with. Stagehand, sweeper, cleaning costumes. Then I began to assist the director. I'm sure Bruno thought it a wonderful bit of folly to have a British lord's son in service to another, but I loved it. Soon enough, they began letting me take charge of the little comedy bits that come on stage before the opera begins—and then before I knew it, I was helping to stage the main show."

"Why, Mr. Merrick, aren't you full of surprises?" Bridget smiled at him. "You are a director."

"Not right now, unfortunately," Oliver replied, unable to keep the grimness out of his voice.

"What ho, there is a story behind that statement," she declared, hopping over a bridge as she did so.

"Really? How can you tell?"

"I have a sister who cannot wait to tell stories, Mr. Merrick. The signs are universal."

"Yes, there is," he conceded. "And actually, this story is related to you."

She cocked her head to the side at that.

"A few months ago, my father wrote me, saying that my elder brother, Francis, had fallen from a horse. It was quite serious, and I was needed at home."

"Oh, I am so sorry. About your brother, I mean."

"Thank you." He inclined his head. "So I resigned my position at La Fenice, packed my bags, and prepared to depart. Carpenini was to come with me."

"And that was when you wrote to me," Bridget surmised.

"Quite so. But a day before we were supposed to depart, I received another letter from my father, detailing Francis's recovery. I was not needed at home after all." Oliver sighed, his voice surprisingly sad. "I went back to La Fenice, but by then they had given away my position. Other opera houses were similarly staffed. So I am currently what I had claimed to not be—a British man living a life of leisure abroad."

He smiled ruefully, but Bridget was silent, contemplative. "Well," she said finally, "I am glad to hear of your brother's recovery, at least. But it must have been terribly awkward for those few weeks. Preparing to change everything, to go home, and then to be told not to."

He paused in his steps, his eyes searching her face, her features. As if she had struck at something true—more true than he himself realized.

"Yes, far more astute than is comfortable," he murmured, and then he cleared his throat. "But I promise you, it is better this way. You must understand, he was the son of my father's first wife, and as we are nearly fifteen years apart in age, we have never been particularly close. He is the heir, and thus he is the one groomed to a life of being Lord Merrick. The good English son. Currently he has only a daughter, so if he had passed . . . I would have been given the role. But I am a reluctant understudy, and I never learned any of the lines."

He gave a halfhearted smile at that small pun, and Bridget had to stop herself from reaching out to him. He was such an imposing figure—taller than most men, and with the strength borne of a boxing regimen; he could have come off as hulking, brutish, with his fearsomely dark hair and complexion. But he was so kind and polite . . . and so open with himself that it belied any such mean description.

"It is hard," Bridget said softly, "living up to the expectations set by elder siblings."

"Especially when they are better at being who they are than you could ever be," he commiserated, as he pulled to an abrupt stop. "But my father . . . well, it turns out I was not wanted in any case."

Bridget looked around herself and was surprised to find that they stood in front of the Hotel Cortile. She had been so engrossed in hearing Mr. Merrick's tale that she had lost all sense of time and—curiously, for her—direction.

Something haunted Bridget. The sad resignation in Mr. Merrick's voice, saying he was not wanted. It had sounded so much like . . .

So much like Lord Merrick's.

"But surely," she tried again, "without your position at the theatre, you could have gone back to England for a visit anyway—"

"No," he stated curtly, and Bridget reeled back at his abrupt speech. "I could not. Not now, likely not ever."

Bridget opened her mouth to speak but was cut off by the wave of his hand.

"Please don't pity me, Miss Forrester," he said, his smile

lightening the depths of their conversation. Impulsively he leaned forward and took her hand in his. It was warm, and she grasped his. "I promise you, I have enough irons in the proverbial fire to make up for the loss of my position at La Fenice. Besides, now I get to listen to you play daily—what could be better?"

Then he leaned over her hand and kissed it before releasing her.

"I can only hope to be so lucky, Mr. Merrick," Bridget replied cordially, her arm falling gently against her side. "Although I have no intention of getting lost in Venice—I was rather hoping to find my way."

He chuckled at that. "Well, you made a good start today, with Carpenini."

"Just as you did, when you met with him in England," she replied. "So . . . same time tomorrow?"

"Indeed, Miss Forrester." He touched a hand to his hat by way of a salute. "Give our—mine and Vincenzo's—regards to your mother and sister."

"Yes, Signor Carpenini—" Bridget bit her lip. "Is he . . . is he always like that?"

"How do you mean?"

"Is he always so—abrupt?" Bridget's mind flew back to how they had ended their session, less than a half hour ago. "He seemed very desperate to be rid of me. Indeed, as soon as lessons were finished, he practically shoved us out the door, *desperate* as he was to get to the keys of his beloved pianoforte and compose, as he had been apparently *desperate* to do all day."

Her tone was light, but it was to cover one simple fact. In that moment, it was as if she hadn't existed anymore, and that had left her momentarily stunned.

But Mr. Merrick's tone was not anywhere near as light as Bridget's. "He meant no insult," he said softly, reassuring. "Indeed, you greatly pleased him today. He simply takes some getting used to."

"Really?" she asked, unsure.

A rueful smile spread across his features. "Yes, Vincenzo can be rather, er, focused, when it suits him to be. He tends to forget everything—people, manners, food—when the mood strikes him."

"If that's the case, I find it hard to believe that the two of you became friends at all," she smiled tentatively.

But the smile on his face fell. "Miss Forrester—I'm sorry, I thought you knew."

"Knew what?" she asked, her brow coming down.

"That Vincenzo and I . . . we are not simply friends."

"How do you mean . . ." she began, and then felt her face go up in flames as realization dawned. Utter horror dripped through her body; she had been making a cake of herself all this time! "Do you mean . . . Oh! Oh, I am so mortified, Mr. Merrick, I had no idea. I mean," she babbled, certain her tongue was running away with her, but unable to stop it in her embarrassment. "I *knew* such things existed. Or at least, Amanda says she once saw my music tutor—ages ago now— kissing a stable boy, but she was so young I thought she was completely mistaken, but then I heard other stories, especially about, er, *theatrical* people, but it never entered my mind that you . . . and he—" *And to think*, her mind reeled, *I had been thinking about the* Signore *in that way . . .*

"As well it should not have!" Mr. Merrick exclaimed, shocked, cutting off her ramblings. Bridget ventured a glance up to his face and could see that he had gone as red under his tanned skin as a lobster in summertime, his hazel eyes wide with shock. And it likely matched her own furious blush. "Miss Forrester, I . . . I am not so, er, *theatrically* inclined."

"Oh," she sighed, relieved. "Then neither is . . ."

"Neither is Vincenzo," he said patiently.

"But," she hedged, "you said that you are not simply friends?"

"Yes. It is well-known here, but I am not surprised my father did not take much to advertising the connection at home." Mr. Merrick's mouth quirked up at the corner, bemused. "Before my mother married my father, she had a child that she left here in Venice, in the care of the child's grandparents."

Bridget's eyes went as wide as saucers.

"Vincenzo Carpenini is my half brother."

Eleven

OLIVER was at a bit of a loss for what to say next.

When they had parted three days ago at the steps of the Hotel Cortile, Miss Forrester's astonishment had been clear. It had obviously never occurred to her that there could be any relation between practical Mr. Merrick and her passionate, demanding teacher, Signor Carpenini, beyond that of a curious friendship—strange bedfellows, if you will. Indeed, his English upbringing had on more than one occasion masked just how similar their features were—they were of a height, their hair the same wickedly dark hue, their skin turned the same gold in just a fraction of sun. Taken at a glance, it was only Oliver's eyes—their light, hazel hue—that betrayed him as anything other than a native Venetian.

It was one of the reasons why Oliver had spent his youth feeling . . . out of step. With both his family and peers. He was dark, they were fair. He liked to sing and read plays. They liked to hunt and ride. His father's insistence that he take up boxing might have saved him from more than one beating from some of the older boys at Eton—both because he knew how to defend himself and, coincidentally, because it was a Very English Thing to do—and he put his heart into it because it was one of the few things about Oliver that his father would brag about.

His mother had petted him and loved him, had reveled in her son's happy talents. But after a certain age, no boy wanted that from his mother. So he tried to be sporting and emulate the more English of his relations.

When Oliver's mother had died when he had just been fifteen, it had been thinking that her son had turned his back on his Italian nature.

After that, the constant feeling of being out of step with the world around him had ballooned in his gut. Part of it was mourning, part of it was guilt. But part of it was also the queer looks he received from everyone upon introduction, and then their expressions clearing as he addressed them in his natural, cultured British accent. Their hypercriticalness, the inclusivity—that they would open up to him only if they knew he was "one of their own"—mocked him constantly.

Meeting Vincenzo and coming to Venice had been a dream. Here he would have a brother in truth, instead of one separated by a decade and a half and no small degree of superiority, borne of his dislike of having a stepmother and half brother to begin with. He could get to know his mother's side of the family, her aspirations, her friends from the stage. Here, in Venice, he could indulge in the passions that he had tamped back down into the earth, hoping they would not spring up at inappropriate times. After all, there was nothing worse than bursting into an Italian opera in the dining rooms of Eton, overcome by the need to sing. Not that that ever happened, of course.

Yes, coming to Venice had been a dream.

A dream . . . that had never quite matched up with the reality.

In truth it was Vincenzo who had opened all the doors to him. If he had come to Venice alone, with his ill-remembered Italian and his English eyes, he would have been marked as a tourist and likely found himself headed back home within a month, with the obligatory "souvenereal disease." Vincenzo introduced him to his friends, to the musicians and artists who populated Venice, and made certain he was included as one of their own.

But it had to be said—it was still there. The look. Even in artisans, in opera dancers, just as there had been in English society. People would look at him, trying to figure out where he fit. Whom he belonged to. If he was truly "one of their own."

Because of Vincenzo, he had passed that test. Because of Vincenzo, he was tolerated and accepted as part of the Fenice theatre world. Because of Vincenzo, he had gained the knowledge and the belief that he could run his very own theatre.

And it was why Oliver felt he could not leave Vincenzo, especially now that he needed Oliver's help. Of course he could not go back to England, as he had expressed—perhaps too vehemently—to Bridget.

But when she had said those words—told him that she knew how awkward those few weeks of thinking he was going home was—it had borne in Oliver such a light of hope.

Finally, he thought. Someone who understood. Someone who did not look at him and wonder where he fit.

And while he had no idea what to say next—to Bridget—Oliver found himself eager for any conversation at all.

Indeed, he could not wait until the next day, when he would endeavor to walk Bridget Forrester home again.

But then, the most curious thing began happening: It seemed as if Bridget Forrester was avoiding him.

It happened the very next day. When he reached down to hand her out of the gondola upon her arrival in the morning, she let go of his hand as quickly as possible, glancing back at her maid. Then during lessons, she was too involved in the music to spare him much of a glance—although when she did, it was short and she turned back to the pages immediately.

But it was not until the lesson was drawing to a close that he knew his estimation had been correct. For the moment the clock ticked three, a knock came on the back door.

For a brief second, Oliver feared it would be Lady Forrester and her youngest daughter, and then they would be sunk. Their party had greatly been reduced since yesterday—Oliver had depleted a good portion of his funds on the circus and therefore could not pay Veronica to come and pretend to be his deaf great-aunt on a long-term basis. Considering that, and the fact that Molly the maid had begun to relegate herself to the kitchens and below stairs—where the air was cool and hearing the same music over and over again was muted, and therefore less headache-inducing—there was little more than Frederico, sitting outside the music room doors to guard propriety.

Not that anything inappropriate would happen. Oliver was there to make damn sure of it.

Still, a brief moment of panic did set in when he heard the knock—but then he was quickly reminded that Lady Forrester and Miss Amanda would arrive via the canal, not the back. Thus, when he opened the door, he found a footman in Forrester livery.

"My mother requested that I meet her and my sister at the Campo Sant Angelo today after my lessons, and sent James here to escort us," Miss Forrester offered by way of explanation, as she gathered up her sheet music and shuffled it into a portfolio. Her tone was quiet, subdued. He hoped for, rather than heard, something apologetic in her voice. Perhaps in truth, she was simply tired.

"Signorina, Rossini's most famous work is *The Barber of Seville*, and it may be comic, but it is also fluid. Even staccato, he is fluid! You must play with fluid grace! Think of that for tomorrow!" Vincenzo was saying, as she was on her way out the door.

Tomorrow came, and Bridget's lessons had consisted of Rossini, Scarlatti, and some reinterpretations of Vivaldi— since the Red Priest composed almost exclusively for strings, his work had to be adapted for pianoforte. Vincenzo had found, after a long morning of inquiry, that Miss Forrester's repertoire was woefully thin on Italian composers, and he felt the need to build her experience there, considering the nature of the competition they were entering. He was particularly horrified to learn she was not a student of the more intricate, layered style that popularized Italian music of the day . . . and that was Carpenini's strength in composition.

"Yes, Signore, I will practice fluidity," Bridget replied.

"No, Signorina, remember! No practicing at the hotel!" Vincenzo admonished before shutting the door to the music room behind them and leaving him to his compositions.

Which left Oliver to escort Miss Forrester, her maid (who had appeared from the kitchens promptly at three), and now, her footman, to the front steps, where he could hail a passing gondola for them.

He opened his mouth to speak to her—but nothing came out. And before he knew it, she was handed into the boat and had cast off from the docks.

By now, Oliver was torturing himself. What had he done—what had he said?—that caused her to shy away? While Oliver had felt a strange connection to Miss Forrester, had she instead found something to fear? What could it have been?

As Oliver ran through everything that had been said and done—where they walked, the actions he took, what she said in reply—on their last walk, he cemented one thing in his mind.

"Tomorrow," he resolved to himself. He would explain himself tomorrow.

But tomorrow it turned out to be no easier to find a moment alone with Miss Forrester.

Vincenzo, it seemed, was dedicated to giving her as much attention as he could in those short hours that he had her. To inject as much of his knowledge as he could, to wrap her up in the notes and phrases so that she had no room for anything else in her mind. Oliver was very decidedly in the way, even when they took their infrequent breaks. Pianoforte adaptions of Rossini, Marcello and, in particular, Scarlatti made up the day's practices.

"I am betting on Scarlatti," Vincenzo had said as an aside to Oliver. "The Marchese adores him, and his compositions are quintessentially Italian. The perfect showpiece to choose for the competition."

"But Scarlatti worked mostly in Spain. Not strictly Italian."

But Vincenzo waved him away and turned back to his student.

Oliver kept waiting for Vincenzo to show himself to be impressed with his student's proficiency, but the man very carefully held back any praise. For his part, Oliver was wholly impressed. Without the crippling fear of stage fright, Miss Forrester proved herself to be incredibly adept. What she knew, she played with energy and grace—and what she didn't know, she learned quickly. Her sight-reading was top rate; after only a few times through she would know a piece well enough to play it with confidence . . . if not with the style and understanding that came from knowing a piece intimately.

As the day's lesson drew to a close, Oliver felt certain he would *finally* be granted an opportunity to speak with Miss Forrester alone—but alas, there again came a knock on the back door.

Again, there was a footman.

"Where are you off to this time, Miss Forrester?" Oliver asked very cordially.

"I'm not certain," she replied, as she gathered up her sheet music and pulled on her gloves. "James, where are we to meet Mother?"

"At the Rialto Bridge, miss," James answered succinctly.

"The Rialto Bridge is a mere few minutes by foot," Oliver said hopefully. "I would be more than happy to escort you."

"Ah . . ." Miss Forrester looked between her maid, Molly, and the footman, James. Their censure had impact, it seemed. "We would not wish to trouble you. Mother is expecting us by gondola, and it would be best to travel that way. Besides"— the corner of her mouth turned up wryly, filling him with an expected hope—"with your sense of direction, we would likely end up there after my family had already left."

And with that, again, she was gone.

It was another full week before he got his chance. Oliver had begun to despair of the idea that he would ever manage to explain himself to Miss Forrester—for he was certain that whatever had caused her to pull back was somehow his doing—when another knock on the door afforded him the opportunity.

Although this knock came from the front door, not the back.

"Vincenzo, where have you been hiding?!" Antonia Galetti cried in Italian as she burst into the music room. Frederico had barely had time to announce the bubbly lady before she burst into the lessons.

"I am so sorry, Signore, I know you gave orders to not be disturbed," Frederico said sullenly, also in Italian, before sulking back to his place in the hall, where he had taken to sitting in a chair and reading periodicals.

"Thank you, Frederico," Oliver muttered. "Once again, I get to question why I pay you."

"You do not, Signore," Frederico muttered back. "At least not enough."

"Oh la, I am not a disturbance to him!" Antonia tittered, oblivious to any conversation that did not involve her. "In fact, I am something altogether more agreeable, aren't I, Vincenzo?"

Oliver shot a look to his friend. At that moment, Vincenzo did not look agreeable. In fact, he looked quite disturbed. He had been seated next to Miss Forrester at the pianoforte, and the minute the doors flew open, he had closed the lid, nearly crushing Miss Forrester's fingers. But Vincenzo's face cleared almost immediately when he realized who it was. And, possibly, how detrimental rudeness to this particular lady could be.

"Of course, my dear, of course!" Vincenzo cried happily. And then, as she practically launched herself at him, Vincenzo seemed to remember that there was someone else next to him at the piano.

"Oh, Signorina Forrester, this is . . ." But he seemed to be at a loss for words, possibly because he was being strangled by Antonia's arms around his neck.

"Signora," Oliver stated, clearing his throat. "Allow me to introduce Miss Bridget Forrester, who is a student of Signor Carpenini."

"Oh!" Antonia cried as she shuffled herself up to a more respectable position, out of Vincenzo's lap. "Are you his student?" She addressed Miss Forrester in her well-taught English. "Everyone has been wondering who you are! You're quite a little thing, aren't you?"

"Everyone?" Miss Forrester squeaked, her eyes unblinking. In fact, Oliver felt fairly sure she had not blinked since the moment Antonia, with her voluptuous, vulnerable manners, had burst into the room.

"Oh yes!" Antonia replied. "All of Venice is desperate to know who the student is that Carpenini will place against the great Gustav Klein."

"All of Venice?" Bridget repeated weakly, only to have her voice be lost beneath Vincenzo's more forceful one.

"'The 'great' Gustav Klein?" he asked, his mouth coming down into a harsh line.

"Now, Vincenzo, do not give attention to that; I have come for a reason. Oh, but Miss Forrester"—she turned her attention to the other lady in the room—"you must be very talented to be Vincenzo's student. Do you think I might hear you play?"

"No!" Vincenzo cried sharply, earning him a knowing, suspicious look from Antonia.

"But, Vincenzo," Antonia said, her voice a challenge. "You

have been locked up in here with the young lady for over a week. I hear rumors—about acrobats, and circuses, and madness, that it makes me wonder if you are teaching her anything at all."

The implied question—that if he hadn't been teaching Miss Forrester for the past week, what *had* he been doing with her—hung in the air, until Oliver himself stepped in.

"Signora, they have been working very hard," he said, bending over her hand. "As I can attest. I have listened to scales, drills, repetition of pieces so much my head is a ringing bell."

He gave her his most charming smile and earned a charmed one back from her. Thus cosseted by a man's—any man's—full attention, Antonia practically purred in contentment.

It took only one sharp look to Vincenzo to get that man on board. "Yes!" he cried, elbowing his way in between Oliver and Antonia. "In fact, we have been working so hard, we are just about done for the day. You"—he leaned forward and kissed Antonia's cheek—"have come at just"—he kissed the other cheek—"the right time."

Antonia giggled. Vincenzo grinned. And Miss Forrester cleared her throat.

"But Signore, it is not yet three . . ." she offered quietly.

"No matter, we have worked hard enough today—remember, Rossini is fluid grace," he said, and suddenly the lesson began to break up. Antonia moved to the side to allow Miss Forrester to stand and gather her things—albeit never letting go of Vincenzo's hand.

"Yes, Signore," Bridget said quietly, unblinking, shuffling papers, finding her portfolio, stretching her back.

"And no—"

"Practicing at the hotel," she finished for him.

"*Buono!*" he cried, and before they realized it, Oliver and Bridget had been pushed from the music room and into the hall. Before the door closed behind them, he could hear Antonia giggle as Vincenzo said in Italian, "Now, *cara*, you say you came for a reason. I wonder what it could be?"

And suddenly, the thing Oliver had spent these last days wishing for, to be alone with Miss Forrester, had come to fruition.

And yet he still did not know what to say.

They stood in the hall for some moments, until Oliver realized they were not in fact quite alone.

"Frederico"—Oliver turned to his unresponsive valet, who, in his chair, seemed to be overly engrossed in that day's press—"could you please fetch Molly from the kitchens? Miss Forrester is going home for the day."

"Oh, but I cannot!" Miss Forrester cried. "That is, James is supposed to collect me at three, and it is not even two o'clock yet."

But just at that moment, another high-pitched giggle erupted from the music room, filling the awkward echoing silence of the hall.

"Perhaps it would be best if I escorted you back to the hotel, where you could rest before meeting your family," Oliver replied.

"Oh, but I . . ." The girl looked torn, not knowing what she should do.

"I will not accept no for an answer," Oliver said, and with the reappearance of Frederico, bearing Molly in his wake, he took Miss Forrester by the elbow and guided her to the door.

As they wandered into the cobbled streets, watchful Molly falling only a step or two behind them, the first question Miss Forrester asked was not the one Oliver expected.

She had been uncommonly silent. Although whether or not it was uncommon, Oliver supposed he shouldn't really know, as this was only the third time he had managed to walk her home. But it seemed like she was tense, and chewing over something in her mind. And he knew, in his gut, it was censorious of him.

He had begun by trying to engage her in mundane things and work his way up to what he meant to say. After all, if he managed to veer in a random direction, it could take a half hour or longer for them to wend their way back to the Hotel Cortile.

"Tell me, Miss Forrester, when you went to the Rialto Bridge yesterday, did you stop by the San Giacomo di Rialto? The building with the clock? If not, we could go back and see it; it is one of the oldest buildings in all of Venice—"

"Mr. Merrick," Bridget said abruptly, bringing the small party to a halt. "Can you tell me why the Signore forbids me to practice at the hotel? I have been turning it over in my mind and I cannot fathom it."

"*This* is what has been bothering you today?"

"Yes!" she cried, her eyes meeting his for the first time that day. "All I want to do right now is go back to the hotel and practice. To sit at the pianoforte for another few hours, to try to work my way into understanding what he means by fluidness. We've been working on it for days. And I think my playing is fluid. What do you think? Is my playing fluid?"

Oliver could only stare at her in shock for some moments.

"Well?" she asked, jarring him out of his stupor.

"No," he finally said.

"No?" It sounded as if her heart broke on the single, short word. "No, you don't think my playing is fluid?"

"Yes, I mean, no—I mean, I find your playing very fluid, but then again, I am not the master," he said in a jumble. Then, clearing his throat, "I meant to say, no, that cannot have been what has kept you in such a twisted state."

"I assure you it is," she promised, a small smile painting her mouth. "I've been torturing myself for days and days, and my mother has been having James bring us to wherever they happen to be to avoid you, and I cannot even pretend to practice!"

"*Your mother* has you avoiding me?"

"Actually it's your fault for kissing my hand, but that still doesn't answer my original question: Why am I forbidden to practice?"

Oliver felt like he had been spun around three times and knocked upside the head with a mallet. Taking a deep breath, he dove into the fray.

"All right. Let us take this one question at a time," he said, and began slowly walking, Bridget falling into step beside him. "First of all, Vincenzo does not want you playing at the hotel because he is precautious of conspiracy."

"Precautious?"

"Yes. And not unjustifiably. Anyone can walk into the hotel and hear you play. If that someone happens to be a spy for the Marchese, or his competition, Klein, then they can report back how well you play, and try to undermine us accordingly."

Miss Forrester raised a skeptical eyebrow. "That seems a bit extreme."

"The musical world of Venice can be a treacherous one, that much Vincenzo does know." Oliver answered darkly.

"While we cannot conceal the fact that you are his student, as you come and go from my home on a daily basis, at least there no one can simply barge in and eavesdrop on your practicing."

"Except for today," she replied under her breath. Ah, she meant Antonia.

"We will work our way back to Signora Galetti," Oliver replied, holding up a hand. "But first, you have to tell me what you meant."

"What I meant by what?" she asked.

"That you've been avoiding me because I kissed your hand?"

"It's not my doing." She sighed. "In fact, it's hers." She nodded to Molly.

"Don't look at me!" Molly cried indignantly. "I'm not the one that kissed you on the hand—*ungloved!*—in broad daylight!"

"When you walked me home, you deposited me at the hotel and kissed my hand," Miss Forrester interjected. "And it was taken by *some*"—her eye flew to a stiffly uncompromising Molly—"as a bit too . . . European, especially from an English gentleman."

"Met the girl not a se'nnight ago, and now you're kissing her hand, without the chaperonage of her mother nearby!" Molly said stiffly. "What's next? A kiss on both cheeks? How long will it be before you have the girl taking afternoon lie-downs on a settee with you?"

"Molly!" Miss Forrester admonished, blushing. "At any rate, Molly took it upon herself, instead of making the affront known to you, to suggest to my mother that we have an escort to meet her and my sister at whatever tourist spot they have decided upon for that day, thus saving me from your lascivious advances."

Understanding dawned, and Oliver felt like laughing. So he did. Long and loud. So long and so loud that he drew curious glances, not the least of which was from Miss Forrester and Molly.

"Stark raving mad. I told you, miss," Molly grumbled under her breath. "This whole scheme. Stark raving mad."

"Miss Forrester, I mean no offense. To you, either, Molly. Your protective instincts for your charge are to be commended.

But I cannot imagine why a simple kiss on the hand would evoke such response."

"That's what I said," Miss Forrester cried happily, turning her attention to her maid. "Everyone kisses everything here. Hands, cheeks—why, Signor Zinni kissed the top of my head once! Although I'm fairly certain he mistook me for his daughter, who works in the hotel's kitchens; we are of a height . . ." Miss Forrester let that thought trail off, refocusing her argument. "Besides, if you are so worried about my welfare with Mr. Merrick, then why do you go down to the kitchens during lessons? There I am unchaperoned with not one, but two gentlemen—one far more 'European' than the other!"

"As long as I can hear you playing, I know you are safe," Molly replied stiffly. "I come running up quickly enough when the music stops."

"Well, that is certainly true," Oliver mused, recalling how, for the past several days, whenever there had been a break in the music, not fifteen seconds had passed before there was a discreet knock at the door, and Molly slipping into the room, usually bearing a tray, unobtrusive but watchful.

"Besides, it is so commonplace," Miss Forrester continued, "I hardly *remember* him kissing my hand. And it is such a rote action for gentlemen here, I doubt Mr. Merrick even recalls doing it."

Well, that was a bit less true. While Oliver did not remember the impulse that led him to take her hand in his and press his lips to its back, he certainly remembered doing so. He remembered more than anything the warmth of her fingers . . . how slender they were, how small and strong and agile.

But Miss Forrester looked up at him, confident, and all he could do was nod with authority. Then, clearing his throat, he turned back to their inquisitor.

"Molly," he said, as deferentially as he could, "I know you are wary and watchful, and it does you credit. But please know and trust that I have no illicit intentions toward Miss Forrester. Her safety and happiness are my foremost concern as well."

Molly eyed Oliver suspiciously, her gaze boring into him as if she could read all of his secrets.

He rather hoped she couldn't.

Instead, he tried to convey a trustworthiness that had been bred into him as an English gentleman, no matter how much he had tried to deny that part of himself over the past five years.

And suddenly . . . he wanted it. He wanted to be trusted by this guard dog of a maid with the welfare of her young lady. He wanted to be worthy of that.

It must have worked, too, because in that moment, the moment something in his body switched over from the feigning to the desire, Molly's expression cleared. Instead of regarding him as an enemy, he knew in that moment she had decided that he could be an ally.

"Well, if you say as much, I'll believe it," Molly admitted, only a little grudgingly.

"So there is no need to fetch us and escort us to Amanda and Mother, wherever they are?" Miss Forrester eyed her maid. "You know I am so tired after the lessons—I can barely keep my eyes open at the churches and cathedrals . . ."

"I suppose not," Molly admitted. Then with a quick glance beyond them, she added, "In fact, do you mind if I go ahead of you? I would like to head off James before he leaves the hotel."

Oliver raised his eyebrow in shock, but Miss Forrester gave Molly her consent, and off she went.

"Well," he drawled, watching the maid's retreating form as she moved nimbly through the crowd. "When Molly decides to trust someone, she doesn't waste any time, does she?"

"I suppose not. Although I don't think she ever did not trust you. She comes from the country, I believe, and her English sensibilities have been shocked into a tizzy by Venice."

"By a kiss on the hand?"

"That was merely the straw that broke the camel's back. You should have seen her when we landed in Rome; the ornateness of the churches sent her back to her room with palpitations." She grinned at him impishly. "In every other regard she is the most practical person I know."

"Well, if it offends her practicality, I promise to never kiss your hand again, Miss Forrester."

Although, did he? It was said in jest, but the notion did not sit well with him in the least.

But she just smiled at him. "That would likely make her feel much better. Although my next request will not."

"Oh?"

"Yes. I implore that you call me Bridget, or Miss Bridget, if you will. I have been the 'Miss Forrester' in my family for almost a year now, and yet I still cannot hear it without thinking my sister Sarah looms over my shoulder somewhere."

"I cannot promise to remember every time." He shook his head. "Although, if you take to calling me Oliver, I'm sure it will help my memory," he replied, a strange warmth filling his chest. Could it be that they were, even in their strange circumstances, becoming friends, of a sort?

It could only be pure recklessness that had him testing this theory with his next statement.

"Miss Bridget, I cannot tell you how glad I am to know that it's Molly's practical country nature that had you avoiding me for the past few days, and not what I had thought," he said, steering her down a different street than they had taken before. Her footfalls followed his implicitly. However, her eyebrows flew up in surprise.

"And what had you supposed to be the reason?" she asked.

"You have no idea what I have been thinking!" He shook his head, laughing. "I racked my brain, trying to think of how our last conversation had set you against me—when I had felt the exact opposite. I thought I had somehow offended you by admitting that Carpenini was my illegitimate brother—"

"I did not realize he was illegitimate." Bridget's large green eyes went wide. "Although I cannot see how that reflects on you. Or Carpenini."

Oliver smiled, and continued. "I thought perhaps I took you into the wrong part of town—that your sense of direction was livid over wandering so far . . . I thought the fact that my father and I do not get along, and that I lack a desire to go home to England, raised your ire."

"My ire?" she replied. "No. Besides, I understand all that."

"You do?" He could not keep the disbelief from his voice.

"Of course. You and I share the same malady."

"Malady?"

"Yes," she replied. "Stage fright."

He jerked back suddenly, coming to a stop in the middle of the square, or *campo*, they had wandered into. "You think I have stage fright?"

"At least in part. I am afraid of what people will think of me when I play for them. That I won't live up to their expectations. You are afraid you will not meet your father's. That he would not, does not understand. So you stay here and carve out your own existence. Even though in every conversation we have had, you still call England 'home.'"

Could she be right? Oliver fell silent, stern. Could he have avoided going back to England so long because he feared the judgment of others? Of his father?

But that judgment had already been rendered, in monthly letters and a quarterly allowance. His father's words might have been kind, but they were also removed. And Oliver knew the money simply said, *Stay away.*

"But your stage fright is easily managed. After all, I think you need not worry as much about your audience as much as I worry about mine. I have to please all of Venice, not to mention Carpenini." She grinned ruefully. "You only have one person to humor, and he seems far more reasonable."

"Really?" Oliver answered, attempting humor. "You met my father only the once. He struck you as a reasonable man?"

She tilted her head to one side. "I was talking about you. You are your audience."

"Oh," he breathed shortly, properly chagrined.

"But I don't know if your father is a reasonable man," she said quietly. "When I met him, he just seemed . . . well, more sad than anything else, I suppose."

"Oh," he said again. Because it was the only thing he could say.

"My father and I . . ." Oliver began after a moment. "In truth I would rather not discuss him." The future. Yes, it was better to think on the future. Vincenzo would win this competition, he would write a piece for Oliver to stage and the Marchese's patronage would return, and all would be well. His father aside.

But Bridget blinked at him, then conceded with a nod.

And with nothing else to say, silence fell between them.

Oliver did not know how to feel about what Bridget had said. To distract himself, he did what he often had when his thoughts were getting in the way—he let the scene overtake him. The people in the *campo*, the cobblestones of the square, the bright afternoon sun.

It was a market day—as was almost every day, excepting Sundays and holidays—and even though it was the afternoon now, there were still a few stalls open, trying to sell that morning's catch or now somewhat stale bread at a reduced price. There was a woman—a fishwife—singing about her husband's prowess as a fisherman. She was fairly entertaining, her voice rich and full. Until, that is, she got to the higher notes, and her voice cracked with its limitations.

The sweet breeze of spring—made all the sweeter because the canals had not yet taken on their pungent summer aroma— came up behind them from the south. It wrapped around Oliver's legs, holding him still in his place. It danced with Bridget's skirts, pressing them tightly against her well-formed lower half, giving him an excellent idea of how they looked. He could not help but notice it—nor could he help the sensation that sight sent through his own lower limbs.

It seemed as if he would be breaking another promise to Molly that afternoon—Bridget's safety and comfort were no longer the foremost thoughts in his mind.

"Where are we?" Bridget said at last, a blessed distraction from his overly distracting train of thought.

"Do you mean to tell me that even with your directional acumen, you do not know where we are?" Oliver said, teasingly. She shook her head. "We are at the Campo Sant Angelo. You should recognize it—did you not say that you were meeting your mother here a few days ago?"

Bridget looked around with a scrutinous eye. "I suppose it is familiar . . ."

"Look, over there—that is the famous well. This entire square was raised up so seawater would not get into the well during a flood."

"Yes, I vaguely remember Amanda quoting something to that effect from her guidebook. She seems to be a great admirer of civil infrastructure." Bridget smiled wryly up at him.

"And that building there—twenty years ago it was the Teatro San Angelo. Vivaldi was impresario as well as composer there."

"Really? One would, I think should, remember that," she grumbled ruefully. "To be honest, though, I was not paying the closest of attentions to my surroundings."

"I am utterly shocked. This undoes all my preconceived notions about you."

"Do be serious," she laughed, belying any seriousness to be had. "Unfortunately I find I simply do not care about wells, and architecture, and other people, when there is music in my head. Even if I cannot practice on the pianoforte at the hotel, I can study the sheet music. I am here to study with Carpenini, not take in the sights!"

He cocked an eyebrow at her. "Perhaps you should."

"But . . ." she began to argue, but he held up a hand to silence her.

"Hear me out. You wish to learn about music. To study. Well, music is *this*. It is an expression of life." He pointed to the singing fishwife. "It is that woman there. Would she not make a perfect character in an opera? And what about our last unconventional walk back to the hotel—what was most memorable about it?"

He could see the wheels turning in her head. "Other than you claiming Carpenini as your brother?"

"Yes, other than that."

She closed her eyes, let memory wash over her. "The . . . sunlight on the wet cobblestones in the alley."

He found himself taking an unexpected step closer to her. His voice was warm, low. "And how would you play sunlight on cobblestones on the piano?"

Her eyes remained closed. "I . . . I don't know." Her voice came out in a whisper. Her fingers, likely unbeknownst to her, began to twitch at her side, as if finding ivory keys in the ether. "It would be high, and light. Earthy, though—muted pedals. Like waking up."

Her eyes opened, and they found his smile. "*That* is something Carpenini cannot teach. Only Venice can."

She took this in, a serene smile painting her lips. In that moment, he was bewitched. Truly and utterly. She, he, and the spring breeze wrapping around their legs. The impulse to lean forward and catch the little smile with his own, to learn what freckled skin tasted like.

Instead, he indulged the only thing he could do in the middle of a *campo* in broad daylight. Before he knew what he was doing, he had reached down, grabbed Bridget's hand, and brought it to his lips.

"Mr. Merrick! Intent on incurring Molly's wrath, are you?" she admonished, playfully, as he released her hand.

"Only when I can get away with it," he replied impishly. And then she smiled up at him, and he smiled down at her . . .

And suddenly they were the only two people standing in the Campo Sant Angelo.

And that idea, that impulse to lean forward and take what those wide green eyes seemed to offer, nearly overcame him.

Nearly.

"Ah . . . Mr. Merrick. Oliver," Bridget said sharply, rushing them out of their haze and back into the real world, singing fishwife and all. "I have to ask you something."

She bit her lip so charmingly, Oliver could do little but reply with a rush of happiness. "Anything, Miss Bridget."

Her next words were like a bucket of ice water over his head.

"The Signora Galetti . . ." she began hesitantly. "Is she . . . is she a woman of importance?"

"She is the daughter of a Marchese . . . she is a very wealthy, influential woman in Venice," he answered slowly.

"No, I mean is she important . . . to Signor Carpenini?"

Oliver felt all of his happy energy drain from his body, out the ends of his fingertips. He could tell her, he supposed, that the Signora and Carpenini were lovers. It would be the truth, after all. He could tell her that Carpenini's fate might very well lay in her hands and could be crushed if Antonia was not properly placated from time to time. That would also be true. But looking down into Bridget's face, the vulnerability laid bare, he instead told the central truth he knew about Signora Galetti.

"No," he replied. "She is not."

He should have realized.

After those words had left his mouth, the rush of relief from Bridget startled him and seemed to exhaust her. At her request, they walked back in a more direct route to the hotel, so she could rest before enjoying the remainder of the day with her family.

"And learning from Venice," she promised him.

He spent the walk from the hotel to his own rented house remonstrating himself for his flights of fancy.

She had not felt the same rush of temptation he had. Nor

had she stepped into a bubble of their own making, as time slowed down and the temptation of her freckles became almost more than he could bear. No, instead she was more than halfway in love with her instructor, Carpenini, jealous of his relationship with another woman, while Oliver fit very nicely into the role of confidante and, more despised, *friend*.

He was alone in his feelings. It was something he could rail against, or he could cut the connection and save himself heartache. But he liked Bridget Forrester too much and felt too protective of her, and, strangely, he knew her to be too important to do anything other than survive them.

Carpenini's actions, on the other had—*those* he could influence.

"Vincenzo!" he yelled, the door slamming behind him, jolting even lazy Frederico out of his chair in the hallway.

He found him in the music room, sitting at the keys, his hands down at his sides. Signora Galetti had apparently made her exit.

"You," Oliver said. "I told you, you have to be more careful with Bri—with Miss Forrester. She's half in love with you already, and young English ladies don't play by your rules."

"It doesn't matter," Vincenzo replied dully.

"It does matter. If you play with her emotions—well, not only will you find yourself without a student for the competition, you could very well—" But Vincenzo cut him off with a pound of fury on the keyboard.

"It does not matter!" he cried. "We have already lost."

Oliver took a deep breath. "How?"

"Antonia brought with her the Marchese's music selection for the competition." Vincenzo's voice broke as he continued, showing the truth of his despair. "We are not to play Scarlatti. Or Marcello, or Vivaldi, or any other honest, pure Italian composer."

Carpenini pounded his hands against the keys again, a thunderstorm in the still room.

"He chose an Austrian. We are to play goddamned Beethoven!"

Twelve

L UDWIG van Beethoven's Sonata No. 23, Op. 57, sat on the pianoforte, like a viper waiting to strike, knowing that its prey had no choice but to come to it.

"*This* is what I am to play?" Bridget asked, all of the air in her body somehow getting stuck in her throat. The notes on the page swam before her eyes, a jumbled stew of black and white. Twelve-eight time. Rapid appoggiatura. An endless stream of thirty-second notes. Natural minor scales changing to major scales with raised fourth degrees at a moment's notice. It used six and a half octaves of the piano. Three separate movements and more than three hundred bars of music—not including repeats and codas! Even if she was playing *allegro*—which at times, she would be—this piece would take more than twenty minutes to play from beginning to end.

"We've . . . *I've* . . . never attempted anything like this." She could feel the panic begin to rise in her chest, sitting up high in her body.

"And yet you will," Carpenini said, his voice clipped. His gaze had been intense all morning, red rimmed—as if he hadn't slept in days—and focused intently on her. Some impulse in her wanted to reach out and smooth the locks of hair from his brow, but the moment she thought of it, it seemed beyond silly to her.

Smooth Carpenini's brow? She admired the man, of course . . .
more than admired, if she was to admit the truth.

She knew very well she had a crush. Bridget had enjoyed
crushes before—or had been tormented by them, depending
on one's perspective. She knew she thought too much about
the man and not enough about the music when she was lying
in bed at night. How could she not—after all, Carpenini had
brought a circus to her, just so she could play without fear! He
had sought *her* out, come to *her* door and seen *her* talent, and
wanted her to play beautifully for him, for Venice. But now
she had this music—this incredible, impossible piece of
music—in front of her, and not only did she have to learn it,
she had to *master* it.

Smoothing anyone's brow seemed ridiculously silly in that
light.

But while she contemplated the ridiculousness of smoothing anyone's brow, Carpenini had been saying something, and
Bridget had to snap to attention.

"I will play it through. You will listen."

Bridget nodded and seated herself on the sofa. Next to her,
Mr. Merrick—Oliver—arranged himself, ready to listen. She
was very glad of his presence in that moment.

Carpenini began to play. From the opening notes, trepidation rose in Bridget's chest. His fingers moved with an impossible mixture of speed and grace. His concentration was
wholly on the page.

And Bridget's stomach began to turn.

I cannot do this, her traitorous mind whispered to her.

What had she been thinking? That she was any good at all?
She would never, ever, not with a hundred years of practice, be
able to play Beethoven's Sonata No. 23!

She had been too rash, too prideful, thinking she was above
the other young ladies who displayed their talents in drawing
room musicales across London. This was a piece meant for
concertmasters, not little girls. What was it she had said to
Lady Worth, full of the false bravado of a nerve-racked performer? Oh yes, that she was "that good."

That good. What a laughable thought.

And so she did. She laughed, a small bubble of hysteria
escaping her lips, and another threatening to overtake her.

Suddenly, a warm hand covered hers—which had been

pressed into a white-knuckled fist, unbeknownst to her. It was Oliver's hand, and somehow, it had the effect of tethering her back to the ground, before her imagination could put her feet to a run and have her out the door and off the island as soon as possible.

"Take two deep breaths. Slowly," came Oliver's deep, gentle voice. "The first, to steady yourself."

She inhaled, slowly, letting the air fill her body, letting sensation into places that had previously gone numb from fear.

"Now, the second, to focus on what comes next."

She took the second breath, and let herself hear the music again.

This time, she looked past the technique, past the difficulty . . . and the music was undeniably beautiful. It had a thunderous, deceptively simple melody, intruding into one's consciousness easily, the way an army would march into a town. Taking over. The second movement was kinder, more of a . . . persuasion. Until a *fortissimo* grace note that signaled the change to the next movement, and once again the listeners were rocketed back to the invasion of their souls.

It was so sad, it could break one's heart—but at least one would know that it was broken not out of despair, but overwhelming passion.

Carpenini's fingers pounded out the final chords, and the haze of music cleared from his eyes. He turned to his audience. And waited.

"I've never played anything like that," she said finally, calmly.

"I never taught anyone to play anything like that." Carpenini answered in kind. "This is a piece for those who show off. For those who have played on stage since the cradle, and twice your years."

"Oh," she replied, unable to form a thought that matched the enormity of what they were about to attempt.

"Signorina Forrester, I will not lie to you." His Italian accent smoothed over the English words, taking any harshness out of them. "I know this piece, yes, but I doubt I know it as well as Herr Klein does. It was likely taught to him by Beethoven himself." Carpenini's eyes bored into her, the way they had when he had asked her to become his student, to play in his competition.

Mesmerizing her.

Persuading her.

"I have been too easy on you the past few weeks. I have been too easy on myself. You are a talented player, yes. But are you this talented? I do not know. We are going to work harder than you ever have in your life. It will be a challenge, one we have no choice but to accept. There will be no more circuses." His eyes flitted to Oliver, then back to her. "No more fiddling about with Scarlatti and Marcello."

He seemed to require some assurance from her at this point—all Bridget could do was give a small nod. Everything else in her body was fixated on what lay ahead.

"Signorina Forrester, we have only two months before the competition. Therefore," he said coolly, "we have no time to waste."

≈

"No, no, no!" Carpenini yelled, his footfalls hitting the floor with such force, it rattled the piano's ivory keys. Bridget's hands jumped back from their positions, startled. Although, she should not be startled; Carpenini had been yelling for a good hour now.

"Faster—the trill has to be faster. Your fingering is clumsy, flat—it has to be light, like air!"

He thundered at her like a dark god. She set her hands and tried again.

"No, no, no!" he cried again. Then, with a harsh breath, he continued. "Tonight, you count how many times you can do a six-note trill in one minute. And whatever number it turns out to be, work to double it."

"But I am not meant to practice at the hotel . . ." she protested gently.

"Practice on the damned dining room table!" he ground out. "You do not need keys to make noise to know that you are doing poorly."

"I am sorry, Signore. I will try again," she said with heretofore unknown patience.

She played it again; this time, he bemoaned the trills but he did not stop her—not until she got to her first arpeggio, which finished with octave-and-a-half-spanning chords.

"You fumble the chords!" he chided with no patience.

"I . . . I am sorry, Signore," Bridget replied. "They are large chords and my hands are small . . ."

"Well, I am sorry, but we cannot have a smaller piano made for your delicate size," he countered snidely. "You must *stretch*. Your hands must become the width needed."

"I . . . I will stretch, Signore." She nodded, then set her fingers back on the keys.

It was as if Carpenini were a different man today, one intent on finding fault with everything she had ever been or done. As if she were not hard enough on herself! As if she were not daunted enough by Beethoven, now she must live in fear of Carpenini!

Bridget could feel the tears pushing themselves to the corners of her eyes, blinking fast to keep them from falling, when the last straw fell.

"So prim! So proper!" the dragon chided, his voice looming behind her. "Signorina, if you are to play that run, you must not keep your elbows locked by your sides. You need space!"

She moved her elbows out.

"No, wider! Wider!"

"Signore, I cannot!" she finally shouted back, a turncoat drop running down her cheek. "It is my dress—the sleeves are not made for one to lift her arms above her head! You must deal with close elbows!"

She turned back to the music and began to play again, her heart soaring from the relief of having fought back. But then, as she began another run, she felt nimble fingers at her back.

Undoing the buttons of her dress.

She stood up so swiftly, the legs of her piano bench screeched across the floor as she whipped around and found Carpenini staring at her incredulously.

No, he wasn't staring at *her* incredulously. He was staring at Oliver, who had crossed the room and grabbed Carpenini's hand, midbutton.

"What is the meaning of this?" the Signore asked, oblivious to offense.

And it was his obliviousness that deflated the situation. The murder left Oliver's eyes and he let go of Carpenini's hand. Instead, he sternly issued a warning.

"You cannot assault Miss Forrester's person in such a manner." His voice, usually a rich tenor, was now low, angry.

"I am not the one assaulting her person! The dress is!"

"Signore, I will *not*..." But her shaking voice was cut off by Carpenini's protestations.

"Bah! If you cannot play properly in your dress, you must remove the dress! That is all there is to it!"

"And do what?" she fired back. "Play naked?"

"If necessary," he replied, his voice cold casualness.

Bridget was so taken aback, she was utterly silent. As was Carpenini and, oddly, Oliver. But Oliver was the first to shake himself out of his thoughts and back into action.

"If you both will give me a moment, I think I have a compromise."

And with a stern look to Carpenini, Oliver turned on his heel and exited the room, the door quietly clicking shut behind him.

Leaving Bridget alone with Signor Carpenini.

For the very first time, she realized.

It was unbelievable, that the man who had encapsulated every single thought since she had first received his letter—or rather, Oliver Merrick's letter—was only now alone in her presence. If she were another sort of girl, the kind that took crushes seriously, she would look at this as some type of opportunity.

And perhaps, a few hours ago, she would have.

But the man who had emerged to teach her today—this overbearing, unforgiving, growling, feral creature who earned none of her sympathy and all of her unhappiness—was nothing like the man who lived in her mind. The man who had belief in her talent, who wanted her to succeed? The man who, in her fevered imagination late at night, bent over her hand reverently once she had played music for him, kissing her mouth, falling to his knees in adoration. (After that, her imagination was appallingly muddled. After all, no man, maestro or otherwise, had ever fallen to his knees in adoration of her. Nor kissed her on the mouth, come to think of it.)

Thus, how could this forbidding, hateful taskmaster be the man who had looked into her eyes and coaxed her into attempting Beethoven's No. 23, only a few hours before?

"Why are you doing this?" she asked simply, her gaze as direct as she could make it.

His dark eyes met hers, a cold, unfeeling challenge in them.

"Because you need it."

But something unspoken hung in the air between them, another simple phrase that did not leave Carpenini's lips but entered Bridget's ears all the same.

Because I can.

Before she could contemplate what he had said and what her mind had heard, the door to the music room swung open, as Oliver entered, practically out of breath, bearing Molly in his wake. In his hand, he held a white linen shirt.

"Molly, would you please help Miss Forrester with this?" he asked very cordially, handing the shirt to her. Molly nodded, taking it, and led Bridget behind a screen in the corner of the room, one that had not been moved since the days of the circus—apparently some of the ballerinas had required room to change.

Apparently, Oliver had explained to the maid what was needed, because Molly wordlessly helped Bridget with the buttons on the back of her dress. Once the dress was unbuttoned to its high-waisted seam, she then helped Bridget pull her arms out of her sleeves.

"Can your arms move now, miss?" Molly asked quietly.

Bridget lifted her arms above her head—yes, there was a great ease of movement now. But it was in no way respectable, to have her dress half off, exposing her chemise and corset! Molly, bless her, seemed to sense her charge's worry and, like a good, practical country woman, was on the task of all things regarding modesty.

"That's what your Mr. Merrick gave me this for. It's his best one." She held up the shirt. Her nose wrinkled slightly. "At least, the best of what's been laundered recently."

Molly tied the sleeves of Bridget's dress around her waist as snugly as she could. The dress was in no peril of sliding down, as it was still fitted to the smallest point of her waist. Rather, it functioned solely as a skirt now, and with Oliver's shirt on, buttoned up to her neck, it was the best possible solution, albeit an oddly disheveled one.

Molly took a step back and surveyed her work. "The shirt is too large. It's practically a nightdress," she grumbled. "We will have to tie it at the waist somehow . . . aha!" Molly's eyes fell on a bit of string that had fallen off one of the circus performers' costumes, weeks ago now. "I hope this came from a shoe and not a corset," Molly replied, her voice stinging with censure, her eyes sliding to beyond the screen.

"Is everything all right?" came Oliver's kind, yet worried voice.

"Ah . . . nearly ready," Bridget answered back.

As Molly tied the string around her waist, she whispered in Bridget's ear. "I'll sit in the room today, if you please, miss," she said, her eyes meeting Bridget's.

Suddenly, Bridget could tell that underneath her practical demeanor, Molly was worried about her, too. Not about propriety, not about the rules. About *her*. And tears began to sting her eyes.

"That's . . . that's all right, Molly. I'd rather have as few witnesses as possible to my humiliation today." While Molly had never been the cause of one of Bridget's panics on the stage, today seemed to be hard enough without tempting fate. "Besides, Mr. Merrick will be here."

Molly gave a short nod. "You're in good hands with that one, miss. He'll look after you. Regardless of his hand-kissing ways. But if it's all the same, I'll not be sitting in the kitchens today. I'll sit with Frederico, just beyond the door." And with a squeeze of assurance on her arm, Molly turned and exited the small space behind the screen, giving Bridget little choice but to follow.

Stepping out from behind the screen, Bridget knew she looked a mess. She was not a wholly vain creature, as her sister Sarah could be, but she did consider it important to look presentable.

This . . . this was not presentable. Even with her waist tied with the string, the shirt was so large and voluminous it gave her no shape whatsoever. She looked as if she were buttoned up to her chin in a puff of cream, her fingertips barely finding their way out from beyond the sleeves.

No, it was not presentable. But it was serviceable, and it would have to do.

"Thank you, Molly," Oliver said, dismissing the maid. Bridget met Molly's eyes, and the practical maid gave a curt nod, letting Bridget know that she would, indeed, be just beyond the door.

"Er . . . may I?" Oliver's melodious voice intruded on her thoughts. His gaze was directed at her oversized sleeves. He approached her with caution, and kindness. Gently, reverently, he began rolling up the sleeves of the shirt. Again, Bridget could not be more struck by the differences between him and his half brother! It was enough to make one start tearing up again.

"I am sorry about the size of the shirt—the shoulders sit practically at your elbows." He gave a small laugh, trying to encourage her to join in. But her eyes were too wet, her nose too stung with withheld tears, that she couldn't laugh lest they fall. "We will endeavor to find something better suited to you, I promise," he continued, his eyes still on her sleeves.

"No, don't," she replied softly, her voice betraying her wateriness. "I like it."

He looked up at her then, his lips pressing into a grim line. "This will not be easy, Bridget." Her name sounded like such a balm, coming from him. "You do not have to do it—you are under no obligation to us. To him."

"Yes, I do," she replied, her voice barely a whisper.

"Then I will tell you a secret," he said, his voice equally low. He dropped her second sleeve, now rolled, and leaned into her ear. His hand fell gently at the back of her neck as he pulled her to him, her skin incredibly aware of his touch.

"I have never, in all my life, heard anyone play the way you play."

Her head came back, and her eyes met his.

"If you let him teach you—if you master this—it will be the making of you."

Bridget could feel all the air leave her body. Those hazel eyes, golden green, kind as they were, found a way to bore into her very self and burn there.

"If you are ready," came Carpenini's sharp tones, breaking into their solitary sphere, "can we play then, yes?"

Bridget's eyes stayed with Oliver's for one more moment. And again, words entered her head that did not leave his lips, but they were somehow said, all the same.

You can do it.

"Yes, Signore," Bridget said clearly, straightening her spine and turning with the grace borne of a Forrester lady. "I am ready."

Thirteen

O NCE Miss Forrester had left for the day, Vincenzo used the spare hour he had while Oliver escorted the lady back to her hotel to brace himself for what was to come next.

"What the bloody hell do you think you were doing today?!" Oliver thundered back into the music room, forcing Vincenzo to lift his hands from the keys.

Of course Oliver came thundering back into the music room. This was Oliver's new pattern. Look like he was being strangled all through rehearsal, escort Miss Forrester home, and stomp back into the music room, full of recriminations. At least it was better now—during the week that he was barred from walking Miss Forrester home, Oliver had been mournful in his spite. Vincenzo would have laughed at him, cajoled him into humor, had he himself not been the target of Oliver's wrath.

"I was teaching today," Vincenzo replied, happy to switch back to his mellifluous Italian. Years ago, as he had taught Oliver Italian, Oliver had in turn taught him English. The past few weeks with Miss Forrester (and Oliver falling back into his native language more and more) had strengthened his English, but it still was a little rough on his tongue. Italian flowed from him. The way music flowed from his fingers and out the pianoforte. Italian was like . . . Vincenzo tried to translate that thought into a little tune, playing a new phrase from the top of his head. Hmm . . . not quite right, but nearly there.

"Would you stop that?" Oliver ground out.

"You want me to *stop* composing?" Vincenzo replied coolly, purposefully teasing his brother. "Consider, it's been so long since I've done so successfully."

"I want you to stop berating Bri—Miss Forrester. I want you to stop trying to break her down. She is doing you an enormous favor."

Vincenzo withheld a withering glance. Really, the way Oliver was wearing his heart on his sleeve bordered on pathetic. "If she wants to play this piece, she *needs* to be broken down. She needs to relearn her fingering. And taken from some perspectives, it is I who is doing her the favor, not the other way around."

Oliver took two gigantic strides (really, it was amazing how oversized and intimidating he could become when he let go of politeness) and hovered above him. Vincenzo kept his fingers on the keys, kept trying to find his way through that not-quite-right musical phrase. What would it become? A melody for an oratorio? Perhaps it would work best as a secondary harmony on something larger . . .

But, of course, there was that looming figure above him. So he sighed, and he did Oliver the favor of taking his fingers off the keys.

"You are talking about a girl who has such stage fright, she barely got past being able to play for *us*. Playing for the Marchese is going to be a hundred times more daunting. You really think criticizing every little thing is going to get her to play better? She needs her confidence built up!"

"No, she needs her skills built up!" Vincenzo retorted. "You forget that I am the teacher, not you! And if the competition were held today, not only would she lose, but she would be laughed out of the room. The Number Twenty-three takes stamina, it takes *passion*, but most of all it takes knowledge. And you are too calf-eyed around the girl to realize I am trying to do what's best for her!"

"How is tearing off her clothes in the middle of a lesson any good for her?" Oliver spat back.

"Oh, that?"

"Yes, *that*."

"She did need to move her arms," Vincenzo shrugged. "Besides, it had the added benefit of proving you wrong."

Oliver flinched back. "Proving me wrong? About what?"

"That girl is not in love with me," Vincenzo responded, unable to keep away any longer and letting the tune that was tempting him flow again. "Whether she thinks it or not. If she were, she would not have jumped up in fright at the sensation of my fingers on her back."

"You are used to dealing with actresses and whores, Vincenzo. A young lady of quality, who is pure and good, could only react as she did."

The seething anger came off Oliver in waves—enough so that if Vincenzo hadn't already walked so far down this road, he would begin to feel a little fear. But as it was, he could only prod that little bit further, and smile knowingly as he did so.

"Well, then perhaps my doing so will help awaken the passion she needs to play the Number Twenty-three."

He saw the fist before he felt it. A fraction of a second in between—not enough time to do more than widen his eyes in surprise. It landed just below his temple, on his cheekbone, cracking with force.

Damn, he had forgotten that Oliver knew how to box.

He stumbled to the floor, out of his seat at the pianoforte. He tried to orient himself, but the rising panic brought on by the exploding pain in his cheek didn't allow for it. He had never been hit before, no matter how many people wanted to—and likely there were many. And he had certainly never provoked someone of such even temper like Oliver to violence.

But then again, nothing about Oliver had been the same since the arrival of Bridget Forrester.

Vincenzo finally found his feet. And when he did rise, and managed to focus his vision, he saw Oliver with his hands down at his sides.

"I . . . I apologize," Oliver said hoarsely. "If you wish to hit me, I would understand."

"Are you mad?" Vincenzo grumbled. "I am not risking my hands." Turning to the pianoforte, he began to busy himself with gathering up his pencils, his papers—those lined sheets that had sat devoid of music for far too long.

"If you really must fall on your sword for finally expressing your feelings," he said, trying to keep the shaking out of his voice, "you can allow me to teach Miss Forrester the way she needs to be taught."

"But her stage fright—"

"Will disappear when she knows the music like it's a part of her body," Vincenzo returned. "But if you insist on it, work on curing her of her anxieties. It will keep her occupied." *And you, too*, he thought, but kept it to himself. Yes, it would keep Oliver occupied, and in the only place where he seemed comfortable of late—Miss Forrester's presence. "I have other work to do."

Oliver seemed to consider this compromise, even if he knew full well that it was no compromise at all—it would let Oliver do what he wanted to do so badly but couldn't see. And it would let Vincenzo do what he needed to do.

"I will let you teach her," Oliver finally decided. "But I will be damned if I let you assault her again."

Vincenzo merely bowed in acquiescence, which seemed to placate Oliver, because after an acknowledging nod, there was little else for the man to do but turn on his heel and leave Vincenzo alone in the music room.

Which was exactly where he needed to be.

Because the one thing he had learned today was that he needed a new plan.

The selection of Beethoven as the music for the competition had taught him that much. It was a slap in the face, a direct hit, harder and more insidious than the one that was leaving a swelling bruise on his cheek.

The Marchese didn't want him to win. He favored Klein. He favored the new. And therefore Vincenzo might as well no longer exist in the city of his birth.

Klein. He had likely learned the No. 23 from Beethoven himself. *His* sheet music was probably filled with little pencil marks in the deaf old maestro's hand, telling him where to hit harder, where to crescendo, proper fingering, and when to apply a half pedal. Oh, of course, Vincenzo's sheet music had all of those signatures, too, but they were printed from a Berlin press. Nuance was lost to printed sheet music. Whomever Klein was teaching to be his protégé at the competition had Klein's knowledge as an advantage.

It wasn't that Vincenzo didn't like Beethoven. Far from it.

The man seemed to combine a sense of romanticism and narrative strength that so many other composers couldn't master. But it wasn't *his* music. It was not from his world. And it was very much from Klein's. And Vincenzo had to admit, it had been years since he had tried the piece—not since he'd last been in Vienna. His memory of its strengths and movements was fuzzier than he could let on in front of Oliver and the girl.

Oh, Vincenzo would still teach Miss Forrester. He still had to present someone, something to the Marchese—and Vincenzo had to admit the girl had some talent. But it was not going to be enough.

Had she been born a man, she would have been allowed the musical education that would have placed her firmly on the stage, playing concerts for audiences across Europe, the way Vincenzo himself had. But she was a woman, and so her education was sorely lacking, part of her brain filled up with such fluff and nonsense as society, propriety, and shame.

Ridiculous things that simply got in his way.

Another thing that was getting in his way was Oliver. His brows came down in an angry line at the thought. Oliver, who was usually so tractable, so easily pleased with the marvels of Venice that he could be talked into anything. Now, he was already three-quarters in love with Miss Forrester. And that swayed the rhythm of their friendship so that Vincenzo was having trouble keeping time.

It grated against Vincenzo that Oliver would so abandon him—now in his hour of need! And after he had promised him a symphony (or an opera, or a concerto) to stage. Now he was stepping further and further away from Vincenzo, from his own flesh and blood . . .

Well, that was fine. Vincenzo didn't need him. He had never needed anyone. Not the mother who had chosen her English son over her Italian one, not the grandparent who had paid for his music lessons with money she sent and their drink with the rest, and not even the Marchese—he had made his own name and written his own work well before meeting him or his tempting daughter Antonia.

All he needed was the music . . . and for people to love him for it again.

Therefore he needed to write. When he presented Miss Forrester to the Marchese—whether she played well or not—

he had to have something held in reserve, something to give to the people who had once loved his music, and would again.

He needed to compose, and that need was coming back to him like a burning fever. Maybe it was this tune he had been fiddling with—still not quite right, but he would find a way for it to get there. Because the most important thing to Vincenzo Carpenini was not his brother's feelings, or the girl, his student, succeeding.

It was that he could not, would not, fail again.

No matter what.

Fourteen

OVER the next several weeks, Bridget Forrester, Oliver Merrick, and Vincenzo Carpenini settled into a routine, which very quickly began to feel normal for them. Whether Lady Forrester and Amanda found it normal was open for debate, but they chose to keep their own council and go about their holiday.

Bridget would wake up with the sun, which was getting earlier and earlier as spring took full hold of the city. She would spend the first hour of her day stretching her hands, pressing them down against the table at impossible angles. And stretching out her arms, working out the kinks that had formed overnight. As she stretched, Molly would bring in her morning chocolate and fresh water, and Bridget would perform her morning ablutions as she hummed a movement of the No. 23, point and counterpoint, backward and forward—especially the sections she would be working on that day. She was ready to greet the rest of her family usually before seven in the morning—however little they were ready to greet her.

At the hotel the Forresters had an entire floor to themselves, including a sitting room, dining room, breakfast room, and ladies' parlor, not to mention their bedrooms. Therefore, Bridget had a whole breakfast room to herself, where she was eventually joined by her mother and her sister, who would lay out their plans for the day, what part of town they would be taking in, where Amanda was in her guidebook, and with what member of the British ton who happened to be visiting Venice they would have the pleasure of dining that evening.

And meanwhile Bridget would absolutely scarf down her food.

The work made her ravenous. She was always hungry. And it was not as if she were putting on flesh—far from it! She was, in fact, reducing—a circumstance Molly noticed when Bridget's corset laced half an inch tighter than it had before. But the energy, the concentration required for her lessons required constant fuel.

Soon enough everyone would be ready to head out the door and begin their day. Oftentimes Lady Forrester and Amanda would wave Bridget off, as they were sitting in, or receiving guests that day—it amazed Bridget how many people her mother managed to collect, British and Venetian alike, in so short a space of time. But oftentimes they would be getting into one gondola as Bridget and Molly got into another, to be conveyed to Mr. Merrick's house.

Once there, Molly would join Frederico down in the kitchens—Bridget secretly suspected she was berating the lazy manservant into doing more work, because the music room seemed to be dusted with far more frequency, and suddenly, one day a cheese plate was delivered at noon to the famished musicians. The cheese plate had made an appearance every day since.

Meanwhile, Bridget *worked*. The sheet music for No. 23 was smudged at the corners with her fingerprints. It was marked over and over again with her handwriting, with Carpenini's handwriting, placing emphasis on phrasing, fingering order, and the word *passion!* written at several points and underlined for emphasis. Carpenini leaned over her shoulder, moved her hands when necessary, would demonstrate a particular run and then expect Bridget to play it perfectly immediately.

It was, without question, utterly exhausting.

And while Carpenini would rap her knuckles or move her arms to the positions they had to hold, he kept his fingers off her buttons. Because before the day's lessons began, before Molly went down to the kitchens, the first thing they did was step behind the screen, where Oliver's shirt was waiting for her.

It always smelled of soap and starch, which Bridget found funny. Did Oliver have poor Frederico wash the shirt every day? But it also smelled of something else, something held so deep within its fibers that no amount of washing could take it out. It was salt and wood smoke and grease paint. It smelled like Oliver.

Sometimes she caught Oliver watching her from across the room during the lesson, and caught the scent of his shirt at the same time . . . and it was like he infused her with his calming, happy presence. She would smile, and he would smile, and . . .

And usually Carpenini had to rap her hands again to get her attention back to where it should be.

Carpenini. Much to Bridget's surprise, he had not gone back to the seductive creature who mesmerized her with his words, his promises. No, now that he was making good on those promises, he was a ruthless taskmaster. And once the lessons were done at three o'clock, he shut the doors on them and worked unapologetically on his own music. No distractions. No wine. No Antonia Galetti. It was such an astonishing turn that Oliver and Bridget had taken to mimicking him on their walks home.

"No, Signorina!" Oliver said, pitching his voice to Carpenini's more gravelly tone. "You must play with your ring finger and pinkie! Now, go home—I must compose!"

Bridget giggled. She loved this time. The time when she was exhausted from the day's work, when she had poured out her being onto the keys and was drained. Therefore she was freed from the nagging feeling that she wasn't doing enough for these few moments, when the only thing she had to do was walk home and enjoy Oliver Merrick's company.

And enjoy it she did. He was a remarkably easy companion, making her laugh with his impressions. He did a remarkably good one of Frederico being taken to task by Molly.

"Frederico!" he would cry in a falsetto that was eerily similar to Molly's true pitch. "Your laziness is a testament to your continental nature. You should be ashamed by the state of this rug!"

"Oi—enough of that," Molly grumbled from behind them. Then added, "Although he should be ashamed."

Sometimes they would walk toward the east, back to the hotel, but meandering in their path. On other days, Oliver would have thought of some beautiful old building, or square, or bridge that Bridget absolutely *had* to see—her trip to Venice could not be complete without it—so they would head in the exact opposite direction of the hotel and find themselves wandering their way back hours later.

If it was early enough in the afternoon by the time they reached the hotel, Bridget would change quickly, go out with James and Molly, and meet her mother and sister at whatever architectural marvel Amanda insisted on exploring that day. Lady Forrester had taken to complaining that Amanda was turning out much like their father, what with her newfound passion for art and architecture.

Bridget had never had this kind of freedom before. Oh, of course she never went anywhere alone—there was always Molly or James within arm's reach. But as the middle child, she had always been braced on both ends with forced companionship, and all of a sudden, she was given permission and free rein, in the foreign city, to choose her own way.

And being by herself, or with Oliver, she got to see Venice in a different light than she would have if she had been with her mother visiting in tedious drawing rooms, or with her sister and her guidebook.

She saw workmen smoking tobacco pipes, relaxing after unloading a large cart at a shop, their white teeth showing under dark beards as they laughed at some mellifluously told joke. Or at least Bridget assumed it was a joke; her Italian had not improved nearly enough in the intervening weeks to be able to tell.

She saw the way the afternoon sun hit the stones of the city, lighting the city like the center of a candle's flame. She saw fishermen, grizzled old men half seaborne, bringing their nets into the shore. On still days, she saw the reflection of the buildings in the canals, a mirrored world, as much above as it was below.

And all of it, to her, looked, sounded, felt like music.

Bridget told her mother that the lessons were going well—quite well—and Lady Forrester, obviously seeing the marked change in her formerly desperate, unhappy child, was well pleased and did not interfere. In fact, all talk of possibly moving on to Milan, Rome, or Naples (mostly from Amanda) was put to rest. Their holiday was now not spent exploring the Italian peninsula, but firmly entrenching themselves in the scene and society of Venice.

In the evening, they would come back to the hotel and dress for dinner. They might dine at the hotel; Signor Zinni always seemed to have an entire repast prepared for them—or, rather, prepared to impress Lady Forrester. If they were dining out at the home of one of Mother's new friends (she had found a social circle of British visitors that expanded daily), Bridget would more often than not cry off, begging exhaustion.

"I swear, Bridget, if Carpenini is working you this hard, is it worth it?" Amanda asked one evening, pulling on her gloves—which were rather tight. It seemed than Amanda, despite their hopes, was not yet finished growing.

"Yes," Bridget answered simply. And that was the truth.

It *was* worth it. Bridget had not known she could push herself this far. That she could work this hard at anything. And that it could pay such rewards. She was beginning to feel the music—feel it in ways she hadn't before. Carpenini was teaching her theory—not only that the notes were placed in a certain order, but why. They had even had exercises testing her pitch, making her name a single note's pitch and octave blindfolded.

Carpenini's compliments were rare, but when given, they meant something because of their rarity. She felt like she understood music better—but that did not mean she would ever understand Carpenini.

In fact, more often than not, Oliver had to act as translator. Not for Italian, but for her instructor.

"But I do not understand what he meant by 'throwing slop,' when I was playing that one phrase," Bridget had said on one afternoon walk. Shame came over her: "Did . . . did he mean I was playing like slop?"

But Oliver had simply laughed. "No—in fact, he wanted you to play like slop."

"And now I do not understand you, either," she replied sardonically.

Oliver went over to a nearby fishmonger and, after a quick negotiation, handed the man a coin and came back with one (thankfully empty) wooden bucket.

"There is an arc," he said, leading her down a short set of steps to stand even with the canal, "when one throws a bucket full of water, or slop if you prefer—and Carpenini does, because he likes to perpetuate the myth that he grew up on a farm, which is laughably untrue."

And indeed Bridget did laugh.

"Anyway," he continued, "that arc, followed by the impact at the end—that is what that phrase is supposed to feel like. Being airborne, and then crashing down." And then he demonstrated, filling the bucket of water from the canal and slinging it out, an arc of water flying through the air, splatting into the canal—narrowly missing a gondolier.

"*Scusi!*" he cried, while Bridget suppressed giggles.

Oliver never failed to make her laugh.

"Here," he said, handing her the bucket. "You try."

She had taken it, biting her lip to hide her smile. "I wager I can throw farther than you!"

Her body was beginning to respond to the work, too. Her upper arms took on a muscular definition that on most women would be unseemly—but Bridget liked it. It was proof of her hard work. Her fingers could span an entire whole step farther on the keyboard, thanks to her constant stretching. After her mother and sister left for the evening, Bridget would come back to her rooms and stretch her fingers some more while studying the sheet music for No. 23—it was always with her, carried in her little portfolio. Carpenini made her tuck it inside some less challenging music, just in case spies were following her on the way home, but to Bridget it seemed silly. If they knew she was his student, they knew this was the piece she had to learn. No reason to hide it. But she obeyed his more nervous cautions, if only to keep his ire in check.

She would fall asleep, often still in her clothes, the sheet music around her and music in her head.

When she awoke, she would be humming a tune.

But it wasn't always No. 23.

Sometimes, another tune sneaked into her mind. One she had not heard before. Or one that she had heard a thousand times, in a thousand different ways. In a fishmonger's wife's shrieking call, or in the way a gondolier's paddle moved gently through the water. She heard it in the way her footsteps resonated as they crossed a bridge over a canal. She heard it pouring out of windows and on the salty breeze that came in from the lagoon.

To Bridget Forrester, it was the sound of a foreigner awakening to Venice and falling in love with its cacophony.

It was this tune that tempted her, distracted her from what she needed to concentrate on—Beethoven's No. 23, and her lessons.

That tune was stuck in her head for three days before she resolved to do something about it. And really, the only thing to do was to get it out.

It was the only thing that ever worked. Bridget had written down little tunes here and there in the past, nothing with any formality or structure—just the tunes that would come to her, and annoy her until she put them to paper. It would never interfere with her life overly—it would just irk those around her, her family and her sisters who had to listen to her incessant humming. Once written, it was as if her mind gave permission to let it go, and invariably she would begin humming some new tune under her breath, aggravating her sisters.

But this tune was much more persistent than any before, and the way that Carpenini was grumbling at her that day, she could easily blame it for her lack of concentration on following his instructions.

"No, Signorina!" he corrected, as she played through the run again. "You must attack this section. You must stay a bare breath ahead of when the beat falls!"

The notes themselves had long ago been perfected in the lengthy piece; now Carpenini was turning his attention to bringing out the meaning behind them. But after a long day of Bridget's being slightly behind the beat, the Signore's temper was shorter and shorter.

In fact, it had been three days that she had been slightly behind the beat. Three days since she had heard a hard-won compliment from Signor Carpenini. Three days, instead, of his unbearable temper.

"Yes, Signore," she answered, and attacked the notes in a manner she hoped would please him. But, master player that he was, he saw through that immediately.

"No! You cannot play to please me, you must play because that it how it is in your heart!"

She spared a glance up and saw that Oliver was not there.

Strange, he was always in the room. She frowned, a little bereft at the idea that he was not watching over her. But at that
moment, he came back into the music room, carrying a box in
his hands.

The rap of the door closing caused Carpenini to look up
sharply. He spoke very curtly to Oliver in Italian, and Oliver
answered in reply, holding up the box as evidence of his ire.

Bridget had been in Venice long enough now to be able to
pick a few choice words out of the dozens that flew above her
head—*paper*, *account*, and *payment* chief among them.

Before she could question the brothers about their squab-
ble, the clock chimed three, and everyone in the room visibly shifted. The lesson was over, and the next part—the best
part—of the day would begin.

"Signorina, for tomorrow, practice attacking the arpeggio.
Think ahead in your mind when you read the music," Carpenini said, all fight gone out of his body.

Molly came in, Oliver put the box down, and in the flurry
of activity of gathering up her music, changing back out of
Oliver's shirt, and finding bonnet, gloves, and reticule, Bridget
could not help but sneak a glance at the box that had broken
up the lesson. Oliver and Carpenini were engaged in a low
conversation in Italian on the other side of the room; there was
no reason she couldn't peek inside . . .

Imagine her confusion at finding a box of simple paper.

Imagine her delight at finding it was ruled with lines. Lines
for the musical staff. Bridget could piece together the meaning
of the overheard conversation now. Carpenini must have ordered this special paper, printed with staffs for his own compositions! And there was an entire *book's* worth of paper here.

Now Bridget could have easily gotten her own paper and
lined it herself. For that matter, so could Carpenini—this was
an extravagance. But since this was here, surely he wouldn't
miss a sheet or two? It would even be a help to their lessons,
because she could get the tune out of her head quickly and
move on to more important things, like attacking her notes
with proper attention.

She was just slipping two such sheets of paper into her
music portfolio (or perhaps it was three) when Oliver's voice
made her jump.

"Miss Forrester? Are you ready to depart?"

"I saw that, you know."

They were walking through the Piazza San Marco, one of Oliver's favorite places in the city—and now, one of Bridget's, too. Bridget brought her head down—her eyes had been fixed on the intricate facade of the Doge's Palace. Molly hung back a few paces behind them, always mindful of propriety, but blessedly unobtrusive. Oliver had been happily conversational so far in their ramble, but his topics were terribly mild. Until now, apparently.

"Saw what?" she asked, trying for innocence. And failing.

"I saw you hastily stuff something into your portfolio—and really, it was the hasty nature of the stuffing that gave you away." He grinned at her. "You would make a terrible spy."

Bridget raised her eyebrows and mentally made a note to apply to her brother-in-law for training in more covert tactics. He would likely tell her to suppress the blush that was at that moment rising over her cheeks.

"Now, what could you have stolen that would have required such haste?" he chided further.

The dam burst.

"I'm so, so sorry, Oliver, I couldn't help it, I looked in the box and there was this lovely blank music paper and I have had this tune in my head that I simply need to get down! And if I don't, my lessons are just going to get worse, I know it, so I thought that the Signore would not mind if I took one or two sheets out of that box, and of course I didn't need to steal it, I am perfectly capable of making my own sheet paper, but I thought, it was there, and I could use it—do you think he'll be terribly cross at me?"

Oliver blinked, which he tended to do whenever her speech ran on. He then took the expected steadying breath, and it steadied her, too. In a city built on water, Oliver seemed to be a grounded point.

"Bridget," he began quite properly, as he always did when he was about to be quite proper, "do you mean to tell me that this rushed speech of contrition is because you pilfered some paper?"

"Yes," she nodded.

"Some *blank* paper." He clutched his hands behind his back.

"Some blank lined paper," she corrected and giggled.

"And is your guilt the reason for your relative silence today?"

"Yes." She frowned. "Well, no. It's because of the tune."

"The tune."

She sighed and threw up her hands. "I have a tune in my head, and I have to put it down on paper to get it out. And then maybe I'll be able to attack the notes of Number Twenty-three properly."

He regarded her quizzically. "Is it the tune that goes like this?"

He sang a low melody, shocking Bridget, his lovely tenor making each note warm and full.

"Yes!" she cried. "How did know?"

"You've been mindlessly humming that tune on our walks for three days." Oliver smiled at her, reaching out to tuck a wind-caught curl back behind her ear. His touch was careless, as if he hadn't noticed he was doing it.

However, Bridget noticed. And the jolt of warmth that passed from his naked fingers to the tip of her ear shocked her.

"Do . . . do you think he'll mind?" she stuttered, bringing herself back to the present, back to the piazza. "Carpenini, I mean."

Oliver's hand dropped to his side. "Bridget, he'll never notice. He's been going through paper like a newspaper press." He gave her a quick reassuring smile. "As far as I'm concerned, you can have every single sheet in that box. I paid for it, after all."

That last was grumbled low, under his breath. Bridget cocked her head to the side quizzically. "What do you—"

But he just shook his head. "A mix-up in billing at the *papier*'s. It's not worth the trouble it takes to think about it." He squared his shoulders and changed the subject. "But I did not know you composed, as well as your other talents."

"I do not." She shook her head. "Not really. Sometimes a melody will come to me, though, and the only way to make it quiet is to put it on paper."

"And these are just melodies? Not full compositions?"

"Well," she hemmed, "occasionally I amuse myself by making an arrangement out of it, adding harmonies and counterpoint, but . . ."

"That sounds remarkably like composition to me," he interjected. "And then what—these arrangements simply sit in a drawer, never to be heard?"

"No one wants to hear what I've written, Oliver," she laughed.

"I do," he responded, quite vehemently. "In fact, I want to hear this tune that you've been humming for three days—because it is as much in my head now as it is in yours. I want to see what it can be built into."

Play. One of her own compositions? For other people's ears? The thought practically had Bridget jumping out of her skin.

"I . . . cannot," she protested. "The very idea . . . fills me with more dread than playing naked in front of a thousand people!"

"Actually, that gives me an idea about how to combat your lingering stage fright—but I digress." He grinned wolfishly at her. "You will not be playing naked, or in front of a thousand people. And I would very much like to hear it."

She could say no, and she could do it so forcefully, Oliver would regret pursuing the issue. But along with the dread that felt a close cousin to when her nerves would fail her, there was a spark of something new. Of . . . hope? No. Ambition. A glimmer of that energy that drove her to want to be a great pianist. She wanted to get this tune onto paper. This tune, so much stronger in her head than the others, springing almost fully formed! It was worth being shared. It was worth being shared with Oliver.

Out of everyone, he was the one she felt safe hearing the contents of her mind.

"All . . . all right," she said finally. "You can hear my music."

The next morning, Bridget arrived early at Oliver's home.

Shockingly early.

"Signorina Forrester," Frederico said, meeting them at the gondola. "Signors Merrick and Carpenini are not yet down from breakfast!"

In fact they were not even down *to* breakfast. Carpenini was fast asleep. Oliver had been abandoned in the middle of his morning shave so Frederico could go meet the gondola. He quickly wiped away the soap that lathered his face—which had not yet been touched by a blade, so even though he came down to greet Bridget scruffily, it was at least even.

"I'm so sorry!" she cried upon greeting him at the base of the stairs. "But I could not sleep any longer! I'm not permitted to play at the hotel, and I have to know how this will sound on the keys!"

She held up her sheet music—where yesterday it was blank lines, today it was marked heavily with staccato rhythms, time and key signatures, and a bold clear melody.

"Well, let's hear it, then," he said, stifling a yawn, and gestured for Bridget to lead the way.

She practically vibrated with energy, he thought, watching her—it was debatable whether she had slept last night, such was her anticipation. There was a slight waver of nervousness in her voice when she finally spoke.

"Now please bear in mind, I haven't been able to play this yet—I've only heard it in my head." He watched passively, unobtrusively as she seated herself at the piano and smoothed the pages out before her.

"I understand," he replied with a smile. "Although you may wish to remove your gloves before playing."

"Oh," she said, surprised to find her gloves still on her hands. Not to mention her bonnet still on her head and her lightweight spencer still on her back.

She quickly removed the gloves, although the bonnet and spencer would have to wait. And then, with one last preparatory breath, she began to play.

And Oliver let her music wash over him.

It was by no means a full, refined piece. There was too much repetition in the second half, as if she hadn't yet figured out what to do as a counterpoint resolution to her melody. Oh, but that melody. It started quietly, peacefully, like the morning sun just touching the waters to the east of the city. Then it built with the bustle of a day spent being met by new things, surprises, happy exclamations. Then the falling into night, a quieting down again, a delighted exhaustion. It had a romantic sensibility but a classical soul. And Oliver knew as soon as her fingers left the keys where she had found her inspiration.

"That was Venice. Wasn't it? An ode to Venice."

She looked up at him, her eyes shining with happiness. "Yes! I hoped you would be able to tell."

"How could I not? It sounded just like it to me."

"Really? Strange, it sounded to me like a student who has not been practicing the Number Twenty-three."

Both Bridget and Oliver whipped their eyes to the door of the music room, where Carpenini stood. Or, more accurately, leaned. He was hastily dressed in trousers and a shirt, much like Oliver. But whereas Oliver had been awake for at least a little while, Carpenini blinked into the light like a disgruntled bear waking from his cave.

"Is this"—his hand waved vaguely to the music on the piano—"what has been distracting you the past few days?" Oliver thought he caught Vincenzo sliding a glance toward him, but he could not be sure—what with Vincenzo's half-closed eyes.

"Er . . . Signore, I apologize," she began, but cut herself off. "Yes. But it won't be a problem anymore."

"Good," he grunted with a nod. "Since you are here, Signorina, then we will get to work."

Fifteen

IF Bridget had hoped to have her head cleared by putting her "Ode to Venice" on paper, it was not to be. At least, it was not to be that day. Or the next. Or the next.

Bridget did manage to get ahead of the beat and attack the notes as she had been struggling to do for the last few days, even earning a few of those rare, "*si, si*"s from her instructor.

But once she had defeated these old dragons, a new one reared its ugly head.

"Signorina, how many times do I have to tell you— *appassionata!* With the heart, the fever! Build with the crescendo!"

Oliver observed from his usual perch on the worn, faded velvet settee. He was always there, always listening. Most people would find sitting through other people's lessons boring, but he found it surprisingly compelling. He had never watched Carpenini teach anyone before—at least not this in-depth. And he had also never been privy to a student with the same talent as Bridget Forrester.

He could watch her hands move on the keys for hours. The way her brow came down as she pushed through a long, complicated run. That stray curl coming undone from her coiffure, and the way her tongue slipped out and pressed against her upper lip when she was concentrating.

Yes, watching Bridget Forrester was certainly the most interesting way to pass the time.

And watching *over* Bridget Forrester, the best.

Oliver knew he wasn't wholly useless in his current position, because both Bridget and Vincenzo would look to him as the objective auditory party.

"That crescendo doesn't start until here!" Bridget exclaimed, pointing to the music.

"*Si*, but is better if you start before, and slow down the build. It is in the gut, the liver. I am right, Oliver, yes?"

It amazed Oliver how Vincenzo's Italian would suddenly get worse when he was trying to win a point. Not that his English was perfect by any means, but five years with Oliver and as many weeks with an English-only student had made him infinitely more understandable than in the past.

"I think it sounds strong either way," Oliver said diplomatically. There was absolutely no way he was going to enter the fray between Vincenzo and Bridget—at least not when it came to music.

He could do that for her, he decided—as much as he itched to jump to her defense, to argue with Vincenzo in a way that five years of friendship had taught him would work. Instead, he let Bridget fight her own battles.

And the amazing thing was, she had begun to. She had begun to trust her own ear, and judgment, and began to play the way the piece spoke to her. It was only here and there at first, during phrases one could tell she truly enjoyed, but the fact that her confidence was building was undeniable.

"No, no, Signorina! It is weak, tired! It does not have the *appassionata*!"

What was also undeniable was the fact that Bridget was having a harder time than before beheading this particular dragon.

"Signore, I am putting as much feeling into the piece as possible," she began, her voice rising with her ire.

"Then you do not have the right kind of feeling!" Vincenzo retaliated. "It is about making love. Falling out of love. Pain! Greatness!"

"What a marvelous number of adjectives that mean very little strung together," Bridget replied sardonically, and Oliver could barely suppress a laugh. When Vincenzo tended toward dramatics, they were rather . . . dramatic.

He managed to catch Bridget's eye and saw that she was hiding her own smile, too.

He would have to make a note of today's display, to imitate on their walk home. He supposed he should feel a little guilty about making his half brother—and Bridget's renowned instructor—the butt of a joke, but it just seemed to him that the more human Vincenzo was to Bridget, the more she would be able to relax in his presence, and the better she would play. And hopefully, the more she would enjoy the process, too. She took it, and herself, so seriously! And of course, it was worthy of being taken seriously, but not at the expense of her health or her sense of self-worth. Balance had to be met. If Vincenzo was harsh, rigorous study, then Oliver would be the counterpoint.

Thus Oliver considered it his duty to earn smiles from her. Even if it had to be at Vincenzo's expense. He was certain that had Vincenzo known about their little jokes, he would forgive him. Especially if it helped Bridget play.

But Oliver did not know if *he* would be able to forgive Vincenzo for what happened next.

"How can I explain this to someone such as you!" Vincenzo threw up his hands, and then buried his head in them. Dramatically, it went without mentioning.

"Why do you not show me, instead," Bridget replied patiently, indicating the keys in front of them.

Vincenzo's head came up from his hands, as if struck by a light. "*Si*, you are right. One cannot explain passion to a virgin. One must show her!"

And with that, Vincenzo turned Bridget Forrester in her seat, held fast to her shoulders, and kissed her hard on the lips.

Oliver was out of his seat before he knew what was happening. But before he made it two steps, Vincenzo broke off the kiss.

"Now, Signorina, start the crescendo earlier—and play that feeling as you do," Vincenzo commanded in a self-satisfied manner.

Bridget looked around the room, blinking, as if in a trance. Oliver desperately tried to meet her eyes, but their usual un-

spoken communication during her lessons was in no way ad-
equate.

"Miss Forrester—Bridget," he ventured, his voice coming
out strangled.

"I . . . I'm fine," she reassured him, and then, refocusing on
the music before her, she began to play, but whether she played
the crescendo as Vincenzo wanted, Oliver could not hear.

Because his blood was thrumming in his ears, and his
mind rushed with words that formed thoughts he couldn't
fully comprehend.

Are you all right? he wanted to ask. *Are you safe?* pulsed
through his system. But underneath all that was a darker
thrumming, an anger that could not be laughed away.

Mine, it said. *She is mine.*

❧

It could be a surprise to no one that both Bridget and Oliver
were uncommonly silent on their walk home. And remarkably
slow of foot, too.

"Miss, do you mind if I walk ahead?" Molly said, breaking
into the awkward quiet that covered them. "It is your mother's
day to receive callers, and the hotel's girls don't know their
stoneware from bone china."

"Of course, Molly," Bridget replied. "I apologize, we
should not dawdle today."

"Do not trouble yourself, miss, I'll just move ahead if you
don't mind."

And with that, Molly gave a short curtsy and, elbows tucked
to her sides, began to dart through the afternoon crowd.

Leaving Oliver alone with Bridget.

Either Molly was immensely sensitive to the thoughts of
her employers, Oliver thought, or she was uncommonly obtuse
to them and lived in a world of happy coincidence. But given
the look she slid to Oliver on her way past him, he rather suspected the former.

And he was given to believe that the practical, Methodist
maid was, strangely, on his side.

"Well," Oliver began, not one to let awkwardness detract
from opportunity. "That was an interesting day."

"Yes," Bridget mused, her eyes still on her feet, although it
seemed she was not truly watching where she was going. She

seemed to lag, to stumble over cobblestones, her mind clearly elsewhere.

Oliver could guess where.

"Did you feel that the lesson today was . . . useful?" His voice strangled the last word.

"Yes," she replied, by rote. Then her head came up; her feet came to a stop. "No."

"No?"

"No. It wasn't useful. I don't understand what he wants." She slumped mournfully. "I don't think I ever will."

Oliver took a half step toward her but, mindfully, kept his arms at his sides. "What don't you understand?" He tried to keep the curiosity out of his voice.

"This . . . this *appassionata*!" she exclaimed. "This inflamed gut—which, by the by, sounds like a disease"— Oliver could not help smiling at that, as she continued—"try and I try, and he still does not like the run. And then he *kissed* me, and I play the same run again, and it sounded no different!"

"Bridget—" Oliver began, his voice taking on those proper tones that made him sound like her father, not her friend. He quashed said tones immediately. "What are you getting at?"

"What does Carpenini want?" she asked breathlessly, turning her green-eyed gaze directly at him. "What does he want me to feel—to understand? Do you have any idea?"

Oliver felt every muscle in his body tense in awareness. He could count his heartbeats as he weighed his response.

"Perhaps I do," he replied finally, his eyes never leaving Bridget's face.

"What is it? Can you . . . translate for me? As you did with the buckets of water—er, slop."

"No," he replied, considering. Her face fell, an adorable plaintive look. "It cannot be explained. Not with words."

"Oh," she replied, her brow coming down in confusion.

"But perhaps I can show you," he offered. Careful to keep his hands behind his back. Careful not to touch her. Not yet.

"Would you, please?" Bridget's face lit up like she'd just been offered an invitation to a private box at the opera. One that she didn't have to share with her sisters.

"It's . . . a physical feeling, converted into music. That is what he's after," he warned her. He wanted her to have a chance to walk away. Even though it would kill him if she did.

"Is it like a touch? A . . . a caress?"

She reached out her hand and touched his arm, at the elbow, pulling his hand free from behind his back. As electric as the feeling of her hand on his coat—the gentle pressure she placed there, barely more than a bird's weight—he couldn't help but laugh.

"Not quite. That's a good place to start, though." He looked around them. "This lesson cannot be taught in the middle of a footbridge, however. Come."

He held out his hand, and she hesitantly slipped her smaller one into it. They were in the middle of Venice, in the middle of a busy day on a busy street, where everyone could see them. Granted, most of the people who saw them would not care beyond how they blocked their path, but he did not wish to disgrace her to that small percentage that would care very much.

He pulled her down a side street and into a quiet, unpopulated alley.

"This is that alley," she said, her voice a whisper—which the environment seemed to call for.

"What alley?"

"They one you first showed me. With sunlight on the cobblestones and impatient windows."

He glanced around them. "So it is," he murmured. An appropriate enough place. After all, it was just about here that the itch—that itch he was about to take the opportunity to scratch—came into being.

He dropped her hand but remained close at her side. He wanted to instruct her properly, and that meant . . . anticipation.

"So . . ." she asked, unable to come up with the rest of the sentence.

"So." He exhaled slowly and closed the meager distance between them. "The feeling that Carpenini wants is internal. It's a blooming feeling of love. Of lust."

"Well, I know that," she said, exasperated.

"Do you?" A single eyebrow flew up skeptically.

"Well, yes." Her hands went to her hips, a defiant stance.

"I'm not completely ignorant. I've been trying to think about that . . . emotion, while I'm playing, but it just falls short."

He cocked his head to one side. He leaned in, ever closer, still holding himself just that barest distance apart, still holding his hands at his sides, no matter how much they ached to come up and rest on the skin at her wrists, her throat, her cheek.

"What are you thinking of, specifically, when you are playing?" His voice was little more than breath.

Bridget looked sideways, seemingly loathing to admit. "A crush," she mumbled.

"Pardon me?" Oliver's voice went up in pitch, his heart skipping a beat.

She rolled her eyes. "Oh, this is so embarrassing. I used to have a bit of a . . . a crush, on my sister's now-husband. Before they were married," she hastened to add. "I try to think of what it felt like to have a crush on him. A crush on anyone, really."

"Well, then, that's the difficulty." He smiled at her, his lips shockingly close to hers. "You are not meant to think of anything at all. You are simply supposed to *need*."

Her eyes were nearly black, with a feeling she could not yet know how to comprehend. But she would.

"Need what?" she asked.

And then . . . his lips met hers.

There was no sensation in the world quite like this. This first of all kisses, this first time when their hearts and breath would mingle, and the need to touch overwhelmed.

Oliver finally gave in to that need to touch and gently let his fingers rest at the back of her neck, threading through her dark curls. He might not be her instructor, he might not have Carpenini's refined ear for music, but he could teach her this.

Gently, his thumb danced along her jaw, the slightest pressure urging her mouth to open, to let him in. She did, a small shudder of surprise moving down her spine. Feeling it through their contact only made Oliver want to bring her closer. And so, with his other hand, he reached around to the back of her waist, pressing her body into his, holding her in a stunning, needful embrace. He deepened the kiss, their dance. His hand fisted in the back of her dress.

And then, he felt it. The tentative touch against his coat.

The slide of her arms up to his shoulder, her fingers threading through the dark hairs at his neck, her embrace a copy of his.

"Good," he murmured against her mouth. "You're learning."

"I was always a good student," she whispered back, a little shakily.

"Ready for something more advanced?" He did not wait for a reply, of course. Instead, he let his lips fall away from hers and moved them to the tantalizing line of her throat.

She gasped in surprise. *In pleasure.* He grinned against her neck.

He took a step forward; she moved with him. Suddenly her back was against the wall of the alley. He sought relief to the hard ache that had grown in his cock, pressing himself, through their clothes, against her softness.

She sighed, an echo of want in that empty Venetian street, with only the cobblestones and the impatient windows to hear.

He wanted to explore. He wanted to roam across her skin and find all the spots that would make her sigh like that. But some small, still-intact part of his brain made him resist the impulse. Made him stay right there, in the alley, in the here and now. Made him pull back and meet her eyes.

Normally bright green and probing, those eyes were now hooded, glazed with passion. Her breaths were coming in short, hard bursts, much like his own.

"That is what the music is supposed to feel like," he said, unable to keep his hands from framing her face, from feeling her. "That wanting. That *need.*"

"I think . . ." she said after a moment, unable to tear her eyes away, "I understand now."

Oliver found himself straightening. Had he gone too far? Was she dismissing him? Doubts began to creep in, but he forced them away. He would not allow anything, especially his own conscience, to rob him of the joy of what had just transpired. Of what he felt.

And whether she recognized it or not, he knew she'd felt it, too.

"I have to go," she said suddenly, clearing her voice, setting him back on his heels.

"Oh . . . of course," he replied, forcing himself back into the English Gentleman character he had let slip for a few brief precious moments. Although his body, still coursing with lust, was not as receptive to the idea. He began to pace, to move, trying to settle himself down. "Give me a moment, and I'll escort you."

She looked confused for a moment, and then her eyes traveled lower on his body, leaving a trail of innocent heat in their wake.

"Bridget, staring doesn't help."

She blushed the deepest crimson before shooting her gaze away at the evidence of his baseness.

"Oh!" she cried. "No, do not . . . trouble yourself. I'm . . . I have to go."

And before he could stop her, before he could get his body under control, she shot out of the alley like a ball from a cannon, taking those few short blocks back to the hotel with impossible speed.

Leaving Oliver standing in the middle of an empty, sunlit alleyway, his body still coursing with need, his mind muddled by a thousand thoughts. But one thought managed to find its way through the fog to the front of his mind.

She had just run away from him.

Bridget burst into the hotel, her only goal the piano. Oh, she knew it was forbidden, she knew that she was not permitted to practice at home, lest prying ears overhear, but she could not bend to the Signore's overly worrisome whims just now. Because right now, she had to get to a piano. She had to play that run again and put what she had just felt into the keys.

She had never been kissed before. Never really wanted to be. It was the unfortunate circumstance of limiting one's emotional curiosity to music. In music, especially opera, if a lady is kissed, she is likely dead by the time the curtain falls. To equate the press of a man's lips to hers with death hardly promoted romanticism. But to be kissed twice in one day, by two entirely different men—and to have two such different reactions to them!

It was actually a bit untrue that she had never really *wanted* to be kissed. Of late, she had been thinking about it quite a bit. She had lied slightly to Oliver. With her now-defunct crush on her now-brother-in-law Jackson, lips hadn't figured into her fantasies—that was really more about getting someone to notice her who had only noticed her sister. But for the past several weeks, spending every day in the presence of the great Carpenini, his passions becoming hers, his voice filling her head, it was only natural that her mind would turn to wondering about his touch.

She considered a slight crush on Carpenini logical. Even if he proved severely trying.

But when that touch had actually happened . . . well, to say Carpenini's kiss was a disappointment was akin to saying that the tower in Pisa was only slightly off center. She had been shocked more than anything, and then sort of felt bruised by the whole thing—as if she had been hit across the face with a piece of raw meat. It would get one's attention, certainly, but it would hardly inspire passion.

And to think, this was the man whose dark eyes burned into her, his voice a mesmerization—so much more so than his brother's! Strange as it was, Carpenini, who had brought her to Venice, who had seen in her a spark of something special, who had brought a circus into the music room for her . . .

Wait.

She came to an abrupt stop on the main stairs in the foyer of the Hotel Cortile, oblivious to any servants or guests who might have been around her.

Had it been Carpenini who had brought the circus into the music room? If he was so unloved in the Venetian music scene, would any of those performers have leaped to his call? Besides, from what she'd gathered by her time spent in the house—by the fact that Oliver had to pay his bills for paper for his compositions—Carpenini was without enough funds to pay for such a circus act. It was Oliver who had the connections to the theatre, Oliver who could make such a thing possible. It was Oliver who had done so for her.

Oliver, who made her laugh. Oliver, who was a steady calm in the sea of volatility that was Carpenini's world. Whom she could talk to and enjoy time with. Whom she could ask to help her understand what she couldn't before.

And it was Oliver whose kiss had run through her blood and rattled her senses.

Little pieces of the puzzle that was Bridget's life for the past several weeks began to fall into place, like the shapes of city blocks on a Venetian map.

But she couldn't think about that now. No—right now, she had to play.

Bridget made her way to the Forrester rooms, occupying the entirety of the second floor. She remembered fleetingly that Molly had said this was the day her mother was receiving callers—and therefore had to avoid the woman like the plague, lest she get roped into visiting with whatever friend-of-a-friend-of-a-friend happened to be touring through Venice that week.

She only prayed that her mother was using the east parlor, which was smaller but far more comfortable in the afternoon, rather than the west, which was larger and held the pianoforte.

She ducked her head into the west parlor and breathed a sigh of relief. It was empty.

Bridget quickly put down her portfolio and pulled out her sheet music for the No. 23. Turning to the appropriate page, she set herself at the keys.

She played it once through—just the few bars she was focused on. Despite the old instrument's need for a good tuning, it sounded the same to her ears. Then she stopped. Decided to back up to the beginning of the movement. To allow for something—want? need?—to build.

This time, when she began with *andante con moto*, she did not think of anything as she was playing, as Oliver had said. She did not think of the cross-hand chords that were coming up in sixteen measures, or the way Carpenini had played the run, trying to imitate him. Instead, she let herself feel.

She could feel the way Oliver's warm breath felt against her cheek as he whispered in her ear. Felt his hand on the back of her neck. She could practically see the light in his eyes when he bent his head down to hers. And then suddenly her heart was beating fast, and pinpricks of awareness rolled across her body.

Her vision lost focus on the music, clouding over with memories unbidden but welcomed. A rush of excitement, of surprise. Her back hitting the wall of the alley. Not knowing what would come next, but wanting that knowledge, needing it breathlessly.

And then she heard it. Heard the need in the music, as if it had always been there, and always been so perfect. It was the sound of getting lost in sensation. The anticipation built with

the crescendo—starting earlier, as Carpenini had kept insisting, and the notes rushing into one another. Each wanting their
turn, each needing to be savored.

She took her hands off the keys in wonder. It was all there.
Everything that Oliver had shown her, everything that Carpenini had been insisting go into the music, had just flown from
her heart straight onto the keys.

She wanted to laugh. She wanted to cheer. She settled for
clapping her hands, allowing herself applause at this small
triumph, only one thought going through her head:

She couldn't wait to play it tomorrow.

But not for Carpenini.

For Oliver.

∞

In the east parlor, Lady Forrester was in the process of receiving the tea tray from Signor Zinni, who had deigned to bring
it up himself. Whether this was a testament to his respect for
the formidable Lady Forrester or the elevated stature of her
guests, she didn't care. What she did care about was that as
soon as the tea tray was set down, they were rudely interrupted
again, this time by music coming from across the hall.

"Signor Zinni!" she cried. "I thought none but my family
and guests were permitted to the second floor. Who is that
playing?"

"*Si*, Signora, but I believe that is your daughter, Signorina
Bridget."

"Bridget?" Lady Forrester's annoyance at her errant daughter's not coming into visit with their guests warred with her
astonishment. *That* was Bridget? That complicated, passionate
piece came from her daughter? It had been so long since she
had heard her daughter play . . . she had always been very
good, but she did not recall her daughter being able to play
like that.

A small, impressed smile played across her features, but
she swallowed it and retained her composure. "Yes, of course,
how silly of me. I simply did not expect her home this early."
She took the teapot in hand and made to pour. "Would you
care for tea, Herr Klein?"

"Please. No sugar," was the man's stiff answer. If possible,
he had grown even stiffer in the past few moments.

"I'm sure Bridget will be very pleased to meet you—she is, after all, a great devotee of music," Lady Forrester said, smoothly pouring out the tea. "In fact, she is a student of the renowned Signor Carpenini, you know."

"Actually, I did know," came the syrupy, feminine voice of Signora Antonia Galetti, whose ingratiating demeanor was a marked contrast to Klein. Ever since they had met a few days ago in the Piazza San Marco, Signora Galetti had been so keen on getting to know the Forresters, and even more keen to have the renowned composer Gustav Klein meet them as well.

Signora Galetti leaned in conspiratorially, her eyes shining with glee. Or at least Lady Forrester thought it was glee, it was difficult to tell without her dreaded spectacles. "But the question, Signora Forrester, is do you know why?"

Sixteen

THE next morning, Bridget could hardly look to Oliver without a blush breaking across her cheek. It was really quite distracting. And she wasn't the only one who thought so.

"Signorina!" Carpenini's voice broke into her trailing thoughts. "If you are going to fly away during your morning drills, God help us during your lessons today!"

"I'm sorry, Signore," she said meekly, warm embarrassment spreading across her cheeks. She had been at Oliver's little house on the Rio di San Salvador for less than twenty minutes, having already changed into Oliver's shirt, taken her seat at the piano, and begun her morning drills. Something so easy, she should be able to perform by rote, but she could not help drifting into the memories of yesterday.

After her illicit time at the pianoforte, she had spent the rest of the afternoon in her room at the hotel, doing her best to avoid her mother and sister. She could not put on a subdued face just then; she had to sort out her feelings, her understanding of everything that had transpired.

Those puzzle pieces that had fallen into place painted a clearer picture now. And that picture took on the form of one Mr. Oliver Merrick—and it boasted significant detail, too.

When her nerves had failed her when first playing for

Carpenini, and she had run away in disgrace, it had been Oliver who had run after her, persuaded her to come back the next day, and thrown her a circus.

When Carpenini had assaulted the buttons and the back of her dress, it was Oliver who had made the whole thing all right by giving her the very shirt she was wearing.

It was Oliver who had encouraged her to write down her "Ode to Venice," while Carpenini had simply sniffed and told her (in so many words) to put such things away.

And when Bridget was in danger of falling into the abyss of practice, practice, practice . . . it was Oliver who—through either subversiveness or a true lack of sense of direction—made sure she experienced some part of the city, of the world outside herself.

And one could not forget that it had been Oliver who wrote the letter that brought her to Venice to begin with.

"Signorina, please!" Carpenini cried. "Pay attention! You have repeated the A-minor scale three times!"

Carpenini was a brilliant musician and instructor, true. But it was Oliver who made the entire experience bearable.

She couldn't help looking at him—not now, not after what had transpired yesterday. Her eyes wanted to dart away, wanted to stay on the keys, but there he was—always so tall, lounging on the worn velvet sofa, his broad shoulders stuffed into a jacket, his shirt open at the throat now, revealing a glimpse of tanned skin in the hollow there. When had he begun eschewing the cravat he always wore? Was it days ago? Weeks?

Although today he looked remarkably uncomfortable under her gaze. His posture was stiff; his eyes avoided hers. Except for those times when they refused to do so, and glanced up, seemingly just to check and see if she was still looking at him. When he did, and their eyes met, both of them darted their eyes away.

"Signorina," Carpenini sighed. "I am going to go outside for a breath of fresh air. When I come back, you had best be ready to work."

When the door to the music room fell shut, Bridget stopped playing immediately. "I'm sorry," she began, but was immediately cut off by Oliver.

"No, I'm sorry." He stood awkwardly. "It will be easier for

you to play without my presence—I can wait outside the door today."

"No!" she cried, rising. She moved around the pianoforte, anxious to stop him. "I don't want you to leave! It's my fault I'm so scattered."

"No, it's mine; I took advantages I should not have and it has made you uncomfortable in my presence."

"For heaven's sake, Oliver, I asked you to help me understand the music. And you did! There was no advantage being taken."

He seemed to relax a little bit then. "Oh. So . . . you feel you understand the music now?"

"Yes," she replied, coloring, unable to help a small smile. "Among other things." But then a thought—a *terrible* thought—came unbidden into her mind.

"You do not—that is, did I take advantage of you?"

A disbelieving smile spread across his features. "No." Then he tilted his head to the side, considering. "Although, I suppose if one looked at it in a certain light . . ."

"Oh, please tell me you don't regret it," Bridget cried, covering her face with her hands. "I would die of complete mortification."

A gentle hand brought hers down; a second tipped her face up to look at his. "I only regret that you felt you had to run away after." His voice was soft, serious. A balm. "I thought I had scared you off."

She shook her head gently. "I had to make sure your theory was correct."

"What theory?"

"That I mustn't think when playing. That I must let need come in unbidden."

His hand was resting on her cheek now, the other deftly twining her fingers around his.

"And did it?"

She nodded. "I can play it for you if you like."

"I would," he smiled.

It was as easy as that, Bridget thought, looking up into Oliver's face. Their friendship was evenly keeled once again, without the awkwardness that had punctuated their conversation. And yet, because of what she now saw when she looked at him—and she saw so much more!—she could not deny that something had subtly, irrevocably shifted. What had once been a pleasant constant in her life now took on an exciting new tone.

This—*he*—might just be important.

How on earth was she going to keep her eyes off him during her lesson?

No, she would be professional, she told herself as she straightened her shoulders. She turned to go back to the pianoforte, ready to play the troublesome run for him, when he pulled her to a stop by their still-entwined hands.

"Wait a moment," he said, a mischievous smile. "Before you begin, do you need a reminder?"

Anticipation quickened her pulse. Well, if he wanted to be cheeky, she could be too . . . No! Professional. Subdued.

"No, I'm fine." But she could not help smiling as she said it.

"Are you sure?" he answered back, a laugh escaping his lips. "I think perhaps you might . . ."

One quick tug and Bridget found herself caught up against his chest, wrapped in an embrace that set every one of her nerves alight. Her eyes fluttered shut as he leaned down and . . .

"We have a problem."

They broke apart quickly, children caught at mischief. Bridget looked around Oliver to find Carpenini rushing into the music room, shutting the door hastily behind him.

"Your mother is here." He turned his dark, angry eyes to Bridget.

"Here?" she cried. "Now?"

"Not far off. I saw her approaching in a gondola, with your sister and Antonia Galetti." Carpenini rushed around the room, putting papers into proper place, moving his chair far back from hers. "How does your mother know Antonia?"

Bridget shook her head, her mind reeling. Her mother, *here*. She'd shown absolutely no interest in the lessons since that first time, had in fact granted Bridget much freedom since then. Since being frightened away by scales and drills, and a non-English-speaking great-aunt, that is.

Oh no, Bridget thought. *The great-aunt.*

"Perhaps it has something to do with the fact that you barred her from the house ever since her last visit," Oliver was saying. "Antonia was always far more clever and spiteful than you gave her credit for."

"Oliver," Bridget said sharply, getting his attention. "What about the *chaperone*?"

Both Oliver and Carpenini came to a sudden halt.

"Send a note for Veronica?" Carpenini asked.

"Unless she arrives in the next two minutes, it is rather useless," Oliver shot back, rubbing his chin. His eyes darted to the screen in the corner of the room, the one with all the costumes from the circus, behind which Bridget changed.

"We can delay—" Carpenini was saying.

"No." Oliver turned to Bridget and ruthlessly began unbuttoning her overshirt.

"How bad is your mother's eyesight?" he asked, taking the shirt off her, and then spinning her around and beginning to button up her dress at the back, making her presentable again.

"My mother's eyesight?" Bridget asked, bewildered.

"She squints all the time, but leaves off her spectacles, am I right?" Oliver spun Bridget back around again. "Do you think, on sight alone, she could, say, tell you apart from your sister?"

Bridget practically snorted. "On sight alone, she could not tell me apart from the Pope."

"Good. Vincenzo, stall as best you can—just give me a few minutes!"

And with that, Oliver quickly grabbed something from behind the screen and swept out of the room, the pounding of his footsteps taking the stairs two at a time receding in the distance.

"Come, come, Signorina, sit!" Carpenini was saying, gesturing to the pianoforte. "Do not worry, Oliver will take care of everything."

Bridget moved to the pianoforte at his command, but her mind was reeling. What would Oliver take care of? What was her mother doing here? How would they explain the lack of a chaperone?

She took her seat and let her fingers rest on the keys. Carpenini motioned for her to play. She had no idea what to play, other than the piece that had been consuming them for weeks, and thus began on the No. 23, starting with the recently troublesome second movement.

Carpenini listened in silence, standing over her shoulder for a tense thirty seconds, listening for any sound beyond the music room.

She kept playing as she heard the approaching noise of a party of females determined to get past a terribly befuddled Frederico, and then, finally, succeeding.

"Just keep playing," Carpenini whispered in her ear, before he straightened and greeted the intruders.

"Ah! Signora Forrester!" he cried. "And Signora Galetti! What a pleasant surprise!"

"Likewise, Vincenzo," Signora Galetti purred, and Bridget barely kept her lip from curling in distaste. Antonia came forward with her hands out, and Carpenini took them in his and kissed them, as expected.

"Well, I am *not* pleasantly surprised!" Bridget's mother huffed. "I am quite the opposite."

"Mother, will this take very long?" came the voice of Amanda from behind her. "It's just that the Church of the Frari is open to visitors this morning and I was so hoping to see it in morning light."

"It will take only as long as Signor Carpenini desires to explain himself."

"Explain?" Carpenini asked, putting on a good show of astonishment. "What requires explanation?"

"First, you can explain to me where Mr. Merrick is—and more importantly, where his great-aunt is." Lady Forrester narrowed her eyes at him—or, rather, in the general direction of him. "Then you can explain to me how my daughter came to be involved in something so base as a musical competition!"

Carpenini seemed struck by the latter of the two charges. But by the way Antonia Galetti was coyly trying to hide her amusement, his astonishment quickly faded.

"Oliver—Mr. Merrick—is out. He pays his calls to friends and the church on Wednesday mornings, *si*, Signorina?"

Carpenini turned to Bridget, and she nodded quickly, playing along to his rhythm. Her fingers continued to flow over the keys, trying to keep from shaking.

"As for Auntie . . . ah! Here she is!" Carpenini cried, herding the women away from the door, allowing Bridget to see who had joined their party.

She almost lost her place in the music.

There, hunched and dressed in an ill-fitting gown, lines painted on his face, and a cap covering strands of hair floured to a dull gray, was Oliver. He murmured greetings in a reedy, high-pitched Italian and, with the use of a cane, hobbled over to the center of the room to greet Lady Forrester.

It was absolutely amazing. If Bridget had not been so close or her eyesight not nearly so sharp, she would have thought for all the world that it was an old woman who entered the room. His posture, his voice, were a perfect mimic of a frail, elderly woman—three things he most certainly was not!

Oliver was a better actor than he gave himself credit for.

"Oh, Signora . . . do you know, I do not know if I ever learned your surname," Lady Forrester mused, as she gave a correct albeit stiff curtsy. Behind Oliver—er, Auntie—came Molly, bearing a tea tray.

"Auntie's last name is Oliveri," Carpenini replied cheekily, earning a reproving stare from Bridget and the great-aunt, "and she was just downstairs helping with the morning repast. No one makes fresh bread like Auntie."

Bridget's mother seemed to consider this, eyeing Carpenini as he gently handed Oliver's "aunt" into a chair by the fire. Oliver pulled Carpenini down to his level and said something to him in Italian.

"*Si*, Aunt," Carpenini said, playing along. "She is playing much better today." And then Carpenini straightened up, truly listening to what Bridget was playing, as if hearing it for the first time. "My God! You played the run!" he cried, clapping his hands. "*Bellissima!* With a gut of fire!"

But while Bridget was blushing under Carpenini's praises, the situation in front of them was growing more precarious.

"Ah, Mother," Amanda was saying, her voice a low warning. "I do not think that this person—"

"Amanda!" Bridget cried suddenly, bringing her sister's attention away from whatever she was about to say. "Come turn pages for me, please."

There must have been something in her voice, in the directness of her plea and her gaze, that had Amanda crossing the room to the pianoforte. Once there, she wasted no time in speaking low to her sister.

"What is going on? For heaven's sake, Bridge, you're not even reading music."

"Please, please do not tell Mother anything. I promise you, nothing untoward is going on," Bridget whispered back, making certain to keep the music louder than their conversation.

"Nothing untoward!" Amanda whispered excitedly. "Bridge, unless my eyesight is going like Mother's, that woman is a man."

The existence of the woman—er, man—in question was at that moment being discussed not only by Bridget and Amanda, but by their mother and a more insidious personality.

"Well, I am quite pleased to find you here, Signora Oliveri!" Lady Forrester enunciated very clearly and loudly toward the great-aunt, before turning back to Carpenini and Signora Galetti.

"You must understand, I was very concerned when Antonia here told me that when she last visited you, she did not see Signora Oliveri anywhere."

"I do wonder if she puts in an appearance at all times," Antonia said, sowing mischief as ruthlessly as the snake did in the Garden of Eden.

"Good point, my dear, thank you," Lady Forrester replied. "Molly!"

The startled maid looked up from arranging the tea tray and seemed as if she wanted nothing more than to melt into the wall.

Lady Forrester pointed to the great-aunt, muttering and rocking by the fire. "Has that person been here, in this room, every day during my daughter's lessons?"

Bridget had been worried for one heart-stopping moment that Molly's fundamentalist upbringing would override her loyalty, and she would leap at the chance to extract herself from the tangled web they currently navigated on a daily basis. Luckily, her mother's choice of wording had allowed her an opportunity to tell the truth without incurring any divine retribution.

"Yes, ma'am," Molly said very clearly, looking Lady Forrester in the eye. Then, with a side-eyed glance to Bridget, she curtsied and made her escape.

"There, you see, Antonia, at least I am satisfied on that score. Although I do appreciate your concern." She patted the lady's hand. Although Bridget couldn't be sure, she thought she heard something like triumph in her mother's voice.

"But there is still the matter of the competition," Antonia was saying slyly. "I was socked when you said you did not know of it."

"I think you mean *shocked*, Antonia," Carpenini muttered.

"Whatever she meant, I was as well," Lady Forrester filled in. "What is this competition, and why do I hear of it only now?"

Carpenini seemed to hesitate for a moment, and from what Bridget could see, it was all Antonia could do not to jump up and crow about it. But then the answer came. From a very unlikely source.

"*E un onore*," came the small voice of the fictitious greataunt, from her place by the fire. "An honor."

Bridget felt Carpenini, Oliver, and yes, herself lance through with fear. After all, the most dangerous thing Oliver could do at that point would be to draw attention to himself. But there was such a sweetness in his old woman's voice. A persuasion. Who could deny him?—er, her?

"*Lei suona il pianoforte—bellissima*," he said, shaking a gnarled hand in Bridget's direction.

"Yes," Lady Forrester replied, her face taking on softer hues. "She does play beautifully," she said, understanding the sentiment without need of translation.

Bridget felt a warm lance of pride run through her. She knew her mother loved her and encouraged her playing, but at some point, she had stopped hearing the praise from her parent. Not that it wasn't said—rather that it was said so often, it seemed commonplace. It was difficult to trust as anything other than a mother's deafness in the face of love.

But for some reason, these few simple words, and her mother's expression, did not seem commonplace. Not this time. Had she truly improved so much?

Bridget kept her head down and concentrated on her playing as Carpenini picked up his cues.

"Yes—we did not wish to tell you, until we knew that she was a strong enough player—but it is truly an honor to be chosen. Signorina Bridget is my best student and will be playing for the Marchese di Garibaldi and everyone else in Venice who loves music." Then, with a nod to Antonia, and with that deep entrancing gaze Bridget knew so well, Carpenini turned his full mesmerizing power to Lady Forrester.

"And I believe she can win."

As Carpenini began explaining the details of the competition and glossing over the less savory parts, the small glow of pride Bridget had been nurturing from her mother's words multiplied tenfold with Carpenini's. Heavens, it was practically exploding from her fingertips, so hard it was to keep her joy contained. She wanted to dance about the room—she wanted to play for days! She wanted to shake the dust off Oliver's head and exclaim how much his imitation of an old lady impressed her—he was truly a great actor. Why, he could be on any stage he desired, from here to London, or perhaps Paris—

"Bridge," Amanda whispered. "I have no idea what is going on, but I do not like it."

But of course, the celebration would have to wait.

She turned to her sister, still sitting patiently beside her, still threatening everything with dark, frightened looks.

"Amanda, if you want to ever see the Frari, or any more of Venice, or Rome, or anywhere, you will please keep Mother in the dark. If she knew the truth, she would pack us up and take us home without missing a heartbeat," Bridget pleaded. "I will do anything. Anything."

Amanda seemed taken aback by this—and whether it was the fear of leaving Venice or the offer of anything she wanted, it seemed to have the effect needed . . . if not exactly the effect intended.

"Agreed." Amanda took on a mercenary gleam in her eye—not unlike their mother's when it came to bargaining. "But you have to tell me everything."

"Everything?" she replied weakly.

"I just want what I've always wanted." Amanda shrugged. "Information."

Seventeen

THE consequences from Lady Forrester's timely visit to her daughter's lessons were threefold. First, she did not, as feared, feel the need to swipe her precious daughters away from the twisting streets of Venice and the exposure of the Marchese's musical competition. Indeed, once she was convinced of the competition's prestige, her reaction was quite the opposite.

"*My* daughter! Playing for the Marchese! Oh, what an honor, what a coup!" Lady Forrester was overheard saying at every available opportunity, and to every possible person they met, whether traveling British or Venetians they met on the street. "Of course, she has always been quite talented, but she has blossomed underneath Signor Carpenini's instruction, simply blossomed!"

However, Lady Forrester's enthusiasm for her daughter's newfound honor also had the effect of making her far more interested in her daughter's lessons. She and Amanda began to "pop in" unexpectedly on the lessons so frequently that it was deemed prudent to rehire Veronica to take up her role as the doddering great-aunt again, happily darning things with crabbed hands by the fire. And Lady Forrester tended to swing by in the first and last hour of the lesson, thereby providing

Bridget an escort to whatever destination they were headed for next. Meaning that the chance for Oliver and Bridget to take a lingering walk went from slim to none.

Bridget found the restrictions on the freedoms she had just been beginning to enjoy more stifling than ever. She was no longer able to enjoy the sights from her morning gondola ride with only Molly and her own thoughts for company. No longer was she able to beg off from an evening spent in boring company—now her mother insisted that she attend and be feted. (Although, thankfully, she always managed to avoid playing for people, as Carpenini expressly forbade it, and her mother was the very best enforcer of Carpenini's rules.) And worst of all, no longer was she able to meander through alleys and enjoy the way the sun fell on cobblestones and the memories that flared to life at seeing them.

But when she mentioned her chafing frustrations to Oliver during one of the few rare moments they found alone, he gave her a long considering look before replying.

"It's probably for the best, you know," he said on a sigh, his hand unconsciously reaching out to play with one of her curls.

"Why?" she asked, unable to keep the longing from her voice.

"Gustav Klein," he answered simply.

Bridget could only sigh in agreement. For the third consequence of her mother's visit was that Carpenini's fears about Klein had been proved right.

After her mother and sister left that day—the former presumably to tell the world about her daughter and the latter hopefully to keep her secrets—Antonia Galetti hung back for a few moments, eager for a private word.

"You've done it now, Antonia," Carpenini growled, once the door closed on the two Forrester ladies.

"What have I done? I simply told a concerned mother what her daughter was involved with," Antonia replied, eyes wide with innocent astonishment.

"Well, your little plan failed—" Carpenini began, but his anger was interrupted by Oliver's rising from his great-aunt crouch and stretching to his full height.

"Vincenzo, Lady Forrester would have to know eventually; Antonia did no lasting damage," Oliver said kindly, smoothing the troubled waters. "If she wanted to, she could have revealed me at any moment."

"Oh, Signor Merrick, I would never do that. You amuse me too much." She shrugged simply. "Besides, if you had not kept me so in the dark, *barring* me from visiting"—she pouted, very prettily—"why, I did not even know for certain that Signorina Forrester was your chosen student . . . at least not until I heard her play the Number Twenty-three yesterday."

The weight of her stupidity fell on Bridget's shoulders like an anvil.

"Yesterday?" Carpenini asked. "When?"

"While I was visiting with her mother at the Hotel Cortile," Antonia replied. "And I was not the only one. Gustav Klein was with me."

Carpenini and Oliver both gaped in astonishment.

"Well, a lady cannot always be alone, Vincenzo," she replied pointedly. "Perhaps if you had been more available to me . . ." She shrugged her little shoulders, seemingly unaware of the rage vibrating off Carpenini.

"Antonia, you did not—"

"I did nothing, Vincenzo. The same as you." She stepped to him, squaring her shoulders. "But as a friend, allow me to give you a warning. Klein knows the girl has talent now. And he will stop at nothing to beat you in this competition."

Antonia turned to leave, pausing only at the door for a brief moment. "*Ciao*, Signores. Signorina, you play very beautifully, and I wish you the best of luck."

From that moment on, Klein had been at the forefront of their worries. And it was not without cause. As Bridget was a member of the British aristocracy, her family was invited to many engagements held by resident Englishmen that her out-of-favor instructor was not. (And now, thanks to her mother's enthusiasm, she had to attend them.) But as Gustav Klein was very much in favor, he had apparently taken to responding positively to such invitations. And he was often . . . looking. In Bridget's direction.

It was more than unnerving. It was disturbing.

However, when she mentioned Klein's attentions to Oliver, suddenly she had a reason to start enjoying these engagements. Because suddenly, Oliver began showing up at them, too.

"Oliver!" she cried, seeing him walk through the door one evening. "Er, I mean, Mr. Merrick," she corrected herself, hoping no one had overheard her slip.

They were at a card party in a palazzo on the Grand Canal—held by some son of some English Duke whose natural climate did not agree with him nearly as much as his adopted one. It was the third such engagement this week, and Bridget was bored of them. This was good entertainment for good people, and they all talked of the same things, be it in English or Italian, none of which really interested Bridget. Oh, now and again someone (invariably her mother) would bring up the competition, but Bridget would smile and change the subject as quickly as possible. The only reprieve was when there was a quartet, or some music for dancing.

But the sudden appearance of Oliver Merrick made the evening much more interesting.

"I thought you were banished from such amusements," she whispered, as he bowed over her hand.

"I am not banished—I have simply never shown an interest before. I am used to trading on my brother's name in Venice, not my father's. But in company such as this, it's his that opens the doors." Oliver smiled, a little grimly, a little uncomfortably. But he was there, and she knew, deep down, that he was there for her.

"It's your name, too, you know," she replied, a little pertly. "Did you never think you open your own doors?"

If Oliver had a reply to that, he did not have the chance to give it, for Lady Forrester and Amanda found them and greeted him happily. And Bridget had to remember to extract her hand from Oliver's.

"Mr. Merrick, how lovely to see you again." Lady Forrester looked approvingly at his evening dress and, with a gleam in her eye, toward Bridget. "Have you come to dance, Mr. Merrick? I hear the musicians are particularly good this evening."

As if taking his cue, Oliver bowed to Lady Forrester. "There could be no greater pleasure. Miss Forrester, would you do me the honor?"

They had been in company together for months, they had explored every corner of the city and had a glorious lesson in passion besides, but for some reason, the formal act of dancing with Oliver Merrick put the pink to Bridget's cheeks. He put his hand on her waist for the waltz, and all it did was remind her of another such embrace, it seemed like ages ago now, although it had really been little more than a fortnight. In the meantime, her life had been lessons, engagements, and a strange sense of needing.

And it had been so *long* since they had been able to be alone together . . .

"Well, this is pleasant," Oliver murmured in her ear as they spun through the turns. Bridget was by no means a bad dancer, but Oliver had a different sort of masculine grace that gave his steps confidence. "Finally having you alone to myself."

Bridget blushed—had he been reading her mind?

"Not quite alone, unfortunately," Bridget replied softly, her eyes falling on where her mother and sister were standing. While their mother chatted with their host (a rather florid-looking man who enjoyed the leisure of continental living), Amanda watched Bridget and Oliver closely, entirely suspicious.

"Ah yes, your sister," Oliver said, his gaze catching the line of Bridget's. "I am amazed at how you managed to keep her from revealing our small deception to your mother."

"It was not difficult. I simply had to give in to her blackmail and tell her everything."

"And did you?" Oliver's head whipped back around to hold Bridget's eyes.

She blushed through her smile. "Almost everything."

Amanda had been relentless, so Bridget told her everything she could: about how the competition was conceived, about Carpenini's need to win. About how it was simpler not to have any extra ears around during lessons, that even though she was not formally chaperoned, she was completely safe under Molly's, Frederico's, and Oliver's protection.

Especially Oliver's.

Although she kept certain things as vague as possible—she did not think she could easily explain the nature of their meandering walks home, or how having a circus in the music room could be considered completely proper and aboveboard—it felt amazingly *good* to be able to confide her feelings in someone. About how she was playing, improving, learning. About how she found the city brighter and more beautiful because of the way she was allowed to see it. About how she was actually composing little tunes—ones that might be halfway decent, if only in her own mind.

And Amanda reveled in her newfound role as confidant.

"Do not worry about Amanda," Bridget said, as Oliver took her expertly through another turn. "She swore up and down that she would not tell our mother anything."

"Then why is she looking at us like that?"

"Because she wishes she could dance but is not yet out, and is therefore not allowed." Bridget waved away any suspicions . . . although she had them, too. Amanda was frighteningly observant when it suited her purpose. Was it possible she could see straight through to Bridget's thoughts, the way Oliver seemed to be able to?

"Never mind Amanda; tell me, how was it that you were able to sneak away and not raise Carpenini's ire?"

"Oh, I doubt he even noticed I was gone. After your lessons, he has his head in his compositions and does not come out for food or company." Oliver frowned. "It's very good, in a way—it's been so long since he's composed anything; he seems to be back on track now."

"And what is he composing? A sonata? A symphony?" Bridget asked, trying to keep up conversation. Although she was having a harder time of it than she would have liked, because Oliver's thumb was making lazy circles on the back of her gown, leaving a trail of fire on her skin in its wake.

"He plays things, but I do not really hear them." Oliver bent low to her ear, and whispered in the most delicious tenor, "For once you leave the house, all I can think is, 'I wonder what Bridget is doing right now.'"

Heat spread out from his thumb at her back, diffusing through her body. She breathed in sharply. "So you came to find out."

His honey gaze caught hers, and she could feel his body tense under her arm, in the same manner, from the same cause as her own present distress. That fantastic want. That unbearable need.

Suddenly, a movement caught Oliver's eye and his gaze flickered up. Through a turn, she was able to see what garnered his attention. It was Klein, on the other side of the room. He seemed to be very much not watching them, with great attention.

"Is he still bothering you?" Oliver asked.

"He has yet to bother me at all—indeed, he has yet to speak to me," she said soothingly, trying to cage the anger she felt coming off Oliver. "He only stares."

"But it unnerves you."

"Yes, well, most anyone staring at me unnerves me," she replied, hoping to break the tension. But it seemed to have the opposite effect.

Oliver returned his gaze to her, cocking his head to one side, quizzical. "You still find it unnerving? Being watched?"

Bridget knew he was asking about her playing, about her fear of performing. "I . . . I don't know," she replied honestly. "I am much more comfortable, but I only play for you and Carpenini. And of course, Veronica, now. And Molly. And Frederico. I suppose I shouldn't be afraid any longer. Although I fear that I will be. Afraid, that is, when the time comes. Does that make sense?"

"Yes," Oliver replied grimly. Then, with a sudden burst of inspiration, he asked her, "Bridget, do you trust me?"

"Of course," she replied, albeit suspiciously.

"Then I have an idea to help you—but we must obtain your mother's cooperation for it." His smile widened to a mischievous grin as the musicians played the waltz's final notes. All the couples came apart, some more reluctantly than others, applauding the musicians and the dance.

Oliver bowed and offered Bridget his arm. "Shall we go ask her?"

They made their way to the side of the room, where Lady Forrester and Amanda stood with their host.

"Mr. Merrick, I take it you are acquainted with our host, Lord Pomfrey?" Lady Forrester made introductions.

"Of course," Lord Pomfrey blustered. "All of us expatriates know each other—although Mr. Merrick enjoys the company of the natives more than the most of us."

Bridget could feel Oliver bristle, and she kept a steady hand on his arm.

"Interesting to see you here, Merrick! I thought you had forsaken the good life," Pomfrey ribbed, obviously trying for jocular good humor.

But whatever Oliver was feeling, he kept it underneath his skin, because he simply smiled, and replied smoothly. "All of Venice is the good life, Pomfrey. Don't you agree?"

He did, and through his jocular good humor, Oliver began to converse with Pomfrey, finding they had many interests in common, including the opera.

"To that end, Lady Forrester"—Oliver turned to Bridget's mother—"I was wondering if you would permit me to escort you and your fair daughters to the opera tomorrow?"

The opera! Bridget's heart leaped with glee. Oh, it had been too long since she had been to the opera. But then she caught Oliver's eye and the gleam it held. Then, of all things, he winked at her!

Trust me, he mouthed silently.

While her mother was busy accepting and her sister was busy exclaiming at the idea of seeing the famed Fenice opera house, Bridget suddenly felt a pit in the bottom of her stomach.

Somehow, she felt certain the opera was not going to be the delight she was hoping.

Eighteen

For Oliver, stepping into La Fenice was like coming home.
Teatro la Fenice, which meant "Phoenix Theatre" in
English, was a palace to music and opera, a great, lofty space.
Row upon row of gilded boxes lined three sides of the interior.
Every surface that was not covered with ornate scrollwork or
baroque decoration was painted a sky blue, so that when lit
with chandelier and candelabra, it looked as close to heaven as
its architects could imagine. The fourth wall was of course the
stage, its sumptuous velvet curtains hiding a world of mad
preparation and moving parts all in the name of the spectacle
of a well-told story.

Yes, it was like coming home—but to a place where he no
longer lived, and hadn't in some time.

It was that backstage area that Oliver knew best, and to
which he headed now, with a very curious and confused
Bridget Forrester in tow.

And unfortunately, so was Amanda.

"Where are we going now? What do all these ropes do?"
Amanda asked, dodging women in costume and men carrying
props as they squeezed through the narrow passageways that
tunneled through the backstage area. Everyone was preparing

for the performance. And although she didn't know it yet, Bridget was among them.

He had met them at the hotel and escorted Lady Forrester and her two daughters via gondola. Much like London with their carriages, good families in Venice kept their own boats, their quality and design a testament to said family's goodness. Unfortunately, the only gondola of sufficient quality that Oliver could procure in such a short period of time was a borrowed one from Lord Pomfrey.

When Oliver and Pomfrey had begun talking about opera the previous evening, and when he had asked the Forrester ladies to attend, Pomfrey had practically given him the gondola.

At first he thought the man was known to his father and happy to do Oliver a good turn. But no—in fact, Pomfrey was an enthusiastic supporter of La Fenice, and had enjoyed Oliver's staging of an English play last season—*The Clandestine Marriage* by George Colman. Pomfrey, as he said, enjoyed a romance.

"And you need an impressive vehicle if you are to wage your own." Pomfrey had winked.

Perhaps Bridget was right, Oliver had thought. Perhaps he did open his own doors.

However, Lord Pomfrey's gondola was . . . distinctive. He did not like to have a covered boat, but rather preferred the whole world to see his extravagance and wealth on display in the lacquer of the boat and the distinctive red velvet cushions. But it was not to be helped.

However, the ostentatious gondola was forgotten as soon as La Fenice came into view.

He had felt the awe ripple from Bridget as they were guided up to the steps of the theatre, its stones lit gold by torches, its doors thrown open to a short, narrow street that led to the canal. He had glowed with pride when she stepped into the theatre for the first time, completely enthralled.

And he had been tickled by her shock when he made his announcement.

"If you'll permit me, Lady Forrester, I have arranged for Miss Forrester to meet the diva of tonight's opera, Veronica Franzetti, backstage, before the show begins," he said, as he handed Lady Forrester into her seat at the front of the box. "I know your daughter's nervousness about performing, and have persuaded Signora Franzetti to impart as much advice on the subject as she can."

"Oh, what a treat!" Lady Forrester cried, clapping her hands. "No wonder you wanted us to come to the opera so early—why, the common seats are not even filled yet."

Oliver nodded in acknowledgment. "Unfortunately, yes, Signora Franzetti will be too exhausted to meet with anyone after the performance. If you'll permit me, I shall escort Miss Forrester backstage."

"Of course, Mr. Merrick," Lady Forrester replied, waving them away.

Oliver nearly crowed with triumph as he took Bridget's hand. This was going exactly as planned.

"Can I go, too, Mother?" Amanda asked suddenly. "I would love to see the backstage of a theatre—the flies and the sets, and the way everything works."

Of course, Oliver thought. And it had been going so well.

"It may not be the place for someone as young as Miss Amanda . . ." he ventured, trying to be solicitous, but the steely look of shock on Lady Forrester's face told him he had miscalculated.

"If the backstage of a theatre is not the place for Amanda, it can in no way be the place for Bridget."

"I did not mean to imply—"

"I think what Mr. Merrick meant, Mother," Bridget interrupted, "is that it might be rather chaotic back there. People are, after all, attempting to do their work, and not expecting a curious child to wander through."

Amanda stared such daggers at Bridget, he would not have been surprised if Bridget had bruised from it. "But I will be very, very good," she said, her gaze never wavering from Bridget's face. "I will do anything you say, Bridget. Anything."

Those words seemed to have an effect on Bridget, and Oliver knew he had paid witness to some kind of sisterly blackmail, because Bridget discreetly touched his arm, letting him know to accede.

"Miss Amanda, we would be delighted for you to join us," Oliver said, holding out his other arm.

"Don't worry about me," Lady Forrester called after them. "I like nothing more than using my opera glasses to see who's who!"

"That's because it's the only time you can see anyone clearly," Bridget said under her breath, causing Amanda to chuckle.

"Oh, I cannot wait! I want to see where all the sets are stored, and the costumes!" Amanda said—and off they went.

But now he had both girls backstage, and Oliver had the rather complicated task of setting up one with her task, while keeping the other oblivious.

Luckily, he could rely on his old friends at the theatre for help.

"You are late!" Veronica cried, throwing open the door to her small dressing room, stopping herself when she saw three people there, not the expected two.

"What is going on?" she asked Oliver in Italian, keeping her smile up so as to not raise any suspicions in the unexpected second Miss Forrester.

"I need you to distract Miss Amanda for thirty seconds, and then I'll give you Bridget," Oliver replied, also in Italian. The way he moved his hands at the girls' names, he made it seem as if he were performing introductions. Veronica shot him a conspiratorial look before pushing her smile even wider and focusing her attention on Miss Amanda.

"Come in, young lady, come in! You must let me see you, and your lovely hair—and you are so tall! I will talk to you first!" Of course, she said all of this in Italian, so Amanda had little to no clue as to what was happening.

Amanda was barely able to get out a curtsy and the words, "A pleasure to meet you," not realizing that she had met—and ignored—Veronica several times before, in the guise of an old woman, before she was ruthlessly pulled into Veronica's dressing room and the door shut behind her.

"What is going on?" Bridget whispered as soon as the door was closed. "Why have you brought me backstage?"

"To give you a chance to find out if the stage is something you still need to fear," Oliver replied in a level whisper, then nodded over to the other side of the stage, where she could see a familiar pair of jugglers practicing their trade.

"You remember Carlos and his brother?" he asked. "Well, they are performing their routine tonight, as one of the acts before the opera begins properly. And you are going to accompany them."

Bridget's eyes whipped back to his. "Accompany them? Tonight?" she practically screeched.

"Yes—in about, oh, fifteen minutes."

"But . . . But . . ." she sputtered, unable to give voice to any of what must be a number of objections.

"Bridget, what did you say to me when I said you should play your own compositions?"

Bridget shook her head, unknowing.

"Well, I remember—you said that you would rather play naked in front of a thousand people. Now you won't be playing your own compositions—the Bach you practiced with the brothers before should do quite well. Nor will you be naked—in fact, you will all be in disguise."

"Disguise?"

"Yes, Veronica will help you get ready. The jugglers will be wearing carnival masks as well, so it looks consistent." Oliver smiled, taking Bridget's shoulders in his own. "I've worked the whole thing out. This way, your mother and anyone watching will not know it's you—but also, if you fail, no one knows it was you playing. If you succeed, no one knows it is you, either. You do not have to worry about people's expectations because they will not be able to have any expectations of Bridget Forrester. You will simply be another player."

"But . . . shouldn't the musicians be in the orchestra pit? Not on the stage?" She finally managed a weak protestation.

"In general, yes, but I have persuaded them to wheel a pianoforte on stage, just for you." Oliver smirked at her. Then, unable to resist the moment of being alone with her in the mad crush of people and props trying to arrange themselves for the coming performance, he leaned forward and kissed her on the forehead.

It was a mistake, as it was the most physical contact they had been permitted in weeks. All it did was make his body itch for more.

Immediately Oliver drew back, using distance as a means to allow him to regain control over himself. Bridget, meanwhile, was busy blushing to her roots, and she turned her attention to the thick velvet curtain that separated the gathering audience from the clamor of backstage.

"Ah . . . how many people are out there, do you think?"

"Tonight? Not a thousand. But a few hundred at the very least."

Before Bridget could blanch to a proper white at the prospect of playing for a few hundred people, the door to Veronica's dressing room flew open, and Amanda emerged, utterly bewildered, wearing a few pounds of paste jewelry, disoriented to the point of dizziness. Veronica chattered behind her in an unending stream of Italian.

"I have no idea what she's saying, so it's entirely possible I'm going on the stage tonight as a Grecian goddess," Amanda said in a giggly rush. "Bridget, what are you two doing out here? I thought you were here to get advice on performing."

"*Si!* Signorina Bridget! Advice!" Veronica nodded, grabbing Bridget by the hand and taking her into the dressing room.

Amanda turned and tried to elbow her way back into the room, as all good sixteen-year-olds would. "Tell me, Signora, do you think—"

"Miss Amanda, if you would permit me, I would introduce you to the manager of the house—he can tell you all about, er, how the pulley systems work," Oliver interrupted. "Signora Franzetti would prefer to give your sister her advice in private, I am sure. She guards her professional secrets, you know."

"Ohhhhh," Amanda said, clearly not wanting to disturb the diva. "Of course. And I would love to meet with the house manager! Do you think he will let me up to that walkway, all the way up there?" Amanda pointed to the long, narrow footway high above them.

Oliver steered her away, with murmurings of dissuasion from going anywhere near any ladders leading up. But as he did, Bridget called him back for one last moment.

"Oliver, do me a great favor?" she asked, as he stepped toward her.

"Anything."

She exhaled a long slow sigh. "Make certain Carlos knows to catch on the downbeat."

❧

Bridget was too much in a whirlwind to feel anything about her upcoming performance. And that whirlwind's name was Veronica.

"You will be boy, *si*?" Veronica was saying as she stripped Bridget out of her beautiful jade green silk evening gown and threw it over the back of a chair. There in her chemise and stockings, she had an adolescent boy's costume from the last century—richly embroidered brocade, three-quarter-length coat and knee breeches, shoes with heels and buckles—shoved into her arms.

"Go!" Veronica waved her hands, jolting Bridget into movement. "Put on!"

Apparently there was no screen for privacy here—indeed, there was barely space enough to accommodate Veronica, let alone her—so Bridget had little choice but to get dressed in front of the actress.

She pulled the breeches on over her stockings and hopped into the unfamiliar—and alarmingly tight—garments. Stuffing her chemise into the breeches, Bridget caught sight of herself in Veronica's looking glass. "Oh heavens, you can see everything!" She turned in the mirror. Her calves, her thighs—her rear end!—all of those lines were perfectly visible in the boy's knee breeches.

"*Si*, but no one see you—they see Carlos and his brother Dominic." Veronica breezed away her objections and approached her, a long strip of cloth in hand.

"What is that?" Bridget asked. "A cravat?"

Cravat was apparently not a word in Veronica's limited English vocabulary, because she just tilted her head to the side and said, "Is cloth. Now, put arms up."

Bridget looked askance but did as she was told, and Veronica wound the cloth around Bridget's chest, pulling it tighter, binding her breasts down. "Ow!" she cried.

"You must be boy, Signorina!"

Understanding dawned on Bridget, and she submitted herself quietly after that. Once her chest was bound down to an unappealing, and constricting, flatness, Veronica handed Bridget the three-quarter-length coat and motioned for her to put it on. Apparently the costume did not have a shirtwaist to go under it, but as the collar of the shirt was high and the coat sleeves were edged in lace, no one would know the difference from the stage. Veronica reached over to her little table, where a powdered wig from the last century, with side curls and a little bow at the back, rested.

"But my hairstyle!" Bridget protested. It would be impossible to get back to its original style. This was all wrong. She could not go out there with her hair as it was, set into an intricate updo with braids and side curls that had taken Molly nearly an hour to perfect. She would be recognized, no matter what Oliver said . . . she would be recognized and she would fail, and there were hundreds of people out there, and she was meant to accompany Carlos and Dominic in a routine with a piece she had not practiced with any regularity in the past months, all of her time taken up with the No. 23, and—

Apparently, Veronica could see some of Bridget's mounting hysteria finally catching up with her, because she leaned forward and gripped Bridget's hand, hard. So hard that the pain distracted her from her train of thought.

"We will fix the hair after—I promise," Veronica said clearly, calmly, holding Bridget's gaze in hers. "Now, turn."

Bridget did as she was bid and let Veronica place the wig on her head, stuffing up her coiffure underneath it.

"I used to fix hair, you know. When I was in chorus. It will be fine," Veronica was saying. "That was where Signor Oliver spot me. I was in chorus. Then I sing for him, and he say, 'Bruno! Veronica should have role!' Now, I am diva." Veronica moved around to face Bridget again. "I do anything for Signor Oliver for that. Dress you as boy, play Auntie . . . and he do anything for you."

"I don't know about that," Bridget mused, uncertain. "Besides, you are the one doing me the favor. I'm not imposing, am I? On your preparation for tonight?" Veronica gave her a quizzical look, and Bridget knew she had spoken too quickly. She repeated the question in the best broken Italian she could manage.

Veronica snorted in reply. "No—it is Herr Klein's opera. Five hours of music, much singing for tenor and baritone, but soprano? Not so much." She turned Bridget around and began to adjust the wig from the front. "I am Calypso, lead, and I have one aria in act three. One!" Then her eyes met Bridget's, slyly. "And why you not so sure—about Signor Oliver? I am very sure for you."

"Herr Klein?" Bridget asked, fear lancing through her. "Is he here?"

"No—the composer does not come to every performance"—Veronica shook her head—"and you did not answer, Signorina."

"Oh . . ." Bridget replied, turning redder than she liked. "I know that he *likes* me . . . but I don't know *how* he likes me." Veronica gave her that uncomprehending look again, so Bridget tried a different tack. "He likes me as a person, but he . . . we hadn't had the opportunity to be alone in weeks and when the chance came he kissed me on the forehead, like my father would."

Veronica's eyebrow went up, muttering something under her breath in Italian—the only words of which Bridget managed to catch were *men* and *idiot*.

"Signorina, you come to me for advice, so I will give to you. Oliver, he likes you. Very much. More than he knows. But if he treat you as child? You must make him see you as woman."

And with that, Veronica took a *bauta* carnival mask, with the stern male face, and slipped it over her head. Bridget could see well enough out of the eyeholes, so she could see Veronica's smile as she said, "But that is for later. Now you must play."

"And so the entire Trojan horse is only three pieces of thin board?" Amanda was saying from the wings of the stage, where she had cornered Bruno, the theatre's manager, who was being incredibly patient with the youthful curiosity in front of him and confined his annoyed comments to Italian, so only Oliver could hear them when he played translator for all of Amanda's unending questions. He was about to distract Amanda to see if she was ready to return to her seat, when he heard it. Laughter from the audience. And underneath it, a pianoforte.

It was Bach. It was Bridget.

She was playing, and playing well, judging by the way the crowd laughed and cheered at the right times with the routine's bigger moments. Most people did not pay all that much attention to the opening acts—indeed, most of fashionable Venice would not even have arrived yet—but the crowd that was there was enjoying the performance.

Oliver wandered away from Amanda and Bruno, edging his way to the front of the wings, where he could see.

She was there. Not in the spotlight, like Carlos and Dominic, but there all the same. On the stage, and playing Bach with verve and grace. And in front of a few hundred people besides.

Something curious shot through Oliver as he watched her in that decidedly interesting costume, her back to him, as her arms worked the length of the keys, her head occasionally coming up to make sure the similarly masked and costumed jugglers were on beat with her.

She was doing it, she had no fear, and he was so proud. But some little part of him was bereft at the idea that she would not need his encouragement, his lessons for much longer.

But that was not what mattered in that moment. So Oliver let himself watch, and let her playing wash over him, joining with the crowd in enjoying the show.

Returning the ladies to their seats as the curtain was coming up on the first act of Klein's operatic *Odyssey* was not as difficult as expected. In fact, Oliver had managed to wrangle Amanda and get her back to her seat while Bridget was still changing back from her boy costume to herself. Once Amanda had exhausted the stage manager Bruno with her questions, she didn't have much to do backstage anyway. Although, she seemed oddly satisfied to simply hang about and occupy Oliver.

"So . . ." she had begun, "what is taking my sister so long?"

"I do not pretend to know the performing secrets of Veronica Franzetti, or how long it takes to impart them," Oliver ventured, as he squeezed back against the narrow hallway to allow a retinue of ballet dancers through so they could change into costume. Bridget had darted back into Veronica's dressing room after the jugglers took their bows and had not yet emerged. Luckily Amanda's attention had been drawn to something Oliver had pointed to in the other direction at that moment. "If you like I can escort you back to your seat and come back for your sister."

"Well, that would defeat the purpose," Amanda replied pertly.

"What purpose?" he asked.

"Why, playing chaperone to you two." She cocked her head to one side and, for a moment, looked uncannily like her shorter, more freckled sister. "You do need a chaperone, don't you? She has not said as such, but I have a feeling she's been leaving things out of our conversations. Such as how she calls you Oliver."

Damn, but were all the Forrester girls so observant?

Before Oliver could appreciate his opponent's canniness, he was knocked back against the wall of the narrow corridor again; this time Amanda was squeezed up against her own wall, too. All to accommodate a passing shop facade that had to be moved to the other side of the stage before the curtain went up.

And Oliver had seen his opportunity.

"Miss Amanda, this really will not do. We cannot simply linger in this busy thoroughfare; I insist on taking you back to your seat."

Pert Amanda fell away, leaving sixteen-year-old Amanda, who knew little how to argue with such a command. Therefore he managed to get her back to her mother in her box before having to answer any of the child's eerily on-target probes.

When he returned to Veronica's door, he let himself in after a perfunctory knock. There, he found Bridget having pins stuffed into her hair by a hasty Veronica.

"Come, we haven't much time," he said, holding out his hand to her. "The curtain is about to go up and your mother will grow suspicious."

"What about my sister?" she asked.

"She is already suspicious," Oliver replied drolly. "But she is back in her seat."

"*Uno momento*," Veronica said, putting a final pin in Bridget's dark curls.

Bridget quickly examined the diva's work in the mirror. "It looks nothing like it did," she murmured, "but at least it is respectable."

"Bridget, if your mother could not tell me apart from Veronica in an old woman's costume, then she will likely not notice your hair," Oliver remarked, impatient now. "Come, we must go back."

"*Grazie*, for everything," Bridget said, embracing Veronica. For her part, Veronica pulled back and smiled enigmatically at Bridget.

"Do not forget advice," she replied. Then Oliver could take no more waiting and pulled Bridget out the door.

He had moved quickly out of necessity, but part of him wanted to linger for just a bit, knowing that this was as alone with Bridget as he was likely to get for the rest of the evening.

Then again, he was about to be surprised by her for a second time that night.

"You played very well," he whispered to her as they darted through the backstage corridors. "I was quite proud of you. You were in no way nervous?"

"My heart is still pounding from the experience. I confess, I did not have much time to be nervous," Bridget replied on a blush. "But I think that was the idea behind the exercise."

"Maybe," Oliver replied with a smile. "Perhaps I simply thought having a performance under your belt would be worth your while."

"Or perhaps you wanted to see me in breeches and stockings?" she asked, her tone shifting into something new. It was frank, alluring. And it piqued Oliver's interest.

"Actually, I had no idea what costume Veronica had picked for you. You could have been in a druid shroud, for all I knew about it." He turned to her. They had crossed the threshold from the backstage to the front of the house, where fashionable people milled in the ornate entryway, seeing and being seen before retiring to their boxes for the performance. Oliver slowed his pace and released Bridget's hand, forcing himself to a more decorous distance. His voice, however, was everything that was intimate. "It was a happy benefit, however, to find you otherwise attired."

"I'm so pleased," Bridget replied, her gaze unwavering, knowing. "You do know how to arrange a surprise for a lady, don't you?"

"I suppose . . ." he replied, careful to keep his gaze straight ahead as they walked genteelly toward their box for the evening.

"I am afraid I must beg one more arrangement of you." She turned to him, serious.

"Of course," he replied automatically, his brow coming down.

"You will be returning us to the hotel after the performance tonight, correct?" she asked, a little quaver in her voice betraying the nerves behind the boldness.

"Yes . . ."

"I think that after, say, a half hour, you and your gondola should return to the hotel."

They paused at the door of their box, Oliver unable to tear his eyes from Bridget's.

"I should?" he asked, his voice a rumble of anticipation.

"Yes." She stood on tiptoe, to let her lips reach his ear. "I think you would find it worth your while."

Nineteen

To say that Oliver Merrick spent the rest of the evening counting the minutes until that precious hour at which Bridget had commanded his presence at the Hotel Cortile would be an understatement. To say that he was merely eager was blatantly untrue.

It could have started raining frogs, and he still would have shown.

He lay in wait for that interminable half hour, ordering his gondolier (in truth, a fairly unhappy Frederico, but, as Pomfrey's gondolier was needed by the man himself, the best available option) to take a circuitous route through the canals until the appointed time.

"If I may be so bold, sir," Frederico drawled at him in his native tongue, "you may wish to woo the lady with a little more than a boat ride."

"Is this a wooing event?" Oliver replied in the same language, his nerves on edge. "She's the one who set this rendezvous. After all, she could wish to talk about the music, the opera . . . the weather."

"Still—a few flowers, a glass of champagne . . . could turn a conversation about weather to something else."

"True," Oliver mused, his focus fracturing by the minute in

anticipation of what was to come. "But where would one find flowers and champagne this time of night?"

In this, his dour manservant surprised him by steering the gondola back to La Fenice, where women hawking floral bouquets and long-stemmed blooms were gathering up the remainder of their goods and their meager profits after a long night.

Oliver purchased a dozen long-stemmed roses, bright red and fragrant. However, by that point, there was little time left for finding champagne, as they were due back at the hotel.

And lucky that they returned on time, because there, waiting in the shadow of the hotel's awning, was a cloaked figure that came directly up to the gondola before they even came to a stop.

She jumped into the little boat, her movements sure and purposeful. Once she was seated next to Oliver, she waved to Frederico, telling him to push off.

And once they were far enough away from the torchlight of the hotel, Bridget threw back her cloak's hood and greeted him with smiling eyes.

"Hello," she said brazenly.

"Hello," he replied, struck dumb. Under the cloak, she was wearing the same thing she had been wearing all evening— a pale jade dress that made her eyes sparkle like dew-covered moss—and her hair was still arranged in the same fashion that Veronica had managed to cobble together (and one that her mother *had* noticed as different in the box, looking askance at her daughter and asking, "Did Molly try something different with your hair tonight?" to which Bridget paused before shrugging elegantly). And yet, even though she had not changed her attire, she had somehow transformed in appearance. Her eyes sparkled in the moonlight, her cheeks a high flush of excitement. He was captivated by the sight of her. By the nearness of her.

By the fact that he had her all to himself.

No, there would be no talk of the weather tonight.

"Hello," drawled Frederico from behind them, breaking into the silent reverie of the two lovers staring at each other.

Bridget blushed dutifully and met Oliver's eyes—and they immediately both burst into giggles, like children caught at games.

"Er, um . . . so," Oliver said, trying to approach their situation with some gravity. "You should probably keep that up," he said, indicating the hood of her cloak. "I should hate for anyone to spot you."

"It's the small hours of the morning," Bridget countered. "Who is going to spot me?"

"No one you wish to have know that you are out here with me." And with that, he leaned forward, took the soft, heavy velvet hood of the cloak, and brought it up around her face, shading her in darkness. This also had the side effect of bringing his hands to her shoulders—it took very little effort to lean her body into his, to put her lips so close to his . . .

"Are those for me?"

Oliver looked to where Bridget's eyes had fallen. "Oh!" he exclaimed, shaking himself out of his reverie. Damn, but she had him acting like a green schoolboy. "Yes, of course."

He reached behind him and—while avoiding the disparaging look Frederico was no doubt shooting at him—took the roses in hand, pulling one out of the bunch and presenting it to her.

"Would it be an embarrassing admission to tell you no one has ever given me flowers before?" she whispered, taking in the rose's scent.

"Embarrassing? No." Oliver shook his head. "Surprising— very much so."

"Yes, well"—she blushed—"I told you, my first season lacked a certain amount of sparkle necessary to attract the attention of men who send flowers."

"I can only be honored to be the first, then."

Frederico smothered a cough at that moment. Oliver couldn't be sure, but his manservant's hacking sounded suspiciously like the phrase *my idea*. Luckily, either Bridget did not hear the same hidden message or she was happy to ignore it, because she took the rest of the flowers from his hands, put them together with the first, and placed them on her lap. She looked over them reverently as she spoke.

"I feel this is the time in my life for many firsts," she said quietly, before meeting his eyes from beneath her lashes.

A streak of lust lanced right through him, causing his body to tense imperceptibly. What other "firsts" did Miss Bridget Forrester have in mind for that evening?

"I don't suppose I am your first, as well?" she asked.

The tenor of Oliver's racing thoughts before her inquiry had him rocketing back and forth between the wealth of possible "firsts" with Bridget Forrester and the logistics of achieving them in a gondola with the morose Frederico paying witness. Thus, her innocent question brought him sharply back down to earth, making him jump so much in his seat that the gondola wobbled beneath them.

"My first?" he asked, trying to hide the crack in his voice. "No—why on earth would you think that?"

"I . . . I didn't," she replied, blinking in astonishment. "I was just being silly—I assume you've bought flowers for hundreds of ladies."

"Oh," he sighed, relaxing visibly, and then he could not help a laugh. "You meant buying flowers."

"Of course—what else could I mean?"

Oliver decided to ignore that and answer her first question instead.

"Sadly, you are not the first lady for whom I have bought flowers, it is true. The theatre world seems to support the flower markets single-handedly at times, and one way to keep things running smoothly is to have flowers ready at a prima donna's door." He reached out and took one of her hands, brought it to his lips. "But these could very well be the first flowers I've purchased that meant so much."

Something must have caught in Frederico's throat, because his infernal hacking began again, this time with enough lack of subtlety that the gondola stopped moving and drifted over to one side of the canal.

"Have a care, Frederico," Oliver chided, turning to his erstwhile gondolier. "We almost hit that house!"

"So sorry, sir," Frederico replied stiffly, returning both of his hands to the long oar he used to steer and propel.

Oliver returned his attention to the lady in front of him—hooded though she might be, he could still see the light of mirth in her eyes, but now there was something else. A nervous uncertainty. She had surprised him by asking—nay, demanding—this assignation. And suddenly, the light of understanding struck. She had surprised him even more with the prepossession she had displayed up until now. But underneath that—she was completely out of her element. It was as if she had thought out a plan of attack, of getting him alone, he realized. But beyond that—she had no idea what she was doing.

And neither did he. Here he was, acting as nervous as an adolescent, completely enraptured and eager, and having no clue what to do. And he could only find relief in the fact that she was nervous, too. It put them in the same boat. So to speak.

And it gave him the confidence to turn the tables.

"You are smiling at me, sir," Bridget said, biting her lip, her glance unconsciously ending up on his lips.

"That I am, miss," he replied.

They were in danger of simply smiling and staring into each other's faces the whole of the evening. Unless, of course, one of them made the first move.

Oliver decided it should be him.

"Bridget, I am going to kiss you now. Just to get it out of the way," he said, his voice a low grumble.

"You . . . you are?" she stuttered. Her freckles stood out against the pallor of her face—even under the hood.

He did not answer her; he did not have to. All he had to do was slip his hand around her back—which was halfway in place already—and press her to him. He held her near, his lips so close to her luscious, full mouth. Her eyes were wide with wonder, her body tensed to flight, until the moment that a decision was made and she let herself relax in his arms, her eyelids fluttering closed, her mouth parting of its own accord.

Then, and only then, did he plunder. Took what he wanted, what he had been aching to take. This was not the gentle persuasion he had begun in the cobblestoned alley. He did not force himself to keep his hands at his sides until the time was right, nor did he give her time to adjust to his intensity. No, once he had seen her decision made, he wanted her to be pressed against him, to know the full force of his feelings. He wanted to frighten her with it, to entice her. To leave her head spinning.

When he broke the short kiss, they were both reeling, both breathing heavily. He found her eyes in the darkness of her hooded cloak, wild and unfocused. Finally, they blinked their way back into the present.

"My goodness," she breathed.

"Indeed," he replied, bringing his hand up to caress her cheek, resting his forehead against hers.

"I . . . I didn't think you wanted to kiss me again."

"Are you mad?" His voice was strained with laughter. "It's all I had been thinking of for a fortnight."

"I, too. But then you kissed me on the *forehead* tonight—"

He could not suppress his guffaw then. And proceeded to kiss her on the forehead once again.

"You little fool. Don't you know that if I did anything other than kiss your forehead, I would have ended up ravaging you on the floor of the hall? And if nothing else, it would have shocked the hell out of your sister."

She laughed at that, a soft exhale against his skin.

"Well, now that's out of the way," he began, and she laughed again. "What would you like to do?"

"I . . . I do not know," she replied, biting her lip again. "I'm afraid I had not actually planned that far ahead. We are outside the realm of my experience."

He kept his hand on her cheek, secretly thrilled that he had read her correctly. But also, unaccountably, he was made more nervous by the admission. For with it, she had placed herself firmly in his hands.

Confirming that thought, the next words out of her mouth were, "What would you like to do?"

What would he *like* to do? A hell of a lot more than he could in an open gondola. The silly thing did not even have the decency to have a covered box, lending them some privacy from prying eyes. Add to that the visibly distinctive red cushions, and they were not nearly as private as one would like. That was the last time he borrowed a gondola from the flamboyant Lord Pomfrey. Especially if he could not also borrow a decent gondolier.

But the velvet cushions were comfortable, and the openness of the gondola provided them with a view of the city surrounding them and the night sky above them. And with that in mind, Oliver knew precisely what he wanted to do.

"I would like to wander with you," he answered simply.

"Wander?"

"We have been denied a good wander through the city for the past fortnight. And I have missed it."

Her face grew into a tremulous smile. "As have I."

"Then let us wander—unless, of course, you are afraid you will be missed soon."

Bridget snorted. "Amanda, if she wakes up, is firmly on my side these days. And my mother sleeps like the dead. Rousing her at this time of night would take a fife and drum corps."

The corner of his mouth shot up. "Your mother is not only blind as a bat, but sleeps like a corpse. How terribly . . . useful."

"I admit, I have recently found it so."

"It's settled then—Frederico!" he called back to the amateur gondolier. "We should like to wander."

If Frederico had anything to say—or cough—about their ambiguous route, he kept it to himself and propelled them out from Rio di San Marina into the Grand Canal.

It felt right to put his arm around Bridget, so he did. It felt right to lean back in the seat, nestling her against his side and letting her cloak cover them both like a blanket, so he did. And it felt right to look up at the starry sky and let the peace of the night envelop them.

There were other boats on the water, of course—other couples wrapped around each other in illicit fashion, other solitary people on their way home after a long evening, but they paid no attention to them—and they, in turn, paid no attention to Oliver and Bridget. At least as far as Oliver could tell.

They wandered. Through quiet canals dotted with stars. And slowly, those things that they had not been able to say to each other, those things that had drawn them close, began to spill out of them.

"So . . ." he began.

"So . . ." she replied.

"How was your evening?" Honestly, with the way her green eyes were sparkling at him, it was the only thing he could think of.

"Enlightening," she said, after a moment.

"Really? How so?" He tilted his head to the side. "Besides discovering how you looked in breeches, that is."

She blushed. "Besides that. I've never spent any time backstage at a theatre. I know now why you love it."

"It's a very lively place," he conceded.

"And you come alive there," she replied.

"I do?"

"You do. I do not think I truly understood your love of the world of the theatre, of La Fenice, until I saw you moving through the halls and ropes and tight spaces with people who all have the same ambition—to tell a good story." She paused for a moment. "It has such an air of movement. The entire atmosphere is charged, making the hairs on my arms stand on end—one can feel it, like one can feel the lightning before you see it strike."

Oliver looked down at her, her small dark head resting on his chest. "You describe it exactly. Except that working at La Fenice is no longer my ambition. It has not been in some time."

"No?" she asked, confused.

"Can I . . . May I show you something?" he asked, hesitation in his voice. Her head came up, turned to meet his eyes.

"Of course."

"Frederico." He spoke as he turned, to find his manservant's eyes resolutely on the water in front of him. "Take us to the Teatro Michelina!"

Bridget's brow creased in confusion, so as Frederico steered sharply to his left, down a different canal, Oliver endeavored to explain.

"When I left La Fenice, it was to come home to England—although that did not happen as planned, as you know. But when they—indeed, no house in Venice—could take me on in their companies, I decided to follow a long-held ambition . . . and create my own." A strange sense of excitement, of nervous anticipation, began to churn through him, as it always did when he spoke of his teatro.

"While I began as a performer, I know well that I do not have what it takes to make a life out of performing. Those who don't have enough talent have to have naked ambition to carve out a life there. I may have had some talent, but I had only enough to recognize those who had greater talent. Like Carpenini, and like you."

"Like Veronica," Bridget interjected.

Oliver blinked at her in surprise, then smiled. "Is that what she told you? What else did you girls talk about while she transformed you into a boy?"

"Oh, that is for me to know. And you are getting off the subject."

"Right—well . . ." Oliver ran a hand through his hair as he spoke. "It was pointed out to me that I would be well served if I put this particular talent to good use."

Frederico steered them up a smaller, side canal and finally backstroked to counter them to a stop. Oliver pointed in the direction of one of the darkened buildings. It was a tall, flat structure, with a few high windows and a landing that led to barricaded, arched doorways. They pulled up to the moorings and let Frederico hold them there.

"This is my theatre, the Teatro Michelina," Oliver said. "I purchased it."

"You have your own theatre," Bridget intoned. "You want to be an impresario?"

"Well, as Carpenini pointed out, when I did not go back to La Fenice, I did not have a place to stage his composition. So I acquired one. You should see the inside—it is a true beauty. Or at least it will be, once all the dust and decay is cleared away. It is a warehouse now, but it still has the bones of a theatre," he replied, his voice lighting with excitement. "It has been closed since just after the fall of the republic, some twenty years ago. It's a smaller venue, more intimate—it could seat five hundred souls, all come to listen to music, and not distract themselves with the seeing and being seen of the larger opera houses. This would be for true musicians."

"Can I?" she asked. "See the inside, that is."

Oliver frowned for a moment, but then said, "I don't see why not."

He carefully stood and disembarked. He wobbled a bit, but Frederico caught a post at the last moment, keeping Oliver from splashing into the water. Then he took Bridget's hand and helped her out. Hand in hand, they walked up to the dusty, dark teatro, where Oliver lifted the heavy wood beam barring the door and carefully poked his head inside.

"I'll just wait here, shall I?" Frederico called after them— he could not be bothered to hide his bored disdain. Which was fine, as Oliver could not be bothered overly much to care.

Once he ascertained everything was all right, Bridget followed him inside.

The dark space was piled high with crates. And the parts

that were not piled high with crates were piled high with dust. But the stage at the far end was uncovered, lit by moonlight from high windows that lined the backstage.

Oliver pulled Bridget up onto the stage. He held out his hand, as if painting on the air, seeing in his mind's eye what could be, overlaying what was there. "Now you have to use your imagination, but over there, the wall behind those crates will be painted a cerulean blue, with white cornices and a marble-walled entryway. Four rows of boxes, curving around, like a horseshoe. Do you see how close the performers would be to their audience? And this stage will be polished, the curtain—well, it will have to be beaten of dust by a brigade of washerwomen. Then the whole place will be lit by brass lamps, so not a moment is missed."

"Yes," she replied dreamily, her voice echoing in the theatre. "I can see it all. But how did you purchase it?"

"Contrary to how I live, I do have some money." He shrugged, answering as honestly as he could. "My father is very generous; he pays me well to stay away. I could live much higher than I do, but between the allowance that I never spend and the funds I earned at La Fenice . . ."

Of course, saving funds had become far more difficult when he took on Vincenzo as a destitute roommate—money that would have gone into savings seemed to flow elsewhere. Hence he did not quite have the funds for the renovation he saw in his head. But once the Marchese took Vincenzo back . . . perhaps, just perhaps, the Marchese would be interested in investing in Oliver's theatre. Perhaps.

"Vincenzo says that he'll give me his next work to stage—if he ever gets through writing it. And it seems as if—thanks to working with you daily—he's actually making some progress on it."

She blushed dutifully. "I don't know if it's my doing."

"I disagree. Work begets work. Music begets music. And your hard work has influenced him more than you realize."

Bridget blushed again, and fidgeted in his embrace.

"Are you embarrassed?" he asked suddenly. "By what? Praise?"

"No," she cried. "Well, it just seems so strange, the idea that I could have influence over anyone."

"You have great influence on the lives that you touch. And

you should not be so surprised by praise. You are going to receive a lot of it in your life. Much like flowers." He nodded toward the dark, closed theatre. "Especially when I put you on this stage."

But she shook her head adamantly. "No, you will not."

"Of course I will—once the competition is over, you will be in great demand—"

"But it is a demand I will decline," she replied calmly, nimbly negotiating her way down the steps to the main floor. "I do not desire the stage."

He stood up straight, confused. "You do not? If this is about your stage fright—"

"It is not." She smiled up at him, a bright spot in the dark maze of boxes and dust. "Believe it or not. I may not like to exhibit, nor do I desire the life of a performer."

"Then what do you want?" he asked gently.

"The same things other young ladies of my station want. A husband and children, running up and down stairs willy-nilly. A home of my own."

"Then why agree to the competition?"

"A dozen reasons," she replied, her voice becoming thicker with emotion. "I may want the traditional things in life, but I want this one thing first. To be able to look back and say to my children that I had, at one point, done something brave. That I wasn't just one forgotten debutante in a season of hundreds. That I might have been something special."

"You are special, Bridget," Oliver said, following her down the stairs, finding her in the mess of boxes, and taking her face in his hands. "Never let anyone tell you otherwise."

She leaned her cheek into his hand, accepting the devotion he gave, the adoration.

And suddenly, Oliver didn't care that they were in a dusty theatre-cum-warehouse in the middle of the night. He did not care that Frederico was outside, waiting for them. He only cared about the look in her dewy green eyes, and that she was there, in his arms.

This time, there was no warning, no chance for her to tense or to decide. He swooped down and took her mouth with his, letting the dark warmth of her cloak envelop them both. He pressed her to him, letting his hands thread beneath that dark layer, find skin at the back of her neck, at the edges of her sleeves and the low neckline of her gown.

She pressed back, burrowing under his jacket, clutching at his shirtwaist, pulling at the fabric in a desperate need for something she could not define. But Oliver knew what it was, and it burned through him the same way it burned through her.

He wanted contact, so he took it. He took the liberty of finding the buttons at her back and loosening them. Perhaps he was a little too eager. Perhaps he felt one or two buttons pop off the back of the dress, clattering to the floor of the theatre, but he didn't care. And from the way she lost herself in the sensation of his skin against hers, neither did she.

He wanted . . . wanted so desperately. But what he wanted, and what she wanted . . . was it possible?

Beyond the immediate needs. But for the future. He wanted the woman in front of him, but did it supersede the want for the building next to him?

. . . Did it have to?

In the haze of lips on lips, skin on skin, Oliver realized that two lives could meld into one.

And it scared the hell out of him.

"Bridget—" he whispered hoarsely, trying to tear his mouth away from hers, but being lured back like a magnet. "Bridget, we must . . ."

"Yes, Oliver?" Her voice came so sweetly, so hopefully. His name fell from her lips like a prayer, and it nearly broke the little will he had managed to dredge up.

Oh to hell with it! To hell with Frederico waiting for them, to hell with the theatre falling down around them. To hell with anything other than Bridget and him and—

He saw it a split second before it happened. A hand shooting out, setting the tallest stack of boxes to wobbling. Oliver reacted quickly, spinning Bridget around right before the—

CRASH! Oliver immediately covered Bridget with his body, protecting hers with his own. A crate had fallen to the ground, its weak wood splintering on impact, spilling out its contents of cheap ceramic pots, which also shattered.

Correction: A crate had been pushed. And if it had landed as intended . . .

"Are you all right?" he gasped, searching her face.

"I . . . I think so," she said, bewildered. "What on earth happened?"

Oliver quickly scanned the surroundings. It was too dark in the theatre to see far . . . but Oliver would swear on a stack of Bibles that he saw something—some flash of something light-colored—move quickly from the top of one stack of crates to another. Then there were footsteps, running quickly away, out the door. Oliver zoomed his gaze to the front door as light from the outside flooded and gave their assailant a silhouette.

He couldn't be certain—he could not trust his eyes—but even at that distance, Oliver could swear that he saw a man with light blond hair running away into the night.

Twenty

"IT was Klein," Oliver said sharply in Italian. "I know it."
Carpenini looked up from his keyboard, rolling his eyes. It was Sunday, and they were without the distraction of Bridget's lessons for once. Although she was the only thing on Oliver's mind.

"I'm sorry," Oliver replied to Carpenini's eye roll. "But perhaps you do not appreciate the very great danger that your student was in."

"Perhaps you do not appreciate the very great danger you placed my student in," Carpenini replied, his words staccato with emphasis.

Oliver burned with the truth of it. He should not have had Bridget Forrester out in the middle of the night—if she had been safely tucked into bed, she would not have been endangered. Nor should he have allowed himself to become so distracted.

"This is a disaster. And we are so close! What were you thinking?" Carpenini ground out. "Never mind, I know you were not thinking anything at all."

Frederico had seen no one go into the theatre, but when he had been alerted by the crash of the crates, he was about to disembark to come help when he saw the blond man run out.

His fervent description of his features only further convinced Oliver it was Klein who had tried to hurt them.

No. He had tried to hurt Bridget.

In the madness that followed the encounter with the crates, Oliver had wasted no time in getting Bridget back to the hotel. He was loath to leave her but knew it was the best possible place for her in that moment. When he handed her out of the gondola, she was pale and shaking, clutching her cloak about her. At first Oliver thought it was because the popped buttons of her dress had made her appearance unseemly, but then he felt her hands. They were ice cold. She was scared.

And that had been exactly Klein's intention.

"And if I recall correctly, you were the one to warn me against involving the affections of a proper English miss," Carpenini was musing, breaking into Oliver's thoughts.

"A warning that I did not think you heard, let alone heeded," Oliver retorted coldly, his ire rising.

"I did not. But mostly because I did not care. And I do not care now about what you do with the girl. I only care that she can play in the competition."

"Regardless," Oliver replied through gritted teeth, "your protestations and Antonia's warning were correct—Klein will stop at nothing to win, and that includes pushing a crate on top of your protégée!" Carpenini slammed his fingers against the keys, and Oliver knew he finally had the man's attention away from his compositions. "How can we protect her? She lives in a hotel—people can come and go as they please. And if we inform her mother of the danger, she'll be on the next ship back to England before the tide is even in!"

"I do not know," Carpenini replied. "But I do know that if she had not practiced at home, if she had not been out and about and in front of Klein, none of this would have happened. There are only a few weeks left; all we had to do was keep her hidden and we could have triumphed, could have shocked Klein to his knees with her playing. But it did not happen, and now we have to contend with him."

Oliver paused—felt like the breath was knocked out of him by an idea. "You're right," he said, inspiration dawning. "We need to keep her hidden away."

But if Carpenini had heard him, he did not make it known; instead he was mulling something over in his own mind. "Perhaps I can apply to the Marchese, make him see what a scoundrel Klein is. That would do more for taking me back than anything . . ."

"No, Vincenzo," Oliver broke in, determined. "That will not work. The Marchese will only laugh at you. The best thing—the only thing we can do—is *hide Bridget away.*"

"Where?" Carpenini asked suspiciously. "Where in Venice can she go that Klein cannot find her?"

"Not in Venice. I can take her outside the city. Now, listen to me before you fly into high temper," Oliver said seriously. "If Bridget and her family decamp from Venice, it will be seen as a triumph to Klein. He will think that he successfully scared the girl away, and therefore he will not have to pursue her beyond that. You will stay here, and make it seem as if you have been abandoned. Meanwhile, I will make sure Bridget and her family are safe elsewhere, and bring her back in time for the competition."

Carpenini seemed to consider it for a moment. Finally, he replied with a shake of his head. "She has lessons. I must teach her."

"She knows the Number Twenty-three backward and forward. She could play it in her sleep. Can you honestly say that three more weeks of rehearsing, of ridicule, of her thinking Klein is lurking over her shoulder, will do any good?"

"She still doesn't have the emotion of Beethoven. She has parts of it, but not the whole." Carpenini shook his head.

"Then I will take her somewhere that she can learn it." Oliver's eyes lit up. "And how better for her to learn how Beethoven is meant to be played than to hear him played in Vienna?"

Carpenini's gaze shot to Oliver. "You . . . you mean to take her to Vienna?" he cried.

"Beethoven is premiering his new piece there in a little more than a se'nnight."

"It will take you a se'night to get to Vienna!" his brother expostulated. "Then the same to get back, and little more than a few days for Signorina Forrester to prepare herself for the competition. It's madness."

"It's the best idea we have. It's the only way I can think of to protect her from Klein at this point."

Carpenini looked unsure. "It will give me time to finish my

composition," he hedged, finally. Then his eyes shot up from his lap, shining with excitement. "The Marchese will love it—and you will love it, Oliver—it has such strong themes, such beauty. It will premiere in your new theatre to thunderous applause!"

"Fine," Oliver replied, waving his hand dismissively. "But right now, let us get through the next few weeks intact, and then we shall hear your piece."

Carpenini was silent for a moment, his expression its usual inscrutable self. But if Oliver did not know better, he would have said that there was the slightest shift in Carpenini's manner. It was almost as if he were . . . hurt.

But that was just nonsense.

"Just promise me you will get her to a pianoforte in Vienna," Carpenini grumbled, his eyes hard and unfeeling once again. "She will still need to practice."

Oliver grinned, relieved to have a plan in place. "All right, brother. I promise."

Six days later

At last, Bridget thought, her mind and soul completely awake, *Vienna*.

As they pulled in through the streets, her eyes drawn to the beautifully structured classic buildings, lining the curving cobblestone streets that marked the city apart from the small towns and villages that surrounded it, she could not help feeling wholly relieved to have made it to that beautiful city. But no one in the whole of humanity could have been more relieved than Oliver Merrick.

Oliver had made an excellent impression with the ladies Forrester when he met them at the Hotel Cortile with a beautiful boat, larger and far more stable than a gondola, with every comfort provided to make the short trip to the mainland as painless as possible, knowing Lady Forrester's learned dislike of water travel. He made an even greater impression when he handed the ladies up into a spacious and lovely carriage—which Bridget knew must have eaten desperately into Oliver's savings for his theatre. She wanted to demur, to say that it was all too much. But when she saw the hopeful look on his face, the obvious nervous desire to please, she had no choice but to keep mum.

The ride home after their night in the empty theatre had been a blur of shock. And the rest of the night passed sleep-lessly. Bridget was torn between the thrill of her own newly discovered boldness and the sense of guilt she felt for having been so reckless as to have put herself in a position of dan-ger. But all too quickly, as she tossed and turned, a new feeling took over—an uneasy sense of dread. She could have been hurt! She vacillated wildly between anger and fear, and anger was winning out—so much so, that when Oliver came on Sun-day afternoon and presented his plan for going to Vienna, she had balked.

"You want me to flee? To run and hide?" she said low, under her breath. She did not want to have her mother over-hear. Of course, to Lady Forrester and to Amanda, the idea of going to Vienna was presented as a golden opportunity to hear Beethoven in concert. There was no mention of the night be-fore, not only to keep their rendezvous a secret but also to not spread worry about Bridget's safety to her mother, who would take her away in a heartbeat.

"No," Oliver had said, his voice equally low but more mis-chievous. "Removing you from Venice allows us to trick Klein into thinking you have run away."

As Oliver explained his plans, Bridget felt something new—something that had abandoned her in the past day.

A sense of relief. In that moment, Bridget had understood why she had felt so strongly, why fear and anger had begun to rule her actions. Because she had not felt safe. And with one idea, with one touch of the hand, Oliver had restored her sense of safety. Just as he always did.

But after six days of anticipation and being cooped up—however comfortably—in a carriage with her mother, her sis-ter, and Oliver, even that good gentleman's calm and happy reserve had frayed to the point of tenuousness.

It was Bridget's mother's fault.

Apparently, her mother's learned dislike of sea travel had transferred into a newfound dislike of road travel. For a woman who made the journey from Portsmouth to London several times a year, this was discouraging. Every little bump caused a groan to erupt from her mother's lips—and when you have to traverse the foothills of the Alps, there are more than little bumps to contend with.

Amanda was better, but she did not have a guidebook for Vienna with her—and the only ones available for purchase in Venice were written in Italian; thus she had no means by which to obtain the answers to the hundreds of questions she had, other than to ask them.

And as Oliver was the only one of them who had been to Vienna, he was the one to whom they were directed.

"But what about the Schönbrunn Palace? Will we have time to go there? Doesn't it have marvelous gardens?" Amanda rambled, unending. "I don't know where I read that—or perhaps Father said it . . ."

"Perhaps," Bridget said sternly, cutting into her sister's stream of words. "But right now we must adjourn to our lodgings, before the concert tonight."

"Our lodgings?" Amanda asked, confused.

"Yes. We have made it to Vienna, Amanda."

"Thank heavens," groaned Lady Forrester, her eyes firmly shut as they rumbled across the cobblestones.

"Oh!" Amanda cried, and she thrust back the curtains of the carriage and stuck nearly her whole head out the window.

Bridget and Oliver shared a look. They had shared many of these looks over the past week. But unfortunately, looking was all that they could do. Even when they stopped at various inns for the evening, Bridget was flanked by her mother and sister. Finding a moment alone to exchange a word, or even a touch, was nearly impossible.

So it had been days and days of looks. Of unspoken communication. Of Bridget's skin being on fire with the sensation of being untouched.

"Where are we staying, Mr. Merrick?" Amanda asked, bringing her head in from the window.

"Please say it's close," her mother added weakly.

"I have arranged for us to stay at a friend's town house," Oliver answered. "And yes, Lady Forrester, it is quite close."

It was quite close. They were at the front door of a beautifully kept town house in less than a half hour. A good thing, too—as the sun was getting low in the sky, and they would have to leave soon enough for the concert.

Bridget was excited to hear this new work—a new symphony, Oliver had told her. Beethoven himself was rumored to be there, even though the rumor was that he was so ill and so deaf now that he could not even hear his own music.

But that did not stop the man from writing it.

Bridget was musing over melodies and intonations, whether he would use brass or strings or woodwinds, as she hurriedly dressed for supper. She had been installed in a room a bit down the hall from her mother and sisters, and a wing away from Oliver, as was proper. A maid who spoke only German was assisting her, as they had left Molly back in Venice. Which was well enough, because if she had been forced to make small talk as her hair was put up and her gown buttoned, she might go mad.

Because Bridget was again overcome with the feeling that had begun to take shape whenever she looked at Oliver. That this—this concert, this night—was important.

He was waiting for her at the bottom of the steps, checking a pocket watch and dressed in his evening clothes. He glanced up at her briefly, and then, as if struck, his eyes flew back up and held as she came down the staircase.

"What is it?" she asked, suddenly nervous. She touched the row of pearls at her throat, then inspected her mint green silk gown, with the satin bodice and trim of a slightly darker shade. She had chosen it knowing it would bring out her eyes, but there was also the fear it would not travel well. Her German maid had shaken out all of the creases from five days in a trunk—could she have missed some?

"You are beautiful," he breathed.

And for once, she believed it.

Relaxing, she took his offered arm and gave him a small smile. But he did not smile back at her. Instead he held her gaze intently. By the look on his face and the way his hand warmly encompassed her own, Bridget began to get a strange feeling: that perhaps, just perhaps, this was important for him, too.

They walked into the dining room of the comfortable house arm in arm, only to find Lady Forrester and Amanda already seated. Her mother was looking just about as pale as she had on the whole ride, Bridget thought absently as she seated herself.

"Look who I found in the parlor," Oliver said cheerily, masking the intensity of just a moment hence. "And just in time, too; we shall have a bite to eat and then we will have to be off. The Kärntnertortheater is a mile or two away, and the streets will be crowded with other music enthusiasts. We could easily spend an hour in the carriage."

Bridget's mother groaned at that thought. As the soup course was brought out—a bright green pea soup—Lady Forrester's complexion turned from pale white to a matching shade. Bridget did not know whether it was the soup or the prospect of another hour in the carriage, but Lady Forrester suddenly took a decisive stand.

"I cannot. I am sorry, my dears, but I am simply too exhausted from the journey. I cannot attend the concert tonight."

"Mother, no!" Bridget cried. "We came all this way."

"Does this mean we cannot go to the Schönbrunn Palace tomorrow?" Amanda pouted.

"I did not mean to imply that you cannot attend, Bridget. But Amanda will have to go in my place."

When approached with the idea of attending a Beethoven concert, Amanda had shown no enthusiasm for this musical endeavor—and since invitations to the event were hard to come by on such short notice (and how he had managed it, Bridget had no idea—using any number of theatre connections, perhaps?), Oliver had obtained only three. Amanda was going to be perfectly content at the house for the evening with James the footman and various German housemaids for company. But now, it seemed, Lady Forrester had decided to take that comfort for herself.

"You want me to *chaperone*?" Amanda scoffed after gulping a spoonful of soup. "I'm not even allowed to wear my hair up!"

"Mr. Merrick has shown himself to be very trustworthy and honorable," Lady Forrester said on a sigh.

"Well, if he has shown himself to be trustworthy, then why should I go at all?" Amanda countered. "I should much rather explore the library—surely there is an English book about Vienna . . ."

"Amanda!" Lady Forrester spoke sharply enough to cause her youngest to cower a bit. "You are going to the concert, and I am going to sleep. That is all there is to it."

While Amanda sulked, grumbling that they had only one day in Vienna tomorrow and she certainly hoped that she would get to do what *she* wanted to do, Bridget and Oliver exchanged a glance, then a shrug. Regardless of their chaperonage, regardless of whether Oliver and his intentions toward Bridget truly were trustworthy, they would be going to the concert tonight, and they would be going together.

It was going to be a night to remember.

Twenty-one

B RIDGET and Oliver were not in the theatre when it happened.

Nor were they standing in the hall after the concert.

Indeed, they were in the carriage, on the way back to the
town house, when Bridget finally trusted herself to speak
again.

"Five ovations," she whispered. *"Five."*

"Each one earned," Oliver whispered back, equally awestruck. He reached out and took her hand between them. Opposite them, Amanda leaned her head against the wall of the
carriage, clearly exhausted. So Oliver did not hide his actions
when he reached out and took Bridget's hand, holding it close
against his side. She knew it was not a sensual touch or an attempt in any way to seduce. It was a need for contact, for
grounding. And Bridget offered that to him.

Just as he offered it to her.

The evening had begun as expected. A carriage ride that
would have taken a half hour on a normal day had doubled as
they waited in line for their turn to disembark. Bridget had
been nearly jumping out of her skin, eager for the music that
was to come. Even Amanda, who had not given up on her
sulk—likely thinking it would help sway them to her proposed

outing to the Schönbrunn Palace tomorrow—could not help but become enthused with all the nervous energy around them as they finally pulled up to the Kärntnertortheater, the Imperial and Royal Court Theater of Vienna. And the building lived up to that name.

A beautiful structure of yellow brick, it was lit on the inside by a hundred lamps, making the space glow with light. Bridget had felt in awe of La Fenice—and indeed, this space was similar in proportion and decoration. But while her one experience at La Fenice had been of a middling opera by Gustav Klein, the packed crowd at the Kärntnertortheater positively buzzed with excitement. And that excitement was not about who was attending with whom and in what box, or about what the ladies were wearing. No, that excitement was for what they were about to hear.

Oliver led them to their seats on the main floor.

"I apologize, there were no boxes available at such a late date," Oliver said low under his breath, blushing a little.

"Oh, Oliver, don't you realize?" Bridget shook her head. "I'm too excited to care where we sit."

Indeed, even the main floor seats were filled with people of rank and substance, as evidenced by their clothing. Every ticket that could be had that evening had been taken. Bridget watched, waiting anxiously for the curtain to be drawn as Oliver nodded to acquaintances and introduced Bridget and Amanda to those who were within reach. There was a young Miss Unger, who was mingling with guests before she was due to sing—and was found by the Kapellmeister and pulled backstage forthwith. They greeted a Signor Barbaia, who seemed to manage the theatre and whom Oliver called Domenico, as their conversation slipped into Italian. It had not escaped Bridget's notice that Oliver was truly in his element. Nor had it escaped Amanda's.

"Lord, does Mr. Merrick know everyone?" she had said under her breath, as they turned away from the latest in a string of introductions. "My head is spinning." Then, a delightful thought striking her, she said, "Do you think he knows Herr Beethoven?"

"Why Amanda, I thought you had no interest in the music or the musician," Bridget had teased.

"Well, I cannot help it, if every single person we meet—and

we are meeting quite a number of them; Mother will be so terribly jealous to have missed it—mentions that Herr Beethoven is here, and in public for the first time in over a decade."

The idea of Beethoven being in the room, after she had spent the last two months in the company of his No. 23, had Bridget's nerves on the rise again. But she did not have to mount the stage, so the queasy energy that moved like wings in her breast was too strange to be credited. And all too soon, people were taking their seats, and the conductor—not Herr Beethoven, Oliver whispered to her—took the stage to formal applause.

From the first moment, she was enthralled. Two pieces were played before the new symphony, but Bridget had heard neither and therefore let them wash over her. *The Consecration of the House* was followed by the first three movements of Beethoven's Mass—*Missa Solemnis*. They were transcendent beauty, the pinnacle of traditional composition and orchestral music. But Bridget—and Oliver, and yes, the entire room—was waiting with bated breath for what was to come.

As the end chords of the *Missa Solemnis* floated through the air, the applause began impatiently, everyone eager for the chorus to leave the stage and let the orchestra reset themselves for the symphony. But the chorus did not leave the stage.

"It's a choral symphony," Oliver breathed in realization.

The buzz began around the room before the music did. A symphonic oratorio. This was something new and interesting already.

The music began so slowly it was hard to determine where it started. A few notes, as if the violinists and cellists and flutists were simply warming up their instruments. Then a dark theme emerged, an urgency. The intensity of the *allegra ma non troppo* pushed at them from behind and told them all to hurry up and listen! The first movement transitioned with jarring nerves into the second, timpani and staccato violins waking up the room—*as if it needed to be awoken*, her mind scoffed. The darkness of the second movement mirrored the first, but it was more complex, had more wilderness to fight through. But the *scherzo* of the second movement gave it a structure, a plan of attack forming amid that wilderness.

One felt as if some darkness was chasing at one's back, get-

ting nearer and nearer. But the third movement was quieter, a
reflection of peace through oboe and string. An *adagio*, it let
light and peace and hope into Bridget's heart; she knew instinctively, without the darkness of the first two movements,
that such hope could not have been achieved.

And then . . . the melody emerged. A simple beauty, as
basic in rhythm and key as a child's tune, layer upon layer,
instrument upon instrument, joy bursting forth like flames
from the fingertips of the players.

Bridget felt tears begin to sting her eyes. She could not for
the life of her stop her heart from pounding in time to the
music, nor did she want to.

So often, she had found herself transported by music.
She would get lost, lose herself to the time and fullness of the
tones, the way it conjured up air around her as she listened, or
as she played. But this, she thought, one did not get lost in this
music.

One was delivered by it.

By the time the fourth movement came, Bridget did not
know what to expect. She had completely forgotten that the
chorus was still on stage until the bass soloist stood and began
to sing. He sang a poem, a German poem, that Bridget could
not hope to translate, but voiced a definitive, authoritative
sense of goodwill. Then the contralto—Miss Unger herself!—
joined in, making a round of music. Then the tenor, then the
coloratura soprano, and then the chorus, all lifted their voices
in this amazing melody of simplicity and harmony. It built and
built on all the themes, all the feelings the first three acts had
conjured up, until it was almost too large for the theatre, for
the heart, for all of Vienna.

Then, out of the corner of her eye, Bridget saw someone
move, breaking into her fixation on the music. A small white-
haired man rose to the stage, taking hard-won steps. He began
to gesticulate, to conduct, his back entirely to the audience.
His furious gesticulations marked him as more passionately
involved in the music than anyone else in the room.

"Who—" she whispered to Oliver.

"That is Herr Beethoven," he answered, with a squeeze of
her hand—a hand that she had not noticed he was holding.
Because he was such a constant presence, to have him not

holding her hand would have felt more strange. Would have made her bereft.

Bridget had watched as Herr Beethoven moved his head, his hands in time to music he could not hear. The worst-kept secret in the musical world was that the great master was nearly completely deaf. The pounding rush, the whirlwind of the melody, spun the listeners like a pirouette until they were dizzy with it—until, building into triumph, the last notes were played with hard strikes against strings.

The room had burst into applause, clamoring to their feet. Bridget was the first among them, her eyes still wet and her heart still pounding. Beside her, Oliver and Amanda were equally enthusiastic. Oliver especially; Bridget chanced a look away from the stage to glance up at his face. He was flushed, his eyes glazed with passion.

He must have known it, too—known as instinctively as she did. That the symphony—Beethoven's Ninth—was unlike anything the musical world had heard. It was too much to process—it filled the heart and then burst it.

No wonder it had taken until the carriage ride home for Bridget to speak. It had taken Oliver that long, too. One did not feel moved by it—one felt changed.

"When he kept conducting," Bridget shook her head, her eyes still wet, still filled with wonder, searching for something to focus on inside the carriage. For Beethoven had kept conducting, long after the piece ended. His eyes closed, the music played on infinitely in his head.

"I know," Oliver replied hoarsely. "And then Miss Unger stepped forward, and turned him to the crowd . . ."

"That look on his face . . . it was so humbling," she breathed.

"It was joy," Oliver finished for her.

"It was."

Her eyes turned to his then, sought them out in the darkness of the carriage. Her feelings—the music, the night, being with him—overwhelmed her . . . Much the way that his hand on top of hers grounded her. But then, keeping his eyes on hers the whole time, Oliver gently reached over and unbuttoned her glove at the wrist. Then, with painful delicacy, he pulled the soft material off her fingers one by one.

She could hear music in her head. The music that had filled her that evening and left her bared.

He removed her glove as the carriage rolled on into the night. Then he lifted the naked hand to his lips, pressed them against her wrist. She gasped with the sensation. It was as if all the power and passion of the music from that night could be transferred by that simple touch, skin to skin.

Bridget wanted to pull him closer, so she did. She wanted to take her hand and let it revel in the short curls at the base of his neck, so she did.

She wanted his lips on hers, wanted to share in the power of the night and the darkness of the carriage . . .

"What's going on?" Amanda sat up suddenly, a rut in the road jolting her into bleary consciousness.

"Nothing!" Bridget cried, she and Oliver pulling away from each other so quickly that they practically slammed into opposite sides of the carriage. Luckily it was dark in the interior of the carriage, but Amanda was mere feet away.

Thankfully, it seemed she was also half-asleep.

"Oh," her little sister sighed, leaning back against the cushions again, her eyes closing as her body relaxed back into sleep. "That's good."

"We will be home soon, Miss Amanda," Oliver said, trying for blank civility, as his hand sneaked across the gulf between them and took Bridget's. "We just crossed into the Widmerviertel area of town. The roads will be clearer—it should not be long now."

"Oh," Amanda mumbled, through a yawn. "That's good."

Indeed, they rumbled to a stop in mere minutes. Which was all for the best, because if Bridget had to endure any more of the sweet torture of having Oliver's hand play with hers, hidden in the folds of her cloak in the darkness of the carriage, and not be able to do what she wanted—to do *more* . . .

The footman handed her down, followed by a deeply sleepy Amanda. Oliver took Amanda's arm, as it seemed likely she might fall asleep where she stood.

"I don't know if it was the music or the travel that took all the verve out of her," Bridget mused as they made their way into the house.

"I think it was the travel, finally taking its toll. After all, she was applauding as loudly as the rest of us," Oliver whispered back to her as they entered the house and moved toward the stairs. The entryway was lit, and the housekeeper waiting up to attend them.

"Send the household to bed, Frau Reinhaltz, and yourself as well," Oliver said in soft tones. "Just send one of the girls up for Miss Amanda—she's too tired to undress herself."

"Very good, Mr. Merrick," the housekeeper replied, in a thick Germanic accent. "I hope you enjoy ze concert."

Bridget maneuvered around to the other side of Amanda so she could help Oliver with her up the stairs, but his tall strength was quite capable of taking on the weight of a dead-tired practically sleepwalking sixteen-year-old young lady— leaving Bridget to fall behind and do what she could to not admire his form.

Indeed, her nerves were in a strange state of utmost awareness. As if every creak of the steps were something to take notice of, every footfall on plush carpet. Everything, especially, having to do with Mr. Oliver Merrick.

So she tried to distract herself on that endless walk up the stairs and down the corridor to Amanda's room. Tried not to think of the way Oliver's trousers cut across his thighs. Tried not to think about the way his lips had felt—soft and strong at once—against the delicate spot of her wrist. Tried not to remember the way his body had felt wrapped around hers in the gondola during a starlit sojourn . . .

Really, how long was this staircase?

Soon enough, however, they were depositing Amanda at her door, where they were met by the same German-speaking maid who had attended Bridget earlier in the evening.

"*Danke*, Greta," Oliver said, handing Amanda over to her. "And good night, Miss Amanda."

"Goodniiii—" Amanda yawned, and allowed herself to be ushered into her room.

Once the door clicked closed behind them, Bridget found herself unable to move, and unable to turn her gaze away from Oliver.

They were alone. For the first time all evening. For the first time in days.

"So," she breathed, her voice coming out in a loud squeak.

"Shh," Oliver admonished with a smile. "I should hate to

wake your mother—or disturb Amanda before she finds her way to her pillow."

"I told you, my mother sleeps like the dead. And Amanda . . . I do not think even hell itself could keep her from her sleep now," Bridget returned with a smile. But suddenly it felt awkward, uneasy. She had reached this point in the evening—this strangely important, transformative evening—and she didn't know what to do now, except feel bereft at its ending.

They began to move slowly toward Bridget's room, a few doors down the long hall, keeping a breadth of space between them. She picked at her gloves—half off since the carriage ride—until they came away, to be folded and turned over in her hands.

"I suppose you must be as tired as your sister," Oliver offered by way of conversation.

"Quite the contrary," Bridget replied. "I doubt I have ever felt so awake."

He gave a strange cough. "I, too, am strangely awake."

"I do not know what I shall do to fall asleep. Perhaps try to read some German book—there are a few in my room."

"I know," Oliver replied. "Books are in every guest room."

They had reached Bridget's door.

She turned and gave as graceful a curtsy as she could manage. "Well, good night, Oliver. Thank you for the most incredible night of my life."

She expected him to give a quick nod, or a short bow. She thought perhaps he might raise her hand to his lips again, and kiss that spot on her wrist.

But she was wrong.

There, in the darkened corridor of a borrowed town house in Vienna, Oliver Merrick took one languid step, closing the gap between them. He stood there, hovering in her space, letting her revel in his warmth. Then he reached down and took one of her shaking hands.

When had her hands begun shaking?

"Come with me," he whispered, his warm tenor aching with want.

"Where?" Bridget replied, her voice shaking as much as her hand, but her gaze never faltering, never wavering from his.

His other hand reached up, pushed an errant curl behind her ear, then came to rest gently at the back of her neck. Coaxing. Calming.

"Bridget," he said again. "Come with me."

A thousand thoughts rushed through Bridget's mind. A thousand thousand words in reply. But after that long moment, that endless aching, Bridget finally replied with the only word that made any sense at all.

Her gloves fell to the floor as she reached out and took his hand.

"Yes."

Taking her hand, Oliver led Bridget down the hall to another staircase, this one leading to the west wing of the house, the family rooms. He moved with speed, with purpose, but had to be gentle. He did not wish to frighten her with his need. He simply wanted to unleash hers.

They made their way to Oliver's room—a masculine space with dark woods and heavy green velvets that he would take the time to appreciate and compliment the staff for their hard work on at a later time. Right now, all that he cared about was that there was a fire in the hearth, a bed turned down, and Bridget.

He let Bridget go once they reached the room. He let her walk around, explore the surroundings. Get her bearings. She inspected the fire in the hearth, the portrait hanging above the mantel. Then her eyes took in the large, comfortable bed that dominated the center of the room.

She could run, he realized. She could run, and he would let her go. But he knew she wouldn't. She was too brave, too headstrong. She was after all, the girl who had come to Venice, chasing a dream from a letter.

Eons from now, after this night had passed, and a thousand like it, someone would ask him the question of how he had known Bridget Forrester for who she would be—and the answer would be simple. That she was the one person in the whole world he had ever met with who had the gall, the temerity, and the absolute directness of feeling to carry her across a continent on the vague promises in a single letter. Her determination, her talent, and above all, her trust, was something to which he aspired, and it made her shine.

But that was not the foremost thought in his mind. Right now, the only thing he could think was that Bridget was here, she was with him, and she looked very nervous.

"This is your room," she said softly, her voice a bare squeak.

"Yes," he intoned. "We do not have . . . that is, we have all the time—"

"Oliver, will you do something for me?" she interrupted with as much authority as she could muster.

"Anything."

"Will you kiss me?" she asked, betraying her vulnerability. "Just to get it out of the way."

Oliver was not one to refuse such a request. In two quick strides he crossed to the hearth where she stood and wrapped her in his arms. The kiss was deep, an inhale of the life she had and the soul she was so willing to share. She reciprocated, pressing herself into him until he could feel all of her against all of him.

And all it did was drive him crazy.

He thrust his fingers into her hair, letting loose a torrent of pins, each one hitting the soft carpet with a dulled ping. Her hair streamed down her back in a mass of dark curls—so soft!—falling to her waist. He let his fingers run down until they could play with the ends, his hands grasping her tiny middle, lifting her against him. And all the while, never ever breaking that requested kiss.

He was rewarded for his diligence, for his patience. She relaxed in his arms, all sense of nervousness gone. Indeed, as the kiss deepened, as her hair came down and she pressed herself against him, stealing his warmth, her enthusiasm grew. Then it was her hands that threaded into his hair . . . it was her hands that ran down the back of his coat. And her enthusiastic hands that reached under his coattails and plucked at his shirt, seeking the satisfaction that only skin-to-skin contact could bring.

"Wait," he cried, breaking their kiss as her cool hands brushed against the warmer planes of his back.

"What is it?" she asked, biting her lip, unsure. "What did I do wrong?"

"Nothing!" he hastened to assure her, planting a kiss on that delicious lip. "I don't want to rush you."

"I . . . I don't feel as if I am being rushed," she replied, cocking up a brow. "In fact, it could go a bit faster, if you like."

"Well, perhaps then I do not wish to rush myself. I want to enjoy this." He leaned into her ear, whispering. "Savor it."

He could feel through the hand on her back as a shudder of anticipation ran down her spine. He watched as her eyes turned from jade to black with desire.

Delicately, he released his hand from her waist and set her back at arm's length. "We are going to do this slowly. Properly."

"If we were doing this properly, it would be on our wedding night," Bridget said glibly, and then, eyes widening in horror, slapped her hand over her mouth.

Oliver froze. Met her eyes.

"I . . . I didn't mean that," she said, shaking her head. "I was only trying to be funny, and it did not turn out terribly funny, did it—oh blast, now I've ruined everything and you won't—"

Her nervous ramble was worthy of her sister, but Oliver reached forward and silenced her with a kiss.

"Do you want to wait until that day?" he asked hoarsely. "I will happily, if you want me to," he grimaced, unable to lie. "Well, not precisely happily, but I shall."

"No," she said, kissing him back. "I do not wish to wait. But you will have to tell me what to do. I do not know this dance, you see."

He kissed her again. Breaking the connection between them, that had been his mistake. If he just held her, her nerves could not overcome her. If he held her—she was the bravest woman imaginable.

"You know this dance," he answered. "Or, if you don't, at least you know the music."

Slowly, carefully, he pulled back enough to let his arm come up between them and rest on the easy neckline of her evening gown. Running his knuckle gently against the swell of her breast, he let his lips fall against that sensitive spot just behind her ear. She gasped. He took it in.

"I do not wish to rush," he murmured. "Nor do I wish to frighten. All I want to do is wander."

And so he did.

He wanted to let his hand graze against her breast, so he

did. She wanted to let her hand trail down to his rear and press against that strong flank, and so she did. He wanted to undo the buttons at the back of her dress, and so he did.

"Do you know how often I wanted to peek behind that screen?" he whispered, as his fingers deftly worked open one small button, then another. Her dress fell loose against her front, exposing those delicate rosy nipples through her thin chemise. "As Molly was opening up the back of your dress and putting you into my shirt? I wanted to see this piece of skin, right here." His thumb hit the spot in the center of her back, where her chemise began. "See if it was as freckled as the rest of you."

"You never peeked?" she asked.

To that, he only grinned against her mouth.

They began to wander again. To meander, to dilly-dally. His fingers finished with the buttons at the back of her dress, leaving her exposed, her dress hanging from the shoulders. Her fingers took up the call, and threaded themselves beneath his dress coat, pushing it off his shoulders. Putting only as much space between them as necessary for gravity to work, he let his coat fall away at the same time as her dress. Then her fingers, always languid, always following the rhythm he laid out, began to play with the buttons of his shirt, at his throat, at his chest.

Bridget let herself explore, with the curiosity borne from inexperience and delight. Her fingers trailed down the hard planes of his stomach, a contrast with his soft skin and the downy fur of a man in his prime. The firelight let her see only so much; the rest she had to imagine.

She had to feel out the notes.

Like that line, a scar under his ribs—where had that come from? And the way his muscles dipped, the way his shoulders rounded toward her smaller self, as she pushed the shirt off his skin and let it fall to the floor, next to his coat, her gown, and everything else that had come between them, pooling at their feet.

Slowly, Oliver began the dance away from the fire and toward the bed. Bridget moved with him, following his beats, his music, and making it her own.

Shoes, both his and hers, fell away as they climbed onto the bed. Careful to never break that connection, never let themselves be away from each other, not even for a second. Stockings followed, pantaloons, a chemise. Until they lay together, naked, unable to hide.

She did not yield. Did not shy away. Bridget knew, deep down, that the only way through this bit was to hold on to Oliver and not let go. So she didn't. Instead, she let him, and that melody, that insistent melody that had infected her brain and apparently infected Beethoven's, play in her head. It chased her, spurred her. Drove her into not letting him stop until that part of Oliver—that part of endless curiosity, that part that elders never tell young ladies about, but they manage to find out about anyway—had found its way deep inside her.

Then, and only then, did the music stop.

"Do not worry. Do not worry, my love," he murmured, kissing her hair as he did so. "The pain will end in a minute. It will go away," he promised.

It was on the tip of her tongue to ask how he had such knowledge, but somehow, in the blinding haze of feeling, she managed to remember what had happened the last time she had answered with glibness, and held her question. She was rewarded with a rain of kisses, on her face, her cheek, her neck . . . and slowly, surely, the pain did go away.

"It is all right," she answered finally. "After all, what is pleasure without pain?" Indeed, what was the last half of Beethoven's symphony—the quartet of voices, the melody raised in chorus, in instruments—without the first two movements? The pain of running, or fear, gave way, adjusted, so easily to hope. Just as her body so easily adjusted to his.

"It's all right," she promised him, returning those reverent kisses, giving him the permission he needed. "It is all right. I can hear it again."

He held steady, looked down at her, quizzical.

"Hear what?"

"The music," she replied. That melody of hope, of joy, was slowly coming back to her. Oh yes, it was.

"Are you sure?" he asked, hesitant.

"When I look back on this moment"—she bit her lip, but still was resolved—"I will not see fear. I will see only you."

And indeed, she could hear the music. The pace he set, the rhythm in three-quarter time. The delicate way they moved against each other, their own symphony playing, a mutation, a culmination of everything they had heard before.

It was touch—the plucking of strings. It was sound—the soft cries of one blending into the other. And it was sight—seeing the road before them and not faltering; in fact, welcoming the journey to come.

She let him lead their dance, but he had been right—she knew this music. This music written before time was written down.

And when they finally reached the end, those high, powerful notes, Bridget and Oliver both heard the strain of the music taking over their senses, clasping them in its racing grip and then floating away, letting them fall back to earth, with only each other to hold on to.

And there they held, listening into the night, until the last chords died away . . . clasped, holding tight to each other, unable and unwilling to let go.

Twenty-two

I T was a good few minutes before Bridget felt sure enough of herself to speak. A feeling not uncommon to her, as it was the second time it had visited her that evening.

"I want to play."

She was thrown against Oliver's side, lying on her back on the bed. Her arm lay flung out to the side, the need for air, for relief, acute, but she was unwilling still to break that delicious (necessary!) contact. He was breathing heavily, staring at the ceiling, the tent of bed curtains that surrounded them.

"You want to play?" he asked between deep gulping breaths. "If you wish to play with me, I can only beg a short respite."

"No." She gave a short laugh. "I want to play the pianoforte."

"The pianoforte?" He grinned against the dark. "Why on earth would you want to play the pianoforte now?"

"Because I've got it!" She smiled, sitting up. "I think I understand the Number Twenty-three, after tonight, and the Beethoven of it, in particular." She turned to him, holding the bare linen sheet against her breast, so becomingly that Oliver could hardly help but reach his hand toward it—a hand she swatted away like a fly buzzing about the cream.

"I understand the Number Twenty-three sonata now.

Beethoven—he pushes feeling at you, he does not allow you the leisure of discovering it for yourself. You are already on the ship and riding along before you realize you have joined. And it is a ride." Her determination came up with her color. "There is this hook, just on the inside of your cheek, like a caught fish. You are jerked along until you are finally caught up with him, and all you can do is hold on."

She paused for a moment, leaning back against the sheets.

"I would play that," she said, staring up at the ceiling. "That is, I think I can play that. I think that's what is missing from how I play the Number Twenty-three."

Of course she would want to play now, he thought ruefully, when they were lying in bed, lost to the world, to the night. Her jumpy, fractious nature did not allow for anything else. And that was the woman he loved. So there was nothing else but to go along with it. Or try to find a way to persuade her to stay.

"I do not know if this place even has a piano," he answered lazily, letting his finger trace figure eights on her shoulder.

"Of course you do," she replied. "This is your house, is it not?"

He stilled, letting his eyes meet hers in the darkness.

"What do you mean?"

"This is your room," Bridget breathed, as she met his gaze, coming back down to earth from her musical meanderings.

"Yes," he nodded. "For the time being."

"No, I mean . . . this is *your* room." Her brow came down. "The portrait over the hearth—that is of you as a young man, is it not?"

Oliver felt color creep up over his face. She saw more than he gave her credit for.

"Yes," he conceded. "That is me at sixteen."

"You know all the staff by name. And the streets of Vienna. This is your house."

"This is my father's house," he corrected, leaning back against the pillows in defeat.

She shook her head at him. "Why did you not tell us? You let us think this is Lord Pomfrey's house—or at the very least, the home of a 'friend.'"

Oliver stared up at the ceiling. "I do not know," he said quietly. "I suppose I wanted you to think I had managed all of this by my own measure, without resting on the shoulders—or money—of my father."

"Why?" she asked simply, propping up her head on her elbow so she could look at him properly. Lying naked next to him, having shared their bodies, it seemed to Bridget that sharing other secrets would come without objection. And thankfully, after a moment, Oliver did not object and gave in to her inquiry.

"I know how it is, Bridget. Everyone sees me as either my father's son or Carpenini's brother. And I do live off both of them in some ways. I cannot deny that it is family money that keeps me fed and sheltered, and that I have used to purchase the Teatro Michelina. Nor can I deny that I am going to use my half brother's compositions to put it back on the map." He rose up on his own elbow, meeting her gaze. She took the opportunity to reach out and smooth the hair that mussed about his temple.

"The idea that you do not stand on your own feet is preposterous."

"Bridget—"

"It's true. How did you come by invitations to the concert this evening?" she asked.

"I have met with Signor Domenico Barbaia, who manages the theatre, on several occasions. I called in a favor of sorts," Oliver answered, hesitantly.

"So your father did not fetch them for you?"

"Of course not, but—"

"And Carpenini? He had no influence over this?"

"Actually, Vincenzo and Signor Barbaia have had differences of opinions in the past."

"You see!" Bridget cried, putting a gentle hand against Oliver's chest. "They had nothing to do with it. In fact, Carpenini could have been a hindrance. And he"—she hesitated, not wanting to offend but still needing to make her point—"has been living with you for a year now, exiled from the musical world in Venice. You are the one who is of assistance to him now, not the other way around."

Oliver shrugged. "He is not living with me for free—he will produce a piece to premiere on stage at the Teatro. Besides that . . . he is my brother. He is family."

"You allow your brother such leeway and not your father?" she countered.

Oliver looked at her, pained—unhappy to reveal this little bit of himself. But not unwilling. Nay, perhaps he was even compelled.

"I told you—my father does not understand." His voice was little more than a whisper. "Hell, he gives me an allowance to stay away."

"Are you sure he is not providing for you to follow your heart?" Bridget asked, a fissure in her heart, opening just that much wider for Oliver, for his pain. "That is what families do, after all. They support, even when they do not understand. Do you think my mother understands how I feel about music? Why I felt the need to travel halfway across the world to Venice? Why I am putting every piece of myself into a competition that she did not even know about? Of course she does not." Bridget let her hand rest on his heart, let him feel her presence there. "But she supports me, loves me, to the occasional point of lunacy."

His hand came over and held hers in place against his chest, his thumb making lazy patterns against her soft skin.

"She is not the only one," he murmured, before lifting her hand to his mouth and kissing her palm.

Bridget froze. Did she dare trust her ears? Had he said what she thought he had? But before she could move, before she could think, Oliver had released her hand and thrown himself back against the bed and, with exaggerated humor, covered his face with a pillow.

"When you said you wanted to play, I did not think it would be with my deeply held beliefs about my family!" he groaned, eliciting a giggle from Bridget.

"Well, you are the one who has not provided me with the requisite pianoforte," she countered with a laugh.

That had Oliver sitting up. "Fine," he began with an overly weary sigh. "We shall adjourn to the music room."

Oliver stood up and began to pull on his trousers, letting them hang from his hips in a distractingly lazy manner.

"Ah . . . there's a music room?" Bridget asked, her eyes jumping to his face.

"Yes—and thankfully, it is on the opposite side of the

house from your mother and sister's bedchamber." He looked down at her in the bed, his eyes running over the way she held the bedsheet to her breast, the tangle of her hair. And then a smile crept over his features.

A delightful, devilish smile. One full of ideas.

"But if you are going to play, you are going to do so my way."

Tiptoeing was not easy for Bridget. Especially when dressed in only a bedsheet.

It was longer than her, so it dragged on the floor, catching against her feet. Also, it was wrapped so tightly around her that her steps were mincing and unsure.

They were barely out the door of his bedroom when Oliver gave up hope of her maintaining silence and lifted her in his arms to carry her to the music room.

"This is much simpler," he whispered, as he lifted her against his chest.

"And much more fun," she returned with a wicked smile.

Oliver was able to tiptoe their way to the music room, down the corridor, past Amanda's room and Lady Forrester's, down the stairs and through the living rooms that had been aired out for the younger Mr. Merrick and his guests, and into a room that had not received such attention.

It was a narrow, high room at the back of the house, windows looking onto the small garden that produced flowers and cuttings for the public rooms. But those windows had not been opened in many a week, making the air thick and stifled. All the furniture was still covered in dust cloths.

"Well," Bridget said, as she was put on her feet again, clutching the sheet to her. "At least I match."

"Now, it may not be perfectly in tune," Oliver said as he crossed the room and whipped the sheet off of the beautiful oakwood instrument that dominated the space. As he opened up the instrument, he continued, "Although I do know the servants are under strict orders to have it serviced monthly."

"Why have an instrument tuned if no one lives here?" she asked.

"It was my mother's," Oliver shrugged, as he self-consciously rubbed the back of his head. "They lived here for a time before I was born. Taking in the city. After her death, my father . . . well, he has a sentimentality about some things, at least."

Bridget just shook her head at him as she followed his path across the room and took her seat at the piano bench.

"No, no." Oliver shook his head and held out his hand. "You have to leave that with me."

She looked down to where his eyes had fallen. "You want the sheet?" she asked, surprise lighting up those eyes.

He nodded.

"But I'll be naked."

He nodded again, unable to suppress a grin.

"In the words of Molly, you're stark raving mad," she retorted, and stuck her tongue out at him.

"Keep doing that and I'll find far more interesting uses for your tongue," he growled at her, and took estimable pleasure in watching her blush. Oliver put his hands behind his back, putting his back up straight.

"You are about to launch a logical argument at me," Bridget said before he could speak.

"I am?" he asked, surprised. "How can you tell?"

"You always put your hands behind you and lean back on your heels when you are about to give a lecture." She smirked at him. She looked so impossibly lovely in that moment—her hair running wild about her face and shoulders, the curves of her woman's body exposed by the draping of a single sheet— that Oliver had difficulty keeping his hands behind his back. But he'd be damned if she wasn't right about his posture.

"All right," she sighed, waving her hand, and almost lost her grasp on her sheet. "Er, convince me why it is logical that I play naked."

"Again, shall I revisit your statement to me about rather playing naked in front of a thousand people?" He grinned at her. "Well, you have played before a thousand people, now you have the opportunity to complete the other half of that prospect, in relative privacy." He took a step forward, closing the distance between them. "After this, you can have nothing to fear."

He held her gaze as his fingers slipped deftly below the neckline of the sheet, and he slowly pulled it away from her. Leaving Bridget standing there, in the dark, in her full, freckled glory.

Brava, you, he thought as she continued to hold his gaze—refusing to shrink or to cover her body with her arms. Instead, she took a measured breath, then squared her shoulders and turned to the pianoforte.

Light gold freckles covered her from head to toe. Hell, his trousers (his only clothing at the moment) were not going to do a damn thing to hide his admiration.

Seating herself on that glorious rear (of which she had afforded him a fabulous view with her defiant walk to the bench), Bridget began a quick scale, feeling out the keys, making sure the instrument was in tune. She picked out the insistent melody they had heard that evening in Beethoven's Ninth Symphony. She giggled as Oliver moved across the room and found an old taper and candlestick, lighting it quickly with a nearby flint and bringing it over so she could see the keys better.

Once the light was on her, once the room had stilled, she took a steadying breath, followed by a second for what came next; then she asked very simply, "What should I play?"

Oliver raised an eyebrow. "Play . . . play your 'Ode to Venice.'"

"In Vienna? Surely this is some kind of sacrilege. You know, Byron wrote an 'Ode on Venice,'" she stated, placing her fingers in the first position for her own ode.

"Yes, but it is quite long-winded. I like yours better."

She smiled and began to play those soft, awakening notes, the tune so much a part of herself, so full of her idiosyncrasies, that it was hard to tell where the artist stopped and the art began.

It was only a few minutes in length to play, so when she was done, she turned to him again.

"Perhaps it should be renamed. Perhaps it can be the 'Ode to Vienna' after tonight," he teased.

"No, I shall write Vienna her own ode. This one belongs to Venice." She shook her head at him. Then, with consideration, she asked, "What next?"

He cocked his head to one side. "Play what urged you down here. What you wanted to play when we lay so cozily next to each other in bed."

She regarded him for a short moment. Then, with infinite care, she placed her hands on the keys again and began the No. 23.

With those few opening chords, the music took over her body. There was no hesitation. There was, indeed, nowhere to hide. Oliver leaned against the instrument, weakened by the beauty of it. She exposed every ache, every plunge, through the highs and lows and rapid appoggiaturas. It was well played, as always. But this time, something was very different.

Instead of sitting back and letting the feeling come, as before, this time, she pushed the feeling at the audience, the way she had described Beethoven doing in his latest symphony. Whether she could do this because she was naked, or because she had only Oliver listening, he could not tell, but the only thing he could think was that he was so terribly grateful that he got to be the one to hear it.

She let her fingers rest after the first movement, taking them off the keys. She let the power that she had unleashed into the air seep back again, falling like light, settling around them.

When she finally turned to him, her eyes were shiny with tears.

"You're crying," she said to him. Oliver put his hand to his own eyes. She was right—tears threatened to fall onto his cheek, too.

"That is how you should play it. At the competition."

"That's how I will win?"

He shook his head. "That is how it should be heard."

He moved from his position leaning on the pianoforte and came to gingerly sit next to her on the delicate piano bench. He felt the warmth coming off her, her skin so close to his. She began the second movement of the No. 23. Not pushing emotion or herself this time, just feeling out the notes from memory, letting herself float along with the melody.

"The competition," she breathed, shaking her head. "You have no idea how much I wish that were already over. And yet I dread its coming."

"Do you?" he asked.

"It is all I think about," she admitted. "My entire life has been framed around it, for months. I will be so relieved when it is over, but on the other hand . . . what do I do with myself when it is gone? My lessons . . . do they come to an end? My family—I suppose we go back to England. But if I begin thinking of the after, I become overwhelmed and then ultimately, oddly . . . bereft."

"Bereft," he repeated. "I do not understand why."

She shook her head, lifting her fingers from the keys mid-measure. "Because it means this time—this wonderful, glorious time—is coming to an end. My lessons, playing for a circus, learning from Carpenini and wandering the city with you. My *purpose* will have ended. And I cannot think on that without being a little sad. And then utterly distracted."

He held his breath, waiting. She put her fingers back on the keys again, picked up exactly where she had left off.

"So I do not think about it," she said, letting herself drift back into the music. "I can only think of the competition. And let the after come later."

Oliver let out a long slow breath. He had to admit, he had not been thinking about the after, either. He had only assumed that the way their lives were would carry on. His mind had not let him think of her not taking lessons any longer . . . or of the possibility of her going back to England.

But he knew one thing. He did not want Bridget to leave his life. He wanted that day of family and flowers and a church, and the lifetime of music that followed.

"Bridget, you know that we are going to have a conversation all too soon. About the after. A question that needs asking."

"I know," she nodded. "But not until after. Please."

"All right," he conceded. "Not until after."

She smiled at him and leaned into him playfully as her fingers continued on the keys. He let the music surround them for a few moments, let it whisk her away into feeling. Then, gently, he leaned down and kissed her shoulder. Reverently.

"Thank you," he whispered.

"Whatever for?" she replied, astonished.

"For the most incredible night of my life."

Twenty-three

"**I** do not sleep as soundly as you think I do."

Bridget whipped her head around, eyes wide. Amanda stood stock-still looking out at the lawn of the Schönbrunn Palace. It was their sole full day in Vienna—they were due to begin their journey back to Venice at first light tomorrow—and Amanda had absolutely insisted on getting her way and going to see some of the more illustrious sights of Vienna.

Luckily, the royal family was not in residence, and therefore the touring grounds of the Schönbrunn were open to the public . . . that is, a public that could manage the entrance fee. A price set high enough to keep out the riffraff, yet not too high to discourage the gentry from an idyllic tour. The palace itself was located a few short miles from the center of Vienna, and so talking Lady Forrester into the carriage that morning had not been too daunting a task. A short ride, they told her, and then the wide-open spaces of a well-planned garden. Lady Forrester saw her youngest daughter's insistence, her middle daughter's acquiescence, and gave in.

Indeed, Bridget did not care a fig what they did today, as long as they were out of the house and in company. Because if she had the opportunity to be alone with Oliver, the chances were they would not be able to keep their hands off each other, and then there would be real trouble.

Keeping their hands off each other in the company of her mother and sister had been troublesome enough. Before, while on the trip north to Vienna, they had been itching with curiosity, but now that they both knew what it was like . . . well, suffice it to say, Bridget practically had to sit on her hands during the ride to Schönbrunn, lest she unconsciously find hers wrapped up with his.

Bridget had thought they had done a reasonably good job hiding what had passed between them in the night from the stark light of day and the prying eyes that would know more.

But apparently, they had not.

"What . . . what do you mean?" Bridget asked, aiming for nonchalance and failing miserably.

"I know I was rather dead on my feet by the time we arrived home last night, so I do not fault you for thinking that I would slumber as soundly as Mother does." Amanda shrugged as she began walking. Bridget could only follow, a brisk pace necessary to keep up with her taller sister.

They walked past a hedge line of white roses that surrounded the famed maze of Schönbrunn, Amanda idly touching the blooms, stopping to smell them here and there. To anyone else—and especially, to their mother, who was walking several yards ahead of them, Oliver held hostage on her arm—it would look like they were simply strolling.

It would not look in any way like Bridget's biggest secret was about to be exposed—and by her sister, no less!

"In any case," Amanda continued, her tone as bland as if they were talking about the flowers, "perhaps it was all the sleeping I did during the day in the carriage, but I was shocked to find myself wide awake after only a few hours' slumber. And since I heard the very soft piano music, coming from somewhere in the house, I thought perhaps you might be awake, too."

"Me?" Bridget replied, her voice a squeak. "I assure you I went right to bed. You must have been dreaming, Amanda."

"I promise you, I could not have been dreaming—my imagination is in no way strong enough to have created what I saw from the ether."

Bridget had to restrain herself from asking just what it was that Amanda thought she saw, but she held her tongue. Having her baby sister say out loud that she had seen her playing the pianoforte in such a state of dishabille—there was no *habille* to remark upon—while sitting next to a man who wore little more . . . she did not have the stomach for it. Instead, she decided to ask a far more pertinent question.

"How did I sound?" She turned to Amanda, cocking her head to one side.

Amanda blinked twice, then smirked. "You sounded wonderful."

A hundred butterflies began flapping their wings as she began her next question.

"You haven't told Mother yet, have you? Of course not; if you had, I would be locked in my chamber on gruel and water right now."

Amanda's brow came down. "Where on earth would Mother find gruel in Vienna?"

"It does not matter; she would." Bridget shook her head. "Please do not tell her—not yet; let me . . . oh, let me figure out what to think and I shall cater to your every wish in the meantime. I will go and see every single architectural sight in the Italian peninsula with you, just let me figure out how to speak to Mother—"

"I am not going to tell Mother." Amanda shook her head.

"You're not?" Bridget breathed a sigh of relief. Then, always skeptical, at least when it came to her sister, she asked, "Why not?"

Amanda took her time, but when she did speak it was with the gravity of truth.

"Because you looked happy."

It was Bridget's turn to blink in surprise.

"I don't understand," Bridget replied, unsure. "You are not going to tell Mother what you saw?"

Amanda shook her head. "I have to admit to a certain amount of shock at seeing . . . well, you know. His . . . taking of liberties."

Bridget wanted to cringe. Just how much did her sister see? But Amanda continued on blithely.

"But after I *scoured my eyeballs*," she grimaced, "I let myself remember that Mr. Merrick seems to be a very nice man, and very nice to you. After all, any man who creates a circus in his music room for you must be worthy of some consideration."

Bridget came to a stop. "I never told you that. How did you know . . ."

"Molly told me." She shrugged. "I told you, I like to know things. And when I could not understand why the man should wish to take us to Vienna for a single concert, she told me that he had done much more than that for you, and likely would again."

Bridget felt her heart begin to beat queerly. Her eyes trained themselves on Oliver's back as her mother pulled him along the path. At that moment, he glanced back at them and winked at her. He was handling their mother with aplomb, it seemed.

"And he makes you better." Amanda's gentle line broke into her thoughts.

"Better," Bridget repeated dully, her brow coming down.

"Well, you are not as angry as you once were. As lost, I should think."

Bridget turned to her sister then, regarding her. "And you are not as young as you once were, are you? I do not think I can handle you being quite this grown up?"

Amanda shrugged, in that way that still marked her youth, and Bridget was glad of it. "I simply do not see the point in denials. I prefer you happy, Bridge. It makes life so much easier. So the question remains, does Mr. Merrick make you happy?"

A breeze picked up at that moment, stirring the skirts at her ankles, winding around her, then moving forward to wrap the pair walking ahead of them up in its life.

"He does make me happy," she admitted quietly. "I'm in love with him, Amanda."

"Oh," Amanda breathed. Then she frowned. "Although I would not let that buy him forgiveness for taking liberties."

"So . . . you approve of Mr. Merrick?"

Amanda turned up an eyebrow at her. "I do not know if it is my place to approve. Just as it is not my place to tell Mother what I saw. Although I think you should."

"I will . . ." Bridget whispered desperately, and meant it. Perhaps she would not tell the particulars of what had transpired between her and Oliver, but she should at least speak her feelings. "At the right time. We have not . . . that is, not discussed . . ."

This time Amanda came up short. "You haven't discussed? For heaven's sake, Bridget . . . How can you not know his intentions? Do you even have any clue what you are doing?"

Bridget's face flamed with shame and not a little bit of anger. Explaining herself to her sister was not on her list of activities for the day.

"Yes, I know what I am doing," she said sternly. She knew his intentions, after all. Didn't she? Granted, the question of marriage had been skirted around—although that was Bridget's doing and not his. And if they did get married, where would they live? Would they remain in Venice? Would Bridget ever be able to go home to England and see her family? Her heart was sick at the idea of not being near her father, her sisters . . .

But no! This was exactly why she did not want to think about what came after the competition. Why she had requested a stay on the judgment, a stasis. A note held without transition.

Oliver glanced back at them then. A smile flashed over his shoulder—and a slightly desperate plea for rescue. She could only giggle as she watched him try to placate her mother with smiles and nods, touched by the solicitous way he always made certain that Bridget and Amanda were fine and within sight.

What on earth did she have to worry about? She shook her head at own foolishness. Oliver had never been anything but wonderful to her. Her safe harbor when it came to her own nerves. Her silent anchor when her lessons became overly intense. Her champion when she exposed that littlest bit of herself with her own compositions.

He was the one person she could truly trust. Even with the most sacred part of herself.

"Yes, Amanda," she said again, but this time more kindly. "I know what I am doing."

And she could only pray she was right.

Twenty-four

THE competition. It loomed in the brains of all parties concerned like a dark portent—one could never be too prepared, because it *was* coming. While Vienna had been a respite, a holiday from the pressures of what they faced, almost as soon as the carriage doors had closed and they took off that next morning at dawn did it become obvious the competition could no longer be pushed out of their thoughts.

Lady Forrester spent the ride alternately moaning in agony, deciding which dress Bridget should wear to play and whether Molly should be required to add any fluff or furbelows to make it shine like it should, and plotting which of their new-found friends in Venice should be present at this competition.

Amanda spent the six-day journey back to Venice keeping a watchful eye on Mr. Merrick, and just as watchful an eye on Bridget, beside whom she insisted on sitting the entire journey, forcing Oliver to take the seat next to their mother. While she may have been willing to trust Bridget that she knew what she was doing with the gentleman, she in no way was under any obligation to trust Mr. Merrick, especially given that he had not yet had the temerity to speak his intentions toward her sister! Although she did find him kind and solicitous and every bit the gentleman, and he did make her sister happy . . . well, suffice it to say, Amanda's maturing mind was at a loss how to categorize Mr. Merrick, and therefore she thought he warranted watching. That was all.

Oliver, meanwhile, spent the journey worrying over Bridget's state of mind, that she was contented and unbothered by anything that could distract her from her playing, all the while his mind completely engrossed in the different tangential possibilities of the future. Also, he could not help wondering why Miss Amanda kept staring at him, as if he were a piece of crown molding to be studied and watched for signs of rot.

And Bridget could only think about how the music was supposed to sound, about the rhythms that came to her from the way the carriage moved with the ruts in the road, and how much she wished she could reach across the space of the carriage and take Oliver's hand.

Every night spent on the road was more and more torturous for the young lovers. Not because their passions overwhelmed them, but because as they got closer and closer to Venice, the worry returned, the grim lines around Bridget's mouth became deeper. It was not without notice that the ability to simply hold each other would do her a world of good. As it would Oliver.

A night of rain made the roads slow going, which added a day of travel to their journey. And which, when Oliver finally walked through the door to his house, had apparently wreaked havoc upon Carpenini's sensibilities as well.

"Where the hell have you been!" he cried, his speech a rush of Italian. "You said you would be back yesterday!"

"I know," Oliver replied, exhausted. They had taken over fifty miles of road that day to reach the banks of the lagoon before dusk settled in. They found a ferryman to take them across the lagoon to the city, and he had just delivered the ladies to their hotel, where Lady Forrester had been appalled to learn that Signor Zinni had let one of the unoccupied rooms on the second floor while they had been away. From the way she blistered Zinni's ears, Oliver had the feeling the poor hotelier was going to have to remedy that problem immediately.

"Rain delayed us," Oliver said in Italian, by way of explanation. "Frederico!" he called out, "I should like some supper, if you please. Sometime before breakfast." He made a move for the worn velvet sofa that he usually occupied, his entire body aching to lie across it.

But Carpenini blocked his path. "And where is Signorina Forrester?"

"Back at her hotel."

"Bring her back here! We have only days until the competition; we must practice through the night!" Carpenini growled, pacing as he sat down at the instrument.

Oliver took in the room. After nearly a fortnight away, he would have expected the place to be an absolute wreck, considering he had left Vincenzo in the deepest throes of composition. Normally there would be balled-up paper everywhere, ink on Vincenzo's cuffs, and a small mound of food detritus—since he would not allow Frederico to come in to clean, if Frederico felt like cleaning anyway.

Oliver turned to Vincenzo as understanding dawned. "You finished your piece."

Vincenzo could not help a small smile. "Yes, I did. And now I should like to concentrate on rehearsing my student before her recital."

"That is excellent!" he cried, collapsing on the sofa while Vincenzo was distracted. "Tell me about it."

"It is a symphony—a full symphony, with weight on the strings, in the beginning, like the dawn awakening . . ."

As Vincenzo began spinning out the description of his symphony, Oliver felt a deep pleasure settle over him. Because not only had he successfully distracted Vincenzo from dragging Bridget to the house for practice at this late hour, but Vincenzo had his piece completed! He had a work that could enjoy its premiere at the Teatro Michelina. And once Vincenzo was vindicated as a musician by Bridget's beautiful playing, the Marchese would back wherever Vincenzo wanted to play . . . Oliver could get him to invest in the Teatro, he could have the place cleaned up in a matter of weeks and be a viable theatre again . . .

As Oliver indulged his fantasies of everything working out perfectly—if not in quite an orthodox manner—he leaned back against the couch and sighed happily.

"So, are you going to play it for me?" Oliver said, stretching his long legs out in front of him.

"Not yet." Carpenini shook his head. If Oliver had not been

so tired, he would have said that his brother was being unusually protective of his work. But he decided better of it.

"Right now," Carpenini said, cracking his fingers, "we must focus on the competition before us. Have the Signorina here at eight o'clock tomorrow."

And she was. Bridget appeared on their doorstep at exactly eight o'clock in the morning, having received Oliver's note the night before, her mother and sister in tow. Now that the competition was so close, their lives revolved around it as well, and they would not leave her side. And Bridget was as restless to play.

Having listened to Vincenzo's recitations all evening about how he was absolutely certain that Bridget had not had opportunity to practice and that her playing would have suffered for the trip, Oliver knew Carpenini was just as eager to hear. But when Bridget sat down and began to play, suddenly Carpenini was singing a very different tune.

"Wonderful! *Bellissima!*" he cried, a wide grin spreading over his face. "I knew a trip to Vienna would bring out what was missing! You hear the master Beethoven and he taught you what was in your heart!"

If Oliver and Bridget happened to exchange a quick glance at that, no one in the room was the wiser. For everyone around them, from Carpenini, to Lady Forrester and Miss Amanda, to Frederico and Molly, who had come to hover in the doorway from the kitchens, had gathered around simply to listen to the transcendent beauty of Bridget Forrester's playing. She had not missed a single note, a single beat, a single emotion. It was all there.

"Just you wait, Oliver," Vincenzo whispered to him, unable to quell the smile on his face. "Come tomorrow, we will show that fraud Klein and whatever poor student he has just who is the better teacher!"

Oliver wanted to roll his eyes at Vincenzo's presumption but could not. Because like the rest of them, he was just happy to let the music roll over him, and think about tomorrow, tomorrow. It would come soon enough.

And it did.

Tomorrow evening came like a rush of stillness, each

minute marked and waited on, gone through with the patience
of those who had only time in their way. Carpenini and Oliver
came to the Hotel Cortile to fetch the Forrester ladies, this
time in a gondola rented for the occasion. Oliver had no desire
to be seen and spotted in as recognizable a vehicle as Lord
Pomfrey's red open contraption again, just in case Klein had
some last-minute ideas in his mind.

They had heard nothing of Klein in the short hours since
they arrived back in Venice. He had not made any overtures to
Oliver or Carpenini; he had not, according to Veronica, come
into La Fenice. His staging of his *Odyssey* had come to an end,
but he had been seen there several times since, kissing the correct hands among the musical patrons of Venice. However,
one could assume that either Klein had been put at ease by the
Forresters' sudden disappearance to Vienna and had not heard
of their return, or he had heard of it and was madly working
to bring his own student up to standard. But either way, for the
journey from the Rio di San Marina along the Grand Canal,
their party was safe.

The Palazzo Garibaldi was lit inside and out with a thousand candles and lamps, making it shine like a beacon over
the sea of gondolas that waited just outside it, jockeying for
position as their tufted and bejeweled passengers made to
disembark.

And Bridget felt for one brief moment that she could not
breathe.

The beautiful palazzo, its reflection in the Grand Canal
fractured by the movement of all the black boats, caught and
held her focus. It was the grandest palace she had ever seen.
Grander than La Fenice. Grander than the homes of the richest
people in London. She had passed the building a dozen times
in daylight and possibly marked its beauty, but now . . . now it
was the setting for the most important night of her life.

It was as if the weight of the palazzo itself settled next to
Bridget in the gondola and would sink them—her—into the
canal.

"Two breaths." Oliver's voice came from her side, a warm
gentle caress. "The first to steady yourself."

She did.

"And the second for what comes next."

By the time she exhaled the last of the second breath, Bridget found that the fear had taken a step back.

She looked up into the eyes of Oliver and took his hand. Her anchor, not caring for once who else could see them. But oddly, no one was paying attention to her at that moment. It had been decided that while Amanda had been permitted to enjoy some of the smaller, more British social functions that Venice had to offer, tonight was too large and uncontrollable an event for someone still sixteen. Therefore she was left in the care of a vigilant Molly, likely one helping the other organize trunks, as they had not yet fully unpacked from their journey to Vienna—possibly because no one knew how long they would be staying in Venice after this evening.

Bridget's mother sat opposite Bridget and Oliver but was concentrating on a distant point on the water, as she had taught herself to do to stave off any uneasiness brought about by the sea travel. Carpenini sat next to her—however, his attention was to the front, on the Palazzo Garibaldi, and the fight that was before them.

The gondola made its way to the front of the line quickly enough. Oliver and Carpenini alighted first, both turning to take Bridget's hand.

"Signorina, tonight you must be by my side," Carpenini commanded, and he brooked no argument. After a moment, Oliver nodded and withdrew his hand.

Bridget stepped out of the gondola on Carpenini's arm and was made a little uneven by it. She was not used to Carpenini's attentiveness in matters other than her technique, her playing, her emotional consistency. Nor did she want Oliver to step into the background.

But on the latter score, she was relieved when Oliver leaned down to her ear and whispered, "And you will be by my side every night after this," causing her to pink with pleasure.

She glanced at him fleetingly as he helped her mother out of the gondola and gave her his arm. They were the words she needed to hear. Needed to know that even though she was Carpenini's student, she was Oliver's in truth. And while she was not on his arm as they made their way into the palazzo, its grand hall and staircase dominating the space, littered with the beautiful and powerful of Venice, he was no more than a step away.

As Carpenini gave their names to the majordomo, a hush came over the crowd. And when the stalwart man bellowed their names to the party, cheers and applause rose with the turning faces of the crowd. Bridget was stunned until she recognized Antonia Galetti making her way through the crowd to their side.

"My darling Vincenzo! Signorina Forrester," she said by way of welcome, bobbing into a scant curtsy as Bridget executed a far more graceful one. Then she extended her hand to Carpenini, and he took it reverently. It was as if through her coquettish smiles and giggles all memory of their previous meeting with Antonia Galetti and her small act of betrayal had been forgiven.

Although, to be fair, she had been away from the Signore for a fortnight . . . who knew how often Antonia had been forgiven in the intervening time.

"Finally, you are here!" she cried in heavily accented English, in deference to Bridget. "We wait, for you," she said, attaching herself to Carpenini's other side. Bridget glanced behind her, finding Oliver there with her mother. Her mother seemed to be taking in the grandeur of the space silently, but not in awe. No, Lady Forrester had no need to be awed. But perhaps she was just a little bit impressed by the ornate hall and staircase, the Tintorettos on the wall, the beauty of the guests.

"For a city in decline, you would not know it here," Bridget heard her mother mutter, and Oliver gave a short chuckle. That was her mother, eminently practical in the face of opulence. And suddenly Bridget felt herself again.

Antonia was pulling Carpenini toward another room through the crowd. Subsequently, he was pulling Bridget, and Oliver and Lady Forrester followed. When they reached the new room, Bridget again found herself rendered speechless—and very, very nervous.

It was a ballroom, but not a ballroom like Bridget had ever seen in a private residence before. The pale blue walls were framed by gilt scrollwork, extending up to a vaulted ceiling floating above them, a celestial night painted on the ceiling above, lit by three massive chandeliers lining the length of the room. But this room had not been prepared for dancing. Rows upon rows of chairs—enough for every person currently jammed into the outer hall!—were facing a polished stage at the far end of the space. And on that stage, which could have fit an entire orchestra, was a single, beautiful, perfect pianoforte. Save their party, the room was empty, except for three men lounging in chairs in the front row, talking and laughing.

"Papa!" Antonia cried across the space. "I have them!"

As they made their way down the echoing space, Bridget recognized one of the gentlemen: Gustav Klein. He was dressed impeccably and seemed to be making the appropriate nods and gestures to his companions, but his stare—that unnerving stare—had locked firmly onto Bridget. Next to him was a younger gentleman—perhaps only a few years older than Bridget herself—just as blond and Germanic as Klein, with a more boyish face. He kept his hands firmly behind his back as he nodded at something Klein said. And the other gentleman, an older man with silver hair and a demeanor that could quell a hurricane, must be . . .

"Papa," Antonia said as they reached the men, holding out her hands to the older gentleman. The Marchese—for it could only be the Marchese—grasped his daughter's hands and kissed them. "I have brought you Carpenini and his little student."

"Marchese"—Carpenini made a deep, obsequious bow—"may I introduce Lady Forrester, and her daughter, my student and entry into this competition, Miss Bridget Forrester."

Both Bridget and her mother stood forward and gave curtsies. The Marchese bowed and did the honor of taking Lady Forrester's hand. "Lady Forrester, an estimable pleasure." The Marchese's English was impeccable, far superior to his daughter's thickly accented speech. Then he turned to Bridget.

"I have heard much about you, little bird," the Marchese said, putting a finger under Bridget's chin, forcing her eyes up from their spot on the ground. His choice of pet name reminded her of the kind captain on the ship over from England. But the rest of him did not. She met his scrutinizing gaze as best she could, knowing that the Marchese was not the only one watching this exchange. "Not only from my dear Antonia. Indeed, everyone here is wondering just what you can do."

Bridget's eyes flicked to the Signore beside her. He nodded

once; she knew what she was supposed to say. "Signor Carpenini has been a great teacher, Marchese," she replied.

The Marchese gave a half smile, a crooked cynicism. "We shall see. He has, at the very least, promised me I shall be greatly entertained tonight. Well, Carpenini," the Marchese said as he turned to that man, "tell me what you think? We could not possibly fit everyone in the music room; thus I had the ballroom refitted to support tonight's events—the stage, the small amphitheater we made of this end here?" He swept his arm over the space, at once owning and dismissing it. "I should like your opinion, too, Mr. Merrick."

Oliver looked away from Bridget for the first time that evening, caught by the Marchese's instruction.

"I am told that you should like to have something like this at your Teatro Michelina . . . if on a different scale," the Marchese continued.

"Possibly." Oliver cleared his throat. "I would accept the Marchese's recommendation for any builder or mason . . ."

As the gentlemen began to move down the length of the room, talking about raised versus sunken orchestras and acoustics (and no doubt, Amanda would kick herself for not being present), Bridget was left with her mother, Klein, and the young unintroduced gentleman, who could only be his student.

"I wish you the best of luck, Fräulein," Klein said, his cold stare never leaving Bridget's face. "You will need it."

Then, before a retort could be issued, Klein and his student bowed and made to join the men in their discussion.

"Heavens, my dear," Bridget's mother said, squinting after Klein's retreating form. "That man just gets more and more unpleasant, doesn't he?"

Bridget's eyes followed Klein as he went, too. Inserting himself between Oliver and the Marchese, making himself the right-hand man of his patron.

"I am afraid he does, Mother."

"I know you must be a little nervous about tonight, my love," she said, nonchalant. "And I know that as your mother, you will think me biased. But I hope you believe me when I say that I have heard you play, and I know you can defeat him."

A giddy resolve began to form in the pit of her stomach. Her mouth became a grim line of determination even as her mother's words seeped into her head, feeding the soil around a seed of an idea that had not really existed before.

She *could* win. It was entirely possible. Before Carpenini, before Venice, she had thought herself a good player—talented, one who understood music at its roots but was felled by an unfortunate case of nerves. But now she knew that to be folly.

Now she was better than she had ever been. Even when she had been free from nervous shatterings, she had never, ever played like this. She had not been lying when she had said Carpenini was an excellent teacher. He was. He was a bit of an ass, in all honesty. He was ruthless, demanding, forcing drills and exercises and study the likes of which she had never attempted before. Before, she was good—but a good dilettante.

Now . . . she was a pianist.

"Thank you, Mother," Bridget said, giving her mother one of her brightest smiles, filled with a surprising honesty. "I fully intend to."

❧

Guests began to fill into the renovated ballroom with the lazy efficiency of the masses promised a treat. As time passed, they began to fill up the seats, chattering and waving to each other, arranging themselves as they thought themselves best presented, choosing which were the most advantageous chairs to take. It was no different than the opera, Bridget thought, except now the assembly did not have boxes to exclude themselves and mingled freely. And rather loudly.

Bridget and her mother were escorted to a small antechamber where the players could hold themselves away from the crowd to "compose their minds," as the Marchese had said. It was a pleasant chamber, with sofas overlooking wide windows that faced an inner courtyard. A perfect place for serenity—even if the occupants would never be at all serene. The crowd beyond could still be seen and heard through the doorway, but no one was coming over to wish Miss Forrester luck—all of the attention was on the Marchese and his two dueling maestros.

Bridget watched as the Marchese, standing in front of the stage, conducted the room. Everyone came up to him before taking their seats, causing a queer sort of receiving line—

queer, because everyone had been received in the outer hall already. To his left stood Klein. To his right, Carpenini and Oliver. Oliver was the only one who glanced their way, making certain they were all right. More than once, he made to step away from the group, but was always pulled back in by some comment from the Marchese, and then by someone who had come up to them in line.

He was like he was at La Fenice, Bridget realized. He was alive, in the presence of all these musically inclined people. All the people he needed to know if he wished to run a theatre.

Carpenini was no different. But while Oliver was good-humored and making people laugh, Carpenini was impressing everyone with his verve and passion. He gesticulated wildly, speaking with enough animation to turn his eyes bright and his cheeks flushed. Occasionally he would indicate Oliver, draw him into conversation. Oliver would do the same with whomever he was talking to, throwing deference back on Carpenini.

The two worked together like a pair of hands. Partners in their social front, ready to take on the world.

"He seems to be enjoying the attention," her mother said in her ear. They were perched on a sofa near the door, both peering (her mother squinting) out into the ballroom.

"He needs it," Bridget replied, her eyes never straying from the pair. "Everyone knows Carpenini needs the Marchese to reinstate his patronage. He must be loved."

"I meant your Mr. Merrick," her mother replied grimly.

"He's not my Mr. Merrick," Bridget protested, but it was futile.

"My dear, I may have left off my spectacles, but I can still see what is truly important," her mother admonished. "I should have thought that he would have had you out there, by his side."

"I do not wish to be out there," Bridget replied. She did prefer it in their little antechamber, where it was cool and nominally quiet. Why, it even looked out onto a calm, pleasant little courtyard. "But if you wish to be, I would understand," Bridget said to her mother.

"You do not want me to stay with you?" her mother asked. It was not a question filled with hurt; it was, however, filled with concern. Bridget squeezed her mother's arm, thankful for that kind tone in her voice.

"Actually, if you would not mind, I think I would prefer to be alone," Bridget replied. "It will be easier for me to concentrate."

"Are you certain, my dear? I would not leave you if you need me."

"Go, Mother. I will be perfectly all right here," Bridget replied. "Besides, you need to go stake your claim for the best possible seat."

Her mother gave her one last squeeze and then pecked her cheek.

"You will be brilliant, my dear. I know it," she whispered, before moving off into the glittering crowds, ready to smile and chatter with the best of them, laying praises upon her daughter all the while.

Leaving Bridget to stand at the door, unable to move forward or back, standing on the edge of the gaiety but not part of it. Not yet. No, she would wait, running through the themes of the music, the trills, the crescendos and decrescendos, letting it play again and again in her mind.

Until it would be time for her to play on the stage.

❧

"When the hell are we going to begin this thing?" Oliver whispered to Carpenini, as the hundredth person came up to them, congratulated them, happy to see Carpenini back to being in his element, eager to see Miss Forrester play against Klein's protégé.

Oliver was eager, too, but his eagerness was also filled with a sense of dread. As much as he enjoyed the flattery of having the Marchese place him firmly there, his entire mind was on Bridget, who by now would be alone in the antechamber, in a state of nervous anticipation. And picturing Bridget nervous made Oliver anxious as well.

"Desperate for it to be over already?" Vincenzo whispered back to him.

"Aren't you?"

"No—this could be our only chance to enjoy any accolades."

"You have so little faith in Bridget?" Oliver shot back, making sure to keep a strong grin on his face.

"Am I the only one prepared for the eventuality that we could lose?" Carpenini replied.

"Are you?" Oliver questioned. "Prepared for what will happen if we lose?"

After all, they could be run out of Venice. At the very least, Carpenini would never play there again, and Oliver would be punished for his support of his brother and likely have to wait another eon before the Teatro Michelina could have an orchestra playing on its stage . . .

"Of course I prepared," Carpenini was saying. "Why do you think I worked so hard to finish my symphony? Even if the Signorina fails, I will play that piece for the Marchese and he will be forgiving of me."

Oliver had to keep from grinding his teeth. "I wish you would have more faith in your student. Do you not remember how she played the room to tears only yesterday?"

"I do. And I will be praying she brings the same confidence to her playing tonight." Vincenzo sent Oliver a sympathetic look. "Do not worry, Oliver. She will play magnificently. My new piece is only in case of true disaster."

Oliver let out a long-held breath. He should not be as harsh on Carpenini as he was—after all, Carpenini had finished his composition *before* Bridget had come back from Vienna with her . . . musical education completed. And considering the importance placed on this competition, it was perhaps right to not have the entire weight of it placed on Bridget's slim shoulders.

"Anyway, it looks as if the wait is over," Vincenzo murmured. Oliver followed the line of his eyes. The Marchese had moved from his spot at the front of the stage to standing upon it.

"Ladies and gentlemen," he cried, in his fluid Italian, "if you would be so kind . . ."

With a wave of his hands, a dozen liveried servants melted off the walls, ornate handheld lamps in hand. They moved the light from the room itself to the stage, placing the lamps on the edge of the stage, effectively lighting the stage and at the same time darkening the room.

The crowd hushed immediately, settling into their seats.

"You are all here because months ago, there was a challenge, a question issued. And we were all too curious to leave it unanswered." The Marchese gave a quick, practiced chuckle. "Well, I could not."

The room chuckled with him.

"Signor Vincenzo Carpenini, Herr Gustav Klein?" With those words, the two composers moved to join the Marchese on stage.

Oliver, seeing his chance, left his place in front of the stage and moved nimbly over to where Bridget was hovering at the doorway to the little room the Marchese had provided for them.

"Miss Bridget," he said formally, smiling as he kissed her hand.

"Mr. Merrick," she returned, but did not play along. Her attention was too much on the stage. So Oliver contented himself with taking her hand and wrapping it around his arm, holding her close to his side.

"I am a bit unclear on who issued the challenge," the Marchese's voice boomed across the room, "but Carpenini has said that he can produce a female student who can best a male student of Herr Klein's at the pianoforte. An interesting choice of weapon for dueling, to be sure." The Marchese gave a wry smile at Carpenini. Vincenzo simply gave a fluid bow to the audience, of which they heartily approved.

"And a piece of music was chosen," the Marchese continued, "that both students learned. And now, it is only for us to introduce them!"

Applause came from the crowd.

"Are you ready?" Oliver asked, leaning down to her. She nodded, her eyes resolutely ahead.

With a breath of resolve, they began to walk up to the stage. Bridget did not pull away or against him—she simply moved with light grace, as if floating, until she came to a stop next to Carpenini, lit by the lamps on the stage.

"May I present Miss Bridget Forrester, lately of England," Carpenini said in Italian, his words intoned so the whole room could hear. From the audience, there was one person who applauded enthusiastically at the name—one could only assume that it was Lady Forrester herself. Bridget smiled wanly when she heard her own name—as much as she had spent the last months in Venice, she had not learned the language nearly enough to follow the conversation.

Of course, it had been known for weeks that Bridget was Carpenini's student—her mother had paraded her around the British expatriate houses of Venice with that information. But there was some speculation as to whether Bridget would appear that evening, and thus the wave of murmurs that followed Lady Forrester's applause was particularly gratifying to Oliver's ears. He looked down at Bridget—she was blinking out into the darkness, trying to see the audience in the dimness. Her face was rigid, unsmiling . . . and alarmingly pale.

"And Herr Klein? Your student?" the Marchese asked.

While Bridget had been a known entity for a little while, Oliver had it on good authority that no one knew which young man he would present. Klein enjoyed innumerable students in Venice, not to mention those he had taught previously in Austria.

But what he said next was not expected.

"I am afraid," Klein said, also in Italian, "that the student I have prepared—Josef, come here—cannot play."

The young man they had met earlier that evening walked up onto the stage, his hands held, as always, behind his back. But when he reached his place beside Klein, he brought his hands forward—the right one wrapped in a huge bandage.

"As you see, the young man has injured himself, just yesterday," Klein said, as a hushed roar of titillation came from the crowd. "And I have no other student who knows the piece."

"What is going on?" Bridget asked in a low whisper. She was watching the proceedings, her eyes glued to the bandage on Josef's hand.

"Klein's student cannot play," Oliver whispered back.

"What does that mean?"

"I do not know," he replied. "Hold on, we may find out yet."

The Marchese was holding forth, turning over Josef's hand in his, inspecting the wound. "This is unfortunate indeed. An unforeseen circumstance that does not please me, Klein."

Klein flushed with chagrin at being admonished by his patron, but charged ahead. "I apologize, Marchese, but it cannot be helped."

"Oh dear." Carpenini chose that particular time to join in

the conversation. "I am afraid that means that you will have to forfeit. How unfortunate, Gustav."

"I do not intend to forfeit, *Vincenzo*," Klein ground out. Then, drawing back into his usual reserve, he said "I would instead take the boy's place myself."

The dull murmurs from the crowd became thunderous at that point. As thunderous as the look on Carpenini's face. But he did not lash out. Instead, he threw back his head in laughter.

"Oh, Gustav, you have been in Venice for months, and you have finally left your rigid, humorless ways back in Austria. Well done."

"I am afraid I do not make fun," Klein replied. "Why can I not—after all, the rules of your challenge state that I must produce a male student. Well, I am male, and I taught myself Beethoven's Number Twenty-three. I am arguably my very best student."

The Marchese, who stood between the two men, watched them intently. Then, with the air of a judge making a decision, he turned to Carpenini. "Gustav has a point," he said, fingering his chin in contemplation. "Besides, I should not like to have my party ruined because it lacked its entertainment."

"Marchese," Carpenini replied, attempting to be as ingratiating as possible, "if Herr Klein is to play in his student's stead, then I must request the same privilege."

"Oh, but your student is to be female," Klein piped up. "You cannot play . . . unless you mean to reveal something even more shocking to us tonight."

The crowd tittered at that. And Bridget dug her hand into Oliver's arm.

"Oliver," she said, her eyes pleading up at him, "I don't understand."

Oliver took a deep breath. "What has happened is that the competition will go on—and your competitor will be Klein himself."

He watched as any faint color that Bridget might have had drained out of her face. Her eyes whipped straight ahead, latching onto Klein. Klein, meanwhile, had done the same, locking eyes with Bridget, staring, unblinking, at her.

He was making his way inside her head, Oliver knew. And

by the way Bridget paled and her hand began to shake, it was working.

Her eyes broke away from his and flew to the audience, just beyond the threshold of darkness. Searching for anyone . . . anything. But there was nothing she could see, only the hazy movements of people, and she could hear their voices, their whispers, amplified against the walls of the ballroom.

"I'm not ready," she whispered to Oliver, her voice shaking.

"Well, now that that is decided," the Marchese was saying, controlling the room with the elegance of a ringmaster, "shall we agree on the order?"

"Oh, since I have caused such difficulty," Klein was saying with an obsequious bow, "let me cause no more, and offer Signor Carpenini the advantage. Ladies first."

"Oliver, I'm not ready," she repeated, her fear palpable in her voice. He reached down, tried to hold her hand against his arm, tried to steady her, but she jumped at his touch, pulled herself away, and fled the stage.

The crowd, already on the edges of their seats from the dramatics—before the music could even begin—began standing and pointing when Bridget left the stage. She ran to the small antechamber where he had collected her and firmly shut the door.

Oliver turned to Carpenini. "Buy her some time. I will calm her down and bring her out—that goddamn Klein is playing head games with her, staring her down, becoming her opponent—"

"I would bet his student's hand was injured by his own," Carpenini grumbled darkly.

"Probably, but it does not matter—you just need to buy us some time!"

"How?"

"You're the one who prepared for this," Oliver replied, exasperated. Then he turned to the Marchese and said, in a loud voice, so everyone could hear, "Marchese! Er . . . Before the competition begins, the Signor Carpenini has a gift to offer you!"

Carpenini's face seemed to fall into a grim line. Then, decision made, he opted to go along with it.

"*Si*, Marchese," Carpenini said with a bow. "With your

permission, I should like to play for you the main theme from my new symphony."

The Marchese looked over at them with a bemused smile.

"You have something new, Carpenini?" he said. "How utterly rare."

"Er, yes. I hope to stage it with a full orchestra in the fall, but I could not wait that long for you to hear it."

"You hope to stage it in the fall . . . I can only guess where," the Marchese replied, his eyes falling on Oliver. Then, with a wave of his hand, he said, "Very well. Let us hear this new piece."

As Carpenini made his bow to the Marchese, then to the audience, Oliver could wait not a moment longer. He took three long strides to reach the edge of the stage and ran down the steps, flying into the antechamber and after Bridget.

Twenty-five

BRIDGET felt like a fool. A complete and utter fool. She had spent all that time convincing herself she could do this, training and becoming a better, stronger player, and one small hiccup and a stare from Klein's ice blue eyes and she was undone.

It was utterly ridiculous! She *would* go out there, and she *would* show him, Klein, Carpenini, her mother, the entire crowd gathered for the gala—that she could do this. Despite the enormous pressure she was being put under, despite the strange way her body felt both light and heavy, both hungry and full and fluttering—she would go out there.

In a moment.

She instead sat on the sofa, looking out the long windows onto the courtyard, and let herself breathe. Once to steady herself . . . A second breath for—

"Are you all right?"

Bridget turned in her seat. Oliver stood by the door, slipping the latch shut.

"Yes," she replied with a smile. "I just feel foolish, is all."

"Foolish," he repeated, as he came over to her, seating himself beside her. "For what?"

"For thinking I had this conquered," she replied, shrugging sadly. "For letting myself give in to my fears and run."

"You do have this conquered," Oliver replied, resting his hand over hers. "Klein is a bastard. He has played a game with this competition and is hoping to play one with your head. He must know that you are too good a pianist to try to best you honorably."

"I know." She shook her head, trying to smile. "In my mind, I know that. And perhaps, as I'm playing, the rest of me will catch up." She rose then, steeling her resolve.

"You don't have to play quite yet," Oliver whispered warmly, not letting go of her hand. "Vincenzo has bought us a few minutes' reprieve. He is playing his newest composition for the Marchese. Listen."

Bridget did—and heard the magnificent pianoforte, its music drifting in from the large ballroom to their small, still space.

"This is new?" she asked, letting herself listen for a few moments. "It's lovely."

"He's been working on it for a while, finally cracked it while we were away. He's quite proud of it."

"And you are of him." She sat back down by his side.

"I have to say, I am pleased that he has found his way back to music—and that he is keeping his promise to me, in letting me stage it in the fall." Oliver gave a small frown. "If I ever manage to get the Teatro back into shape."

"You will," Bridget replied. "Once the competition is won, Carpenini will be welcomed back into the Marchese's fold, and you will benefit from his patronage as well."

"I do not wish to think about that right now." Oliver shook his head, and she knew he meant the competition aspect of it. The fact that it all rested on her shoulders. This great favor she was doing for them.

"Nor do I," Bridget replied. "In fact, I would like to think of nothing at all." She looked up at him from under her lashes. He reached up, letting his knuckles graze lightly against her cheek. It was the first time in ages that they had been alone together. The first time since that night that they had no fear of being seen. They could be themselves with each other, at last.

Oliver leaned forward, took her mouth with his, and
Bridget bowed into him, grateful for the contact. He kissed her
lips, her eyelids, the easy spot beneath her earlobe—every one
a thank-you, every one a gift.

His gentleness, his reverence nearly undid her, but more
than that, it gave her strength, made her bold. She took what
he offered and let herself go to the sensation. Let herself be
in that moment. Not the one that would follow, and not the
months of hard work and conquering fear that had preceded it.
But simply being there, in that little room, at that one minute
in time, it was all the comfort she could have ever asked for.

"Bridget"—he broke away, her name on his breath a
prayer—"you're thinking again."

"I am," she admitted, biting her lip. Oliver's thumb moved
lazily against her jaw. "I was thinking about how much I like
this moment, and how I wish the next were over, so I could
have more moments like this instead."

Oliver's hand stilled. Then after what seemed an age, he let
out a slow, long-held breath. "You want moments like this one."

"I do."

"Forever?" he asked, his voice becoming ragged.

Now it was Bridget's turn to go still. Oliver carried on.

"I told you that once this was over, I would have a question
to ask you." His thumb began to move again—a caress, a persuasion. "Would you like me to ask you that question now?"

Bridget looked into his eyes, could not look away. And suddenly she wanted to hear the question. She wanted to face
what was coming and not stall it, not put it off, not be *afraid*.

She had spent so much time afraid.

Afraid of performing for people. Afraid of not measuring
up to her sister Sarah. Afraid of being judged. Afraid of
losing—be it a moment in time or a competition. She had spent
so much time afraid that it overshadowed any accomplishment
that she had made in that time. After all, she had performed
on the stage of La Fenice! She had learned Beethoven's No. 23.
And she had somehow managed to get this man to fall in love
with her—and vice versa.

She had a single point of bravery that had changed her life.
She had come to Venice—perhaps at the time she had been
running from failure in London, but she had come to Venice
and it had altered everything. Because it had introduced her to

this man, with whom she would never be afraid. Never be judged. He could always be trusted and she would always be safe.

She opened her mouth to let him know what she felt, to tell him to ask the question he so wished to ask. But before she could, something else came into the room.

Something that would change everything, once again.

At some point, in those few blissful minutes, Carpenini's playing, floating in from the ballroom outside, had changed. He had shifted from the opening movement—a bright, cheerful march—to the second, which was deeper, more complex in theme. The notes came to Bridget as if through a fog. It started quietly, peacefully, like the morning sun just touching the waters to the east of the city. Then it built with the bustle of a day spent being met by new things, surprises, happy exclamations. Then the falling into night, a quieting down again, a delighted exhaustion.

To Bridget Forrester, it was the sound of a foreigner awakening to Venice and falling in love with its cacophony.

It was her "Ode to Venice."

"What is that?" Bridget asked, horror breaking over her mind. "Is . . . is he playing my 'Ode to Venice'?"

Oliver seemed as shocked as she was. He dropped his hands from her face, standing abruptly.

"Do not worry," he said, turning to her—his face nothing but worry, turning quickly to anger. "Give me a moment. I will get to the bottom of this."

And he stood and exited the room, closing the door quietly behind him.

The next few minutes, Bridget went numb. She knew that she heard her 'Ode to Venice,' woven through this movement and the next, built within the layers of the piece. She knew that at some point, the music stopped and the applause began. And she knew, without a doubt, that Oliver and Carpenini would be coming into her antechamber next, to fetch her to play.

And suddenly the room became too small for her.

Air, she needed air. Fleetly, she moved to one of the long windows—actually a door—overlooking the courtyard and stepped out into the night air. A small fountain bubbled in the center, but she did not care about the peace it brought. She instead let herself lean against the cool stone of the palazzo just outside the door, trying to calm down, trying to compose herself.

Carpenini had stolen her music. Her composition. It was as if he had taken her *child* and put his own name upon it. Then he had thrust it into the middle of his symphony, and the world had applauded his originality. If she could she would rip his teeth out, the lying wretch!

But no, she stopped herself from thinking violently, and futilely. Even if she had the strength and attitude to rip his teeth out, it still would not stop him from playing. Or from passing off her music as his. No, the only thing that could stop him now was Oliver.

Oliver. Just thinking of him calmed her nerves. Of course. He would find a way to fix this. He would, she had no doubt.

Unfortunately, at that moment, her faith would prove unjustified.

"Oliver, come now—" Carpenini's voice floated into the antechamber, the click of a door opening preceding it.

"Can you really have no idea just what you've done? She is nervous enough as it is," Oliver's voice answered harshly. Then, calling out into the darkness, "Bridget? Are you here?"

But Bridget, still in a daze, could not move from her spot on the wall. Her despair kept her rooted, kept her listening.

"Did you see her come out of this room?" Oliver was saying, his anger and frustration showing in his voice.

"I was not looking, I was too busy playing and being applauded," Carpenini replied with a sniff. Because Oliver was speaking English, Carpenini was, too—his frequent use of it over the past few months with her had made it as common to him as Italian. "Did you not hear them? They loved me, they loved the music!"

"Yes, I did hear them. What I did not hear was any acknowledgment from *you* that you did not write it."

"I wrote every note of it!" Carpenini growled. "Everyone borrows from other composers, builds on their themes. There was also some Bach in there, some Haydn . . ."

"The difference is, when you borrow from Bach or Haydn, people say, 'Oh, he's reinterpreting old masters.' When you 'borrow' from a young unknown, no one says anything!"

"A bit hypocritical, coming from the man who helped me do it!"

"What the hell are you talking about?" Oliver bit out.

"You knew she was talented, had her play her piece, knowing I would overhear—"

"That's not—"

"Then you remove her from Venice for a fortnight so I have time to work in peace—an arrangement you enjoyed as well, do not think I have not noticed."

"Damn it, that wasn't—"

"Tell the truth, Oliver," Vincenzo spat out. "You are not angry at my having borrowed her piece—you are angry that I played it in front of her, and it upset her. Enough to run away, it seems."

"I am angry at all of it, damn you!" Oliver replied in a ragged whisper. And then something fell, or was pushed, because a thud and crash followed, the sound of something heavy—flesh? books?—hitting the floor.

Both men fell silent for a moment, the tension in the air palpable, floating out into the courtyard. Suddenly, she could hear someone let out a long-held breath.

"What do you wish me to do, Oliver?" Carpenini asked, all aggression gone from his voice. "All you have wanted me to do for the past year is compose. Hell, you bought a theatre for it! You have been pushing me, day after day after day. And I finally have, and it is *great*. Hell, the Marchese was so impressed he took my hand. We may not even need the Signorina to play now!"

Carpenini paused, as if trying to collect his courage. "If I go out there now and tell him that it was not my original work . . . the Signorina could play as if Beethoven himself possessed her, and we would not win back his favor. I would never have his patronage again, and you, by your association with me, would never be able to open your teatro. Even if you had it outfitted in gold, one word from the Marchese and no one would dare set foot there."

Oliver gave a grunt, perhaps in a scoffing manner, but there were no words to counter Carpenini's persuasion.

"It is done now," Carpenini said softly. "Can we not just move forward?"

The words hung in midair, taking up all the space. Bridget could no longer hear the babbling of the fountain in the courtyard, nor, from the opposite direction, the murmurs of people in the ballroom beyond the door. No, the whole world was those few words.

And the world was brought low by what Oliver said next.

"Fine," he conceded. "We shall move forward. For now."

"Thank you, Oliver, my brother," Carpenini sighed in relief.

"Let's just get this ghastly night over with," Oliver said grimly.

"Yes, please!" Carpenini gave a short laugh. Then, a little hesitation entered his voice. "What shall you tell Signorina Forrester?"

"God only knows. I'll make up something for now about how you intended it as a sort of honor, I suppose," Oliver replied. "That is, if we can find her."

"There is no need, gentlemen," Bridget said, her voice as strong and resolved as she could make it. She lifted herself off the courtyard wall and presented herself in the doorway to the courtyard, in full view of the occupants of the small room.

Carefully, she moved through the door, her head held high, her back straight. And her eyes were absolutely dry.

"Signorina!" Carpenini cried, the slightest of nervous quavers invading his demeanor. "Thank goodness, we worried. Did we not, Oliver?"

Oliver came over and tried to take her hand. She moved politely but definitively out of his grasp.

"Bridget," Oliver tried, his face grave. "What you heard . . . I cannot explain—"

"So do not try," she answered. "I should hate for you to have to 'make up something.'"

There was sufficient ice in her voice to throw Oliver off his balance. In fact, he looked visibly struck.

"You know, I do not know which of you is worse," she said, very calmly, almost passively. She settled her gaze on Carpenini. "You, who would steal music from your student." She turned to Oliver. "Or you, who would let him."

Oliver looked ill—then began to say something. But before any words could be formed, a soft knock came at the door.

"I'm so sorry." Bridget's mother stuck her head in. "But they are waiting for you, my dear." Her mother's eyes found Bridget's in the darkness. "The Marchese seems anxious for the competition to begin."

Bridget nodded once, sparing her teacher a cold glance. "So it seems you do need me to play after all."

"Signorina," Carpenini began, letting go of any pretense they might have had. "Please, I beg you forget what you just heard. Play well. Play your best. I know you can do it. And it would be lifesaving for me—for Oliver! Come, Signorina— show mercy upon us."

"Oh, Signore," Bridget sighed, her voice a steel blade. "Don't you understand?" She lifted her hand delicately, indicating the ballroom beyond. "This has never been about you."

And with that, Bridget squared her shoulders, painted a look of pure serenity on her face, and joined her mother in the ballroom.

The room hushed as she emerged, everyone settling into their seats. Her mother walked with her until she came to the stage; then she let her daughter carry on alone. Bridget held her head high as she mounted the stage and came to stand before the pianoforte.

She looked down into the front row—past the stage lamps she could see the Marchese sitting next to his daughter Antonia Galetti, who smiled smugly. The Marchese gave a nod, giving her leave to proceed.

Bridget gave the room a short curtsy. Then she turned and seated herself at the pianoforte.

Somewhere, in the back of her mind, she knew she could do something horrible, something little right now. She could play terribly on purpose, to destroy any hope that Signor Carpenini had of winning the competition. She could do that, she supposed, and walk away with a spiteful heart. But somehow, she also knew that if she engaged in that kind of revenge, it would only end up hurting her. After all, it would be her failure at the keyboard, not Carpenini's.

So she had to play. She would not give him—either of them—the satisfaction of bringing her low, of making her petty. Regardless of the way her heart was beginning to hurt, she had to play.

And so she put her fingers on the keys and began.

Almost at once, she knew something was wrong. She had begun too fast; the rhythm was rushed. Someone in the audience coughed, jarring her. She hit her first grace note before the beat, not on it. Then, not eight measures in, she flubbed a slur and hit a wrong note.

Hands shaking, Bridget lifted her fingers from the keys. Her eyes swam. Her heart beat like she faced a firing squad. Her nerves had never left her, it seemed, never given up the fight for her attention.

She turned her head to look out into the audience, where just beyond the veil of darkness a few hundred people sat, waiting.

Her judges.

"I'm sorry," she said, her voice thick with the threat of tears. But just when she wanted to run, as she had done in the past—hell, in the last half hour!—she forced herself to stay rooted to the spot.

Her nerves would not get to win this time.

"I . . . I should like to start again," she said firmly. Then placed her hands over the keys.

There was a point, between the end of a failure and the beginning of a new attempt, where one could allow change to squeeze in. Where a decision was made—between letting oneself fall or picking oneself up again. And it was that point around which whole worlds revolved.

One breath, to focus yourself.

In that moment, Bridget let her mind sharpen, her eyes firmly on the keys, letting them grow in her vision, just beyond her hands. She saw them clearly. She saw the music clearly.

A second breath, for what comes next.

And then she played.

At first, it was just the notes, just the way they were on the page, that filled her head. She could see them, just beyond the keys, guiding her measure by measure.

But it was not long before the notes floated away, leaving her with what she knew by rote, what she felt, and how she had gotten there.

The first few stanzas of the No. 23 were her trepidation. Her fear of being in a ballroom in London, of being compared to her sister. Of living a comparative life to her sisters. Then, a great thundering crash, a start of something rushed, and falling . . . like a tree through the front room of the Forrester town house—letting cold air in and waking her up. Waking Bridget up.

She let her fingers transition into the driving, thunderous undercurrent of eighth notes, sixteenth notes, a sense of drive, of spirit. Of something reckless and new.

She stepped out of the boat onto the streets of Venice. And hunted down her object with a hope and certainty only the naïve could have.

A change of key, into a minor step—expectations are not always met.

Oliver standing at the door, surprised.

And sometimes, you lay eyes on someone so important and yet, in that moment, you do not see them as such. And yet, you recognize them.

And then, everything changed. The music evolved into its second movement, a strange peace overtaking everything. A reprieve.

Oliver, walking her home, after lessons. His enthusiasm for the city infecting her.

She played with the stately grandeur of someone who knew the path that was laid out before her and enjoyed the details one can see only when one is no longer lost. A trill here, a small crescendo there—she could make this section her own.

Wandering the streets of Venice. A kiss in a cobblestone alley. A circus.

Falling in love leisurely, without realizing it was happening.

The music changed once again—the reprieve, the grace of the second movement was always too short-lived for Bridget's liking. Now came the rush of necessity. Of moving through the mud and finding yourself only inches farther away than you were before—but much, much stronger for it.

Lessons, drills, hand exercises. Working harder than she had ever worked in her life.

Finally, she reached the epoch of the run, the notes that were written on a scale about the scale. A mad rush of finger work that took all of her strength, all of the length of her arms. Thank heaven for the fashion of short sleeves in evening dress and summer wear, because Bridget did not have Oliver's shirt to save her this time.

The music slowed suddenly, a *ritardando* that brought the

drive up short and forced the listeners to catch their held breath. A descending scale of notes, a falling dream in the middle of a sleepless night.

A daring, stolen gondola ride, under the stars. A wander by water.

But it ended in a crash of terror, this short reprieve immediately sent back to the beginning of the movement, a split refrain. Only this time, the pressure increased. Since it was a repeated movement, one knew what was coming. But one did not know the heart-pounding level of power that refrain could have.

Hearing Beethoven's symphony for the first time. Making love with Oliver. All of it. Power. Joy. Need.

She pushed all of her emotions, her memory of that one transcendent night into this section. Into this repeated movement. Into its speed, its precision. But something else was there, too, something she had never had before, when she played.

Sadness. Loss. Throwing everything away with a few short words.

And that was what she did. She threw the notes away, the keys. Threw them far into the air and let them fall in an arc like water, a spiraling ascent and descent pushed through herself at impossible speed and ejected. Let go.

And it was glorious, because it set her playing free.

She didn't want it anymore. She did not want this piece. And she did not want the applause that came in a massive wave once she hit those last notes with such force and verve they vibrated in the air long after she had finished.

It took a moment for Bridget to realize what was happening. Her breaths game in hard gulps, her hands still pulsing with the need to play, calluses forming from how hard she was striking the keys. A gleam of perspiration sat upon her brow. She had never, never played with as much feeling in her life. She had never before gotten that lost in the music, in the world she built around it.

And the reaction was breathtaking.

Once her eyes managed to adjust, she could see beyond the dark veil and into the audience; she could tell that they were all on their feet. Not one of them was seated, and every single one was applauding wildly. Bridget could even see some ladies waving their handkerchiefs—and then one of them threw hers upon the stage! A favor thrown for a musical performance by a lady was strange in and of itself, but for Bridget . . . it was wholly alien.

She bent to a curtsy, the only thing she could think of to do, gathering up the thrown handkerchief while she was bent low. Then, to cries of "*Brava! Encore!*" Bridget left the stage as quickly as her shaky legs could carry her.

She found her mother emerging from the sea of the applauding audience. Lady Forrester wrapped her in a hug, then took her by the shoulders. "Bridget, that was magnificent! I have never heard you play like that—I . . . I was crying!"

And indeed, she had been. The telltale shine on her cheeks gave it away, but the smile on her face told her it was tears of joy.

A giddy lightheartedness began to invade Bridget—it was happiness. It was, more than anything, relief.

"Indeed," came a voice from behind her. A simple touch on her shoulder told her who it was. And suddenly, that lightheartedness began to feel hollow. She spared a glance over her shoulder. Hard, so hard for her to do.

"I have never heard playing like that," Oliver said, his voice cracking with emotion. It seemed he had a few tears as well. "Bridget, please, let me explain . . ."

Behind him, Bridget could see Carpenini, as energetic as a schoolboy, happily shaking the Marchese's hand. She could see Klein, too, just beyond the Signore, looking murderous, and nervous. Carpenini saw it, too, and could not help a gloating smile.

"There is no need to explain," Bridget said simply. "You chose him. Threw in your lot. You always have. Go, revel in your success."

"What is that supposed—"

"Mother, I'm suddenly very tired," she said, turning to her mother, who was following the conversation raptly—and not without concern. "I should like to go now, if possible."

"Er, you do not wish to stay?" she asked. "To hear the rest of the competition?"

"No," she answered succinctly. "I would like to go home."

"Of course, my dear," her mother conceded. And without another glance over her shoulder, she let her mother lead her through the crowd, still applauding, still talking, their voices the squawking of a thousand excited geese in Bridget's mind, to the doors, and out into the night.

Away from the party.

Away from Carpenini, away from Oliver.

Away from this movement, this chapter of her life.

Away, indeed, from Venice.

Twenty-six

"WHAT do you mean, gone!?"

Oliver cursed in Italian, pulling Signor Zinni, the poor and currently quite frightened owner and operator of the Hotel Cortile, off his feet by the lapels of his coat.

"They left at dawn tide, Signore," Zinni answered, as politely as he could. "They had all their trunks still packed from their trip to Austria, and when Signora Forrester wants something, she finds a way. So when Signorina Bridget said it was time to go back to England, it was no difficulty to secure passage on the next ship . . ."

Oliver let go of the little man, with a bit more vehemence than he likely should have. Zinni stumbled back, catching himself on his heels.

"I am sorry, Signore," Zinni said, straightening his jacket. "But they rowed out and met their ship before the sun had risen. They are well into the Adriatic by now."

Oliver cursed himself as he left the Hotel Cortile. He cursed himself for waiting until the following morning to seek out Bridget. He cursed himself for his stupidity in what he had said, in what he had conceded last night. And he cursed himself most of all for listening to Vincenzo.

"Let her go," his half brother had said, as Bridget and her

mother disappeared into the crowd of the Marchese's ball-room. "She is too overwrought from the performance now." He took Oliver by the arm and pulled him toward their host. "Trust me. I know. I cannot speak for hours after a performance like that. Come, the Marchese wishes to congratulate us."

And so, he let her go. Stupidly, foolishly. The rest of the evening was spent in hollow conversation. In a glass of wine or whiskey too much, trying to soothe his ragged senses. In coming home too late, and sitting up all night, waiting until such a time as it was appropriate to come and call. He had spent the evening racking his brain, trying to figure out what to say to Bridget, how to defend his detestable actions, how to get her to forgive him.

And she had spent it fleeing the city.

Fleeing *him*.

She had played amazingly last night. He had heard her play beautifully before, he had seen her play naked just for him and seen her play in front of a thousand people at La Fenice, but nothing had had the power, the defiance of her performance at the Marchese's. She had deserved to be the one receiving the praise, to shake the hands of the nephews of kings, the elite whose family name had once been written in the golden book.

But she wasn't. She didn't. She had not cared a whit for it, the thing that would have made her a name, a shining star among her peers. The thing that Carpenini fed from. The thing that, if he harnessed it, would put the Teatro Michelina on the map.

He turned a corner. Then another. Trying to lose himself in the city that he loved. But now, every corner reminded him of a wander, a lost afternoon.

Of Bridget.

He was reeling, lost in his own city, lost once again on the streets, missing a guiding force he hadn't known he'd needed.

He had ruined it. It was well and truly his mess.

What was he going to do now?

His mind was a blank, reeling pit of blackness as he crossed a footbridge and his own dilapidated little house came into view.

He did not want to go home. But he had nowhere else to be. He walked through the door and was immediately surprised to see that Frederico was not only awake, but at his position near the door.

"Well?" Frederico said, oddly anxious. "Where is she?"

"Sailing down the Adriatic," he answered flatly. "Bring something to eat to the drawing room. I need to figure out what to do."

"How can you think about food at a time like this!" his manservant cried.

Oliver was so shocked, he stepped back and stared at Frederico. The look on his face must have been something to behold, because Frederico immediately retreated a few steps.

"Er, that is . . . I'll go see what can be got from the kitchen," Frederico stammered, then moved with a fleetness of foot Oliver didn't know he had, away from him.

Just as Bridget had flown away from him.

Oliver entered the music room and was nearly bowled over by sadness. Everything in this space was Bridget to him. Hell, his shirt that she had worn was still hanging behind the screen!

He went to the screen, grabbed the shirt in his hands, and collapsed on the worn velvet couch where he had spent so many mornings and afternoons. Completely and utterly numb.

"What are you doing?" Vincenzo's voice came from the doorway. "Aren't you supposed to be smoothing things over with your Signorina?"

"She's gone," Oliver said bleakly. "They have left Venice. They are on their way back to England."

"How is that possible?" Vincenzo asked, and Oliver filled him in on what the hotel proprietor had said.

"I'm so sorry," Vincenzo said, pressing a hand to his heart. But then he straightened. "Come, you must cheer up. And you must clean up—bathe and shave. Else we will be late."

"Late?" Oliver growled. "For what?"

"For the Marchese!" Vincenzo rolled his eyes. "A note came while you were out. We are to meet him and Antonia at your teatro. He is very curious about what must be done to turn it back from a warehouse into a theatre." Vincenzo moved over to the window, using the glass to inspect his reflection, straightening his coat. "We only have today; the Marchese will be leaving for his house on the mainland for the rest of summer soon. He wants to fund the production of the symphony, you know. Klein was livid . . . but I doubt he'll be in

Venice much longer, so that blond, humorless statue will not matter soon."

Oliver watched his friend, his half brother, in complete silence.

"Vincenzo, I'm not going with you."

"Not dressed like that, you're not," Vincenzo answered blithely. "Is that the same coat from last night? Did you sleep at all?"

"No. Vincenzo, I'm not going with you. Ever."

Vincenzo rolled his eyes and heaved a great sigh. "And why not?"

"Are you completely insane? I have to go find Bridget."

"Her again," Vincenzo said under her breath.

"Yes," Oliver said, rising to his feet. "Her. Or have you forgotten her already? The student who played the Number Twenty-three better than even you could last night. The student you stole music from in the very same breath."

"Damn it, Oliver, I thought you said we could move past this!" Vincenzo grumbled.

"Well, we cannot. It's too large. We betrayed her. You and me, and if you had any decency, you would own up to it."

"What are you going to do, Oliver? Chase her all the way to England?" Vincenzo scoffed.

"Yes," Oliver said, realization dawning. "That's precisely what I'm going to do. Frederico!"

He bellowed his manservant's name, and Frederico appeared within seconds, a tray of meats in his hand that Oliver had forgotten he wanted.

"Arrange passage for me on the next available ship to England. Whatever the cost, it will be met." Oliver reflected for a moment. "You are welcome to come with me, or you may stay and serve Signor Carpenini. He'll likely be moving back to the Marchese's palazzo—the lease on this house will be given up, at any rate."

Frederico nodded, and then, after a moment's hesitation, spoke. "Er, if it would be possible, Signore, I would prefer to come with you." Frederico turned a rather unseemly shade of red. "It's just that . . . Signorina Molly is with her mistress, and I—er, that is . . . we developed a rapport . . ."

Oliver's eyebrows shot up. "Very well. We can be lovesick

and irritable at sea together. Molly did do wonders at making you a better manservant."

True to his newly improved skills, Frederico said nothing to this and instead bowed his way out of the room, presumably to go set up their passage.

"Are you mad?" Vincenzo asked. "What about the Teatro? What about all the money you have put into it?"

"Hang the Teatro," Oliver said grimly. "I will build a new theatre in England. It will take years, but I will do it, for her."

"I don't believe you." He threw up his hands. "The Marchese is within our grasp, and you wish to go chase a petulant girl halfway across the world? She doesn't matter, Oliver!"

"That's where you are wrong. She does matter. She matters more than anyone." Oliver turned to his friend, seeing him with new eyes. And they were not kind. "What is it—was it the fact that she is so talented? That she played so well, composed such a beautiful 'Ode to Venice'? Or was it that she preferred me over you? When did you stop giving a damn?"

"Oh, Oliver," he sneered. "I never gave a damn. Not about her feelings. Not about the fact that you were bedding her. All I cared about was how she played, impressing the Marchese, and getting my rightful place back."

"And there it is," Oliver said, clapping his hands together in mock applause. "Finally a little truth from behind the facade. I know you don't care about much, but foolishly, I did think you cared about me."

"About you? Oliver, I *made* you! I brought you to Venice! I got you your place at La Fenice!"

"And in the past five years, you've never let me forget it!" Oliver shouted back. "You have spent the past year living off me and my father's money like a parasite, and I allowed it, because of familial feeling. Making empty promises—"

"Empty? Ha!" Vincenzo cried. "I am making good on those promises right now!"

"Falsely. You stole the music of the woman I love, and a woman who trusted you as a teacher. You have no shame, do you?"

"Not if it gets me what I need." Vincenzo rounded on him. "You had our mother, you had a father with money, and you have never known what it's like to claw your way to your position."

"And you have never known what it's like to care more about someone else than about yourself. I did that, for you. I chose you, Vincenzo. Every time. Over my father, when he did not want me to come to Venice with you, when he thought it might be foolish. I did not even know you, but I was so excited at the prospect of having a real relationship with a brother—"

"You felt pity for me, because you stole our mother away from me," Vincenzo snapped.

"Maybe I did," Oliver conceded. "And you used that pity to your advantage. But I also chose you over every other person in Venice, when you were cast down and had no one. And last night I *idiotically* chose you over Bridget Forrester, something I will regret forever. And if she does not forgive me, so help me Vincenzo, I will never forgive you."

They stood toe-to-toe, eye to eye, fists clenched. Brothers— same hair, same complexion, but so different in every other respect. In how they treated people. In how they thought about others. It was many long seconds before Vincenzo finally broke his gaze away.

"Fine!" he said, throwing up his hands. "I will go meet the Marchese myself." He went back to the window, began straightening his coat again. "Have fun chasing the girl across the country. Have fun dealing with your father again. I don't need you, Oliver. I have never needed you. I have never needed anyone."

"No, Vincenzo," Oliver said sadly. Resigned. But relieved. "It is I who do not need you. And knowing that makes me free."

And with that, he turned on his heel and left the music room, ran upstairs, and began the hasty process of locating trunks and throwing things in them.

After five long years, he was going home.

Twenty-seven

"**I** declare, Miss Forrester, why have we not met before? You are far too fine a gel to be shut away in the country!" Mr. Hartley was grinning at Bridget with a dewy look in his eyes, as if he were in some kind of wonderful daydream. The nice, chinless, younger son of a Baronet from Yorkshire led her through the turns of their quadrille with, if not precisely grace, at least well-practiced concentration.

It was the middle of the regular Season, and apparently, the warmth that had eluded England in the winter had visited early and often in the summer. So much so, that most families had already quit the unpleasant growing stink of the city for the more comfortable climes of their country homes.

When the Forrester ladies had arrived back in town, it was to find Lord Forrester ecstatic to see his family again and their town house whole once more, but the front sitting room had not yet been refurbished (Lord Forrester wisely said he was waiting for his wife's return, because if he attempted to decorate it himself it would simply be undone once she came home at any rate). Sarah Fletcher—née Forrester, Bridget's elder sister—was thrilled to see them as well, if for no other reason than their father had taken to having dinner at the new-lyweds' house, and most newlyweds would have preferred at least a modicum of privacy.

Lord and Lady Forrester, when reunited, proved rather newlywed-like, too, and thus, when Sarah informed them that they had been invited to Lady Phillippa Worth's house party at her country estate in Effingham, Surrey, they were more than happy to have Sarah act as chaperone to her two sisters while they stayed in London.

It was an enormous to-do, the way everything that Lady Worth did turned out to be, and it seemed as if everyone Bridget had missed the opportunity to meet over the Season was in attendance, to make up for that lack.

But there were a few people she had met before.

"Mr. Hartley, I am shocked that you do not remember," Bridget replied cheerfully when they came together again through the movement of the lines. "We met in the Little Season, and I remember you and your friend Mr. Coombe."

"Coombe?" A queer look crossed Hartley's face. "And you say we chatted?"

"Yes, Mr. Hartley, we chatted very amiably." Then Bridget decided to cut Mr. Hartley a little slack. "But it was right before we left town to go to Italy, so I do not fault you for not remembering. One meets so many people in London, it takes at least two or three introductions for anyone to stick."

"I should imagine you would stick, Miss Forrester," Mr. Hartley replied. "You are too bright a diamond to be out of anyone's mind for long."

Bridget blushed prettily and shook her head at the compliment. A diamond, indeed. Oh, Bridget knew she wasn't a diamond by any stretch of the imagination, but since coming back a week ago, she had been much . . . calmer, she supposed. Less easily rattled, less confrontational. She smiled more, because she was no longer afraid.

Ever since that night at the Marchese's palazzo, she had lost any sense of fear of being judged. Because no outcome could be anywhere near as heartbreaking as the one that night.

Therefore, there was absolutely nothing to fear from any of the young men who filled her dance card—and they did fill her dance card—she thought, as Mr. Hartley led her off the floor, leaving her with her sisters (Amanda, it seemed, had talked Sarah into letting her *finally* wear her hair up) to wait for the gentleman who had her next waltz to come and find her.

"Here you are," her sister Sarah said, as she came to stand beside her. "You will be quite interested in this. Mr. Fairleigh here was just telling me about this new symphony by Beethoven. Apparently it's all the rage in Vienna."

"And I was telling Mr. Fairleigh that we *know* already," Amanda piped up, but Sarah shot her a look of sisterly affection (which from afar might be interpreted as a look of death) and instead turned and presented Mr. Fairleigh to Bridget.

Sarah did not know what had transpired in Venice—unless, of course, Amanda had broken her promise not to betray Bridget's confidence, but Bridget did not think that was the case. Because if she had, Bridget doubted Sarah would be as eager to present eligible gentlemen with similar interests to Bridget. (No, she would likely have her husband, Jack, track down Oliver Merrick and drag him through the Grand Canal by his teeth.)

Not that Bridget minded. New gentlemen, that is. Since they saw her as pleasant now, they were pleasant to her and eager to please. Mr. Hartley was one, and Mr. Fairleigh—a pleasant landed gentleman from Cumberland, not yet thirty—was another. And it seemed he did have an interest in music.

"The symphony has a beautifully strong theme, a message of hope and love. Music set to poetry," Mr. Fairleigh was saying.

"Yes, I know," Bridget replied. "For you see, my sister is right—we were fortunate enough to hear the premiere in Vienna."

"Did you?" Mr. Fairleigh replied, his interest profound before but now suddenly piqued. "I thought you traveled only to Italy." Mr. Fairleigh set a questioning glance at Sarah. Sarah simply shrugged, also uninformed.

Perhaps it would be wise to tell Sarah herself that more had happened while they were abroad than the taking of a few piano lessons. But if she did, it would be like reliving the whole thing.

And she could not do that. It all hurt too much.

"Mostly we remained in Venice," Bridget explained, keeping her answers as vague as possible. "But we took a trip to Vienna, especially to attend that concert."

"They have given the symphony its own name," Mr. Fairleigh replied. "After the poem that is sung. They are calling it the Ode to—"

"Joy." A warm tenor filled the air behind Bridget, making her heart stop. Bridget did not have to turn to know who it was, but some force of gravity spun her on an axis and brought her around to see his face.

"They call it the 'Ode to Joy.'" Oliver Merrick stood there, looking down into her eyes. And it was as if the whole room, the whole party, the whole world, came to a sudden stop.

"You're here," Bridget breathed, her shock complete, and raw.

"Yes, I am," he answered, unable to keep the bemusement out of his voice.

"I . . . What are you doing here?" she accused.

A small smile lifted the corner of his mouth. "I am here to collect my dance partner."

He brought one of his hands out from behind his back and held it out to her.

"I . . . I don't believe . . . that is, Mr. Fairleigh—" Bridget stammered, trying to unfold her dance card, her hands failing her in time. Because at that moment : . .

"Mr. Fairleigh is going to dance with me!" Amanda cried, wrapping her arm around Mr. Fairleigh's, much to that gentleman's bewilderment.

"Amanda—you cannot dance," Sarah said under her breath to her sister.

"Why not?" Amanda replied. "If I can wear my hair up, I can dance. Right, Mr. Fairleigh?"

And a gentleman he was. "Er, I suppose. That is, I should be delighted to dance with you, Miss Amelia," he said.

"Amanda," she corrected, under her breath, but she kept the smile pasted on her mouth and shooed Bridget and Oliver away. "You must hurry if you are to take your places. We shall, er, catch the next one."

Bridget wanted to rail at her sister, but Oliver's hand was suddenly on her elbow, and she was too afraid she would jump out of her skin for want of his touch to do anything but follow where he led. As she was being maneuvered to the dance floor, she heard Sarah exclaim to Amanda, "I have the feeling I am not being told something important."

"I know!" Amanda answered gleefully. "And for once, I do not!"

Once on the dance floor, Bridget could do little but stare at Oliver as they waited for the music to begin. She simply could not believe it was him. And that he was here. Looking as handsome as ever, damn him.

Although he did look a bit thinner than he had before. Was he not eating? Was he well?

"I can see you thinking, Bridget," he said quietly, as the music came up and he stepped forward to take her in his arms.

"I was thinking . . . that you look as if you have been ill," she said awkwardly, unable to find a benign lie.

But he smiled. "No—well, a touch of *mal de mer* once we hit the open waters of the Atlantic, but I've been fine ever since we docked."

"Oh," Bridget replied, stupidly. "And when was that?"

"Three days ago. Long enough for us to track down your address in London, discover from your mother your where-abouts, ask your father a question of some importance, and travel here."

"Ask my father a question?" Bridget's voice squeaked.

"Yes, but we can save that for later. First, I would like to show you something," Oliver said, as he deftly spun her out of the dancers and away from the crowd.

They stepped into a corridor—Lady Worth's country estate was just as labyrinthine as her oversized home in Mayfair, and therefore this corridor could lead to the card room as easily as it could the courtyard or the kitchens. Bridget had been in residence for almost a week and she still got lost.

She never got lost.

But for once, Oliver seemed to be the one who knew where he was going. Genially, properly, he offered her his arm, and Bridget took it.

"So," he began cordially, "I told you about my voyage. How was yours?"

"It was . . ." *Horrid. Sad. Lonely.* "Fine. No *mal de mer*. Well, except for my mother."

"You made good time; I daresay I left less than a day after you." He mused. "However, I took a different route, crossing the mainland to Rome, hoping to catch you there. But you had already gone on."

Her heart beat a rapid staccato. He had come after her in less than a day? "Yes, the captain said we caught a good wind. We were in England before I realized it," she answered vaguely.

"And how long was it before you missed me?"

And it was that one question, that one simple question, that broke through the armor, the wall that was propping her up and keeping her safe.

"Oliver, please don't," she implored, her thickening voice betraying her. Tears threatened to fall down her cheeks.

"For me, it was practically the moment you left the Marchese's ballroom, proud and triumphant. You won the competition, you know."

"Did I?" She laughed sadly, trying desperately to hold on to some measure of control.

"Yes. After you performed, Klein did not even touch the piano. He conceded without playing. Now, tell me, how long was it before you missed me?"

"Three days," she replied quietly. "I was so angry for three days, on board the ship. And then, I wasn't anymore."

Indeed, it was the morning of the fourth day, when she had awakened to find tears in her eyes. Tears that would not stop. It was as if all the anger had fled, leaving her hollow, and everything else rushed in. And he was right . . . the thing that overwhelmed her the most was the sense of vacancy in her heart, where he used to stand firm.

The missing him.

"I cried for days over you, Oliver. How could you do it?" she asked, more tears flowing now, tears she could no longer hold back. "How could you have let him do it?"

"Hush, my love," Oliver said, his own voice breaking. He pulled her over to the side of the corridor, a small alcove providing a modicum of privacy if anyone should happen by. There, he took her face in his hands and kissed each tear that fell on her cheeks.

"I am sorry. I am so sorry. I will always regret what I did. I . . . I am trying to make amends. Please, will you let me try?"

"How?" she said, between sniffles. She felt horrible, weak-willed. Where was the Bridget who held her head high? Where was the Bridget who could turn away from him disdainfully?

Left at sea, she supposed.

"First of all, you have to know—I never asked you to play your 'Ode to Venice' so Carpenini could overhear. Nor did I take you to Vienna to get you out of his way so he could make use of it. I swear," he breathed, his hands still framing her face, gently brushing back a wisp of hair here, a tear there. It was as if he could not give up touching her, now that she was in front of him.

Bridget did not think she could give it up, either.

"I *wanted* to hear you play, that was the only reason," he continued. "And I wanted to be by your side when we first heard Beethoven's Ninth. You are the only person with whom I can imagine sharing any of that, whom I would ask to share themselves so wholly with me."

"I know," Bridget replied, her heart a bit lighter. "I did not credit those accusations." She gave a short frown. "Eventually, at least. But that hardly matters."

"No, it does not," he agreed grimly. "What I did—letting him steal your music—that is a gross betrayal for which I cannot hope for forgiveness."

"Forgiveness?" Bridget cried. "Oliver, how am I supposed to trust you? You would make the same use of me Carpenini did, taking what you want for your own advantage."

"No!" Oliver cried. "No, I will not. Bridget," he said, running one hand through his dark locks. "I am not going back to Venice. I have decided to sell the Teatro—well, the warehouse that would have been the Teatro."

"You have?" she asked. "Why?"

"Because if that was what I was willing to do to get it, it is tainted. I don't want it anymore. I don't want anything without you." Oliver met her eyes again. "I don't want anything *but* you, Bridget. I love you. I have loved you since you showed up at my door, all determination."

"I love you, too," Bridget said in a rush. "I keep getting lost without you."

He laughed and threw his head back in delight. "That's amusing. For you see, it is only because of you that I managed to find my way home."

He leaned down and kissed her then, and a thousand questions that had been lined up in Bridget's mind instantly fled. To be in his arms again was the only right she could think of.

After a time, they broke apart, too happy to do anything

other than smile and touch. Let their fingers intertwine and their bodies enjoy leaning on the other.

But as they smiled and twined and leaned, a few of those questions came back to Bridget's mind. "What are you going to do, Oliver? Without the Teatro?"

"Well, I thought I might work toward opening up one here. In London." He hesitated, then blew out a breath. "I have been talking with my father."

"Your father?" She blinked.

He smiled. "He was much . . . happier to see me than I anticipated. We have much talking to do. He came with me here. I should love to have the opportunity to introduce you to him."

"You forget, I have already met him once. But I should be happy to again." They abandoned their nook in the corridor and moved down the hall slowly, savoring each other's solo company.

"Is that what you meant by 'us'?" she asked suddenly. He looked down at her quizzically. "You said that three days was how long it took 'us' to find me, and so forth."

"Oh!" he cried with a smile. "Partially. I also brought Frederico. It seems he was just as heartsick for Miss Molly as I was for you . . ."

"That explains so much about Molly's temper during the voyage," Bridget gasped. "And here I had thought she was simply anxious to be on land again."

"Yes . . ." Oliver hedged. "But I also brought someone else."

They had traversed the hallway and found themselves standing in front of a door—and there was the distinct sound of a pianoforte coming from the other side.

Playing a suspiciously familiar tune.

Bridget warily pushed the door open and found herself in Lady Worth's music room. It was populated by a rapt audience—Lady Worth was there, as was Lord Merrick, among others. And somehow, in the intervening time, both of Bridget's sisters had migrated here as well. And everyone's attention was caught and held by Signor Vincenzo Carpenini, up at the pianoforte, playing his latest composition.

The same one that had, upon her hearing it at the Marchese's, nearly broken Bridget.

"What is he doing here?" she asked, her voice suddenly quite hard.

"Do you know, I am not entirely sure," Oliver mused. But his hand had grown more firm around Bridget's arm, making her stay still, anchoring her to the spot, whether she liked it or not. "When I told him I was leaving Venice and coming after you, he adamantly refused to come. But then he came to me and said that since the Marchese was going out of town for the summer, he would rather come with me to England than be left homeless in Venice, if he could. I, of course, placed some conditions on his coming, but he agreed to them."

"Conditions?" Bridget asked, unhappy. *Why was he playing this piece?* It broke her heart even to think of it.

"Hmm," Oliver evaded. "Either he needs people more than he thought, or perhaps he just did not wish to be alone in the world. Or perhaps he grew a dust-mote-sized bit of conscience. In any case, he is here now."

"I don't understand. Did you bring him along so I could strangle him?" Bridget bit out.

Oliver chuckled quietly. "If you wish, but first, perhaps we could go back to the matter of that question I asked your father."

Bridget felt her head spin and her heart stop. "You wish to cover that ground now?"

"It was similar in purpose, although not exactly the same as the question I am going to ask you now."

She whipped her head around to him, wide-eyed. Held her breath. What was he going to ask? And what would she say?

"I would like to know how you would have your name written," he said.

Well, that was not exactly what she had expected. "I don't understand," she replied, once she was able to speak. "My name?"

"Yes. On the publication of the music." He reached into his breast pocket and pulled out a piece of paper, recently printed by the looks of it. He handed it to Bridget.

It was the cover sheet to a piece of music. Across the top it read, *Symphony No. 4, in G Major. By Vincenzo Carpenini.*

And then, underneath that, *With variations and themes by Bridget Forrester.*

"We took a guess that you would want your full name, not 'B. Forrester' or 'Miss Forrester,' or the like," Oliver said quietly.

She looked up at him, in complete shock, unable to reply.

"If I could go back in time and stop Carpenini from playing your piece that night, I would. But he did, and what's more he played it in front of half the musical world. The best way we could make amends was to make certain your name was on it, too," he explained softly. "We made certain his music publisher in Venice knew that you should receive half the royalties and commissions. And we made a quick stop with Carpenini's music publisher in London as well."

"My name is on a piece of music," she whispered in awe.

"Yes," Oliver answered. "A rather good one, too, if you would have my opinion."

"How did Carpenini take this sharing of credit?" Bridget asked, hiding a sniffle. "How did the Marchese?"

"I have no idea how the Marchese took it—one assumes he's heard by now. As for Carpenini . . . well, it's about time he learned to share, don't you agree?"

Bridget smiled and laughed. "Yes. Although I venture to guess he's agreed to it because he thinks he'll make more money this way."

"Maybe so. A young English lady composing a symphony—it would certainly sell tickets," Oliver replied, unable to stop smiling, letting out a slow breath of relief. As if he knew that he had done enough to win his way back into her life, and all he had to do was work just as hard every day to stay there. "I hope you find our solution acceptable—"

She smiled back at him. "I daresay I do."

"Good. Because there is one other question I have long held off asking you. And one that can wait no longer."

For the second time in as many minutes, Bridget's heart stopped. *This* was it . . . this was the time . . .

"Ah, there they are!" came a cry from across the room. "Ladies and gentlemen, the Signorina Bridget Forrester has finally arrived!"

They had not even noticed that the music had come to an end, but now, with Carpenini's delighted cry, they most assuredly had an audience. Every head swung their way and a smattering of "ohh!"s turned into a rather jovial wave of applause.

Carpenini stood up on the piano bench, his Italian accent exaggerated, his theatrics in full effect, and those in the room loved every minute of it. "Friends!" he cried, "if you were unaware, if she was too shy to tell you herself, allow me. Signorina Forrester was briefly my student in Venice these past few months. She set the city aflame with her playing, she played on the stage of La Fenice, and she played for the Marchese di Garibaldi, winning his musical heart. She even helped me compose what you have just heard."

Impressed murmurs spread through the music room. Bridget caught Sarah's shocked gaze across the audience and watched as Amanda leaned down and whispered an explanation to her.

"And perhaps, if you would be so kind as to help me, we can persuade her to come play the piece, the Number Twenty-three by the Maestro Beethoven, that made all of Venice—and my friend Oliver—fall in love with her!"

The roar of applause that lifted the room set Bridget back on her heels. She looked from her sisters to the faces of people she had just met, looking at her with new eyes. Then she finally swung her gaze around to Oliver.

"Go," he said. "Play your piece, and take the bow you have earned."

The crowd parted like the Red Sea, making a path for her to the pianoforte. But before she took a single step, she turned back to Oliver and firmly planted a kiss on his mouth.

In front of everyone.

And they only cheered louder.

"Bridget Merrick," she said, once she pulled away.

"What?" he replied, stunned.

"I think my name should be written as Bridget Merrick." She bit her lip to hide her grin.

A slow easy smile spread across his face.

"As do I, my love. As do I."

And she played. And it would be the music that would guide them through the years. Bridget took her bow, and took a new name with it. Oliver took a chance, and began mending fences with his father. He would buy a little theatre in Covent Garden, run-down, and turn it into the premier stage for the new

and the exciting, especially the popular Italian operas. By the
time he was ready to retire and hand his business over to his
sons, it would have grown threefold, and now had stages in
Edinburgh and Paris to his credit. His only stipulation would
be that, as it had always been, the London stage played a concert of Beethoven's Ninth at least once a year—a gift to his
wife.

Yes, there would be children, and children's children. There
would be success, and despair. Their family would grow
strong with time, their bonds unable to be broken by distance
or death. There would be concerts, and performances. There
would be more works written, some written with her infuriat-
ing brother-in-law, and some that Bridget wrote and published
on her own. Carpenini would take up residence in London and
spend the next twenty years composing happily and complaining unhappily about the stuffy English weather.

There would be sorrow, and hope. There would be six long
years between the death of her husband and Bridget's hearing
Beethoven's Ninth once more. But for the lifetime that preceded them, there was an infinite amount of love.

And that love would manifest in everything they ever did.
Every song they ever wrote, every theatre they ever built,
every child they ever brought into the world.

And throughout it all, like golden thread woven in fabric,
there always was, and always would be, music.

Dear Reader,

The declining world of Venice and the rising world of music became the background for the passionate story of Bridget and Oliver, one of my personal favorites. I was as meticulous as possible in researching both these worlds, but as with any historical novel, the intersection of fact and fiction has to be traversed to tell the story. Sometimes history was massaged to this end, and I am sure there are some outright mistakes (which I claim as my own) but for the curious, here are some of the more interesting tidbits of historical information I came across as I wrote Let It Be Me.

Ludwig Van Beethoven's Ninth Symphony, the "Ode to Joy," is arguably the most famous piece of music in the world. Its simplistic yet refined and infinitely variable central theme is why today it is the official anthem of the European Union. It is also one of the first instances of a choral symphony—the entire fourth movement being the 1785 poem "Ode an die Freude" sung by a full choir. But on May 7, 1824, at its first premiere in Vienna, no one knew what to expect. Beethoven had not appeared in public for years. He was possibly mad. He was most certainly deaf. Thus everyone was curious, and everyone showed up.

The description that Bridget and Oliver give of Beethoven conducting past the end of the music, and being turned around by the contralto Caroline Unger to five ovations of applause, is an anecdote oft reported but never verified. However, I like to believe that it is true, and thus I included this version of events in the story.

Beethoven's Piano Sonata No. 23 in F Minor, Op. 57 was composed between 1804 and 1806, and is colloquially known as the Appassionata. *One of the best known sonatas from Beethoven's middle period, it was given it's name because of its wide range on the keyboard and its extremes in both tempo and volume, as well as its breadth of feeling. Unfortunately it was not called* Appassionata *until 1838, and therefore it is only referred to as No. 23 in this work. Just listening to it, one can tell it is among the most complex and emotional pieces of music from the early 1800s; thus it would be perfectly suited to the Marchese's musical competition.*

The Bach Minuet in G Major that Bridget plays variations on is more famous to today's generation for being the basis of the 1960's pop song "A Lover's Concerto," recorded by the Toys. It was composed sometime in the early 1700s. Interestingly, there has been some dispute in the later part of the twentieth century about whether or not Bach was the actual composer, but in 1824, Bridget Forrester would have easily accepted the attribution of the Minuet in G as being by Johann Sebastian Bach.

One of the things Venice is famous for—besides its history, architecture, and canals, of course—is Carnival. Up until the end of the eighteenth century, Carnival was a six-month-long festival throughout all levels of Venice society, leading up to Ash Wednesday, where the revelers would become penitent observers of Lent. (Think of it as an extremely long Mardi Gras.) Carnival participants enjoyed wearing a variety of traditional masks, disguising their appearances—on any given day a duchess could be dancing with a shop clerk, and no one would know.

In 1797, Napoleon invaded Venice, and stripped the city of many of its ornaments and traditions—including Carnival. When the Wars ended, Venice was no longer a Republic, instead finding itself absorbed into the Kingdom of Lombardy-Venetia and under Austrian rule. The grandeur and spectacle of the Carnival of Venice never fully recovered. In 1824, Carnival would have not been six months long, but a few weeks of frivolity at most. And the revelers were limited to the rich and the tourists, and only those on the main island of Venice. By the midpoint of the century, Carnival would have disappeared from Venice almost altogether, only to be resurrected in the 1970s as a grand tourist attraction to the city.

But even while Venice's long decline had taken a sharp descent after Napoleon, it still retained a charm and grandeur that attracted seekers of beauty. Lord Byron was one of its most famous seekers during this period, enjoying the attractions (and women—he once said that Venice's Carnival had given him the one bout of gonorrhea he hadn't paid for) of Venice, and spend-

ing long periods of time there between 1816 and 1819. He even composed a poem in three (long) parts—his "Ode on Venice," which Bridget mentions as being rather boring.

The Teatro la Fenice—or the Phoenix Theatre—was the most prominent opera house in Venice of its day. Unfortunately, it lived up to its name, and burned to the ground. Twice. The theatre that Oliver Merrick worked at would have been the first La Fenice, which burned in 1836. The second lasted until 1996, and was quickly rebuilt with the version of the opera house that exists today.

There is so much more that went into making Bridget and Oliver's world come alive, from well-known impresario Domenico Barbaia to the history of the phonograph to walking the grounds of Schönbrunn Palace (and if you enjoy these details, there are more posted on my website at www.katenoble.com), but as with all stories, the characters live at its heart. I hope that Bridget and Oliver came alive for you as they did for me, and that their story, in the end, makes you sigh, smile, and hear their music.